HEAT DEATH

THE BULARI SAGA

JESSIE KWAK

This is a work of fiction. Names, characters, places, and incidents either are the product of the author's imagination or are used fictitiously. Any resemblance to actual persons, living or dead, events, or locales is entirely coincidental.

First edition March 2020

Cover art by Dusty Crosley

Cover design by Robert Kittilson

Edited by Kyra Freestar

Map by Jessie Kwak

www.jessiekwak.com

For everyone who voted that
I should include the murdercopters.
You're my kinda people.

N
W E
S
To the Maraka Valley
Geordi Jimenez
Space Terminal
Jet Park
Casinos
Downtown
To Julieta Yang's

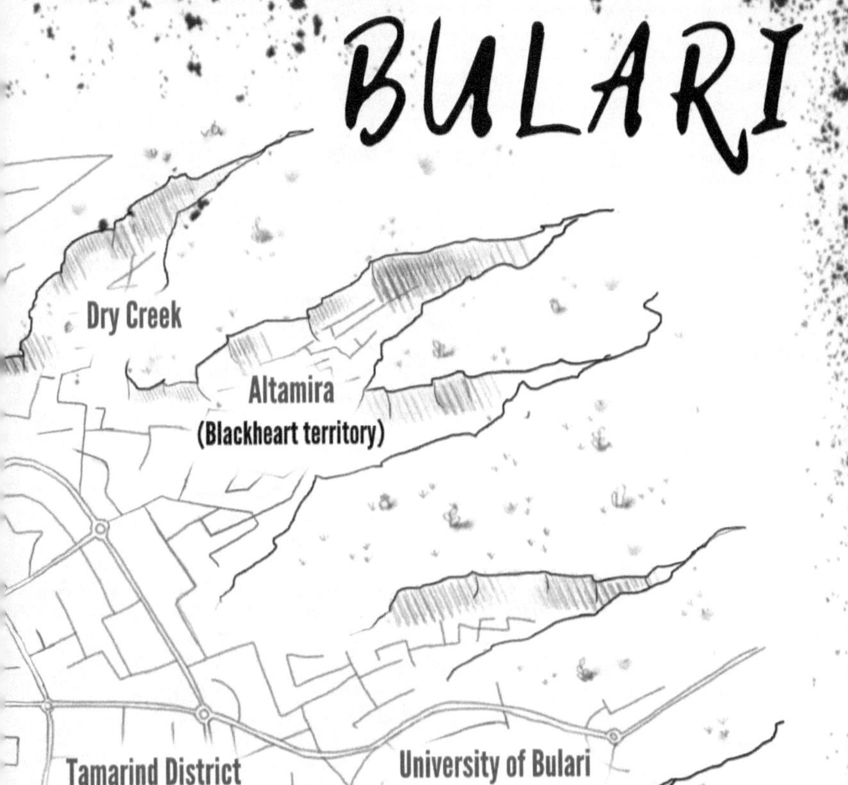

BULARI

Dry Creek
Altamira
(Blackheart territory)
Tamarind District
University of Bulari
Carama Town

PROLOGUE

Phaera D doesn't know how her mother is managing to sleep with the constant whir of machines and irregular beeping; the sedative the doctor gave her must have been strong. Her hand in Phaera's is cool and dry, her breathing even, her eyelids translucent and bruised.

She's so peaceful, but it's all Phaera can do to stay calm herself. She wants to scream, to rage, to tear the room apart until she collapses with exhaustion.

Chief Justice Geum-ja Leone will pay for bringing her mother into this fight.

The last time the doctor came in, she told Phaera her mother was going to be fine, and Phaera doesn't get the impression that Dr. Giaconda Áte makes false promises to make people feel better. Maybe she's right and they're in the clear, but Phaera can't relax. The drive out to this secluded medical complex in the desert was harrowing, even with Oriol's calming reassurances and banter to distract her mother. He's sitting near the door now, a book on his knee, though he's spent most of his time typing a drawn-out conversation on his comm, expression darkening with each exchange.

Steps in the hallway, and Dr. Áte slips through the curtain. In the hours since they arrived, it's only ever been Dr. Áte who comes to check on them. No other doctors or nurses, though Oriol assured her this was a bustling teaching clinic. It could be the hour — it's well after dinner — or it could be the fact that they're here as a favor to Willem Jaantzen and so being kept out of sight.

"Still sleeping?" Dr. Áte asks, and Phaera nods. She squeezes her mother's hand out of reflex, gets a gentle snore in response. "Good. Rest is what she needs right now." Dr. Áte slips a medical supply bag off her shoulder and hands it to Oriol. "Garage on the far end of the airfield. I'll be there in a few."

Oriol stands easily and slips his comm into the pocket of his suit trousers, shoulders the medical bag. "Your mother's in good hands, ma'am," he says quietly to Phaera. "I'll be back soon."

Phaera wants to ask what's wrong, who else is injured that Oriol needs to take care of, but he slips through the curtain before she can.

"Have you eaten?" Dr. Áte presses the back of one dark hand gently against Marjani Harris's clammy brow, then calls up a screen to examine the readouts from the monitors.

"I'm fine," Phaera says. "Where did Oriol go?"

"Ms. Harris," the doctor starts.

"Phaera."

A sharp nod. "Your mother's results are looking much better. Let's let her rest through the night and see how she's doing in the morning, but I'm cautiously optimistic."

"What's wrong with her?"

At the clinic her mother normally goes to, they'd told

Phaera her mother had simply had a shock. Phaera hadn't believed that, and neither had Jaantzen, which is why they're here. Dr. Áte is one of Jaantzen's people, Phaera tells herself. She won't lie to her.

"A concentrate of cardiac glycoside, though it doesn't seem like she drank enough to cause permanent damage. Your mother was poisoned." Dr. Áte's watching her to see how the words land.

"They didn't believe me, at the other clinic. I don't even know if they looked."

Dr. Áte's lips thin. "Oriol snagged me her files — they saw the same thing I saw. Which means either they didn't want to worry you until they knew for sure what they were dealing with — "

"Or they lied to me."

She expects Dr. Áte to tell her she's overreacting, but the doctor nods. "A possibility. I asked some questions. The lead doctor there has some serious financial ties to Leone."

"She poisoned my mother." Furious heat is rising; Phaera drops her voice to a whisper. "And my mother's doctors were going to let her die."

Dr. Áte doesn't answer that. "I'm running some tests to find out exactly what she used. So we can — " A muscle twitches in the doctor's cheek. "So you all can be a bit more prepared next time."

"Next time?"

Dr. Áte swipes away the screen. "Your mother's going to be fine once she gets some rest, Phaera. I'll get you set up in a guest room, but first . . . Do you have a coat?"

When Phaera shakes her head, Dr. Áte hands her a long thermal jacket from the hook beside the door, then takes a lighter jacket for herself. "C'mon." She disappears through the curtain. Phaera kisses her mother's brow and follows.

Phaera hadn't been paying much attention when they arrived, she'd been focused on her mother. Oriol had driven them up a winding road, through a formidable gate, to a freestanding clinic building on the north side of the complex. Now, Dr. Áte leads her to a squat ORV and heads back out the front gate, following a road around the complex wall to an airstrip beyond. Phaera shivers as the wind whips through the open cab, pulls the coat closer — she's still dressed for lunch with her mother, in a sundress and heels. Not the outfit she would have picked for exploring the desert after dark.

A cluster of buildings at the far end of the airstrip reflect moonlight; one has lights on, and when Dr. Áte cuts the engine, voices drift from its open door. Oriol's low tones, Manu's laugh. Phaera's heart rate quickens as she follows Dr. Áte in, but the two men are alone. Manu's sitting on a workbench in shirtsleeves with a blanket draped over his shoulders. Oriol's digging through the open medical bag Dr. Áte sent him here with.

Oriol glances back. "He needs stitches again," he calls.

"Goddammit, Juric." Dr. Áte shakes her head in mock exasperation.

Manu smiles, but it's missing something. The collar of his shirt is spattered with blood, the lower hem soaked black. "Good to see you too, G. Phaera, how's your mom?"

Phaera's lips part, emotions warring: fear for whatever happened to Manu, and disappointment and worry that he's here without Jaantzen. She forces herself to answer. "Dr. Áte says she'll be fine."

Dr. Áte sets her bag on the workbench beside Manu and takes the blood scanner Oriol hands her. "Good news is Ms. Harris doesn't seem to be facing any long-term damage." She whistles low at the scanner results. "But she only had a couple of sips orally, not a whole syringe-full directly in her bloodstream. Jesus, Manu." The doctor sets the blood scanner aside and pulls a suture kit from her bag.

"It's the same poison," Oriol says softly, and it's not a question.

"What happened?" Phaera asks. Oriol glances at her, but before he can answer, his gaze slides past her. He nods faintly at someone behind Phaera, then turns back to Manu.

"Phaera." The voice behind her is rich and deep and edged with exhaustion.

Phaera turns and wraps her arms around Jaantzen. He folds his arms around her; his breath stirs her hair.

"How is she?" he murmurs in her ear.

"I think she's going to be okay. Is Manu . . ."

He doesn't answer, but his hand on the back of her borrowed coat tightens.

"Gia, do you need us here?" he asks.

"Nah, boss," Dr. Áte says. "There's a bench out back."

Jaantzen releases Phaera, hands smoothing down her arms. The callouses on his hands rasp against the coat's rough twill fabric. Before today, she'd never thought to wonder how a man with a desk job got callouses like that. She never even noticed them, not until those hands were roaming her body last night — was it only last night? How these days are blurring together.

And his touch is gone.

Jaantzen holds open a door that leads out to the far side of the garage, where the building blocks the light from the rest of the compound and the sole illumination is a warm yellow glow spilling from the stasis-wrap-covered windows. A few pinpoints of light mark houses kilometers away; the moon silvers the desert's rolling hills and distant cliffs. Above them is a glorious spill of stars. So many stars.

Phaera sinks onto the short bench beside the door and pulls the coat tightly around herself. Jaantzen stays standing, hands buried deep in his coat pockets, dark face shadowed in the dim light.

He clears his throat. "After Tierren poisoned your mother's tea, she caught Manu by surprise. This we know. I'm still not sure if her original intent was to kill him or to talk, but either way, she threatened him with a syringe full of poison. When I arrived, she handed him the antidote and injected him to buy herself time to get away. I nearly wasn't fast enough."

"Why not kill him?"

"Because I would have hunted her down instead of staying with Manu." He sighs. "And she told me Leone wants to turn me into an object lesson. She was that way with Coeur, too — I would've been happy to assassinate Coeur, but Leone wanted to see her humiliated. Torn down and running to the very Alliance she despised for help. She wants to see me dead, but not right away."

"Is Manu going to be all right?"

"I don't know."

His voice is flat, businesslike, but Phaera's seen enough of his interactions with his lieutenant to know how deeply this must be affecting him. She wants to touch him, but he's standing out of her reach. She wraps her arms around her ribs.

"When we were having drinks at the Jungle and plotting our moves against Leone," Jaantzen says, "I don't suppose you thought it would end with us out in the desert like this." There's a hint of wry amusement in his voice.

"Why do I suppose you did?"

"We've been making plans to find a more secure place since Acheta's attack on Cobalt Tower."

"Here?"

Jaantzen shakes his head. "Nearby. I won't make trouble for Gia."

The strange absence of other people in the clinic, even though the facility seems well occupied? The fact that Dr. Áte is meeting her seriously injured friend in a secluded garage rather than bringing him into her medical facility?

"Do you have many friends whose homes you're not allowed into?" Phaera asks.

Jaantzen's laugh is soft. "More this week."

Phaera leans forward, elbows on knees, hands clasped and knuckles pressed to her lips. "You said you've been making plans since Acheta attacked Cobalt Tower. Which means you were making plans even after Acheta was dead. Before Leone began targeting you."

Light glints in Jaantzen's dark eyes as he watches her, waiting for her to ask. But things are starting to fall into place as she plays through the events of the past few weeks. Acheta arriving at Leone's dinner party and announcing he had killed Naali Hinoja. The trouble at Julieta Yang's after that. The plan Jaantzen didn't clue her in on but which resulted in Thala Coeur back on her throne. Acheta's attack on Cobalt Tower.

Something more is going on than a battle for territory.

"What did Acheta want at Cobalt Tower?"

And when he speaks, she can barely believe the story he's telling her — if she hadn't lived through parts of it herself, she might dismiss it completely.

The Dawn hired Thala Coeur to steal something from the Alliance, Jaantzen says. She double-crossed them and tried to keep it for herself by smuggling it to New Sarjun in a shipment for Jaantzen's restaurant supply company. The Dawn kidnapped Coeur and brought her back to Bulari in order to recover their stolen goods, but Coeur's sister asked Jaantzen to rescue her. And he did.

He glosses past that decision with a wave of his hand and Phaera makes a mental note to pry more in the future.

"Afterward, the Dawn worked with Julieta's youngest daughter to lure me to her house," he continues. "They held Starla, Julieta, and myself hostage for Coeur and her stolen goods." Jaantzen clears his throat. "They were unsuccessful."

"Unsuccessful?" Phaera asks. "This must be the daring and exciting rescue story I keep hearing rumors about."

"It's hardly thrilling."

"You'll have to try me sometime."

Is it a trick of the light, or has she managed to make him smile?

"Let me guess," she says. "The Dawn's leader in Bulari was killed at Julieta's, and that's what caused the power vacuum that let Acheta get out of control?"

"Correct."

"Which is when I came to you for help."

"It's also presumably when the Alliance got involved. They sent an agent to infiltrate Acheta's organization and convince him to attack Cobalt Tower. To get back what Coeur stole."

Phaera blinks at him. "The Alliance was behind the attack on Cobalt Tower?" He nods. "How bad was it?" He'd told her Acheta was dead, that they'd stopped him in the lobby, but she'd sensed a heaviness in the following days that Jaantzen had refused to talk about.

"I lost people," he says. "But we stopped them before they succeeded."

Her eyes go wide. "You killed an Alliance agent?"

"No." He rubs a hand over the back of his neck. "We detained her."

"You — " Phaera presses her thumbs to her lips, trying to think. "The bombing on the Alliance Embassy, that wasn't you." She doesn't mean it as an accusation, but for a moment she fears he'll take it that way.

He shakes his head. "I don't know who planted the bomb."

"No wonder they'd blame you, though."

"I think the accusation came from Leone, not the Alliance." Jaantzen smiles wryly. "I have a tentative truce with the Alliance, for the moment at least. That warrant for my arrest will disappear soon."

None of this can be real. Phaera frowns at the ground. She's starting to shiver, but she can't tell if it's from cold or information overload. "You have a truce because you have one of their agents hostage."

"Not hostage. But she's been willing to give us some very damaging testimony they'd rather not see get out to the public."

"So you, Willem Jaantzen, are in a tentative standoff with the entire Alliance, and you still have possession of whatever Blackheart stole. And now Leone is trying to get her hands on it, too?"

Jaantzen pauses, thinking; Manu's laugh drifts from the garage behind them. Phaera's glad someone's having a good time tonight.

"A very good question," Jaantzen says finally. "And I wish I had the answer."

"Okay, that's fine." Phaera takes a deep breath. "What did Blackheart steal from the Alliance?"

Jaantzen's shoulders rise, fall. "I can't tell you."

Phaera's jaw sets. "Because you're afraid I'll go to the cops? To Leone?"

"Of course not."

"I came to you originally because we both had an Acheta problem," Phaera says, trying to keep her tone calm. "I wouldn't presume to think you needed my help, but I definitely needed yours. And I'd been thinking for some time that having a closer relationship with you could be very good for business. Was it calculating? Of course. I hadn't meant for it to get so personal, not at first. Not until — " But she bites back what she was about to say — this isn't the conversation they're having. She holds up a hand before he can say anything. "I underestimated what you were involved with, but I would have made the exact same decision to come to you about Acheta if I'd known about Blackheart. That said?"

She pierces him with a glare. "That night we were sitting at the Jungle, making plans? You should have fucking filled me in on what I was getting into." Jaantzen glances at the door, and she lowers her voice. "The Alliance? Did you think that wasn't going to come up? That it wouldn't be incredibly dangerous to me? Yes, it's a lot to take in. Am I going to go running to the cops or Leone? To the goddamned *Alliance*? I hope you know me better than that."

There's such a look of pain on his face that she feels a stab of guilt.

"Unless that's not what you meant," she finishes.

Jaantzen takes a deep breath. "It is."

"Okay." Phaera leans back against the metal wall of the garage; the cold bites through the coat into her shoulder blades, whispers over her bare calves. "Well, you can trust me. Sit down, Jaantzen."

At first she thinks he won't, but then the weathered wood creaks as he sits. Though the bench is small, he still manages to leave a space between them.

"I apologize," he says.

Phaera laughs tiredly. "At least this time you didn't have Juric and his twitchy trigger finger over to help interrogate me."

"I apologize for that, again."

"It's fine. I know how protective you are of your people." And she's not one of those people. She thinks she kept the bitterness out of her voice, but it's a long time before he responds.

"Phaera." Her name in his mouth is a faint breath. "Leone needs to think this thing with your mother is your last straw." He looks out over the desert. The moonlight has cooled the warm undertones of his dark skin; his profile is sharp against the background light. "Or maybe this is your last straw."

In the distance — but not far enough for comfort — a lone dziva hound howls. Nothing answers.

She lays her hand on his thigh, and after a breath he covers it with his.

"It is my last straw. But not how you mean." He turns his head, curious. "Don't take this the wrong way, Jaantzen, but this has nothing to do with how I feel about you. I will do everything it takes to make sure Leone can't hurt anyone else."

His fingers tighten around hers. "The plan hasn't changed. Leone will play dirty, but we have to play clean if we want to take her down without destroying ourselves. You know about the prisoners who've been sold to Redrock. Calanthe and Letizia are working to tie her to that scandal, and we have some evidence she may be personally benefiting from this trade agreement with the Alliance. With the right luck and timing, we can strip her of her support." He lets that settle between them. "Which will leave a power vacuum."

"You have support."

"So do you."

Phaera looks at him sharply, but he's not joking.

"You have the respect of the business owners you work with. The other casino and entertainment business owners — Cavy, Ayisha. The cab drivers union. All those politicians who gamble at the Devil's Table. Not Leone's old money crowd, but the people who are truly driving business in this city."

"You can't mean to suggest I take over Leone's web of power."

"We."

Phaera stares out over the desert, the vast empty expanse making thoughts of power plays in distant Bulari seem both unreal and actually possible. In this black, lonely night, anything could happen. Sure, why couldn't a glorified waitress go head-to-head with the chief justice of the Supreme Court in a battle for the respect and loyalty of Bulari's most successful businesspeople? What does she have to lose? She wants to burst out laughing at the absurdity.

But she's not exactly alone. Her name may not carry much weight, but his does.

"What's your plan, Jaantzen?"

His voice holds a smile. "Let's start with a dinner party. Perhaps in a week?"

The clenched fist of fear in her chest is a familiar friend by now. She takes a deep breath to loosen it. "I'll start shoring up the guest list."

"Thank you. I trust your judgement." His shoulders rise and fall with a breath she's learned means he's carefully considering his next words. "You started to say earlier you hadn't meant this to become personal. Until what?"

Phaera leans to close the final gap between them, shivering against his solid warmth. "You caught my attention because you were so different from the rest of the stuck-up old money crowd at Leone's. And you're easy on the eyes." A faint line sketches itself between his brows and Phaera laughs. "But it was how you were with Julieta that made me . . . well." She's not hanging any heavy words on this feeling, not yet.

"She doesn't tolerate fools, and she's obviously very fond of you," she continues. "You're so careful and polite, but sometimes I'd catch a glimpse of a completely different person when the two of you were together. And I found myself counting the days between those glimpses." She's glad he can't see the heat rising in her cheeks. "That sounds ridiculous."

She can feel his heart beating between them, steady.

"Julieta said something at Leone's last dinner party," he finally says.

"Yes?"

"She teased me for not being able to recognize when a woman is coming on to me."

"She's right. You're very slow."

"And she told me you would be good for me."

Phaera's breath catches. "I don't know about that."

Jaantzen's calloused fingertips catch in her hair as he brushes it back. "So far she's been right," he says, and before she can answer his lips are on hers, fingers threading through her hair, thumb smoothing along her jaw. She shifts against him, cursing the awkward narrow bench. And freezes at the knock. Jaantzen pulls back slowly, and the cold desert night rushes in to fill the space between them once more.

"Hey, boss," Manu says apologetically, his lanky frame silhouetted in the too-bright light spilling from the doorway. "Gia's kicking us out. Says I gotta sleep and I can't do it here."

"Tell her we'll be on our way."

Phaera frowns. "I don't want to bring trouble. Do we —"

"You and Oriol are fine," Manu says. "Gia said something about you being 'respectable.'" He throws up air quotes with a wink, but even his expression is pinched with pain. "Take care, Phaera. We'll see you soon." He disappears, leaving the door open.

Jaantzen tastes like the cool desert air and a hint of salt, and when he follows Manu inside, Phaera stays on the bench, arms wrapped around herself. Feeling utterly, dizzyingly alone. The dziva hound howls again, farther away now, still searching for its pack. Nothing answers but the wind.

1

———————

NEW SARJUN

The night is cold, but Starla Dusai's out in the yard anyway, kicked back in one of the sunbleached chairs that came with the Maraka Valley property she and Jaantzen and the rest of them are currently calling home.

The chair — and the property — have both been through better days. This old thing's been left out on the porch come shine or dust storm or occasional rain and she can feel it creaking with her weight every time she shifts. She kicks her feet up onto the chair's even sketchier companion, tilts her head back at the midnight sky.

The Maraka Valley may be hours from Bulari and feel even farther, but Starla loves it.

Maybe because it's isolated, like the space station she grew up on out in Durga's Belt.

Maybe because she finally actually feels like her family's safe here.

Maybe because it's brilliant with stars.

The air is still tonight, the near-constant haze of the season's dust storms cleared away. The moons are slivers low on the horizon; a few lights from other houses glimmer across the valley.

More lights than Starla expected — the Maraka Valley isn't quite the wasteland people paint it to be, though it hardly feels like civilization. And as far as Starla can tell, just as New Sarjun was settled by folks who were too ornery for easy life on Indira, the Maraka Valley is where people who felt too stifled by Bulari ended up. Case in point? Even though there's an energy co-op, more than half the valley's residents are too suspicious to use it, including the man who built the series of booby-trapped underground bunkers they're living in now. Starla and Toshiyo have spent the past week slowly making this deathtrap more habitable by disarming devices, bringing the security features into this century, and getting the generators up and running.

Despite the house lights, their nearest neighbors are dozens of kilometers away. The result? Almost pure darkness.

Above her, the sky is inky black and glittering.

Starla wraps her arms over her torso, glad she packed her warmest coat.

The night sky always makes her homesick, each bright star a cousin made hazy by New Sarjun's atmospheric forces, each flash of a shooting star potential debris from her childhood home, scattered frozen and drifting through the Durga System.

Her gauntlet buzzes and she jumps, startled out of her thoughts. She triple-blinks her lens on to check the notification, and a line of text scrawls glowing across the stars.

Video message received

Starla sits up straight. Mona? Starla's been waiting for a response from her wayward cousin for days now. It's not unusual — Mona's constantly on the move throughout the system — but Starla's latest request for her is time-sensitive.

She opens the attached video, plays it on her lens against the starry backdrop of the night sky, and at first she barely recognizes the face in front of her. The fifteen years since Silk Station was destroyed have been good to her Auntie Abbie. Her mother's cousin looks strong and healthy as ever. Pale face glowing against the stars, cloud of black ringlets floating out behind her in the low-G of wherever she's recording this.

"Sweetheart, I hope you're doing well," Abbie signs. "Mona said you wanted to know about your mother's necklace?"

The stone amulet around Starla's neck is a cool weight against her breastbone. She can't feel the lines carved into the smooth surface through her layers of sweater and coat, but she knows the shape they make: a stylized winged creature with a tail, spiraling towards the heavens.

The resemblance to the alien now living in the bunker deep below her feet is uncanny. And, Starla suspects, not accidental.

"It was a keepsake from a job. I'm afraid I don't know where she and your father were working. But I did find out the job was for someone named Felipe Zacharia."

Abbie fingerspells the name, and with each letter, Starla's chest tightens.

"I know the job went bad, I remember Las saying the Alliance got involved? I'm sorry I don't have more information." Her aunt is still signing, catching Starla up with little pleasantries to finish out the conversation, but Starla's already chasing down her suspicions over the deathtrap's shaky network.

Felipe Zacharia, long-imprisoned prophet of the Dawn.

The man whose nightmare brother, Bennion, had been running the Dawn's operations in Bulari until recently. Until her godfather killed him.

Starla pulls up Felipe's mugshot from Redrock Prison, stares into the ice-blue eyes that had found her in the virtual museum full of alien artifacts, eyes so similar to the pair that had taunted her in Julieta Yang's greenhouse.

Thirty years ago, her parents had worked a job for the man who would go on to found the Dawn from his cell at Redrock Prison. And whatever they'd discovered must have had something to do with the alien artifacts — and organic samples — Felipe Zacharia had based his religion around.

It's late; Caba Regina burns high overhead, the tip of the Crooked Spear eternally chasing Arctas and Prixa Minor across southern New Sarjun's sky. This time of year the ecliptic cuts through the Fisherman, and icy Bixia Yuanjin is currently caught in his net. The Egret is ascendent, the spiral galaxy of its eye brilliant.

She scans the ecliptic out of habit, only this time she's not searching for remnants of her childhood home. Somewhere out there in the debris of Durga's Belt, her parents worked a job for the Dawn's prophet and came home with an alien artifact.

She sits shivering beneath the stars as Abbie's message ends, then watches them for a long time after with REPLAY MESSAGE Y/N blinking in her tear-blurred vision.

Phaera has had plans to turn the rooftop at the Devil's Table into a bar since the day she signed the building's lease, but she's never quite brought herself to do it. It would be a draw, of course. Both for the elite gamblers filling the tables in the casino below her feet and for a new market: a dinner and cocktail crowd looking for a unique experience and a gorgeous view of the casino drag and Bulari's glittering downtown core.

But the rooftop currently acts as an impromptu employee break room. It's furnished with things that don't quite belong in the casino: repaired chairs, wobbly stools, retired tables. Tonight a pair of dealers and a busser are enjoying their shift beers on a stack of crates, laughing without worry of disturbing guests. Vanessa Dosantos, the Table's front-of-house manager, is leaning against the railing with smoke curling out between ruby red lips, red leather gloves tucked in the back pocket of her trousers, red-smoked glasses pushed up on her dark brown forehead. Black finger waves still perfectly in place despite it almost being the end of the night.

The rooftop has a worn-out, lived-in, private feeling Phaera isn't quite willing to let go, no matter what a boost to her bottom line opening a bar would be.

The rooftop is her employees' place — not her patrons'.

It's *her* place.

How many nights has she come up here for a nightcap and to stare down the drag, to admire the glittering lights and holograms of the other casinos and nightclubs, thinking of the people who own them and amazed she has the gall to number herself among them.

Vanessa smiles as Phaera steps out onto the rooftop, and holds out her cigarette, eyebrow raised. Phaera joins her at the railing and takes a deep pull, closing her eyes as she sighs out smoke with pleasure. She hands the cigarette back, folds her arms against the railing next to Vanessa.

"Best view on the drag," Vanessa says. Smoke curls up between them.

It is.

On the farthest end is the glitter of the Desert Gem's cut glass and the liquid illusion of the hologram waterfall at Phaera's other casino, the Lorelei. She's always thought the ever-exploding hologram at Orveto's Thousands was a bit too much, but she does love the Aterciopelado's sinuous curves. Tonight, Ayisha's Palace sends a spear of light into the night — the plaza in front is packed with people queuing to see whatever superstar Ayisha has booked to sing.

Phaera turns back to Vanessa with a contented smile; the other woman's frowning.

"You've lost weight, Fay," Vanessa says.

"I don't think so," Phaera lies. But food tastes like ash since her fight with Acheta began. Phaera is eating when she remembers, or when someone reminds her, or when she wonders why she's nauseous. She hasn't dared to weigh herself, but she's starting to have trouble finding clothes in her closet that fit right.

She gives Vanessa a game smile and gets skeptical pursed lips in return.

She and V have known each other since the Aterciopelado, almost a decade ago. They've each worked at most of the joints up and down this drag, though the 'Tercio was the only casino where they overlapped. But they had remained friends no matter where they worked, and while Phaera stuck to waiting tables and dealing, V's done everything from cocktail waitress and cashier to valet and security. She was the first person Phaera hired when she opened the Devil's Table.

Vanessa obviously has more to say about Phaera's

weight, but before she can, something catches her eye. She lifts her chin over Phaera's shoulder. "Cowboy's about to tell you to step back from the edge." Vanessa straightens and hands Phaera the cigarette. "And he's probably right."

Indeed, Oriol Sina is walking towards them, that apologetic quirk to his lips saying he intends to herd her. With his sharp suit and rakish good looks, he doesn't stand out on the floor of the Devil's Table, even right at her side. But here, with her employees, he looks exactly like what he is: her bodyguard. Phaera's getting used to Oriol's near-constant presence, but she still doesn't think in terms of a bullet around every corner — and she doesn't want to. She doesn't want to worry someone might try to kill her on the rooftop of her own damn building. It's secure. She's supposed to be fucking safe here.

But she takes another drag of Vanessa's cigarette and steps away from the railing, brushing a sheen of sand off a crate to sit there instead; the view vanishes from sight. Oriol settles nearby once she leaves the edge of the building, in a watchful parade rest, and it's too much. Phaera waves for him to join them.

"How's it going, cowboy?" Vanessa calls. She gives Oriol a warm smile, and he finally closes the distance between them, though he never stops scanning the rooftop.

Moonlight glints on the new ring on his left hand. In everything that happened right before Jaantzen and Manu left town, Phaera can't pinpoint exactly when Oriol started wearing it, and she hasn't had the heart to ask. Nothing she says will bring Jaantzen and Manu out of hiding before they're ready.

Last week she'd had only a casual relationship with Jaantzen; tonight she can't stop wondering where he is. If he's safe. She hasn't heard from him, and so far she hasn't had anything to report, so she hasn't tried to contact him herself. She needs Leone to think things are over between the two of them. She has no idea how closely Leone is watching her — if she has spies on her staff — but she and Jaantzen had agreed it would be best to play it safe.

And she hates it.

"Any sightings of our mystery woman?" Oriol asks Vanessa.

"Negative." Vanessa directs a stream of smoke away from him. "I've been asking up and down the drag, nobody's seen her."

Phaera isn't sure if it's good or bad that the woman with the heart-shaped face, Victoria Tierren, hasn't been seen in any of her disguises since the day she poisoned Phaera's mother. Because surely she didn't leave town herself — and Phaera can't imagine she's content just running Jaantzen away.

"But that reminds me. A courier brought this by before I came up on break." Vanessa reaches inside her vest and pulls out a slim envelope. "Wanted to make sure you got it tonight."

Phaera reaches for it, but Oriol clears his throat. With a wry smile at her, Vanessa hands it to him instead.

Oriol pulls a thumb-sized scanner from his pocket; light plays over the thick paper. He frowns at whatever he sees on his comm, then flicks open a knife and slits the top, hands her the envelope.

Her name is written in flowery script on the back, a hand she doesn't recognize. Inside she finds three mystix cards. They're from the Lorelei, backs printed with a gold-leaf river against a sapphire background.

Phaera turns them over one by one on the crate beside her. Even in the dim light, the cards are unmistakable.

The first two are the Loup-garou and the Lorelei, not one of the unbreakable marriages, but still a formidable pair to have in your hand. She'd bet large on their strength alone.

"Nice," says Vanessa, then shakes her head sadly as Phaera flips over the third card. "Better luck next time."

The third card is one of the three fortune killers: the Mask. It's also one of the few directional mystix cards, meaning its impact on a hand changes depending on how it's dealt.

It's facing her with tragedy ascendant: Those you trusted have betrayed you, those you believed protected your back have put a knife in it. Your hand's over, if not your game.

Phaera stares at the three cards, trying to comprehend the message. She might be the Lorelei, the always-adapting enchantress, the woman who takes what she wants. Jaantzen's probably the Loup-garou, the hunted and hunter, the man who lives two lives. Whether the Mask is meant to be a warning or a threat, who can tell.

And while the Mask is untouched, there's something wrong with the other two cards. The Lorelei has been defaced, a noose drawn around her neck in thick black marker. And the Loup-garou — she holds it up to catch the light spilling out of the rooftop's doorway. Something is splashed over the figure's face and body.

"Is that . . ."

Oriol takes the card from her and scratches a fingernail over it; deep rust flakes away. "Blood," he says.

"When's the last time you heard from him?" Phaera asks, heart beginning to race.

Oriol doesn't answer, but he's pulling out his comm, putting through a connection request that continues to ring.

Victoria Tierren waits until Phaera's bedroom light is off before she unfolds herself from her surveillance position and slips down the far side of the building.

She's had a pleasant night — she enjoys the hunt almost even more than the kill, which is good because this isn't a usual headhunter job. She rarely does straight hits these days — she prefers complicated cases that let her special blend of patience, perseverance, and creative thinking shine. She dissects. Peels back layers of skin and muscle and false identities and secret trails. Prods at organs to find the pain points, tugs on the severed ends of tendons to uncover a web of relationships, fears, hopes, secrets.

When Leone's original call came up on the head-hunting boards, Tierren had been intrigued. Leone didn't want her target killed; she wanted him destroyed.

The job was perfect.

She's digging the wide range of personas she gets to play. The fascinating knot of emotions and loyalties and liabilities among Jaantzen's crew to untangle. The chance to spend some quality time in Bulari.

Honestly, there haven't been any downsides to this gig.

Well, besides getting shot.

Tierren never likes to get shot, but she's not holding any grudges — it was fair play, and now she knows to be faster on her feet around Manu Juric. And her arm is healing nicely; Detective Timo Cho did a good job on the first aid.

She pauses at the door to Phaera's local corner store when her comm chimes. It's Leone.

"I'm working," Tierren says.

"Have you found him?"

"I'll let you know when I do."

Leone makes an annoyed noise. "Maybe it's time for a stronger approach. Phaera is the weak link, she must know where he is. I suspect you're skilled at . . . that sort of thing."

Tierren is. But if she thought Jaantzen's girlfriend knew where he was hiding she would've cut it out of her already. Tierren slips into the corner store, smiles at the clerk. "I've been watching," she says to Leone. "They haven't met."

"Then use her to draw him out."

Tie her up and dangle her over a cliff so Jaantzen comes riding in to save her is probably what Leone means, but there's no fun in that. The chief justice lacks imagination; Tierren does not.

"I'm working on it," she says.

"Do I need to find someone who can deliver?" That hint of an Arquellian drawl Leone gets when she's giving orders ghosts across her Bulari accent.

"If you just wanted him dead, you would've hired another headhunter," Tierren says. She smiles at the clerk's startled look. "But you hired me. I'll get results if you stay out of my way, unless you want to go back to the job boards."

Silence on the other end of the line, and for a dizzying moment Tierren thinks Leone is finally going to snap and fire her. That she'll call her bluff — because it is a bluff, if Tierren's being honest. She's enjoyed the past few days of untangling knots, but she lives for the hunt, and it's about to get good. Despite her threat to walk away, Tierren isn't entirely sure she can. She's already in too deep.

She tasted blood tonight, it's still caked under her nails and coppery on the back of her tongue.

"You have one week," Leone snaps.

"It won't take that long," Tierren says. "I can feel it."

She cuts the connection and sets her haul of InstaMeals

and instant coffee on the counter. When she swipes credits from an unlinked chit, the cashier frowns at the splash of rust on the inside of her wrist.

She grins, and whatever he sees there makes him look away.

There's a perfectly good reason no one's answering his calls, Oriol tells himself, but he's both exhausted and wired when he palms the lift door at Manu's apartment building at the end of the night. The network out at the property is sketchy at best, and this isn't the first time he hasn't been able to get through to Jaantzen or Manu. He'd half considered driving out to the Maraka Valley to see for himself after dropping Phaera off, but he forced himself to head home, instead. He's not one for head games but he recognizes one when he sees it. The mystix cards could mean something is wrong. Or they could be trying to get him to rabbit out into the desert and lead Tierren straight to Jaantzen.

The lift scanner pulses to let him know he's cleared for the thirtieth floor, and even with the ring on his finger he gets the usual pang of surprise when his credentials still work. He never understood why Manu kept opening his door every time Oriol came home from yet another attempt to scratch his travel itch, but he's grateful all the same.

Each floor has a dozen units, and with the hours Oriol

keeps, he's never met any of Manu's neighbors. Tonight the hallway's empty as always. He palms the pad beside Manu's door; it clicks open.

And Oriol freezes.

The lights are off, as he left them. But music is playing faintly over a traffic hum that says the balcony door is open. Objects in the hall have shifted: coats hung up, paintings straightened, shoes pointed toe-first at the wall.

As he listens from the doorway, the song finishes. Starts again.

Could be Manu snuck home and is creepily listening to music on repeat by moonlight. Or he's already gone to bed . . . and didn't close the balcony door and turn off the music. Maybe his comm is dead, or disconnected, and that's why he's not answering any of Oriol's calls.

Any number of completely rational things Manu has never done before could be the reason for the darkness, the unanswered calls, the music on repeat, the open balcony door. The faint scent of smoke and iron.

Blood rushes in Oriol's ears, drowning out the music. He breathes in, out. In. Out. Scans the empty hallway once more and draws his gun. Shuts and locks the door quietly behind him.

Steels himself for whatever he's about to find.

Oriol doesn't turn on the lights — he doesn't need them. The windows are set to go transparent at night, so the living room and kitchen are flooded with Bulari's ambient light, the hallway silvered. The bedroom door is a gaping maw of blackness and Oriol pauses, listening for anything to betray someone hiding in the darkness, then covers the bedroom and skirts past on the other side of the hall. He'll circle back once he knows the rest of the apartment is clear.

The song fades again and restarts, and Oriol finally

recognizes it: moody and instrumental, a karabéi group Manu was into years ago. Oriol hasn't heard him play it for a while — he hasn't heard him play any music lately, let alone a song on repeat. The string chorus pulses like a wailing ghost in the otherwise silent apartment.

Oriol's grip tightens on the pistol. He swings into the living room — corners clear, good sight lines around the couch, no one in the kitchen. If someone's in the apartment, they're hiding in the bedroom or out on the balcony. And they definitely heard him enter.

The living room is as tidy as the entryway; someone put things away, shifted furniture back into precise lines. Oriol catches a whiff of garlic. A couple of takeout containers from Jade's are standing neatly on the counter, a single plate and pair of chopsticks set out like Manu was interrupted while fixing himself something to eat.

Oriol's heart rate spikes.

God, no. If anyone up there is still listening, please no.

He shifts against the far wall so the couch no longer blocks his view of the balcony. Beyond the open door a figure is slumped in the woven rattan chair, feet kicked out. Head lolling to the side.

"Manu," Oriol says quietly.

The figure doesn't move.

Oriol forces himself to keep going slowly, even as every nerve in his body is screaming, because he's seen this scene before more than once. A person interrupted at their routine, then staged to be found. The song on repeat, the dinner left uneaten. The way Manu's suit jacket is folded neatly in its place over the back of the couch, the way light glints off the coffee table — details are cataloguing themselves with searing precision in Oriol's mind for him to sift through again and again later.

"*Manu,*" he hisses.

He has a clear view, now. The balcony is empty but for Manu's still figure, sprawled in the chair with one slim hand spilled over the side, lazy like he's lying in a boat on a warm Arquellian summer's day, trailing his fingers in the water. The music loops eerily over the otherwise too-silent scene.

So peaceful.

So still.

Oriol's pulse pounds in his ears. It takes every ounce of willpower to continue his sweep, and an entire lifetime of training barely wins out over the desire to run to Manu's side. Oriol scans back through the room behind him — he didn't sweep the bedroom, but the rest of the small apartment doesn't have space to hide. If it's a trap he'll have a good vantage from the balcony to see them coming.

It's not a trap, though.

Even before the strange note sent to Phaera on the roof at the Devil's Table, Oriol's been waking from nightmares — and flashbacks — of this exact horror every night. The vise around his lungs tightens; a small voice lectures him about inbreath, outbreath, but fuck that voice.

He steps onto the tiny balcony, mouth dry, stomach churning as he prepares to see his husband's throat slit, a bullet through his head, his eyes wide and staring. His guts folded neatly beside him.

Manu's eyes are closed.

His body is unmarked — he's wearing shirtsleeves folded up against dark forearms, partially unbuttoned to show a smooth swath of his chest. A plate at Manu's elbow holds traces of Jade's chicken and black bean sauce, an empty bottle of Darius lager sits on the floor beside the chair.

Manu's chest is rising and falling evenly.

His breath catches in a little snore.

Relief rushes through Oriol like a tidal wave and he slumps against the doorframe, murmuring a fevered prayer of thanks in case someone's still listening to him. When he trusts himself to move again, he shoves his pistol back in its holster, then kneels beside the chair. He smooths a hand over Manu's cheek and the other man's eyelashes flutter. Manu's lips pull back in a smile.

"Bout time you got home," Manu murmurs.

Oriol doesn't let him say anything else. He covers Manu's mouth with his, his fingers working his way down the buttons of Manu's shirt as much because of how much he needs him as to see for himself that Manu's all right, to run his hands over every inch of him to make sure he's whole.

After a moment, Manu pushes himself upright in the chair with a hiss of pain and Oriol breaks the hunger of his kiss. Sits back, fingers stilled on the button of Manu's fly.

"What's wrong?"

Manu winces and kicks out his right leg. "Foot fell asleep," he says. "And my neck is killing me."

Oriol lets out a breath shaky with adrenaline. "There are better chairs for taking a nap."

"I didn't plan to doze off." Manu leans elbows on knees and rolls his neck. "I was watching the city. The stars are amazing out in the desert, but gods I miss this."

"Somebody could have seen you."

A wink. "You think I can't break into my own apartment building?"

"You scared the shit out of me."

"Sorry. I should've turned on some lights to let you know I was here."

Let him think that was it — that Oriol was startled to

find him back in the apartment. Not that Oriol's been having visions of finding Manu's body torn to pieces.

Oriol forces his breath to calm. "No worries," he says lightly.

"You should've changed my code. What if — "

"It's fine." Oriol tries to smile. He can't talk about this right now. He gets to his feet and holds out a hand to help Manu stand. Manu swears and kicks out his right foot again, and Oriol's watching his every movement, evaluating. Manu might simply be sore from sleeping in the rattan chair, but Oriol isn't taking any chances.

"Let's get you into a real bed," he says. "Though you might need to give me a minute to find it."

"I already cleared it off." Manu cracks his neck and yawns. "Weren't they supposed to teach you how to fold your clothes in the military?"

"I spent the last eight months living out of a shoebox." Oriol can do jokes, if that's what they're doing; his heart is still hammering. "Plus, it's easier to choose what to wear if it's already out on the bed."

"You only wear workout clothes."

"I'll have you know I own three suits now."

Manu laughs. "Yeah, I found two on the floor and hung them in the closet where they belong." He lounges against the doorframe, hands in pockets, shirt draped open. His muscles have lost some of their tone in the last few weeks of injuries and attempts at recovery, but he's still fit. A bandage is taped above his right hipbone.

But he's fine.

He's here.

Something deeply knotted in Oriol's gut twists loose and he's just this side of throwing his head back and laughing until he sleeps for a week.

But that would look crazy, and Manu's watching, an evaluating smile on his lips as his gaze slips down.

Oriol's wearing his favorite of the new suits, gray on gray, classic enough to blend in with the Devil's Table crowd, comfortable enough he can still move well. He did actually spend some money on the thing and got a recommendation for a tailor from the Table's head of security, Hiro Matapang. If he's any judge of his own wardrobe — and he's really not — he doesn't look half bad.

Manu's lips quirk to the side appreciatively as he takes Oriol in. Apparently Hiro's tailor has a good hand. "I'll give you a tutorial on how the closet works," Manu says. "We can practice with this fine-looking suit."

Oriol shrugs his jacket off and tosses it onto one of the armchairs; it crumples to the floor. Manu shakes his head in mock despair. "Let's not waste time tonight," Oriol says as he starts on the buttons of his shirt. "How long are you staying?"

"Through tomorrow — I'll head out when you go back to work."

Not long, but longer than Oriol had dared to hope.

"Got a busy agenda?" Because surely Jaantzen sent him back to Bulari for something. Oriol's got nowhere to be before late afternoon, though, so maybe he can help out somehow. Capture back those few spare moments they have, even if it means running errands for Jaantzen.

Manu shakes his head.

"Nah, man," he says with a slow smile. "Just you."

3

STARLA

"The Zacharia brothers are originally from New Sarjun," Toshiyo says; Starla's only half watching the transcription as she reads over Toshiyo's shoulder. Toshiyo's fingers are flying over the keyboard, sifting through a sea of information at a rate that's putting immense strain on the Maraka Valley deathtrap's network connection.

She stops and flicks a file from the stream onto her desk. "I've had crawlers gathering information on them ever since Bennion Zacharia showed up at Julieta's greenhouse, but . . ." She shrugs. "I haven't had time to sort through it. Sorry."

They've all been busy. Starla doesn't bother saying it, and Toshiyo's not looking at her anyway. They're in Toshiyo's makeshift office in the deathtrap, one of about eight rooms they've managed to make habitable. Starla isn't actually sure how many more rooms there are, but she's reasonably confident they've disabled all the booby traps. She's warned Manu and Jaantzen not to go off wandering without her or Toshiyo, though.

It's been less than a week since they bought the property, and Toshiyo's new office looks almost identical to her old, with drifts of interesting clutter and half-assembled projects. Toshiyo somehow works best when her office is full of potential distractions, when her mind can wander subconsciously through the many disparate pieces in the room and come up with something brilliant.

A transcription starts flowing across Starla's lens once more.

"Here it is," Toshiyo says. "Both brothers served time in Taufang-Set Penitentiary for murder and extortion, but after their release there's no further official record of either of them until Felipe was arrested by the Alliance."

Starla leans in to examine the Alliance arrest record. Felipe Zacharia was picked up out in Durga's Belt after an anonymous tip. *Subject recovered without a fight,* reads the log.

"He'd been showing up on Alliance most-wanted lists for at least five years prior, after he destroyed an Arquellian passenger ship." Toshiyo's pulled up one of the old lists. Felipe Zacharia's ice-blue eyes shine out from the chart of mugshots. At first Starla doesn't recognize anything of the wizened old prophet she saw in the virtual museum. But if you added a beard to cover the vicious curve of the mouth, then softened the intensity of those icy eyes with age and wrinkles, the resemblance is there.

Toshiyo is about to sweep away the most-wanted list when another face catches Starla's attention. She stays Toshiyo's hand, heart beating in her throat.

Raj Dusai. Deserter. Wanted for piracy. Reward, 5 million Alliance credits.

Toshiyo's eyebrows shoot up. "That's a lot of money."

Starla smiles faintly, with an odd sense of pride that her father's bounty was more than double Zacharia's. Her father's rakish grin cuts deep, leaving a dull ache below her sternum. "Mom told me once they turned Dad in for the bounty, then broke him back out. I think it went up even more after."

"Well, nobody got Felipe Zacharia's bounty," Toshiyo says, paging to a different record. "He was found on an anonymous tip and no one ever came forward to claim credit. I wonder why not?" Toshiyo glances back at Starla. "What's wrong?"

"The date." An uncomfortable electric buzz is building between her shoulder blades. "My amulet? Auntie Abbie said Mom got it on a job for Zacharia, and Mom called it her fertility goddess because . . ." Starla makes a face. "It was about nine months before I was born."

After a second Toshiyo's lips part in surprise, then she winces. "She told you that?"

"Gross, right? Nobody needs to know that. Anyway, when I asked, Auntie Abbie said the job went bad and the Alliance got involved. My parents got away — but Zacharia didn't."

"Do you think your parents tipped the Alliance off about where to find Zacharia? Or were they partners and he got the bad end of the deal?"

"You mean, are my parents the reason Zacharia is at Redrock Prison?" Good riddance, if so. "I have no idea."

The stone amulet around Starla's neck is the last physical link she still has to her parents. Since Toshiyo discovered the alien, the pendant has gone from a strange-but-pretty accessory to an artifact that's more unsettling with every new fact she learns about it. Starla's dying to know what her parents found out there in Durga's Belt, but her parents — and anyone and everyone who served on the *Nanshe* with them — are dead. Auntie Abbie, the one person she thought might actually know the story, doesn't have any details.

She'd been losing hope of finding out the full truth. But now, one of the people who was there when her parents found this amulet might still be alive. Locked up at Redrock Prison. With a potential grudge against her parents, a definite grudge against her godfather, and an army of cultists at his back.

"I have to talk to him," Starla signs.

"Zacharia? Good luck. As far as I can tell he's being held in solitary confinement, even if you could walk into Redrock with a visitor's pass."

"He found me in the virtual museum," Starla signs. "If he's in solitary, who's giving him network access?"

"He must have some friends up there," Toshiyo agrees. Now that she's not messing with the files anymore she's fallen into her patois of USL, fingerspelling, and speech. "As far as I can tell, he's been running the Dawn's operations outside Redrock since his brother died."

"I thought Coeur shut them all down?" That had been part of Jaantzen's plan in reinstating her, at least — if not the only reason he did so. Bennion Zacharia had aligned his cult with the Dry Creek crew and Coeur's lieutenant, Acheta, then tried to do the world a favor by killing Coeur. Under normal circumstances, trying and failing to kill Thala Coeur would have been the biggest mistake of his life. But he also tried and failed to kill Willem Jaantzen. After Jaantzen took Bennion out, he'd put Coeur back in power and let her apply her own efficient vengeance to wiping out the last traces of the Dawn cult.

Or so she'd told them. Starla knows Coeur has been useful, but the woman has left too many scars on too many of Starla's friends for Starla to trust her. No matter what Jaantzen's new arrangement with her is.

"She got rid of the Dawn in Bulari, at least." Something closes down in Toshiyo's expression, like a window going opaque. "Remember that news story you found a while back, about the poisoned water shipment?"

While the Alliance seems to be focused on developing terraforming from the alien technology, the Dawn had been fixated on the alien's venom and its ability to enhance humans' healing abilities and reflexes. Either that, or kill them — as far as Starla can tell it's a toss-up, and not a risk she's interested in taking. But they called it the Gift of the Fallen, and according to their holy books, they were trying to perfect the formula to create it at a scale large enough to "purify the world." They started their experiment by delivering it to some no-name company mining town last week via the water supply.

"They're doing it again," Toshiyo says. "Or still."

She pulls up another file, then sits back, expression impassive.

It's a news story from Ruby Basin. Two separate corporations lost contact with their operations a few days back and sent out representatives to investigate. The first corporation, Ouro Vermelho, discovered fifty-three employees dead. One hundred and thirty-seven were found dead at the Blacklode mine.

Blacklode.

Starla's gaze cuts instinctively to Toshiyo; she's studying a chip in her black nail polish.

Blacklode was the corp Jaantzen had bought Toshiyo's indenture from, about five years before Starla came to live with them. Toshiyo never talks about her time there, but given the small amount Starla's been able to dig out of

Manu, she's not sure if she should feel happy or horrified Blacklode got hit.

Horror wins out as she reads on. One hundred and thirty-seven people dead from what the news feeds are starting to call the Brujería Syndrome, after the pusher in the Brujería nightclub who'd been publicly poisoned by the Dawn's tainted shard. The article lists the symptoms, which basically amount to becoming a blistered pile of charred flesh. Same as the man Starla watched writhe to his death at the nightclub.

Whoever hurt Toshiyo probably died years ago. And even if they didn't, nobody deserves to go that way.

Toshiyo hasn't moved since she pulled up the news report for Starla; she's barely breathing. Starla squeezes Toshiyo's shoulder and the other woman jumps at the touch.

"You all right?"

"I'm fine." Toshiyo cracks the ring fingers of both hands, then reaches for her keyboard again. "I read through the coroner's reports and compared them to both the original shard pusher and the last poisoning. They're changing the formula each time, and I think they're getting closer."

"What?"

In response, Toshiyo taps a finger against the last sentence of the news article. Starla leans in to reread it, skin crawling as she realizes the significance.

Ouro Vermelho is still searching for the whereabouts of four missing miners.

"Where did they go?" Starla signs. There's nothing around for miles, and the pusher at the Brujería had died within minutes of taking a tainted shard tab. Hardly long enough to run.

Toshiyo pulls up another link in lieu of an answer.

Starla begins to read, nausea churning in her gut at the account of a murdered homesteading family nearly ten kilometers from Ouro Vermelho's company town. The lone survivor, a ten-year-old boy, described a man who ripped through their front door and couldn't be stopped. Just like Bennion Zacharia's supersoldiers, who'd healed miraculously and kept fighting long after they should have been dead.

She's read and reread the Dawn's holy book enough times that Felipe Zacharia's words come unbidden to her mind: *Through the Fallen, God has given us the means to create heaven on earth, to transform this broken planet and its unfaithful people as one. It is the duty of the faithful to fulfill the prophecy by spreading the transformative power of the Fallen to cover the planet and its inhabitants. And after the fire burns away the impure, the pure will become devout. And when the pure become devout, we will see a new era unlike anything humanity has ever experienced.*

Bennion Zacharia may be dead, but his brother is still trying to spread the Gift of the Fallen throughout New Sarjun. And Starla isn't so sure she wants to live in a world with all of its impurities burned away. Especially when surviving the serum apparently means being turned into a monster.

"What can we do to stop him?" Starla signs.

"Zacharia? He's about as safe as he can be at Redrock."

"But he has access outside the prison. Can you get into his records?"

"Not the current ones, but I cloned everything I could access through Ximena's account before they finally shut it down."

Starla leans in as Toshiyo begins sifting through another torrent of data, pulling files onto the desk. Something nuzzles insistently against Starla's leg, and she lifts Mango into her lap. The cat's purr thrums against her chest, rough tongue on Starla's chin, whiskers tickling her neck, the small gestures of affection becoming more insistent and annoyed as Starla's hand stills. Starla barely remembers Mango's in her lap as she understands what she's reading.

Felipe Zacharia had been given a life sentence when he was arrested thirty years ago, and he's been granted considerably more privileges throughout the years for good behavior. Including a massive leap about fifteen years back for, according to the record, *collaboration on ongoing case B-259.087.*

The timestamp on the record is as familiar to Starla as her own birthdate. It's the day Silk Station was destroyed, her parents were killed, and she was taken to Redrock as a prisoner by the Alliance.

"This collaboration?" she signs to Toshiyo. "What case is that?"

Toshiyo opens a search in another screen. "Case B-259 dot . . . o . . . 87. Here it is." She pulls it up, and her eyes go wide.

Alliance case B-259.087 is closed. The targets, Raj and Lasadi Dusai, are listed as killed resisting arrest. Their network is listed as dismantled and neutralized. Their daughter, Starla Dusai, is presumed dead after attempting escape from Redrock Prison.

Starla stares at the file blankly, seeing but not understanding the scroll of transcription on the bottom of her screen as Toshiyo speaks to her.

In the back of her mind, she's always believed the Alliance could never have found Silk Station without help. A few times over the years, she and her cousin Mona have even traded dark conspiracy theories about who in her parents' crew might have been the traitor. Felipe Zacharia may have been at Redrock for almost fifteen years by the time he collaborated with his captors to bring down Starla's parents, but he must have still had some network outside the prison that he could tap into in order to direct the Alliance to the right place.

A fifteen-year-old grudge finally laid to rest when he used the Alliance to wipe out the Dusai clan.

Felipe Zacharia is the reason her parents are dead. That her aunts and uncles and cousins are dead. That everyone who remains is scattered throughout the system.

He's also the reason hundreds of people are dead by poisoned water — and in his ideal world he'll kill millions more.

She blinks back into reality when her gauntlet buzzes: Jaantzen reminding her their meeting with Leti and Calanthe is about to start.

"We're stopping him if I have to go to Redrock myself and find him." Starla stands. "I have to go see Jaantzen. Find a way for me to get to this asshole."

Toshiyo's already turned back to her keyboard. "Working on it."

4
____

JAANTZEN

"The worst of the bleeding's probably over," says Lo é Njeri, voice crackling with static. Her image on Jaantzen's wall screen is banded and grainy. "We might see a few more resignations still, but unless there are any more big bombshells, anyone who was going to quit on pure principle already has. And the recruiting agency I hired is sending me good candidates." Lo shakes her head with a laugh; she's finally becoming more relaxed about delivering her endless litany of bad news to Willem Jaantzen during their daily meetings. "But silver lining? Cedra finally quit."

Jaantzen knows the name, though he's never met the office manager Manu has complained about for years. "Then who's handling admin at RKE?" He suspects he knows the answer.

"It's being routed through me for now," Lo says. "But it's fine. After the initial batch of people calling to cancel orders, it's been business as usual there."

Rosco Kudra Enterprises, Jaantzen's restaurant supply business, took the biggest hit when the news first came out that he was the owner. Unlike the Jungle or Admant Security, the name Willem Jaantzen had never been associated with RKE. Customers — and employees — were caught by surprise.

Business is steadying quickly after the initial uproar though. Most Bulari restaurant owners care more about getting a good deal than who their money goes to.

Admant Security has been a different story. Employees and customers alike knew who they were working with, but the double punch of shard allegations and Jaantzen being implicated in the Alliance Embassy bombing has earned him sudden cold shoulders. Appointments canceled, prospects gone cold, budgets "dried up." Fortunately, while RKE has seen an exodus of staff, he hasn't lost a single employee at Admant. Maybe because everyone there feels like they work for Starla, not him.

All his businesses are under investigation, but Jaantzen isn't worried. Every shielding unit and security-grade electric barb Admant Security supplied was legally acquired and documented, and the few times someone like Phaera or Julieta needed something above and beyond, Starla acted only as a facilitator to help the client meet her old friend Absolon Chevalier, Arquellian arms dealer.

Not to mention Admant's clientele include respected business leaders like Mizal Seti and Lhasa Demosga. Public figures like the mayor's sister. Important places like the prime minister's summer home. Politicians like Chief Justice Geum-ja Leone. His staff at Admant Security has been very helpful in sharing those names with authorities and reporters.

Lo scrolls to the next item on her briefing list. "Pupura finally broke their contract, good riddance," she says. "But I've already shown the office space to two of the companies on our waiting list today — I'll have it filled by the end of the month."

"Thank you. And the retail spaces?"

She laughs. "There were some grumbles at first, but nobody's complaining now. They're getting *so much* new business. Foot traffic is up by forty-three percent — notoriety isn't all bad."

Lo winces, like she's stepped over a line.

"I'll take what silver linings we can find," Jaantzen says, and she relaxes a fraction. He doesn't want notoriety; he doesn't want fame. He wants a quiet, peaceful life with all his people safe and cared for.

But he'll play the hand he's been dealt, like he always has. And he'll win.

"Send me a list of open positions by priority, but don't wait on me. I trust your judgement to hire whoever you need."

"Thank you, Mr. Jaantzen," she says, and her smile seems genuine. "I'll talk to you tomorrow."

His penthouse was a quiet place, but when Lo é Njeri cuts the connection, the silence of this desert bunker is oppressive. He can't help but think of the meters and meters of soil and sand over his head, the wind-scoured kilometers between this place and their nearest neighbors.

When death comes in on the desert wind —

He blinks as the words slip in and out of his memory; a fragment of a poem he'd heard years ago. It's gone before he can grasp for the rest.

The property feels like death on the desert wind, indeed. A few lone buildings make it look like a bare-bones homestead from the outside. Defensive shielding below the surface hides the bunkers, which were dug by hand into a paranoid warren over decades.

Toshiyo and Starla made a thorough sweep of the place and have at least mapped all the rooms even if they haven't been fully explored. Some of the older rooms are rustic, but the later work is clean and meticulous, the work of a man who spent the better part of his life building extensively. Hiding? Or simply contrary? Jaantzen supposes a certain sort of person appreciates being so self-reliant that they create their own power, filter their own water, and even install scrubbers to keep the oxygen levels right lest they all suffocate. They might as well be on a space station, cramped and claustrophobic with nothing but a thin layer of foil between life and death.

Something brushes against his leg and he nearly shouts out before he feels the tiny pricks of claws kneading his calf.

Pepper. One of Starla's pair of cats who've also been relocated to the Maraka Valley indefinitely while he and his crew prepare their counterattack on Leone. Pepper and Mango at least seem happy with the arrangement. Plenty of mice and spiders for them to hunt out here.

Jaantzen flinches back in his chair as the cat leaps into his lap, then picks it up gingerly before the delicate claws snag the threads of his suit pants. He sets the thing on his desk, where it sniffs at his coffee mug and swishes its tail across Jaantzen's nose.

In a strange way, the fallout over the last week has been a blessing. For years he's wondered which of his employees would quit if they knew who they actually worked for. How much of his business would dissolve once his name was attached to it. Now he has a number. It's a blow, but it's not as high as he'd expected — and at Admant the damages wouldn't have even made a blip except for Leone's false allegations.

He hadn't realized how long he'd been holding that breath.

He may not have to hide who's behind his businesses anymore, but he's still hiding from Leone, and from the Alliance — though the latter more because they want the alien creature than because of the warrant out for his arrest. It hasn't been officially rescinded, but it was deprioritized almost as quickly as it was announced. Alliance Deputy Chief of Mission Marquez ó Lauris had sent a hasty message to Manu that his agreement with Jaantzen was still in effect. That there was no need for Jaantzen to attempt to derail the current trade talks between New Sarjun and the Alliance by allowing the Alliance agent who'd attacked Cobalt Tower to testify and expose the Alliance's unauthorized attack on — and murder of — New Sarjunian citizens.

And as far as Jaantzen can tell, ó Lauris is correct. The consequences of playing that card vastly outweigh the benefits, which means that, for now at least, he has an uneasy truce with the Alliance.

Silver lining, as Lo would tell him.

He checks the time, then pings Starla and nudges Pepper off his desk to make his next call. The connection request cycles, maddeningly slow, but finally it goes through. Calanthe Yang, the daughter of Jaantzen's mentor Julieta and a lawyer extraordinaire, appears on one half of the screen. Starla's friend, the PR shark Letizia Diamante, appears on the other. Her interpreter doesn't join them for these video calls; the transcription software is good enough to keep Calanthe in the loop and fill in the gaps in Jaantzen's USL.

"Good morning," Jaantzen signs and says aloud.

"Good morning," Leti signs back. "And good news: We got our first mainstream hit on your connection to Leone."

That is good news. Leti has been pushing Admant's connection to Bulari's high-profile figures — particularly Leone — all week. The gossip rags are eating it up, but so far the mainstream feeds have shied away. Jaantzen scans the story she sends. It's brief, but it's original research rather than parroting the gossip rags. And it hints that Jaantzen and Leone's business relationship began around the time Thala Coeur was removed from power.

Jaantzen almost allows himself a smile.

If Leone is hell-bent on taking him down, he's taking her with him. And he has much less of a distance to fall.

Footsteps in the hall, and he turns to see Starla hurrying in, waving a quick "Sorry." She looks haunted, but she turns on the shine when she slips into the seat next to him and greets Leti and Calanthe.

"Good work," Jaantzen signs to Leti. "The prisoner scandal, any progress?"

She makes a face that says, *Good news, bad news.* "Do you know Kumail Anh?" The name vaguely rings a bell; Jaantzen shakes his head. "Legendary reporter, and friend. He's broken stories all over the system — wars, organized crime, insurgent groups. He's been digging into the missing prisoners and found evidence New Sarjunian citizens are being illegally sent to Redrock in exchange for kickbacks. At first he thought this was some sort of labor thing, for the manufacturing they do up there?"

"I recall." The labor issue's been hitting the news again in light of the trade agreement negotiations, some New Sarjunian protest group accusing the Alliance of international crimes against humanity for using Redrock prisoners as unpaid labor. They're calling for New Sarjun not to renew the Alliance concession, but that will never happen.

"But it's weird. Kumail has found transfer records *to* Redrock, but no official record of prisoners arriving."

"They're not at Redrock?"

"The Alliance isn't just using these prisoners for labor, they're disappearing them," signs Leti. "This could be bad for Leone. 'Criminals get worse sentence than usual' isn't going to make a splash, but if the chief justice of the Supreme Court is involved in a cover-up with the Alliance?" Leti tilts her head, dark hands paused dramatically mid-flourish. "I'm dying to find out what they're hiding."

Alien technology. A paradigm-changing terraforming operation. And who knows what else — maybe even a training facility for supersoldiers. Coeur's sister, Ximena Nayar, had told Jaantzen she'd been requisitioning extra rations and shipping them on for years, never asking questions about where they went. Playing her own part in covering up the illegal labor provided by people the Alliance — and Leone — didn't think society would ever miss.

"Is there a connection to Leone?" he asks Leti.

The face she makes says, *Not quite.* "Kumail is trying to nail down who the kickbacks are going to."

"Thank you. Calanthe, have you been able to speak with Leone's former secretary yet?" Breaking the scandal in the press is one thing. Building a legal case for Leone's involvement requires careful work. If they can find an eyewitness like Leone's former secretary Orris Moss, someone who was in on her kickback scheme before she sent him to rot in Taufang-Set, it could be their golden opportunity.

If they can get in to talk to him.

"They've been stonewalling me," Calanthe says. "But I

called in a favor and got an order to speak with him. I'll have that in hand tomorrow. They can't deny him counsel if I make a stink about it, but it's been hard to do without alerting Leone I'm trying to see him."

"Call me tomorrow, after you see him."

He hates the strangled pace required to make their move without tipping their hand, but Willem Jaantzen is nothing if not a patient man. Leone's been flinging false allegations his way, assuming it won't take much mud to tarnish his reputation. Jaantzen's attacks on her need to be airtight if he is to have a chance to beat her at her own game.

"Thank you both. Is there anything else?"

Calanthe shakes her head. Leti lifts her hands. "Kumail isn't the kind of reporter who sits at a desk all day," she signs. "He's going to try to speak to someone at Redrock in person."

Starla straightens beside him, preoccupied expression dropping away at this new development. "Maybe we can help," she signs. She lifts her chin at his disapproving look. She's been dropping hints for days that she wants to take a team up to Redrock to see if they can learn anything more about the alien wreckage, and every day he's been telling her no.

Now she's found another reason to insist on going.

"We'll talk later," he signs, out of view of the screen. They can argue about this when they're not in front of Leti and Calanthe. "How soon?" Jaantzen asks Leti.

"As soon as he can find a ride."

He ignores Starla's pointed look. "Keep me informed. Calanthe, can you stay on a moment?"

Leti's screen goes dark and Jaantzen turns to Calanthe. Even in the staticky picture she looks exhausted, lips pinched and dark bruises under her eyes. The last few weeks have been hard on the Yang family, and even polished Calanthe is showing cracks.

"How is your mother?" Jaantzen asks.

Her lips thin. "Not good. That night in jail was hard on her. It looked like she was recovering, but she's started to slide. The doctors . . ." She sets her jaw, either choosing her words or working up the courage. "She wasn't strong to begin with, and between Leone and my sister" — she spits out the word — "her health has plummeted. They're not sure how much longer she'll hold on."

"Is she still at the hospital?"

"We're trying to bring her home today. Maybe tomorrow." Calanthe clears her throat. "She'd rather be here, when . . ."

"It will be good for her." The words sound hollow. "I wish I could be there."

"She would like that."

Jaantzen casts about for something more to say, but nothing will change the fact that Julieta Yang is dying and he's not at her side. "Let me know how it goes with Moss," he says. "And give your mother my love."

Calanthe's sad smile breaks his heart. "I'll tell her." The screen flickers to dark and Jaantzen leans back in his chair, the slow fury that's been banked in his chest for days kindling into hot flame.

He hates this, being trapped in the desert. Hands tied while Lo manages his businesses, while Calanthe argues her way into Taufang-Set Penitentiary, while Phaera pleads his case to his former allies, while Letizia sends reporters digging for answers.

While Julieta lies dying.

All because he refused to be Leone's lapdog, and she went to war with him rather than take no for an answer.

Her fight is with him, yet she's put everyone he loves in the crosshairs. If Leone doesn't kill him, the stress of sitting and waiting will.

Starla's watching him, and his chest tightens. Ah, yes. He forgot to add Starla's desire to return to the hellhole he rescued her from fifteen years ago to his list of things he cannot control.

Starla lifts her hands before he can tell her she absolutely cannot go.

"Toshiyo has been trying to figure out the missing piece of the terraforming puzzle," she signs. "The serum the plans call for? It's not the liquid the baby alien incubated in. It's not the alien's venom. She went through the plans again, and figures it's an organic material the Alliance found on the alien ship. We have to get a sample if your business plan with the Demosgas is going to work."

He folds his hands, waiting.

"The reporter? Leti was telling me about him — when he digs his teeth into a story, he doesn't let go until he knows the truth. Getting him to Redrock will be very good for us."

"And what else?" he asks.

"We need to know more about Lucky. The Alliance has been studying the aliens for longer than we have, they will have answers."

She's about to sign something else, her hands pause ever so briefly before she drops them into her lap. Jaantzen may not have had the benefit of knowing Starla as a child, before she became his tempestuous teenage ward, but by now he's familiar with this too-innocent body language. She's trying to sweet-talk him without revealing her full motivation. He considers pressing, but that's the best way to get her to close up. Better to approach it from the side.

"What's your plan?" he asks, and the corner of her

mouth twitches in triumph, another look he knows well. Despite his best intentions, he's rarely managed to keep Starla from executing her schemes.

"The reporter will need to go legally, right? So we find someone making a delivery to the prison — I already pinged Manu about it." Of course she did. "Then Simca, El, and I jump before they land and sneak into the alien research facility." She waves his hands back to stillness before he can respond to that madness. "With our satellite up in the air, we have maps, locations scouted, all of that. Toshiyo and I have been talking routes and logistics for days. The only thing that changes is the reporter helps make things more legitimate."

There's a reason she almost always wins: Her plans are rarely half-baked.

"Supplies?"

"Gia has most of what we need. I'm going to pick it up this afternoon."

"This afternoon? And when were you going to talk to me about it?"

She shrugs. "Today. This was good timing." She leans forward and kisses him on the cheek. "I'm heading out. Do you need anything from Gia's?"

"No." He catches her arm as she starts to rise. She couldn't have thought she was getting past him so easily. "Tell me this is just about Leone and the aliens." Cracks appear in her careful expression. "Starla. What's going on?"

She presses her palms together in her lap, composing a response or composing herself, he's not certain. Finally she lifts her hands, and her eyes go hard. "Felipe Zacharia? He sold my parents to the Alliance. He's the reason my family is dead."

He was the one?

The Alliance couldn't have found Silk Station without help, and in the early days Jaantzen had tried to track down the informant who murdered Raj and Lasadi Dusai. But then the civil war had happened, things got bloody at home, and by the time he had the energy for it once more, all the trails had gone cold.

"You're certain?"

She tugs at the cord around her neck and pulls out the stone necklace she's taken to wearing. "They found this amulet while working a job for him. The Alliance got involved, he was arrested. Fifteen years later, he helped the Alliance find Silk Station. Somehow my parents are connected to these aliens, and I have to know how."

"Some mysteries stay buried."

"I have to try."

"Not if it puts you at risk. Listen to me carefully." A muscle jumps in her cheek. "I need you to bring home a sample for the terraforming plans, to assist the reporter, and to find any data you can about the aliens. When Leone's no longer a threat, we'll figure out what to do about Zacharia. Your parents' death will be avenged. But do not put your mission in danger to do so."

He expects her to argue, but she nods once, slowly, and closes her hand around his. "I love you," she signs with her free hand. "And I promise."

"I love you, too." He sits back in his chair, struck by a sudden weariness that has nothing to do with the anxious days pacing the prison-like bunker or the haunted, sleepless nights on an uncomfortable bed. "We'll go over plans tonight when you're back from Gia's."

5

___

PHAERA

The first time Phaera sat across a table at Lucky's Palladium Coast from Wiljo Cavenaugh, she'd been terrified.

Unlike most of the other casino owners Phaera had worked for over the years, Cavy walked the floor of his Aterciopelado and socialized with the people dealing cards and serving drinks to his patrons. Phaera had been dealing in the high rollers room, where he preferred to spend his time, so she'd gotten to know him a bit better than most. When she decided to open her own place, he was the first person she approached for advice. She knew enough to know she couldn't go it alone, and Cavy was the best around when it came to creating exclusive experiences that attracted the gambling elite.

It was a risk, telling him about her vision to one-up the 'Tercio's high rollers rooms, but she'd sold it as providing one more reason for the filthy rich crowd to come planetside rather than staying up in Aiax Demosga's orbital casinos. Cavy had been immediately enthusiastic about the idea, and Phaera's gamble paid off. The Devil's Table might be busy, but the 'Tercio is busier yet.

Still, who had she thought she was, asking the oldest, most respected man in the business to mentor her? And who does she think she is now, asking Cavy to give up his careful impartiality and choose herself and Jaantzen against one of the most powerful women in the city?

When she'd come to him for business advice, he'd met her request graciously. Today, he's frowning at her as he slowly chews a bite of pineapple.

Phaera doesn't flinch, doesn't let her chin drop, doesn't backpedal.

Her mother has recovered. Her parents are safely on "vacation" in Alusina. And Phaera's secured her first round of meetings on Jaantzen's behalf. She started with Cavy not because she believes he'll say yes — she doubts he will — but because Cavy won't play games. He'll give it to her straight, even if it's not what she wants to hear.

Cavy sets his chopsticks down beside his plate, lining them up precisely in a way Phaera has learned means he's sorting through possible responses. He's dapper as always in his ivory three-piece suit, with a glossy green silk shirt and an ivory tie embroidered with abstract swirls. He leans his elbows on the table and folds his hands, each gnarled brown knuckle sporting a jewel. The tips of his silver braids brush the table.

"Acheta brought his fight to my drag," he finally says. "And I am sorry I didn't act sooner to support you. But you're talking about stepping into a fight that's not mine. That's not in my neighborhood or with my people. I'm sorry, Phaera."

"I'm not talking about picking a fight. I'm talking about

a meeting of like-minded businesspeople who want to make a difference in this city."

"That's what the Casino District Business Association is for."

"And we've discussed expanding to include Jet Park, yes." Phaera leans forward. "But advocacy is one thing. Action is another. The city ignores the concerns of anyone outside the downtown core, you know that. Even after Acheta shot up the Lorelei, the police didn't do anything to help me."

"So you went to Willem Jaantzen."

Lucky's Palladium Coast is loud and no one is nearby. For all the restaurant's faded cushions, garish gilt-and-cut-glass decor, and mediocre food, it's a popular meeting spot for a reason. Casino workers come here because it's off the drag and the tourists are too nervous to go inside. Business owners and underworld players come here because Lucky's is regularly swept for bugs and the regulars keep their curiosity to themselves.

Still, Cavy said Jaantzen's name in barely a whisper.

"I asked him for help because I've known him for years through Leone, and I knew he was also having difficulties with Acheta. That, and no one in the Business Association would help me except for Dal Jaxon and the cab drivers union."

She doesn't bother keeping the frustration out of her voice, and Cavy's face softens. She's not angry with him — she knows why he was reluctant to help in her fight with Acheta, and he'd shown up when it mattered the most. She'd probably be dead if it wasn't for Cavy, but she's not going to win him over if the conversation stays centered on Jaantzen.

"I also went to the police, which didn't get me anywhere. Cavy, when's the last time you actually got a response from the BPD? They came out when Ayisha had that stalker, but she's basically a national treasure. Remember when Herran got robbed at gunpoint? The police didn't even call him back. Or those poor girls who kept showing up dead in Dry Creek Ravine a few years back? The only reason that sick asshole got caught was because Naali Hinoja put her crew on finding him." She raises an eyebrow. "And we could give the police every address of every shard operation in Jet Park and they wouldn't lift a finger."

"You think Jaantzen will solve our problem."

"No, Cavy. But I'm saying no one else is going to solve our problem. I'm saying me, you, Ayisha, Mizal Seti, and the other Jet Park business owners — and, yes, Jaantzen — we can solve our own problems."

"And Coeur?"

She blinks at him.

"Thala Coeur," he says again. "You mentioned Naali taking matters into her own hands, but Naali's dead, now. Blackheart's back."

She and Jaantzen haven't spoken about Coeur. If he was planning on involving Blackheart — the flamboyantly vicious crime boss turned mayor turned . . . whatever she is now — Phaera assumes it'll be through some arrangement of his own. Bringing her into a room full of the people Phaera is collecting would be disastrous. But she can't discount the possibility Coeur will become involved, whatever her history is with Jaantzen. Which means Phaera needs to know exactly how disastrous it would be.

"I don't know anything about Coeur," she says. "Have you met her?"

"I have," he says. "Shook her hand once when she was

mayor. She was a competent mayor, but too rash." Cavy picks up his chopsticks once more. "Crime's down in Dry Creek and Altamira since she's been back, which means it's down on the drag. I can't complain." He stirs thoughtfully through the dregs of his fried noodles. Phaera knows from experience she has one last shot to influence those thoughts.

"I wasn't looking for a fight," Phaera says. "But it came to me. So I'm seeing the opportunity here — not just for business, but to actually make a difference. You're already leaving a legacy, and when you finally retire they'll build you a statue on the drag. But will anything actually change? The politicians will keep ignoring us, the police will keep ignoring us."

"Who are you doing this for, Phaera?"

The tips of her ears are burning. "I'm sorry?"

Cavy sets down his chopsticks. "I've never been in politics, but everyone I know who has says the same thing: Geum-ja Leone will either make your career or destroy you. Is this a fight you want to pick?"

"Or is he using me as a shield, you mean?"

Cavy spreads his gnarled hands in a shrug, rings flashing.

"Do you remember how many people tried to invest in the Table in those first few years? I turned them all down because I wasn't going to let anyone tell me how to run my business. That includes Leone — and Jaantzen. I'd rather rebuild from ashes than let her keep thinking she owns me. I understand if you can't help, but I'm not stopping."

Cavy's expression softens. "You have a whole life ahead to gamble, but I'm an old man. I'm happy, and I'm not going to make an enemy of a woman like that when I'm this near the finish line. But I'm flattered you asked me." He sighs. "I suppose you hoped for another answer."

She hadn't, not really. "I understand."

"You're fighting an uphill battle, Phaera. I don't think crossing Leone is wise, but I wouldn't expect you to roll over for her. If there's another way I can help you, let me know."

A way that doesn't put your skin on the line, she thinks, but it's not fair to say. Wiljo Cavenaugh mentored her when she wanted to build his competition, he championed her when other casino owners dismissed her out of hand, and he stepped in between her body and a bullet when Acheta's man tried to kidnap her. Cavy doesn't owe her anything more.

"You can help by promising to always to give me your honest opinion," she says.

Cavy laughs, a quiet chuckle. "I don't have any other kinds."

"And thank you for meeting me."

"Always. I wish there was more I could do."

"I understand." Phaera swipes marks onto the table to cover their meal, and he lays a hand over hers.

"Be careful, Phaera," he says softly. "You're messing with fire."

"I always am."

The furrows between his brows deepen. "Careful, or messing with fire?"

Phaera winks and squeezes Cavy's hand. Both. Neither. She gives him one last smile to push aside the feeling she's in far over her head, then weaves her way through Lucky's, dialing up a cab on her cuff. Oriol falls into step beside her when she passes the bar, where he's been waiting.

"No luck?" he murmurs, and Phaera shakes her head. This meeting with Cavy had been a long shot; her meeting with Mizal Seti could be an even longer one. Depends on whether Mizal is more scared of Leone or Jaantzen.

Despite the ten-minute cab ride between the casino district and Jet Park, the neighborhoods feel worlds apart. Jet Park is nearer to Geordi Jimenez Space Terminal, and anyone who could afford to moved out of the path of the never-ending shuttle launches decades ago. The cheap real estate means endless development opportunities — or so Mizal has been telling her for years.

Much more of the neighborhood is under construction than the last time Phaera was here. Work has halted in the heat of the day, turning Jet Park into a wasteland of cranes and safety fences and heavy equipment. The road is pitted with potholes where it's not torn up to lay pipes and wiring.

Maybe now *is* the time to get in on the Jet Park gold rush. She'll think about that if she survives Leone.

"We've passed at least a dozen construction sites," she says to Oriol. "It can't all be Seti."

"The man has property out here," Oriol says.

"An old spinner dealership, right?" She leans forward to the cab driver. "Do you know of an old spinner dealership that sold recently out here?"

"I try not to drive out here," the woman says, but she slows at the next intersection and points down a wide boule-vard. "This used to be Jet Park's main drag. That might be it."

The building has architectural value, if not the benefit of location. Three stories tall with a pure glass facade, the windows wrapped for stability. It's surrounded by the same trappings of construction as the other sites in the neighbor-hood, though the workers here aren't on a midday break. Angry red Stop Work Order signs flicker behind the hazy glow of a no-trespassing field.

"They say it's going to be a brewery," the cab driver

says. "Though I don't know who the hell's gonna come out here for it."

A block later, they pull up in front of a glossy black building that stands out in stark contrast to the rubble around it. Juvex Spa Center, reads the massive sign in glowing gold letters.

If Mizal was going for relaxing, this monolith of a building is not doing it. But maybe that's because she's not an ultrawealthy Indiran tourist looking for gentech treatments illegal in Alliance territories.

This stretch of sidewalk is newly poured and well-groomed, and freshly landscaped with local desert plants. In other parts of Bulari, tall buildings, trees, and woven shade screens dull the sun's edge, but standing in front of Mizal's black building at noon is nearly unbearable. Above them, the building's facade ripples with heat; sweat dampens Phaera's brow. Fortunately, security buzzes them in quickly.

The lobby is as soulless as the exterior. Glossy black tile and white marble columns, ostentatiously posh furniture that can't be comfortable to sit on. And a hologram AI receptionist so the tourists don't even have to talk with a real New Sarjunian as they get checked in. Charming.

"Mr. Seti will be down in a moment," the AI receptionist tells her as she approaches the desk. Its face lights up in a smile. "Would you like a drink? Green tea? Water? Champagne?"

"I'm fine, thank you."

The receptionist turns to Oriol. "Anything for you, Mr. Sina?"

Oriol frowns at it and doesn't answer. Facial recognition? Or did Mizal program it to know who was coming? Either way, this place makes Phaera's skin crawl.

"The way of the future," says a man's voice from behind

her. She turns, startled, and Aiax Demosga grins. He pumps her handshake. "Good to see you, Phaera."

The big man is as much bombast and bluster as ever, straight white teeth glittering in his leather-tan face, his obnoxious print shirt unbuttoned at the collar. Aiax Demosga's casinos, including the *Dorothy Queen* and the *Little Brother*, orbit New Sarjun. Phaera's been — they're honestly not as nice as the Devil's Table, or Cavy's high rollers suites in the Aterciopelado, but the plus for Arquellians is they don't have to set foot down on New Sarjun. As little as she likes this spa, it will be another draw for Bulari's economy.

"I was in town and Seti said you'd be stopping by," Aiax says. "Do you mind if I crash your tour?"

"Of course not." Phaera's been in customer service and gambling her whole life, she can lie with a straight face like the best of them. She'd requested a meeting with Aiax days ago and had heard nothing back.

"Good, good." Aiax turns his broad salesman's smile on Oriol. "Have we met?"

"No, sir." Oriol holds out a hand.

"I hired Mr. Sina during all the unpleasantness with Levi Acheta a few weeks back."

"Smart move," Aiax says. "This is a tough business and I'm happy to see a lady like yourself taking safety seriously. Oh, here's the man of the hour!"

He turns away to greet Mizal, and Phaera suppresses her eye roll. Plenty of men would have meant it as a dig. The worst thing about Aiax Demosga is that even though she knows he didn't mean it like it sounded, he has a talent for coming off like a pig no matter what he says.

She shares a look with Oriol, and steels herself for an aggravating hour.

What she doesn't know is why Aiax ignored her message only to show up here — and whether this changes her plans to talk with Mizal about Jaantzen. She knows the Demosgas and Jaantzen had been planning to do business, but that was a week ago, and Aiax Demosga is as capricious as a sandstorm. He may be ready to back Jaantzen's new business venture, or he may be in Leone's pocket.

She'll play it by ear.

Phaera turns a smile on Mizal Seti. He's a decade younger than her, though his dark hair is already flecked with silver strands and he has deep furrows on his brow and around his dark brown eyes. He's dressed impeccably in a pale blue suit with a lavender shirt; he grins, perfect teeth.

"Phaera, glad you could make it." He ignores Oriol and waves them all past the receptionist's desk and into a hall marked Private. "A quick tour, if you don't mind?" He doesn't wait for a response; Aiax grins at her like they're sharing a joke.

Mizal's dress shoes and voice echo down the sterile white hallway. "We have a dozen private suites," he's saying, "fully equipped with everything you need for your stay. It's a nice getaway for the entire family."

"So Dad can get cybernetic eyes, Mom can get a massage, and you can put little robot flippers on the kids?" Aiax laughs at the disapproving look Mizal shoots over his shoulder. "I'm kidding, Seti."

"We do it all," Mizal says in response. He pushes through a door into the spa, which is a sharp contrast to the rest of the building. It's lush and tropical, and Phaera's skin drinks in the humidity. The decor is all rich blues and flashes of gold, with trickling water features and plants filling every corner. Tasteful signage advertises specials, and the air is scented with an exotic mix of oils that manages to feel both spicy and relaxing.

"This is lovely," Phaera says in surprise.

Mizal doesn't try to hide his pleasure at her reaction. "You're welcome any time you need to unwind," he says. "Compliments of the house."

"I hope you do couples' packages." Aiax winks at Phaera. "Because I think we're all going to need to unwind after this shitstorm with Leone is over."

"Not in a million years, Demosga," says Phaera.

"Why, Aiax, I thought you'd never ask," Mizal says at the same time. He squeezes the other man's elbow. "Give me a call. When this is over."

Aiax laughs, but the mention of Leone has tarnished the levity of the moment.

"My office is this way," Mizal says, leading them through the far end of the spa reception area, up a set of stairs, and to a chic waiting area. He stops outside his office door with a pointed look at Oriol. "Your guard can wait here," he says to Phaera. At Phaera's nod, Oriol settles easily on a couch across from the office door.

Mizal's office windows are frosted; the view of the Jet Park street can't be pleasant. He waves them into a set of modern chairs upholstered in rose gold around a white marble coffee table.

"The primary challenge I'm facing is image," says Mizal. "With the Alliance ban on mod surgeries, most genmod facilities on Indira are underground chop shops. Unsanitary, high mortality rates. So whether my patients are here for a lifesaving treatment, accessibility gentech, or a vanity mod, I need to make sure they have such a fantastic time they can't wait to tell their friends."

"Or, they can tell their friends they're going for a spa getaway," Phaera says.

Mizal nods. "And Indiran customs agents."

"Then you must be up in arms about that Alliance trade agreement, too," Aiax says. "The bit about restricting gentech trade."

"It's frustrating, yes."

"You've got the image nailed," Phaera says once they've settled in with refreshment. "Except for when you're driving through the neighborhood, when it definitely feels like you're about to be chopped up and sold for parts."

"I told you you should've done this in orbit," Aiax says. "My clientele, they don't even have to come down to the surface."

"I need consistent gravity," says Mizal. He shoots Aiax a look. "And maybe I'm not embarrassed by my own planet."

"But the neighborhood?" asks Phaera.

"Is why you and I are talking."

"The Casino District Business Association has been an incredible boon for our neighborhood," Phaera says. "And expanding it to include Jet Park would give us an even stronger voice, because then we're talking industry. Manufacturing. Medical tourism. We might be able to get the government to take our issues seriously."

"Issues like Thala Coeur?"

Phaera takes a deep breath, ready to go to battle.

But Aiax laughs. "And what do you expect anyone to do about Coeur? Declare a national emergency and invade the Fingers? What I hear, she's been good for peace."

"Crime is down on the drag, Mizal," Phaera says. "Foot traffic is up. I've spoken to several of my colleagues who've just had their best week in months. There may have been a burst of violence right after Coeur took power, but there hasn't been so much as a mugging reported since."

"I think 'reported' is the key word."

"My chief of security at the Table grew up in Dry Creek," Phaera says. "He says it's night and day difference now when he goes home." She holds up a hand. "Mizal. We're not diminishing your personal grievances. But maybe wait and see before stirring up the pot with her."

"Being angry at Blackheart is like being angry at an earthquake," Mizal says slowly. "It doesn't do a damn thing — but I thought I could trust *him*."

"It was a difficult decision," Phaera says, because it must have been — not that Jaantzen let her in on it at the time. But surely he didn't decide on a whim to work with the woman who killed his wife and children.

"A decision he made on his own," Mizal says. "She killed my father."

"We know, Mizal," says Aiax gently. She hadn't expected him to have her back in this conversation, but maybe she and Aiax Demosga are the only people in Bulari Coeur hasn't personally pissed off. "But you know how Jaantzen thinks. He's a humorless bastard, but he's always a dozen moves ahead, and he doesn't roll on anyone he's given his word to. If he needed Blackheart in place, it's for something we can't see yet."

Mizal is watching him warily. "What deal did you two make?"

"A good one, and I want Leone off my back so I can see it through." Aiax tosses him a grin. "I thought you'd also made a deal with Jaantzen."

Mizal frowns at his hands. "I haven't been able to get many people to invest in Jet Park — they can't see the potential like I do. But I knew if I could get him interested, I could sell other people on it. Everyone knows he doesn't make bad business decisions."

"Except for pissing off Leone," says Aiax. He turns expectantly to Phaera. "Which is why I'm guessing you're here today. To explain how we can loosen Leone's grips on all our balls without shooting ourselves in the head."

Phaera sits straighter, cold calm flowing through her. "I've been thinking a lot about politics lately," she says. "About the way power transitions from one generation to the next. A tight fist can choke a community's vitality. It can stifle revenue growth. And I don't know about you, but I'm getting tired of ultimatums about how I run my own business. She thinks she's the sole center of power in this city, and right now that's true. But only because the rest of us are too scared of her to band together."

"We're smart to be scared," says Aiax. Mizal nods in agreement. "If she finds out I met with you, she'll shut me down." Which explains why he's here; Phaera and Mizal have reason to meet, but Aiax couldn't come up with a reason to see her without inciting Leone's suspicion.

"You're going to let her keep control of you?" Phaera asks.

"You're suggesting I give Jaantzen my leash instead?"

"Of course not. I'm suggesting you take it back for yourself."

Mizal studies her. Aiax studies the ceiling. And Phaera's heart thuds as she waits for their response.

Mizal clears his throat first. "Tell him I would like to apologize for my rash acceptance of the rumors about him. But his support of *her*" — the way his lips twist at the word, there's no mistaking he's talking about Coeur — "feels like a betrayal. I don't understand it and I will never accept it." He takes a deep breath. "But I am not his enemy."

Cool disappointment settles in her gut. Phaera turns to Aiax.

"The bastard's crazy," he says. "And you're crazy for listening to him."

"But he's always a dozen moves ahead, right?" she asks, though both men have made up their minds. "And you know you can trust him to have your back if you have his."

"You can trust him to have *his* back," Mizal says. "He's leaving you out to dry, Phaera."

The words hit her like a slap; years of schooling her game face keep her from reacting. "That's not true."

"Even if it isn't, it won't matter," Aiax says. "He's picked a fight with Leone and she's already crushing him. He's looking to spread the blows between the two of you, and I don't think I want in on that game."

He's looking to spread the blows between the two of you.

Jaantzen's not thinking that way, Phaera knows it, but — isn't she partly playing the role of a distraction to keep Leone's attention while he makes his plans in the desert? She pushes the thought aside and gets to her feet. She can't let Aiax knock her off her game.

"You'll side with Leone, even if it means missing out on your big business deal?" she says to Aiax. "And you both know she's pushing that new trade agreement with the Alliance. What if she decides it's a bigger payday to get in bed with the Alliance than support her allies here on New Sarjun? All of your client base, Mizal, gone in a flash because you were too afraid to cross her."

"But Coeur," Mizal says, frowning.

"Is the least of your problems," says Phaera over her shoulder as she crosses to the door. "You both know how to reach me."

6

JAANTZEN

Jaantzen's suddenly aware of how hungry he is. It's well past lunch and he hasn't heard any noises out of the kitchen since Starla left hours ago, which means Toshiyo probably didn't eat either. It's not the first time a meal has been skipped when the two of them have been left alone together.

The kitchen is just down the hall from the room he's staked out as an office, and though it's not much to speak of, it's certainly better supplied than when they arrived. Jaantzen owns a restaurant supply company that's currently in a downturn — he had a few units to spare to outfit their safe haven.

Where they've gone to ground, literally. From the top of Cobalt Tower to being buried in the earth. He's not missing the irony.

Or the penthouse, he's surprised to find. It was comfortable. It was secure. He liked it, but it was just another temporary place to store his clothes and make plans. Only, unlike the long chain of abandoned warehouses and ratty apartments and safehouses he'd lived in before, the penthouse had a fantastic view.

But it hadn't been home.

He'd had a home, once. A narrow, three-story townhouse on Seventeenth Street, out towards Carama Town. It had been old but well tended, the faux-wood floors patched with love, flea-market art hung over walls they'd always meant to repaint, the carpets on the stairs worn threadbare. Mismatched furniture Tae insisted they didn't need to replace even as their incomes stabilized and they could afford to. A tiny kitchen with brightly painted cupboards and well-scrubbed tile counters Tae complained about every time she rolled out dough.

It was a tight fit for family dinners with Gia, Toshiyo, Manu — Oriol if he was in town — especially when they added a pair of toddlers into the mix. But no one had complained about the lack of elbow room if it meant a chance to sample one of Tae's feasts.

So strange to think he could once gather everyone he needed to protect under a single roof. At nights in this bunker, knowing Manu and Toshiyo and Starla are all asleep down the hall, he can almost pretend it feels the same. But in actuality he has employees across multiple companies whose families rely on him for their income. Phaera trusts him to make the right move, and therefore he now feels responsible for her parents, for the people who rely on her. He has Julieta and her family — he knows it's not fair to her to include the Yangs in his tally, but if their friendship has led Julieta's family to harm, then it's his responsibility to fix.

Jaantzen roots around in the refrigerator and finds leftovers from the hearty soup El Anahoy made yesterday afternoon — he's turned out to be the best cook among them and now supplies them with leftovers when he comes out to visit. Jaantzen sets the soup to warm and washes a pair of bowls from the pile in the sink.

"Hey, boss," Toshiyo says behind him.

He straightens, startled out of his thoughts.

"I wasn't sure if you had lunch," he says. The soup is starting to sputter on its burner; he switches it off.

She smiles. "A snack. I heard you in here and thought I'd see what you were scavenging up." She takes the bowl he offers. "Looks like you were pretty deep in thought."

He ladles soup into his own bowl, considering how to answer. He finally settles on the truth. "I was thinking about the house on Seventeenth," he says, and Toshiyo's smile saddens, but doesn't fade.

He hadn't slept there again after Tae's death. He had returned only for a few possessions. Toshiyo convinced him to let her pack up the rest before he sold it — it had been her home, too, for the first year she lived in Bulari. He's never asked what she kept and what she sold.

Toshiyo settles at the kitchen table. "You eating here, or going back to work? I got the latest batch of satellite scans, and so far they look amazing." She thumbs on the tablet she brought with her and sets it on the table in front of her.

"It's still flying?" Jaantzen asks, setting his bowl across from her.

"Mm-hmm." Toshiyo swallows. "I mean, I'm proud of our cloaking job, but if we make it to the end of the week without the Alliance shooting us down it'll be a miracle. Still," she calls up an image and taps a finger on it, "this is gold."

Due to the nature of the treaty that granted the Alliance land to build their prison, the skies above the Alliance concession on northern New Sarjun are kept purposefully free from satellites. No one but Alliance prisoners and prison staff lives in the uninhabitable land north of the Jupari Desert, which bands New Sarjun's equatorial zone. It must have seemed like a good deal to New Sarjun's government at the time. Give the Alliance some useless land, get a nice check each year. Of course, they had no idea the discovery of a lifetime — an alien spacecraft — was buried in those sands. Whether or not the Alliance did is another question.

If New Sarjun's government knew about the technological bounty in the northern hemisphere, they might think twice about renewing the Alliance concession as part of the trade agreement.

There's no way this secret stays hidden forever. And surely there's a path forward that doesn't get everyone he loves killed by Leone, the Alliance, or both.

Jaantzen zooms in on the spot Toshiyo is pointing at. A spot they could have missed were it not for the fact they knew where to look, thanks to the intel Ximena Nayar had brought them. The shielding is rudimentary: simple tents and optical disruptors, designed to keep anyone from looking deeper. One of the images Toshiyo shows him is dotted with heat signatures beneath the shielding; in the other he can make out the elegant, alien lines of what they've come to believe is the crashed alien spacecraft.

Jaantzen studies the images with a growing sense of dread. "What will Starla find up there that she can't learn from these?" he finally asks.

Toshiyo sets her spoon back in her bowl and presses her lips together. "We need that sample, boss. As far as I can tell, the Alliance is using an organic material they found on the ship to terraform, and we need it, too, if you want your plan with the Demosgas to work. We also need to know everything the Alliance does about the aliens before Lucky and our other little buddy get much bigger." She picks up her spoon and stirs the soup a moment before setting it back down without taking a bite. "I don't want her to go either. But even without all that, Leti's reporter needs to find out what's happening to those prisoners."

She zooms out on the images, tracing a faint line with the tip of her finger. "This is the flight path. They'll come in low enough that when Starla and the others jump, they should be pretty well obscured by this mountain range. We drop them with the murdercopters, and it won't take them more than a few hours to get to the crash site and terraforming operation."

Jaantzen frowns at her. "With the 'murdercopters'?"

"The, uh . . ." Toshiyo points at the ceiling, like she's indicating something stored over their heads. "Those helicopters that came with the property, the personal-size ones that fold up? They're in the hangar."

He has a vague memory of helicopter blades stacked in a corner. "They run?" And more importantly: "They're reliable?"

"Oh, yeah, we've been playing with them. I thought you knew."

"And you call them 'murdercopters' because . . . ?"

"The blades. They're below the rider." She waves a hand at his wide-eyed expression. "They're safe. Just . . . sketchy. Looking," she quickly amends. "Anyway, they get the intel, they rendezvous with the ride home. Starla and I have already gone over all the possible routes and come up with the best options."

Jaantzen takes a deep breath. "What do you need to be ready for them to leave tomorrow night?"

"I'll keep getting more detailed scans on every pass.

And with luck the Alliance won't notice our satellite for a few more days, so we can maintain communication."

"What are the odds?"

Toshiyo shrugs. "There are a lot of unknowns, boss."

"Is it worth it?"

"Yes."

"Thank you."

Toshiyo folds her hands in front of her, pressing knuckles to her lips. The pale undersides of her forearms are marked with the welts of angry red scars, a web of lacerations from the night the Alliance agent nearly killed her. The gash on her left palm is no longer bandaged, but the scar still looks red and sore.

Something about this place is making him nostalgic, apparently, because he can't help but think of the first time he sat across from Toshiyo Ravi. At another bare metal table, in another stifling bunker buried out in the desert. Twenty years ago, she'd been barely nineteen, less than half his age, though she'd seemed younger still, shivering in an oversized sweater with sleeves past her knuckles. He and Gia had trekked all the way out to Ruby Basin in search of a certain ops tech with a reputation for brilliance, only to find himself sitting in front of a waif who looked like she could be knocked over by a breath.

All her nerves had faded away when she ran through a test scenario for him, though. Jaantzen could see her mind working in rapid blinks as she made split-second decisions. The trembling in her hands stilled, the calmness in her eyes and the tenor of her voice never wavered even as systems began to fail, her ragged, dirty nails blurring as she typed.

None of the other candidates had achieved perfect marks on the impossible scenario. Toshiyo Ravi had done it without once losing her cool. And then she'd melted back into a shell of herself once more.

At first he'd thought she was scared of him; later, he would come to realize she was just exhausted and malnourished, and the haunted look had far more to do with the faded bruise on her cheek than interview jitters. And that the oversized sweater hid layers of fading yellow, deep purple, and angry, fresh red, revealed by the slip of her sleeve when she shook his hand to agree to take the job. Later, when Tae began to share with him what little Toshiyo was willing to tell her, he'd learned that compartmentalizing was less an innate genius and more a survival trait.

Twenty years later, he doesn't know what he would do without her calm voice in his ear.

Toshiyo sighs pointedly, and he tears his gaze away from her arms.

"I'm fine, boss," she says.

He forces his clenched jaw to relax. "I promised you'd be safe if you came to work for me."

"And I have been."

"You were shot within the first week." During the disastrous job he'd originally hired her for, the one where Coeur had double-crossed him the first time. "You nearly died."

"No I didn't. Oriol and Gia were there."

"Why did you stay with me?"

"You know."

"Tae."

For some reason that makes her laugh; she picks up her spoon once more and digs into the soup. "C'mon, boss. Anyway, I'm ruined for working for anybody else. Who'd get me my own satellite?"

"I didn't get you a satellite." Jaantzen frowns. "Frankly, I have no idea where you got it and I've been afraid to ask."

Toshiyo grins. "Starla traded for it from Absolon."

Absolon Chevalier, Indiran arms dealer and old friend of the Dusais.

"Ah," Jaantzen says.

"You thought we stole it."

Jaantzen opens his mouth, closes it. "I'm not sure where else one gets an Alliance satellite," he says finally. He never deals with Chevalier personally; he certainly didn't know the man had that kind of thing in his catalogue.

A chime cuts through the moment, an alarm on Toshiyo's tablet. "Time to feed Lucky."

"Do you need any help?" He's relieved when she shakes her head. He takes her empty bowl to the sink with his own and begins to wash them both. "Once we're through this, it may be time to find someone with a bit more expertise to help us with the creature."

"We should talk to that professor Starla's been seeing," Toshiyo says.

Jaantzen turns, curious. It's a strange way of phrasing it, and he's about to ask her to clarify when he notices her chagrined expression.

Oh.

"'Seeing'?" he asks.

"I mean. Getting information from." She drops her face into her hands. "I'm bad at this girlfriend thing. She's met with him a few times, but she seems into him."

Jaantzen can't even recall the man's name; he hadn't realized he'd need to.

"Does everyone know but me?"

"Boss, 'everyone' right now is me and Manu. And if I somehow noticed, Manu definitely knows."

Jaantzen smiles ruefully. "Are you saying I'm less observant about relationships than you are?"

"Hey!" Toshiyo laughs. "I didn't see *you* at girls' night. Thanks for lunch."

The water is still running; he shuts it off and considers the disintegrating soapsuds in the sink. Starla's never brought home a serious relationship, which he always assumed was because she hasn't found the right person. Now he wonders if it's not her, but him.

A conversation for a happier time. Jaantzen forces his shoulders to relax, hands going through the motion of washing the bowls. He can fret about his goddaughter's happiness when his bandwidth isn't consumed by worrying whether or not she'll come home.

7

STARLA

Gia and Tevi's Andel Medical School is tucked into rolling foothills of the mountains by the same name, which rise a hazy red and jagged contrast to the gray-green of the Maraka Valley. The winding road to get to the compound is well maintained, the compound walls painted a welcoming blue. They're also heavily fortified. It's meant to make the students feel safe out here — many have never left Bulari before — as well as to keep the school from looking like too much of a target to raiders. Gia has spent hours with Starla and Toshiyo over the years trying to find the right balance between welcoming and secure, and as Starla drives up to the entrance, she's proud of the end result of design deterrents and hidden defenses.

The gate is open, but the way the gate swings out forces her to drive through a twenty-meter chute edged with disruptor fields. A touch of a button and those fields will crisscross the entire chute, disabling any vehicle and sending waves of nausea through the occupants. Even though she knows where to look, Starla can barely see the disruptor's panels built into the otherwise rustic walls.

She does good work.

Too bad none of this can go in Admant Security's portfolio. All Jaantzen's donations have been carefully laundered to keep his name from being associated with the school, and Gia uses the money to buy supplies from one of Admant's competitors. Safer for her that way.

A cheerful sign points the way to emergency services, student housing, and the office. Everything is built around a central plaza, with the student housing tucked away from the public buildings for a sense of privacy. A hangar is built into the far wall of the compound. Out here, it's faster to travel by air than by the poorly maintained dirt roads, so many of the Maraka Valley's citizens have a hopper or two for getting around. Not to mention the patients who get airlifted in from farther-flung places outside of Bulari.

The deathtrap property has a hangar, too, and though the murdercopters have been fun, Starla's dying to get her hands on a hopper. Until then she'll have to be happy with the ancient ORV cargo hauler they found on the property. It didn't take too much magic to get it up and running again, and it tackles the pitted-out roads in the valley marvelously.

Somebody's walking out of the office to greet her, and Starla slows her cargo hauler in the center of the plaza to wait for him. She slides down the window — a blast of midday heat pours in — then taps a finger against one tattooed ear and shows him her comm.

I'm here to see Dr. Ate. She's expecting me.

He gives her a thumbs-up and beckons for her to follow, then helps her back the hauler against a loading dock. "Wait here," he says, or she thinks he says. He's exaggerating the words, lips stretched and barely readable.

Starla cuts the engine with the mechanic's prayer to the

gods of ancient machinery running through her head: Don't die on me now.

She settles into the broken-backed seat to wait, pulling up a string of new Admant Security messages on her lens. Last-minute work to wrap up and hand off while she's gone — maybe it's a good thing business is so dead right now. She's finishing up a delicate message shutting down a current client who's inquiring about discounts — there's been an uptick in those lately — when Gia appears at the driver's side window.

Starla presses Send and lifts up the door with a grunt. She knows it's reinforced for rugged driving, but it also makes for impressive armor. This hauler is fantastic.

"Good to see you," Gia signs. "C'mon in." She vaults easily onto the loading dock and holds out a hand to help Starla up.

The warehouse is small and packed to the brim but neatly organized, every box on a shelf and labeled except for four stacked near the loading dock.

"These are yours," Gia signs; her hands are hesitant and her USL primitive but reasonably clear. "Everything you asked. Want to open?"

Starla nods and flips open the knife at her hip.

"This one's all medical supplies." Gia's words appear on Starla's lens as she slices the seal of the first box. "Is your lens on? Okay. First aid, a suture kit, you need a refresher?" Starla shakes her head. "And you've used a universal splint? Good." Gia holds up a silvery vial. "Coag nanites, please be careful with these. Any questions about anything else?"

Starla digs through the rest of the supplies but doesn't see anything she's not comfortable enough with.

"Next box is more of the same," Gia says. "Bandages, et cetera."

Starla believes her, but slices it open to paw through herself anyway. Burn spray, wound sealant, bandages, antiseptic, tourniquets. She'll take this all up to Redrock, but if everything goes well, these two boxes can sit unused on the ship. Satisfied, she reaches for the third box.

"Desert survival supplies," Gia says. She doesn't release the box, though, and Starla looks up. Gia's expression is vintage *Don't bullshit me*; Starla feels like a teenager again. "You having trouble with the life-support systems over at the property?"

"It's good to be prepared," Starla signs. Gia seems to understand — like Toshiyo, she's learned to understand USL better than she can speak it. Knowing what Starla said doesn't seem to diminish her skepticism, though. But she releases the box.

"Water reclamation masks. Thermal sleeping bags, emergency shelters in sand camouflage as requested. Sand camouflage?" Starla gives her an innocent look. "This last box is the wastewater reclamation system — you're really planning for trouble, huh?"

Starla shrugs and pokes around the wastewater reclamation system's mess of tubes and containers. She really hopes that thing doesn't come in handy.

Satisfied, she sits back on her heels. "Thank you."

Gia holds up a finger — *One last thing* — then reaches into her pocket for a data chip. "I thought you might be missing something from your list. A map." She holds up a hand to fingerspell "Redrock."

Starla tilts her head to study her.

"Please tell me I'm wrong," Gia says.

"I have a map," Starla signs. But she takes the data chip from Gia's fingers and slots it into her gauntlet, calling it onto her lens to examine side by side with the one she already has loaded into her system. "It's the same."

"It's inaccurate."

Starla blinks the maps away and lifts her chin for Gia to go on.

"I looked everywhere, but you're not going to find an accurate map of that place. The employee complex outside is probably right, but the prison itself is wrong." Gia gives her a searching look. "And there's nothing of the surrounding area. Though you're probably not going to the prison itself, anyway. Not if you're looking for . . ." She fingerspells "aliens."

Starla begins closing boxes — she'll reorganize once she gets back to the deathtrap property. "Thank you for your help," she signs.

"You need someone who knows not just the prison, but the surrounding area," Gia says. "I was on enough work crews, I know that place like the back of my hand. I still know people there. And if you're going to get into some shit, you need me. Plus, I'll sleep easier knowing you're not going to accidentally give someone thrombosis with the nanites. If you — "

The light in the warehouse changes suddenly as bright sunlight washes in through the far door; Gia glances over her shoulder and calls something back to whoever entered. Starla slips the data chip with the map of Redrock Prison into one of her cargo pockets as Tevi Sharaf rounds the corner.

Starla hasn't seen Gia's husband for a few years, and in the interim his prematurely salt-and-peppered hair has gone completely silver. It's working for him when you add it to his golden skin, youthful features, and lean runner's frame.

Tevi opens his arms as Starla reaches for a handshake, and they settle on an awkward half hug, half arm clasp.

"Good to see you," he signs — or kind of signs; Starla understands what he's trying to say. He gives her one of his signature gentle smiles, then switches to speech. "Did you get the supplies you needed?" Over his shoulder, Gia's fierce glare says, *Don't you dare bring this up with him.* Like Starla wants to get in the middle of that fight.

"Yes, thank you," she signs.

"Happy to help," he says, though his discomfort is clear. If anyone but Starla had come for this shipment, he wouldn't be in this room, but he took a liking to her when they met ten years ago on Maribi Station. After she'd helped save his life, but before he realized who her godfather was. "How are things?"

The way he stumbles on such a simple question tells her he knows about their recent move to the Maraka Valley and isn't thrilled with how the neighborhood's going downhill. Despite the fact that it's still at least a forty-minute drive on rough roads between the medical school and the deathtrap.

Starla smiles brightly, gives a *Fine* flick of her wrist, then types, How's the new crop of students?

She listens politely as Tevi describes the newest cohort, half reading the transcription, laughing when he laughs. Her thoughts are on the other side of the planet.

Gia will be instantly recognizable in the Alliance system if they get caught, but then so will Starla. And at least Gia's a free woman rather than a fugitive. Bringing her along doesn't escalate their risk in the slightest — and she'll be an enormous asset. And Starla will breathe a bit easier knowing they have a medical professional along. And at being able to pick Gia's brain for information about the region.

Last time they worked together, though, Starla was barely out of her teens, and Gia had been an overbearing babysitter hired by her godfather. Starla's already nervous as hell. She knows El and Simca will follow her without question, but she's also taking unknowns with her: the pilot, the reporter. People she's going to need to command with absolute authority to keep them all safe.

Will Gia follow her orders? Or will having her there be a disruption?

And Jaantzen's been trying to get Gia out of operations as much as possible. How will he react if Starla says yes?

Tevi seems to be wrapping up on a high note, so Starla gives him a friendly smile. "That's great," she signs, then pretends to notice the time. "It was good seeing you, but I gotta go. Long drive back."

"I'll help her load up," Gia tells Tevi when he starts to reach for a box. "Can you check on the patient in Room 12?"

"Of course." The warm smile he gives Gia falters when he turns it on Starla, but he gives her another hug goodbye.

Neither she nor Gia move until the door closes once more. Then Gia's lips part — and Starla holds up a finger. She types out a message, she needs to make sure Gia completely understands this.

I would be grateful to have you at my back, but you're not coming to protect me. You're working for me.

Is that relief spreading over Gia's face? "I understand," she says.

Starla locks her eyes on Gia's and presses Send again. You'll take my orders.

"Of course."

And Tevi needs to be fine with you going.

A muscle jumps in Gia's cheek, but she nods.

We're leaving tomorrow. Be there by dinner with supplies for three days.

Starla frowns at Gia, considering. It'll raise red flags if Gia goes with the reporter and the pilot to Redrock Prison itself, which means she should go with Starla's team, and El can stay with the reporter. Of course, that means she needs caught up on one critical part of their plan.

Actually, come a bit early so you can learn to fly the murdercopter.

Gia's eyes go wide. "Oh, fuck no," she says.

Starla grins.

By the time Starla arrives back at the deathtrap, she has another dozen messages blinking in her queue, but only one she's been waiting on pins and needles for.

From her cousin, Mona.

Starla pulls into the hangar and swipes the vid onto the cargo hauler's screen.

"Hello, love!" Mona signs. "Sorry it took me so long to get back to you! It's been tougher than usual to check messages." She doesn't say where she is — she never does — but either she's not in range for a real-time call or it would be too risky. Looks like she might be under thrust, the way her hair is plastered to the sides of her face. Her hair is new every time she calls, and today it's reddish-brown streaked with black, her curls straightened into a chin-length bob that sweeps around her jaw.

"Did Auntie A get to you? Sorry she doesn't know much, but we'll both keep asking around. We're all good, by the way. Amit's fine, everybody's fine."

Starla's not entirely sure who everybody entails, actually. The last she saw most of her family, she was fifteen. Mona had gone dark right after the attack on Silk Station, but eventually her habit of constantly being on the move turned her into the central hub tying the far-flung members of the remaining Dusai family together.

It was the role Starla had planned to play, but instead she'd landed with Jaantzen and slowly settled into her life in Bulari, become invested in this new family in a way Mona doesn't understand. Starla lets the familiar pang fade; she's got no time for regrets today.

Mona continues on. "As for Deyva . . . No one's heard from him, cuz. Still." Her expression holds pity: *He's dead, he died in the attack, don't make me spell it out.*

Mona says something to someone off-screen, her lips obscured by the graininess of the feed, then turns back to the camera.

"I sent you a link with the other stuff you asked for. Let me know what else you need and I'll call you for real soon. Love you."

The vid goes black.

Starla pushes aside the familiar ache that comes from the brief conversations with her cousin, then finds and decrypts the link Mona sent through. She downloads the files and torches the shared folder. Identity markers for three different guards stationed at Redrock Prison: fingerprint schematics, iris scans, biological data, ident numbers, and passcodes. Starla doesn't know if they'll need them, but you can't be too careful, and her cousin is one of the best identity fixers in the system. And, honestly, even if they don't use these at Redrock, they'll come in handy eventually.

She could wander the labyrinth of bunkers until she

finds Jaantzen, or she could ask, so she pings him and gets an immediate response: In the lab.

The lab is a grand word for the bare room Toshiyo decked out to accommodate their little alien friend and his younger sibling, who is growing at an alarming pace. Lucky is settled in his pen behind a forcefield, sorting colored stones Toshiyo brought in from the desert into two piles. Jaantzen, Manu, and Toshiyo are watching.

"I think it's smooth versus rough," Toshiyo is saying. "Because it's not by color."

Lucky cocks his head at the two piles, then picks one of the rough stones in his talons and drops it into the other pile.

"Maybe it's mineral content?" Manu says. He glances at Starla as she enters. "How'd the trip go?" he signs.

"Good. How's Bulari?"

"I mostly stayed indoors." He winks at her. "But I did get you a ride. Benedicto Kulikutan, the pilot who flew our rescue crew to Julieta's greenhouse. He's got a long-range hopper that can make the trip, and a friend who doesn't mind getting a nice payday for letting Beto's crew take his regular shipment up to Redrock. Have El take the reporter to Geordi Jimenez, and Beto will bring them both up tomorrow by dinner."

Starla grins. "Thanks. You always come through."

"Don't make me regret it."

"I won't." Starla hesitates — she's not sure how Jaantzen and Manu are going to take this part. "Gia's coming with me."

"Gia's going with you." Manu says it aloud as he signs, and Jaantzen and Toshiyo both turn from Lucky to look at her.

Starla lifts her chin, ready with her arguments. "She

guessed at what we were doing and made her case. She'll be valuable on the crew."

Jaantzen and Manu share a long look. "Good," Jaantzen finally signs. He turns back to Lucky. Her godfather has never been easy to read, keeping his moods close and his expressions neutral, even when he's signing. Which has led to misunderstood words more than once. Learning to read him was a master class in nuance. Right now he seems worried. By the alien creature or by the coming events she can't tell. He's still not happy with what she's about to do, but she'd expected more of a fight after the call this morning. And right now.

"I'm going to go call Leti," she signs to Manu. "Tell Beto we leave by nightfall."

Manu nods, then glances at Jaantzen's back. "Understood. Have El ping me and I'll pass him Beto's info."

"Thank you."

Jaantzen is still engaged in his staring contest with Lucky, and it suddenly strikes her that he'd been avoiding the alien since they moved here, as though its paradigm-breaking presence was too much of a distraction. Maybe a distraction is what he needs right now, though.

Starla's plans are in motion, though. Simca Anahoy will be here tomorrow morning to help her pack, El and the rest will be here by dinner, and by nightfall they'll be slinging their way north across the vast, impassable expanse of the Jupari Desert.

To find answers, she tells herself.

And answers only.

8

PHAERA

"You finally got your wish," Phaera says.

"Getting to drive you home every night? It's about time." Vanessa Dosantos is maneuvering her spotless red Magnata Vashti through a steady stream of traffic and late-night revelers on the outskirts of the drag.

"Walking's good for you. And there are plenty of people out. Pickpockets are looking for drunk tourists, not me." Phaera lifts her wrist so the gold cuff gleams in the light. "And you and Hiro talked me into upgrading the self-defense specs on this."

Vanessa gives her a disapproving look; passing neon signs paint the Magnata's cream interior a shade that mimics Phaera's own magenta hair. "I appreciate you giving in to my paranoia," she says drily. She doesn't need to remind Phaera it's not the pickpockets they're worried about, and a self-defense shock isn't going to do shit against a trained assassin.

Phaera's apartment is about a fifteen-minute walk from the drag, in a perfectly safe little residential neighborhood complete with its own korris restaurant and corner store.

She could afford a bigger place — the thought's crossed her mind more than once over the past few years. But she's had a hard time breaking the scrimp-and-save mentality that took her through saving up a nest egg, building out the Table, expanding to the Lorelei, and finally becoming profitable. And it's hard to beat the location.

She doesn't know how Jaantzen can live in the same place he works. Phaera may not be home much, but it's a refuge from the demands of the job. A place where no one needs her attention, where she can leave a dish in the sink for two days and no one cares, where she can truly let herself unwind without worrying if the wrong person will see her let her hair down and lose the respect she's fought so hard to win.

Maybe that's why Jaantzen's always wound so tight. She can't imagine him letting the weight off his shoulders, even for a few moments. Although the other night, when she —

The tips of her ears are burning.

"How was tonight?" she asks Vanessa before she can spend any more time with inappropriate memories.

"Same, same," Vanessa says. "Headcounts are almost back to normal."

Something in Vanessa's voice gives Phaera pause. "What is it?"

"It's been a rough few weeks."

"And?"

"And the rumors have got people spooked." Vanessa gives her a sidelong look, then turns her attention back to the road, her red-gloved hands steady on the controls.

"Rumors about Jaantzen."

"Right."

There's the corner store, the korris joint. Phaera's building is another block away.

"I can't stop rumors," Phaera says as Vanessa pulls up in front of her building. "But I need you to be honest with me. How is staff morale, V?"

Vanessa narrows her eyes at the empty street, thinking. "People talk," Vanessa says finally. "But it's all talk. I've heard a lot of gossip and speculation about you and Jaantzen, but you know how it is. They're going to gossip about something, and at the end of the day it doesn't matter what people talk about in the break room so long as business is good, they're making money, and they're being treated well.

"And no one thinks the thing with Acheta was your fault. But." Vanessa purses her lips. "Fay. You always look for the best in people, but you're too trusting. You need to decide whether or not you want to take this bullet for Jaantzen. Whether or not you want one of us to take it."

Phaera draws in a sharp breath. She hadn't been prepared for the level of violence Acheta had brought in his attack on the Lorelei, and people had died because she'd underestimated him. But Leone? Phaera knows exactly what's at stake here, and she's not just putting herself in the line of fire. Vanessa's job is on the line — her *safety* is on the line. Hiro Matapang. Jae Bakshi. Everyone who works for her is at risk, whether through literal violence or the threat of losing their livelihoods if Leone does decide to shut Phaera down.

But the alternative to standing up to Leone is accepting Leone's leash. And that's unacceptable.

"It's not just me," Vanessa is saying. "Sina's worried about you, too, and he's one of Jaantzen's men."

"The troubles with Acheta were as much my fault as this feud with Leone is," Phaera says shortly. "So was the fight with the Arquellian casino chain that tried to elbow their way onto the drag last year. Somebody thinks I should roll over for them, and I refuse. I may be on Jaantzen's side in this, but any bullets I take won't be for him. They'll be for me. And for all of you."

Vanessa studies her a moment, then nods. "Then we'll give 'em hell together."

Something loosens in Phaera's chest. "Thank you. For the ride, and for being frank with me." Phaera leans across the console to give her friend a hug, then opens the door. "I'll see you tomorrow."

Phaera waves when she's through the gates, and Vanessa eases away from the curb and into the night. Beside Phaera, the building's night guard watches her go. "Glad you're finally getting a ride."

"Not you, too," Phaera says fondly. Diego has been waiting here for her every night for the past five years, watching trashy soaps in the guardhouse and keeping an eye on the building. She squeezes his elbow as he holds the building's front door for her. "Have a good night."

She takes the stairs, relishing the three flights even at the end of a long day. Each echoing footstep is a resounding refrain made up of Vanessa's question and Aiax Demosga's statement from earlier today.

"Are you sure you want to take a bullet for Jaantzen?"

"He's spreading the blows between you both."

Of course, that's the point. For Phaera to keep Leone's attention divided and away from finding Jaantzen, wherever he's off hiding and solidifying the next phase of his plan. She can move freely in the city, she can make the connections they need. It's a risk, but it's a decision she made for herself.

"He's charming," Leone had told her. Implying that everything Jaantzen had done was calculated to win Phaera over so he could use her as a shield. But wasn't it the other way around? Phaera had needed help, she saw an opportunity to get it, and she took what she wanted. She may be getting burned, but nobody tricked her onto this path.

Phaera locks the door to her apartment behind her, sealing the upgraded biolock her father had insisted on installing after the attack on the Lorelei. She kicks off her heels in the entryway and sets them neatly on a shelf beside their sisters, then pads barefoot across the cool terra-cotta tile to the kitchen; ambient light glows to life as she passes.

She loves this apartment. The quaint Coruscan-style geometric borders that have been out of style for fifty years go perfectly with the mismatched furniture. A few pieces are antiques that fit right in with the outdated Coruscan motif, some are modern splurges that caught her eye, and a few — like the liquor cabinet — are salvage. She found the cabinet behind a dumpster a decade ago and talked Vanessa into helping her haul it up to her apartment.

She pours herself a glass of mezcal, taking the bottle with her to the coffee table and settling onto the red leather couch. She has an early morning tomorrow, but she hasn't been sleeping well. Maybe a few glasses and some mindless vids will help slow her racing mind.

She calls up an entertainment screen, then stares blankly at the smiling robot hologram asking what it is she wants to watch. She ignores it for now and brushes a finger over her cuff; a call list glimmers above it.

Today was a bust. Cavy's rejection she'd expected. But Mizal? Aiax? She's watched them at Leone's dinner parties with Jaantzen, jovial laughs and handshake business deals and bravado. She hadn't anticipated their lack of spine.

She'd rather be reporting with good news, but maybe he'll have some of his own to lift her mood tonight.

Or maybe it doesn't matter, because as soon as she chooses his name from the call list, the dialing screen asks if she'd like to leave a message. He'd told her that could be a problem, a result of the unreliable network wherever he's holed up, but still it's disappointing. More so than she'd expected — it's been a while since she curled up on her couch at the end of a long day and willed a man to call her back.

Her cuff blinks to let her know the message is recording.

Phaera watches it blink, hairs rising on the nape of her neck. She glances over her shoulder, but of course no one is there. She's alone.

She cuts the connection.

NOTHING TO REPORT, JUST WANTED TO HEAR YOUR VOICE, she types by way of explanation, in case he sees the failed connection request.

"You want to see the best in people," Vanessa told her. "You're too trusting."

Jaantzen has been up front with her. Although, that night in the desert after her mother was poisoned? All those revelations about the Alliance, Acheta, Blackheart? He'd kept plenty of secrets from her — and he still is. He's refused to tell her what Coeur stole.

And maybe that detail doesn't matter. Or maybe Aiax is right, Vanessa is right, and Jaantzen will never be completely honest with her. He just needs her to protect him from the full force of Leone's anger.

Just like she needs him. Because something shifted inside her that night at Dr. Áte's desert compound, when he'd said those three little words.

"You have the support to fill Leone's power vacuum," she'd told him.

"So do you," he'd answered.

If Phaera is putting Vanessa's job on the line, it's not because of Willem Jaantzen's ambition.

She's finished her first glass of mezcal, hasn't managed to decide what show's going to put her to sleep tonight. The liquor is sitting uneasy in her empty stomach, along with a sensation she suddenly realizes is hunger. It's possible she missed dinner tonight; she can't remember.

She heads back to the kitchen to find something to take the edge off.

And stops, hand on the cupboard.

Something's tugging at her attention, something out of place. She retraces her steps, scanning the room, and spots a white square in front of her door. A note that hadn't been there when she came home.

From a neighbor, maybe? A noise complaint from her walking around this late at night?

She stoops to pick it up, and her pleasant mezcal hum vanishes like smoke. It's a thick paper envelope, her name written in a flowery script on the back. She recognizes the hand — the same as whoever sent her the three mystix cards at the Devil's Table last night. By the familiar shape inside she can guess what's in this envelope, too.

She tears it open, and her fingers know the glossy finish, the embossed shape on one side of the card before she even pulls it out. It's another mystix card from the Lorelei, the second of the three deadly fortune killers: the Fallen Tower. Your stronghold has been breached, the place you thought you were safe is now a trap.

There's another scrap of paper alongside it, a note written in the same flowery hand.

Nice place. I love the couch.

She spins, chilled. But nothing is out of place. Her

curtains are drawn. The door's biolock is still sealed, *was* sealed when she got home. Wasn't it?

It's a head game, she tells herself, as she opens a connection to the guard shed.

"Diego? Someone slipped a note under my door just now. Was it you?"

"No, ma'am. Gimme a minute." In the background, she can hear voices, canned laughter, Diego humming to himself as he checks the security footage. "Nobody's been past your door besides you. Maybe it was there when you got home and you missed it? I'll scan through earlier footage and let you know if I see anything. Are you all right?"

"Yes, thank you. I was curious. Let me know if you find out who it was."

She cuts the connection and wraps her arms around herself, rough goosebumps under her palms despite the day's lingering heat. The note wasn't here when she got home, she knows it — just as she knows Diego's never going to find a sign Victoria Tierren was in Phaera's building.

Was in her apartment?

It's all in your head, she tells herself. She's trying to get in your head. But she downs another glass of mezcal, hunger long forgotten, and settles into bed with a kitchen knife under her pillow. The morning birds are calling outside her window by the time she finally falls asleep.

9

———

MANU

Something's rustling in the bushes as he walks, and that shit is definitely not acceptable. A twig snaps, and Manu whirls with pistol in hand, aiming against the glare of the midday sun at one of those gray-green thorny shrubs with the tiny yellow flowers that make the air smell like honey. It rustles and he tilts his head, narrowing his eyes to see into its shadows.

Another twig snaps.

"Come on, asshole," he murmurs, shifting his weight, and a bull hare as tall as Manu's thigh bolts from the bush, galloping ten meters down the trail before diving into the underbrush. It tears across the desert in a trail of dust and dancing shrubs.

Manu doesn't holster his pistol.

He turns slowly, waiting for any other wildlife to make itself known. Because the lizards and the spiders don't bother him — they're more scared of him than he should be of them. They stay out of the house, he'll let them be. And scorpions are scorpions; Carama Town blends into the desert and Manu grew up shaking out his shoes.

But out here it's all red whips and razortusks and dziva hounds howling in the hills and scratching around the door all night. Bull hares are big but harmless, but if he meets a dziva hound he's filling it full of holes first and asking questions later. He's heard too many stories about them terrorizing the outskirts of the Fingers.

He spent the morning going over plans with Starla and Simca and Jaantzen and getting increasingly frustrated by the lack of things he can actually do. Normally all it takes is a good walk through the city to clear his brain, so he thought he might try a hike around the Maraka Valley property — but between the dusty, rocky trail and the boiling sun, it's putting him more on edge.

Maybe Jaantzen can sit out here and strategize, but Manu's not built for this. He's supposed to be *doing*.

Yesterday's jaunt in the city had scratched that itch. After leaving Oriol, he'd swung by to check on Mirana and Ajesh Paiman and their family, still comfortably protected in a safehouse until it becomes unnecessary to worry about Victoria Tierren. The girls were still a bit rattled after their ordeal, but they're tough kids. They'll be fine. It's Mirana and Ajesh who seem closer to breaking.

The murder charges against Manu haven't been dropped yet, but with Ajesh and Mirana both now testifying Acheta actually killed Naali Hinoja — and their restaurant's internal security footage backing them up — there's no way the charges will stand.

One problem solved, anyway. But Detective Timo Cho was supposed to stop asking questions about Manu and start asking them about Leone, and now the man is dead. Stabbed in the chest in his own apartment by a certain mercenary with a heart-shaped face. If Manu had been a better shot, if he'd been faster, the Paimans would be safe at home and Cho would still be alive.

And maybe Manu would be dead. His heart still beats too fast sometimes when he's lying awake in the middle of the night. A lingering effect of whatever poison Tierren poured into his veins? Or simply a byproduct of the last few weeks?

The asshole nearly took him down. She murdered Cho in cold blood. She kidnapped two girls and left them to rot — and nobody seems to know who she is. He doesn't understand how that can be true, that in this entire city full of criminals and con men and mercenaries who owe him and Oriol favors, nobody recognizes her face.

And nobody's seen her since she caught him in that alley.

He doesn't for a second think that means she's gone away.

Someone calls his name in the distance and he looks over his shoulder to find Gia with her hands in the air. "It's me, don't shoot. The boss — Jaantzen said you were out here."

He shoves the pistol home as she climbs the small rise to join him. She's more sure-footed on the rocks than he, but she did grow up out here, and she's been living here the past ten years. Plus, she's got the right shoes. She looks healthier since she moved back out here, too, more relaxed. Maybe she'd always been a desert creature making do in the city.

He holds out a hand to help her over the last boulder. "How do I know you're not a billion assassin ants dressed in a human suit?"

"My sense of humor. Assassin ants have notoriously bad comedic timing." Gia dusts off her palms then puts fists on hips, turns to survey the valley. "Gorgeous, isn't it?"

"Is it?"

If anyone asks, the desert is straight-up miserable, and if Manu never sees it again after this week it'll be too soon. Fine, the Maraka Valley is pretty, the ribbon of cottonwood and willow following the creek down the middle of the valley, the way the cliffs melt into rainbow hues in the sunset. And there's that moment every evening when the world seems to let out a collective sigh, flowers and foliage unfurling a bouquet of fragrances into the cooling evening air.

But Manu's a stray locked inside, and it's been all he can do not to throw himself against the door until it breaks and he can roam the city free once more.

The brush rustles again and his left hand flashes back to the butt of his pistol. Gia gives him a wry look. "I have a hunting rifle you can borrow."

"I'm not hunting." Manu lets his hand drop. "I'm defending myself against the locals. You're here early."

The quick glance she gives him holds a hint of relief; she probably thought she'd have to break the news she was going with Starla. "It's been a couple days since I last stitched you up. I was getting worried."

"I haven't been gored by any razortusks."

"They leave people alone."

"Doesn't look like they do."

"True," Gia agrees. She jerks her chin back at the complex. "C'mon. Let me take a look at you."

It's a ten-minute hike back to the complex — Manu hadn't let himself lose sight of it — and he greets the cool air of the underground bunkers with relief. The midafternoon sun is killer.

"Do you have a medbay set up yet?" Gia asks when he leads her into the kitchen.

"Nope."

"Seems like an oversight with you lot." She looks around. "This'll do."

"I'm fine, G. All good, no alien diseases."

"I'm not sure you know the definition of fine."

"In no pain, totally healed."

Gia flicks Manu's right bicep. He hisses in pain as her finger connects with the still-healing lacerations left by Toshiyo's hell-beast.

"Up on the table, Juric," Gia says.

Manu sighs and hoists himself onto the table, then begins undoing the buttons of his shirt. Gia unloads her bag onto the kitchen counter.

"Not sure what you need a scalpel for," Manu jokes. He shucks his shirt off and balls it up, tossing it at Gia.

She plucks it out of the air with a glare. "I wasn't planning on using it, but if you keep giving me lip . . ."

"No, ma'am."

Gia frowns at the healing scars on his right arm, but doesn't comment on them. They're not bad. Manu has been keeping an eye on them himself, and despite the deepest laceration still feeling a bit sore, everything else has healed as he would expect. Gia's neat stitches are out, and the shallower cuts aren't bothering him at all. She turns her attention to the gouge Tierren left above his hipbone. It wasn't deep, and it hasn't given him any trouble, either.

No, none of that worries him.

His pulse picks up when Gia pulls out her scanner and begins to examine his chest. He knows what she's looking for, he's been watching for it, too. The faintest stutter, the irregular heartbeat, the slightest indication that whatever Tierren shot him full of, it's still in his system. That it's damaged him permanently. A harbinger telling him that awful clutching sensation of a fist around his heart will come again when he least expects it.

That it will debilitate him when the others most need him.

"All good," says Gia and Manu forces himself to breathe again. "No sign of permanent damage. I'd call that another one of your many lives successfully used up."

"Who's counting?" he asks, a joke and a shoulder roll to ease the tension.

She walks behind him and smooths the cool scanner across his back. "If I were, I'd guess you've spent four. Deep breath."

Manu doesn't dwell on the times he shouldn't have walked away, but it doesn't mean he doesn't have an inventory at hand. "I think you've forgotten the time Jaantzen almost had that scary fucker who was his old lieutenant beat me to death in a basement."

"I *was* counting that. And your pulmonary contusion is healing fine, too." Gia drops the scanner back in her bag, then gives him a sideways look. "For the record, at the time I agreed with Kai. I still can't believe the boss let you live after you tried to kill him. He's too fond of strays."

Manu winks. "Good for you and me both." He hadn't actually known Gia had been on team Kill Manu, but it doesn't surprise him. She's always been fiercely loyal to Jaantzen. He files the information away, though; twenty years later and Gia's still got plenty of secrets locked behind iron bars.

"Then you're definitely not counting the time I was sixteen and my girlfriend's auntie caught me sneaking out her window," Manu says. "Most daring escape of my life."

Gia laughs, and it's genuine this time.

Manu grins. "This is probably the longest it's ever taken me to get you to laugh."

"Is that all you ever try to do?"

"Somebody's gotta lighten you up, Giaconda." He tilts his head at her. "Tevi still making you laugh?"

And the smile's gone. "Anything else you want me to take a look at?"

"Nah, man. I'm good."

Gia tosses him his shirt and starts repacking her bag. "I'll leave this here. I assume one of you all will need it sooner or later."

"Preciate it. Hey." That side-eye again. Manu finishes up the buttons but doesn't hop down from the table. "Things good with you? The clinic, all that?"

"Things are fine." She slams something back into her bag, too hard. "Things are amazing. Tevi's the best thing that ever happened to me, and these years living in the Maraka Valley have been the happiest of my life."

"You look great," Manu says, and she glares at him. "I mean it, G. You look healthy. Happy. Like you found purpose."

Her expression hardens. "So why the fuck am I here?"

He smiles gently. "Who would you be if your family needed you and you turned your back?"

"Happy." She bites out the word like a curse.

Manu doesn't answer, and after a moment Gia takes a deep breath, hands clenched on the edge of the table.

"Tevi doesn't get why I have to go."

"Course not." He kicks a leg out like a kid, it catches her lightly in the thigh and she turns with a scowl. "You wish the boss hadn't asked you back?"

"Yes. And not because it was Coeur he asked me back

for. Because I'd managed to forget how much I missed all this. All of you."

"That why you're going with Starla? Because you miss the adventure?"

"Tosh said she and Starla were making a plan to find out more about the critter, then Starla asked me to help her find some supplies. First aid kits, a bunch of desert emergency shit."

Manu slips off the table, hands in pockets, waiting.

"I figured if she needed all that to find answers about the critter, she was going to Redrock. And I couldn't watch her go on her own." A muscle clenches in her cheek. "Any more than I could let you waltz into Coeur's territory. I can't see any of you hurt, not if I can help. And I know I can."

"What did you tell Tevi?"

She looks miserable. "I told him Starla needed my help."

"Good call. He doesn't know her well enough to know she's trouble."

Gia doesn't smile; he wasn't truly expecting her to. "Biggest fight we've ever had."

"You wanna talk about it?"

"No." She straightens and points to the gleaming band of gold on his scarred left hand. "You two gonna throw a party or what?"

Manu frowns at the change of subject. "We've been pretty busy. And it's not like — "

"Not like you're surrounded by a bunch of people who love you both and could really use something to celebrate?"

Manu's silent a minute. "When you're all back," he says finally. "We'll talk about it then."

"Good. It would be a good time to reintroduce Tevi to everyone."

"I see your ulterior motives."

She finally smiles back. "Everyone likes a party," she says, then sighs. "I need to go talk to Starla. Jaantzen said she was in the hangar?"

"Stairway at the end of the hall."

"Thanks."

"I'll be up in a few."

He watches her walk away, his heart torn. One part pure relief Starla will have Gia at her back, one part fear he's watching yet another friend head into the heart of danger. And there's nothing he can do to help.

He can hear Jaantzen's voice as he approaches the bunker the boss is using for his office. And a woman's. Calanthe Yang.

"I spent the entire morning getting shuttled from person to person while they tried to find him," she's saying from the desk screen. "It's a prison. How do you lose someone?"

Manu catches Jaantzen's eye through the crack in the door and Jaantzen beckons him in. Manu toes open the door, slides shoulders against the wall.

"First they told me he was in the infirmary, then that he'd been released for a court date, and eventually it was a whole mess of guards and security personnel and nurses all yelling at each other to figure out what happened. Moss is gone."

"Escaped?"

"Escaped, or disappeared. Somebody found out I was going to see him and made sure it couldn't happen."

"A pardon, or a conspiracy."

"Willem, I'm sorry."

Manu raps on the door to get Jaantzen's attention. "I'll take care of it," he signs.

Jaantzen's lips press together a moment, and Manu can practically see the desire to keep his people safe warring with the need to find Moss. Especially as his goddaughter is upstairs about to fling herself into unknown danger.

There was a time Jaantzen didn't hesitate to let the people he hired do what he'd hired them for. And there was a time Manu's arm wasn't spiderwebbed with scars, his legs held together with screws. Going up against Coeur had burned them all badly, and Jaantzen has played it safe in the years since.

Still.

Jaantzen may not have asked to get them all into this mess, but they're not going to win if he doesn't let them do the work to get back out of it.

"I've got this," Manu signs. "Let me help Calanthe."

A muscle clenches in Jaantzen's jaw. "What do you need?" he asks aloud.

"I need to know who was there."

Jaantzen nods and turns back to the screen. "It's fine," he says to Calanthe. "Get me a list of everyone who was in the building today: doctors, delivery drivers, everybody. Manu is going to take care of it."

Calanthe nods grimly. "Keep in mind that if you want any case involving him to stick, you need to be careful," she says. "His testimony will seem a lot more valid if he wasn't broken out of jail."

Manu gives Jaantzen a thumbs-up.

"If someone is trying to make Moss disappear, it's already out of the legal system," Jaantzen says. "But we'll be careful. Thank you, Calanthe."

"I'll get that list to you right away."

Jaantzen cuts the connection, then turns to Manu. "What's your plan?"

Manu shrugs, shoulders slipping against the bunker's smooth metal wall. "The usual. Figure out the right people to bother, then have a nice chat about where Moss ended up. Get me that list — I've got a two-hour drive back to town to figure out who to start with, and Tosh can probably help." He gins up a smile and claps Jaantzen on the shoulder. "I'll dig up your man."

"Thank you."

Jaantzen turns back to his desk, and for a minute it feels like old times: Jaantzen needs a thing done, Manu heads out to do the thing, and there's no drama or angst about whether or not Manu should take the risk. Though that's probably because Jaantzen's worries are entirely occupied by Starla. As are Manu's.

He changes first, going from desert casual to a look that's versatile for night shenanigans in the city: suit and shoulder holster, nice shirt, black tie, good shoes. He tosses his tactical vest over his arm, cracks his neck, and shakes off fears for Starla with every step.

The kid's good, she's smart, and she's got a great team at her back. And she's going whether he likes it or not, which means the best gift he can give her is a send-off that doesn't make her start second-guessing whether she should be.

Starla and Simca are in the hangar, readying supplies to be loaded as soon as the pilot arrives. Manu had planned on being here to help facilitate the meeting, but Starla can handle it. And Simca's already flown with the guy.

Starla, a load of heavy coats in her arms, looks up as he crosses the hangar towards them.

"I can't believe you're off to have fun without me," he signs.

She drops the coats on a crate and gives his suit a once-over. "It looks like you're about to have some fun yourself," she signs back. "You can't keep going on dates with your hot husband while the rest of us are doing actual work."

"Hey! I'm doing work." Manu gives her a wounded look. "Moss went missing. I'm off to find him."

"Stay loose out there."

"You too." Manu holds her in a hug for a long time, feeling the strength in her grip, breathing in the sweat of a day's work, the faintly spicy scent of whatever she uses in her hair. He has to force himself to let her go, but when he does, he's got his grin back in place. "Don't do anything Oriol wouldn't do," he signs.

Starla laughs. "Copy that. You too."

He gives Simca a quick squeeze, then turns to find Gia watching him.

"I gotta run," he says. "I'll see you in a couple of days."

Gia's embrace is fierce, her breath hot on his neck.

"Don't do anything stupid," he tells her.

"That's my line."

He breaks the embrace, grins at Starla. "Hey, you got any hornet tags I can borrow?"

Starla shakes her head in exasperation, then reaches into a nearby crate and tosses him a roll. He stuffs it in his jacket pocket and slips behind the controls of the obsidian-black Taosa Scorpion that also doesn't deserve to be exiled in the desert.

He hits the runway and is headed for the potholed road beyond as a shadow passes overhead. When he cranes his neck he recognizes the shape of the ship blotting out the sun above him: the *Coldfire*, piloted by Benedicto Kulikutan. Another good kid, he thinks. Hopefully he and Starla can keep each other out of trouble.

It's out of his control now. He's taught her everything he can, and he found her a ride he trusts. Continuing to worry now won't do anything but get in the way of his own work.

So with a silent prayer to whichever god might still listen to Oriol, Manu turns his thoughts towards Bulari.

10

STARLA

"When's the last time his hair was natural?" Simca signs to Starla. The cloud of dust Manu left in his wake is rolling across the runway and the long-range hopper is on its approach, with Gia guiding it in.

"I don't remember." Starla doesn't think she's ever seen Manu without at least highlights of some wild color in his hair and on his nails. His hair dyed back to black, the matte black manicure — it bothers her. Though he's lost that dangerous, moody edge that had plagued him in the days before they retreated to the Maraka Valley, so maybe it's nothing to worry about.

He'd never tell her if something was wrong, anyway.

Maybe his lifted mood has to do with the forced relaxation out here. Maybe it's a byproduct of surviving his encounter with Victoria Tierren. The usual pang of guilt lodges itself in her chest at the thought. If she'd been faster, if she'd caught Tierren after they found her lair and the Paiman girls, the woman never would've been able to attack Manu.

Simca elbows her out of her dark thoughts and lifts her

chin to the hopper, which is settling gently in front of the hangar, dust roiling beneath its jets. "You didn't tell me the pilot was the guy who dropped us off to save your ass at Julieta Yang's place. The cute one?"

"Sounds like you had more fun than I was having." Starla tries to joke, but at the time she'd thought she — or Jaantzen — was going to die.

Simca's teasing smile softens. "Copy that, you get dibs on the cute boy missions next time around. Unless your hot professor will mind?"

Starla winces, and Simca raises a perfect eyebrow. "Things aren't going good with Sam?"

Good? They're not going anywhere — and how could they be? Starla hasn't had more than two minutes together to figure out if seeing Sam Amrith is something she actually wants to do, let alone *should* do. And that was before they disappeared into the desert. It's not like she can make small talk about what she's been up to.

"No talking about boys on missions," she signs.

Simca claps her hands in delight. "Bullshit! We have three whole days. And, girl, I'm going to find out your darkest secrets." She chucks Starla on the arm, then shouts something at Gia and goes to help guide the hopper into the hangar. Today she's wearing her hair in a thick black braid that cuts diagonally over her scalp; she has on the same sand-colored fatigues as Starla, though hers are adorned with a choker of glittery lime-green disks circling her slim brown neck.

Once the hopper's inside, they'll be safe from prying eyes. There's military-grade defensive shielding in the hangar, which means the guy who built this place was either ridiculously paranoid for a civilian or really had something to hide. Starla wishes she could have met him.

The hopper is a heavily modified Sikuda slingshot hauler, the name *Coldfire* emblazoned across the side. Sikuda slingshots were developed on New Sarjun for efficient long-distance resupply of far-flung outposts by flying a suborbital parabolic trajectory, though now they're primarily used by salvagers taking trips out to the desert to find and pillage wreckage, whether under the radar or on contract to whatever corporation lost a cargo shipment in a sandstorm. Other manufacturers have beat Sikuda out on the passenger transport front — apparently the ride in these old slingshots is much more comfortable for cargo than humans.

Finally the engines cut off, and the rumbling in Starla's chest abruptly disappears, letting her feel the butterflies once more. She ignores them — no time to back out now.

Simca and Gia flank her as the cargo bay door folds down from the tail. The interior is entirely stripped for cargo hauling, and rows of uncomfortable-looking folding seats line both walls. Most of the space is already taken up by pallets of supplies, the ostensible reason for the *Coldfire*'s run to Redrock Prison. The interior of the Sikuda is as modified as the exterior, Starla notes, hoping the modifications are to improve functionality and not just to keep this rust bucket in the air.

El is out of his seat first. He waves a greeting, then crosses the cargo bay to help the other passenger with his blindfold. Must be the reporter: jet-black hair and beard graying at the temples and at the corners of his mouth, warm brown skin lined like he's no stranger to the elements. He's sitting perfectly calmly, although Starla would not be if she were blindfolded for a hopper ride out into the desert. His hands lie motionless in his lap, a mild smile on his lips. El says something to him as he removes the blindfold, and the other man laughs in response, then blinks at the sudden brightness. He undoes his own harness and follows El to the cargo bay doors.

Beyond them, the door to the cockpit slides open to reveal the *Coldfire*'s crew. The pilot, Benedicto Kulikutan, is about Starla's age. Smooth brown skin and intelligent, wary eyes, flight jacket open to reveal a splash of purple lumosilk paisley and a gold saint's medallion. Starla gives Simca a bemused look. She always did go for the ones with the brightest plumage. The woman behind him has dark hair wound in a bun at the base of her neck, a sturdy frame, black eyes that take in everything with distrust.

Starla motions for El to introduce them.

"Starla Deyva, meet Kumail Anh, reporter."

"Thank you for coming," she signs to Kumail after she shakes his hand; his gaze flickers to El's interpretation, but otherwise he keeps his attention on her. "It's nice to meet you."

"Likewise," Kumail says. He bows his head slightly, an oddly foreign gesture for a man whose file says he was born in Bulari. "I appreciate the opportunity."

"Sorry about the blindfold."

His lips quirk in a faint smile. "Not a problem," he says; he seems oddly relaxed, but she's read his résumé. From human interest stories about life in the Fingers to sneaking into places like New Manila and Corusca to cover the Alliance's ongoing not-quite-wars, he's probably done scarier stuff than be flown across the desert blindfolded to meet Willem Jaantzen. And he's smiling easily, but she can tell he's cataloguing details: the piles of crates, the three women standing among them, the barest glimpse of the desert through the hangar door.

El holds out a hand to the pilot, who gives her a sharp

nod of greeting. "Beto Kulikutan," El says. "And Arundhati Si. Ari. They'll be keeping us in the air."

"A pleasure."

Beto Kulikutan gives her an easy smile and a warm handshake, but his co-pilot, Ari, hesitates before taking her hand. Manu's estimation of Beto is positive: fast-thinking and good at doing the job while knowing which questions not to ask. But Manu hasn't met any other members of Beto's crew, and Ari doesn't seem as comfortable pulling this job as her boss is. Starla will keep an eye on them both.

She turns to introduce her team; Beto's smiling at Simca in recognition. "Simca Anahoy," Starla signs. "You've already met her brother, El. And Dr. Giaconda Áte. She'll keep us all in good working order."

"Will we need that?" asks Kumail delicately.

"Never hurts to have a doctor around."

The reporter's lips part as though to ask another question, then shut suddenly. He straightens, his gaze sliding past her shoulder to the bunker entrance. Beto and Arundhati do the same, and Starla has seen enough of those mixed looks of apprehension and intrigue to know who just entered the room. She turns to Jaantzen and waves him in.

"We were making introductions," she signs. She lets El run through them again, steps back so Jaantzen can shake their hands, notes how the knot in Beto's throat bobs as he swallows, and how quickly Ari steps back after, hands stuffed into her pockets. Nerves? Or something else?

"It's an honor to meet you, sir," Kumail says, and he seems like he genuinely means it, even as he's still filing details: Jaantzen's perfectly shined shoes in the drifts of sand on the hangar floor, the type of knot Jaantzen uses on his tie, exactly how many threads of black are shading the brown of his irises.

She'll be keeping an eye on him, too. They need Kumail Anh to help shape the story, but there can be no slip-ups around him. She and Simca have already gone over this with Leti. Starla's relative anonymity among people who don't personally know Jaantzen is about to shatter. She could be recognized in the street, targeted in the club. And depending on how this goes down, Simca's association with Jaantzen is about to become known. Whether that boosts her career or cuts it short entirely depends on how this story plays out.

"All right," Starla signs. "We'll all be taking the same ride up and back, but we'll be splitting up when we get there. El will be leading Team Respectable Citizens on your straightforward mission to drop off supplies and research an article. Kumail, find a reason to need El with you at all times. I'll lead Team Too Recognizable on our secondary mission."

"Too recognizable?" Kumail asks.

"Famous pro wrestler," Beto says with a wink at Simca. "I got that one." But if he knows anything about why the Alliance would recognize either Gia or Starla, he keeps it to himself.

It won't take much digging for Kumail to find out why Gia and Starla want to stay under the Alliance's radar, though, and Starla'd rather keep him digging about the Alliance scandal rather than getting curious about her past. "Gia spent time at Redrock years ago," she says. "My godfather is Willem Jaantzen." She glances at Beto. "Let's get loaded up, Simca can show you what we're bringing."

But Beto has already noticed one part of their cargo: the murdercopters, dismantled and packaged into angular bundles of metal tubing and blades. "What the hell are those? They're not . . ." He trails off as he notices one of the earlier models set up in the corner of the hangar.

"Transport after we jump," signs Starla. Beto's looking at her like she's crazy, but Ari is grinning.

"My wife's a mechanic, and that looks like something she'd dream up." She laughs and shakes her head, like something about the absurdity of the murdercopters has loosened her up. "I used to say I'll fly anything, but I take it back."

"Let's get started," Simca says, heading for one of the crates.

"Gonna be a tight fit," Beto says. When Simca shoots him a faux-scandalized look, his ears flush red. "I mean there's not a lot of cargo room," he says quickly.

"Do not distract him until this trip is over," Starla signs to Simca. "That's an order."

Simca tosses her a salute, then leads Beto, Ari, and Gia over to the supplies. El checks to see if she still needs him, and she nods for him to stay. She has her transcription running, but it won't work without network access, and she wants to get the reporter and the others used to working with El or Simca as interpreter.

"Ms. Diamante speaks highly of you," Jaantzen says to Kumail once the others have left.

"Likewise," Kumail says. "I'll admit I was surprised to learn who'd offered me a ride to Redrock. I understand you gave Leti the initial tip?"

"It seemed like an extremely relevant story."

"All due respect, sir, but it's not." Kumail's hands are in his pockets, faint smile lines around his eyes and mouth. "Leti asked me because I've worked the Fingers beat and I've been beating the drum about how excessive sentences for people from the Fingers are basically our government's way of getting involuntary indentured labor. And no one cares. I'm not surprised to find another link in that chain leading to the Alliance, and I'll keep following these tips and shouting about them until the day I die. But I'd be deluding myself and you if I said this story will make any difference."

Kumail studies Jaantzen, no hint of fear in his expression. "So I'm curious. What's in it for you?"

"A business opportunity," says Jaantzen mildly. "For some years now, the Alliance has been secretly conducting successful experiments to terraform the deserts around Redrock. We believe that's where the missing prisoners have been ending up, which means members of our government have been aiding the Alliance cover-up in exchange for kickbacks. In light of current trade negotiations, the fact that they're hiding this operation from the people of New Sarjun makes your story quite relevant."

Kumail's bushy eyebrows draw together. "You have proof?"

"We do. And we'll have irrefutable proof once we return."

"Your 'secondary objective,'" says Kumail.

"If we're right, your name will be on the biggest story of our lives. You follow your investigation through your normal channels, Starla will see what we can find on the back end. We can share notes once everyone is home."

"You get no say in what I write." Kumail's expression is mild. Starla imagines he's given this caveat to some truly scary people over his career.

"Of course not," Jaantzen says. "We're already getting what we want out of this trip, and hopefully you will, too. But if the story you find is the one we think it is, it will be good for us all."

"I hope so."

They make short work of the rest of the loading, and as the first stars of the evening glimmer on the horizon, they're ready to go. Starla realizes with a sudden thrill that the next time she sees the night sky it won't be the Pangolin or the Sword whose lines she'll be tracing. Her evening companions won't be Arctas and Prixa Minor and Caba Regina, she'll be staring at an alien northern sky few on New Sarjun ever get to see.

Someone moves beside her, and she turns to find her godfather, his gaze following hers north across the desert.

"Do you have everything you need?" he signs.

She nods. "We'll be in touch." Every ninety minutes or so when Toshiyo's satellite passes overhead, until the inevitable moment the Alliance finds it and shuts it down.

"Good." He seems to have more he wants to say, but can't find the words.

She slips her hand into his and squeezes tight. "I'll see you soon," she signs with her free hand, and with a kiss on his cheek she turns her back on the Maraka Valley, turns her back on her godfather, and pours as much confidence as possible into her gait as she joins the others on the *Coldfire*.

11

MANU

Manu slices the sleek black Taosa Scorpion in and out of traffic like a scalpel. He lets himself enjoy it — he rarely drove when he was living in downtown Bulari, but all the trains headed to and from the Maraka Valley carry ore, not passengers.

Toshiyo's been combing through the list of people who were at Taufang-Set at the time Moss disappeared, and she's netted him an interesting anomaly: a delivery driver who deviated from his normal route to make an unscheduled stop at the penitentiary just before Calanthe arrived.

Traffic patterns change as Manu exits the ring road around Bulari and heads southeast down Anjali Lumaban Boulevard. Fewer private spinners, more of the boxy, brightly painted combi vans that race each other along set routes and play a game of chicken to beat each other to waiting fares. They're illegal in every other neighborhood, but Carama Town would grind to a halt without them. Everything's so far-flung, and few can afford their own vehicles.

And it's not like the mayor's office is going to spend

money on public transportation out in the slums. All the nice people in the inner city are spooked Fingers folk would use it to come into town and murder them or throw garbage in their parks. In fact, the passenger train only comes out as far as Anjali Lumaban Plaza because Coeur bullied the city council into it when she was mayor. She's a shit human otherwise, but she did fight tooth and nail to better the Fingers back then.

Maybe she would've gotten farther than a train stop in Anjali Lumaban Plaza if she'd kept her focus on that instead of lining her own pockets and stabbing her rivals in the back.

"Manu, you got a sec?"

Toshiyo's voice in his ear makes him jump; he's been lost in nostalgia as the streets get more and more familiar.

"Yeah, what's up?" Manu deftly swerves as a neon pink-and-orange combi cuts him off, and lays on his horn without any ire. The news feeds are filled with people complaining they'd visit Carama Town except the combi drivers are too unpredictable, but that's bullshit. You just have to speak their language.

"I've been digging into the delivery guy," Toshiyo says. "I wanted to see if he has a history of going to the penitentiary on his days off. And he does."

Even through the bad connection he can hear the excitement in her voice. He slides the spinner through the narrow space between a tourist and a trash collector, then guns it to make a left-turn signal.

"What'd you find, Tosh?"

"Every time coincides with the disappearance of one of the prisoners on our list."

"So he might have some more good intel for me."

"Or Moss might already be on his way to Redrock."

"Let's hope I'm not too late, then," he says. "I'm about there."

Manu didn't have to look up directions to the driver's address — this is his old stomping grounds, though the last time he was out in Carama Town was to do a job well after dark. Now, in the fading evening light, nothing much has changed since he was a kid. That apartment building on the corner? Manu and his friends used to scale the rusty lattice of fire escapes and pipes to break onto the roof and drink stolen liquor, laughing and partying until the building manager was called to chase them away. Then they'd scurry down the side like rats.

The neighborhood's still as colorful as ever, every home a rainbow shade, every inch of public wall space plastered with garish posters advertising fights and concerts and festivals and candy bars and even a few theatrical productions. That old nameless park is more dilapidated than ever, the few plants surviving in the parched soil are scraggly husks.

But there are changes. More anti-Alliance graffiti than he remembers — a lot more — and the street market on Albizia Avenue's gotten a facelift and fresh paint. The vendor stalls are full, flowers in the cement planters. Actually, several parts of Carama Town don't feel quite so desperate as they used to. Streets with actual pavement, old homes remodeled, professionally, not just held together by stasis wrap and metal sheeting and twine.

He barely catches the street name on the crooked sign, skids right, and pulls up in front of the delivery driver's house. Curtains twitch in windows up and down the block.

Manu checks hair and eyeliner in the mirror, shucks off his suit jacket and — reluctantly — his shoulder holster, adjusts the gold chain around his wrist, undoes the top two buttons of his crisp gray-blue shirt to reveal a flash of gold there, too. People from the Fingers don't like to talk to strangers, but he also knows how not to feel like a stranger. He's dressed far too nice for a place like this, but not like a cop or a banker. The casual style, the flash of gold make him look successful at things society doesn't approve of.

He hesitates, then rolls up his sleeves to show off the scars scrawled pale down his left forearm and hand. There's a small chance it'll bring down trouble, but he's willing to take it. If someone doesn't recognize him already, they'll definitely start asking questions about who he is. And people need to know Willem Jaantzen isn't down for the count.

The gossip machine in Carama Town is about to get wild.

He feels naked without the constant weight of his shoulder holster and suit jacket, but the pistol tucked at the small of his back will have to do. After all. He's just here to talk.

The house used to be pink trimmed with magenta, but the paint's mostly faded in the sun and peeled off in the wind. Manu rings the doorbell, then steps back off the cracked front stoop, hands in his pockets. A baby cries. Footsteps approach. He waits, letting the person on the other side of the door evaluate him.

The door finally opens, though the flimsy security screen stays closed and locked. Behind it is a young woman with unruly brown hair tamed into a messy bun, blotches of rosacea staining her pale cheeks, exhausted circles under her eyes. She glances over her shoulder as the baby cries again.

"Ma'am, I'm looking to speak with Andrus. If he's around?"

"What do you want with my husband?" Her eyes

narrow, but not in fear. Just ingrained general distrust; Manu gets the sense this isn't the first time someone suspicious knocked on the door looking for her husband.

"A couple minutes," Manu says. "I'll make it worth both your time."

The woman's lips thin. The baby's still crying and nobody seems to be going to help it, which means either the woman's here alone or her husband's a deadbeat that Manu won't mind getting information out of the harder way.

She looks him up and down, making obvious conclusions about the sort of help he might need from her husband. "We don't want any trouble."

"I'm not bringing trouble, I have a couple of questions. Only way trouble comes is if you're not careful with your spending and people start asking questions about where you got extra cash."

Another pitiful wail from behind her and the woman's fingers tighten on the door — but the mention of money has her attention. Manu holds an unlinked chit in his fingertips and, after a moment, she unlocks the security screen and takes it.

"There's five hundred marks, and five hundred more if your husband answers a couple questions."

She makes the chit disappear into a pocket.

"Andrus is at the Mercury," she says. "He goes there after dinner to meet friends." She doesn't try to hide her undercurrent of frustration.

Manu inclines his head. "Thank you, ma'am. When I see him I won't mention the money I already gave you."

She gives him a small, fierce nod and shuts the door without another word.

The man's out drinking his paycheck away every night while his wife stays home with a crying baby, and those five hundred marks could probably stretch a long way if he doesn't know to look for them. Manu suddenly finds himself hoping Andrus turns out to be uncooperative.

Manu knows the Mercury, it's been around since he was a kid. It's a close-knit sort of place where the regulars have each other's backs and every single head swivels to look when Manu walks in. He exchanges a few nods, then settles at the bar. Ceiling fans and misters ghost the place with the illusion of a fresh breeze.

He lets the gold on his wrist glint in the light. "I'm looking to talk to Andrus," he says to the bartender. "Heard I could find him here."

"Every night." The bartender lifts his chin to a trio of men sitting in a dark booth. "Blue shirt."

Andrus and his buddies look like textbook working men with honest jobs and drinking problems. They've gone back to their drinks after giving Manu the once-over, like everybody except for the table of hotshots sitting near the exit door with a good view of the bar. They're watching him with naked hostility.

Local crew, probably, with some ridiculously macho name. Manu doesn't pay much attention to the minor crews in Carama Town. None of these packs of kids have the organization, the brains, or the firepower to do more than knife each other on street corners. He turns his back on them.

"Two of whatever Andrus is having," he says to the bartender, who reaches for a bottle of black brandy. "And another round for my friends in the corner."

Manu grabs the two drinks and tips the bartender well, then gives the toughs a solemn nod as the bartender delivers the round to their table. Acknowledging turf and letting them know he's not interested in starting a pissing contest — fingers crossed they get the message.

The three men at Andrus's table are watching him approach with mixed looks of curiosity and wariness. The guy in the blue shirt is all ruddy skin, a shock of ashen hair.

"Andrus? I've got a couple questions with money attached. Then I'll be on my way."

"And who are you?"

Manu sharpens his smile. "Nobody you need to worry about." Andrus doesn't invite him to sit, but he doesn't tell him to leave. So Manu turns his smile on the other two men. "You gentlemen mind if I talk to your friend a minute?"

Andrus shifts uncomfortably, then makes his decision. "Give us a minute, yeah?" he asks his friends, and Manu slips into one of their abandoned seats. He sets both drinks down in front of Andrus, lets him pick. Andrus grabs one of the drinks and takes a sip; it doesn't hide the glance he slides at the toughs. Manu gives them an *I'll be out of here soon* wave.

"What do you normally deliver to the penitentiary?" he asks Andrus, and a furrow appears between the man's brows. It wasn't the question he was expecting. "Food, supplies?"

"I don't ask. Place like that needs a lot of things, I fill up my truck and go."

"And on your days off?"

Andrus stiffens. "I don't know what you're talking about."

Manu lounges back into his own chair, takes a sip of the other drink. Tries not to grimace. Black brandy and sickly sweet pear cider, a dash of bitters — he'd been horrified watching the bartender make it but still hadn't guessed it would be quite this terrible. He swirls the ice, evaluating Andrus.

"You think I'm a cop? You think I'm from your employer?"

Andrus shakes his head.

"I don't give a shit what you do with your delivery truck in the off hours. But the guy they put in your truck today is a friend of mine."

Andrus's gaze flickers to the table of toughs again. Politics. It's always politics.

"This has got nothing to do with them, nothing to do with any crew you have ever heard of. I'm not out here to fuck with anybody, and talking to me isn't gonna get you into trouble." Probably.

"But you're from here." You could be connected with a rival local crew, he means. Talking to you could get me in trouble with *them*.

Manu shrugs. "From here, def, but I got out. You ever want to get out? You want your kid to have a chance of getting out? Then I've got a nice little nest egg for you." Manu sets down his drink and fishes the second unlinked chit out of his pocket, holds it glinting between dark fingertips. Greed gleams in Andrus's eyes. "There's five hundred marks on this. Where'd you take my friend?"

"Sawtooth."

The man's testing him, seeing how much of a local he really is. But of course Manu knows Sawtooth, every teenager in Carama Town broke into the old copper smelter at least once. "On Locust Road," Manu says. "That the usual place you deliver prisoners in your off days?"

Andrus scratches the back of his neck, thinking too hard about the answer. Manu slips the chit back in his pocket and starts to rise.

"Normally it's to a private launchpad south of here," Andrus says quickly. He leans forward. "They're sending them up to Redrock. Everybody knows that."

"Everybody?"

Andrus shrugs. "That's the rumor."

"They pay you money to keep quiet?"

"They pay me per delivery, that's all. But I put some of the pieces together." He's preening, now, a guy who likes to be in the know.

"That's fucking huge," Manu says, ginning up an impressed look.

"Isn't even half of it," Andrus says. He's warming up to his topic, and the drink Manu brought him is gone. "The Alliance is doing experiments on prisoners. That's why they want New Sarjunian citizens, it's illegal for them to experiment on their own people."

Andrus goes on to describe the experiments, slicing people up and sewing them back together with animal parts, testing different poisons and nerve gases for when the Alliance finally decides to forcibly annex New Sarjun. Human cloning, drug tests, psychological experiments, this guy is gonna go on for the rest of the night if Manu doesn't cut him off.

"That's wild, man," Manu says when he stops for breath. "You got the address of the launchpad?"

The man rattles off directions and Manu files them away to tell Toshiyo about later. He flips the chit over the tops of his scarred fingers; Andrus tracks it like a hawk, almost twitching with desire.

"That what they're doing to my friend?"

"No clue, it's the first time I've delivered there. But their security is the same. Lots of big guys with guns."

"How long've they been camping out at Sawtooth?"

"I don't know, I haven't been up there since I was a kid."

That information will be easy enough to find, all Manu's gotta do is ask the next Carama Town teenager he sees and he'll get an earful about guys with guns squatting in their favorite party spot. Right now, though, Manu's burning whatever time Orris Moss has left. Because if the Alliance isn't taking him to Redrock, they've probably got something in mind Manu's gonna like even worse.

Manu flips the chit to Andrus. "I'm going to make sure those Alliance bastards don't do any crazy shit to my friend."

"Good luck, man."

As Manu turns to leave, Andrus's friends rejoin him, loudly curious; Manu can hear Andrus's self-important voice behind him talking up the secrets he knows, the edge gone slurred as he reaches for Manu's barely touched drink. Manu puts the man far from his mind. Because sometime while they were talking, two of the toughs vanished. The other two are still watching Manu; one of them smiles slyly.

Manu swears under his breath. He doesn't have time for this.

Manu holds a hand up in farewell to the bartender and walks out the door to find the missing toughs leaning against his spinner. Of course.

They're in their early twenties, if that. One is trying for a patchy red-blond beard, the other has neon-yellow tattoos scrawled into his golden-brown skin. It's expensive work, flashy. Manu can appreciate the kid's style, if not the fact that he's about to attempt robbery.

Manu smiles pleasantly, shoulders loose and gun hand ready. "Can I help you, gentlemen?"

The Mercury's door opens behind him, swings shut

again. Manu glances over his shoulder; the other two toughs have followed him out.

"Nice ride," says Patchy. "I think we'll take it."

"Could be," Manu says. "Or could be we all get on with our evenings."

The two kids leaning against his spinner are armed. Patchy's got a baton — it snaps out with a flick of his wrist — and Tattoos pulls a knife. The long blade glints dully in the last rays of the sun. Manu shifts, trying to get all four of the toughs in his field of vision, but one — a pale guy with a crooked nose and spiked hair dyed red — circles behind him. Manu gives the fourth guy, a kid in a sequin-studded jacket, a genteel nod.

"Unlock the spinner, old man," calls Tattoos. "Let's see what this thing can do."

"Not gonna happen," Manu says. "I got work." He holds his hands out in a shrug, *What can I do?*

"Work," laughs Patchy, but Tattoos's gaze flickers to Manu's left arm and back as the scars flash in the street-lights. His eyes widen.

"What's your name, man?" Manu asks, and the kid's nostrils flare with fear. "I've got a good memory."

Patchy starts to jeer, but Tattoos elbows him. "We don't want trouble," he says

Manu lets his hands slip into his pockets, a liquid shrug. "Then don't mess with people if you don't know who they are." He takes a step towards the two toughs leaning against his spinner. Tattoos flinches back, but Patchy stands his ground. Sequins is frowning at Tattoos, not quite sure what the other kid knows, but spooked enough himself by Manu's lack of fear.

Manu takes another step, and — there. In the glossy

black finish of the Taosa Scorpion, Manu can now see Crooked Nose trying to get the jump on him from behind.

"Get your hands back up," growls Patchy.

Manu doesn't move. He looks directly at Tattoos. "No shame in running," he says. "And no hard feelings from me that way."

Indecision flashes briefly on the kid's face before he grabs Sequins's arm and hauls him away at a sprint.

As Patchy is yelling obscenities after him, Manu spins, decking Crooked Nose in the jaw with his right hand while his left goes for the gun at the small of his back. The kid's teeth snap shut hard; he staggers back and Manu catches him in the sternum with a kick that sends him crashing into a cement planter — and sends fire screaming through Manu's bruised ribs.

He spins, leveling the gun at Patchy. The kid's already charging, baton raised.

Manu bites out a curse — he's not going to shoot somebody for doing the same stupid shit he used to do unless he can't help it. He ducks Patchy's wild swing and drives an elbow into his kidney, cracks him across the back of the head with the butt of his pistol. The kid drops like a rock.

Patchy is down, Crooked Nose is groaning in the planter. The other two are nowhere to be seen. Manu reaches for his door.

And hears a voice behind him, calling his name. Manu draws and spins, the pistol aimed dead between Tattoos's eyes. They go wide in fear, his hands shoot up, and his mouth works a second in silence. Then, "They're saying you and Mr. Jaantzen are dead," he finally blurts out.

Manu lowers the pistol. "No. We're not."

"What are you doing here?"

Manu lets himself smile slow; the kid takes a step back. "I'm the calm before the storm."

"I won't say anything." Tattoos looks like he's about to swear on his mother's grave.

"Tell whoever you want. This isn't the first time I've come back from the dead." Manu pulls open the Scorpion's door, then pauses, half in, half out. Tattoos slowly lowers his hands. "And doing stupid shit like jacking spinners is gonna get you killed. Come see me if you want a real job."

He jams the Scorpion into gear and peels away, letting the chaos of Carama Town traffic soothe his nerves as he puts distance between himself and the Mercury. Surely he'd never been that stupid. Surely.

And he laughs, because of course he had. These hotshots are gonna be talking about the night they accidentally tried to rob Manu Juric for the rest of their lives, but hadn't he tried to assassinate Willem Jaantzen at their age? On purpose?

Live and learn.

He opens up a channel, letting himself smile at Oriol's voice when he answers.

"Hey, you got a few hours tonight for some fun?" he asks.

A brief pause, filled by the background buzz of a crowd; Oriol's at work. "This a booty call or a job?"

Manu grins. "Job first."

"Then definitely. She's at the Table, I'll make sure Hiro's got eyes on her."

"Good. Meet me at the copper smelter on Locust Road, east of Carama Town, and be ready for trouble. Might need a few more hands."

He can hear the smile in Oriol's voice. "For the job?"

Manu laughs. "For the job. I'm looking for diverse skill

sets, discretion, and the ability to handle plan changes on the fly."

"Meaning you don't know what the hell we're getting into."

"You got it. Explosives experience a plus."

"Always is with you."

Smartass. "Phaera have anybody we could tap?"

Oriol pauses so long Manu checks the connection. "I'm not ready to blur that boundary yet. But I got a couple of gals, if they're not already off causing trouble tonight. I'll see you in an hour."

12

———

ORIOL

Manu's here already, leaning against the hood of his spinner, ankles crossed and arms folded, dark face shadowed in the dim light of the city. Carama Town sprawls behind him into the desert south of Bulari proper, the street-lights and house lights a haphazard tumble of gems. The smelter's peaked roofs and chimneys jut up against that glittering backdrop like the teeth of a saw. From the outside it looks completely abandoned. But Oriol did a quick walka-round before coming to find Manu, and someone's repaired the perimeter fence and put up a trip field just inside. A handful of dust and it sizzles, anything bigger than a cat and it'll probably alert the guards.

Manu's got a good vantage point, but his back is to Oriol and he doesn't turn as Oriol approaches, humming softly to himself, to join Manu on the hood of the spinner. Warm breath on his neck in the cooling desert evening, the scent of cologne, the end-of-day sandpaper rasping against his own cheek, the taste of mint before Manu settles back to stare out over the view, radiating heat through the handsbreadth between them.

Oriol smiles, but ignores that heat. The job's first.

"Thanks for coming," Manu says.

"What's the gig?"

"Orris Moss disappeared from Taufang-Set Penitentiary earlier today. A delivery driver claims he left him here."

Oriol runs a hand through his hair, considering the smelter. "So the gig's recovering a potentially hostile asset? We can handle that, no problem."

"Who've you got coming?"

"Couple of gals I worked a gig with when I first got back into town this time. Blowing up a Dawn shard-manufacturing facility."

It takes a minute before Oriol realizes why Manu's looking at him like that. It's been nonstop since he got home from his last trip, and they still haven't caught up about everything.

"Blowing up a what?" Manu asks.

"Nacea, she's got this vendetta against the Dawn. She hired me to help her hit one of their manufacturing facilities in exchange for some intel. I brought Mel along for backup, and the girls hit it off. They've probably hit three more Dawn facilities since."

"You never told me that," Manu says.

"We had a lot going on," Oriol says. He glances down the rustic dirt road. They could use a vacation, but he's long since given up trying to get Manu to leave Jaantzen's side, even for a week relaxing someplace where no one wants to kill them. Normally they at least have time to talk when Oriol comes home, though.

Later. After this job — if not after Leone.

"Nacea's a thief," Oriol says. "Freelance; she likes the showy, complicated jobs. She's not a fighter, but she's fast and sharp and you don't have to keep an eye on her if shooting starts. She gets more emotionally attached to her jobs than she should, and she likes to blow things up." He glances at Manu. "So you've got that in common."

Manu lifts an eyebrow. "The blowing things up?"

Oriol ghosts him a smile. "Sure. Mel and I have worked together for years on mercenary jobs. She's a good sniper and deadly up close, too. Takes orders well, not afraid to improvise, and she'll have your back if shit hits the fan. But she's not going to do anything stupid or out of scope of your agreement. She's level-headed like that."

"I can see why you two get along."

"I like a partner who isn't going to do something rash and cause unnecessary trouble."

Manu slides him a smile. "Do you, though?"

"Predictability saves lives, babe. How many hornet tags did you bring with you?"

"Enough for some fun. Never know when you might need a good distraction. I've tagged a coupla spots already. Oh, and I tossed some to the local kids who gave me intel on this place. Thought they'd have some good ideas."

Oriol sighs pointedly, but he knew this going in — it's always chaos and explosions with Manu. Has been since that first job, and for some reason, instead of walking away, Oriol'd let the kid with the lopsided smile and bad habit of sticking his neck out pull him down head over heels.

Oriol checks the time; Mel and Nas'll be here any minute, and there's one last thing he should get out of the way first. "One thing you need to know about Mel," he says. "She used to run with Zmiya."

Manu blinks at him. "Zmiya? I didn't think any of those assholes were still alive."

"A few stragglers still out there." Oriol's gaze is steady.

"I trust her with my life. But I wanted you to know before you see the tattoos."

Manu exhales a curse of surprise. "She still has the tattoos? I'll try not to stare. How's Phaera doing?"

That's a good question; Oriol's been trying to figure it out himself the past few days. "I can't quite tell," he admits. "I used to think she was a terrible actor, but I think it was just because she didn't bother acting around me. Until now."

"She doesn't trust you?"

"I don't think she trusts anybody."

"The man?"

Does she trust Jaantzen? He doesn't know that, either. But before he can reply, a pair of figures slip out of the shadows. Manu's hand is on his gun, a reflex, but Oriol brushes his arm.

"It's okay," he says. "It's our gals."

Nacea waves; Mel lifts her chin then turns to scan down the path they took up. Oriol steps out to greet them, Manu at his side.

"Nacea Kálas," Oriol says of the slim woman with her hair tied up in a row of messy buns. The thief is dressed in a slim-fitting black jumpsuit. "And Mel Nehrusitha." The larger woman is tall and muscular, bare-armed in the cool evening, snakes coiled around each wrist like warning signs to anyone who remembers the Zmiya crew's sociopathic tendencies from decades back. Oriol hadn't even been living on New Sarjun when they were making headlines, but word had traveled. And *damn*, those were some headlines.

"Nice to finally meet you," Mel says, her gruff camaraderie tempered with a touch of real warmth as she shakes

Manu's hand. She quirks a sly smile at Oriol. "I've heard so many stories."

"What are we up to?" Nacea asks. "Oriol didn't give us details."

"He didn't have any to give," Manu says. He holds out his palm and a data cube there projects the bust of a man. "A guy I want is being held inside, name's Orris Moss. Local intel says whoever's holed up here has been using this place for the last three months. Security's tight. A fence and trip field — I tested that, it's legit — and guards on a regular rotation. I know this place, it's the local Carama Town kids' party spot. My guess is they're holding him in the engine room in the basement."

He points to the southern end of the smelter, where double-story bay doors loom halfway open though it must have been decades since railcars filled with ore glided in and out on the tracks that snake from its mouth and out into the hills. "They have a guard post in the shed at the doorway."

"Where there's no good way to sneak up on it," Oriol says.

"Which means we enter the way the kids do — through the windows." He points to the second story. "It lets you out on the level of the smelter ovens, where there's plenty of cover. We can get to the guard post from the back. Scaling to the window isn't a problem, and the fence isn't a problem. But the trip field?"

"Also not a problem," says Nacea.

"Good. We sneak in through the window, then take control of the guard shed." He glances at Oriol. "Who stays back to monitor as we grab the target from the basement?"

"Nas, you cool with that?"

"I got it."

"Good," Manu says. "Any questions?"

"Two," says Mel, the snakes on her crossed arms black in the dim light. "The target want to come with us?"

"I'm not sure."

"Got it. And who are we potentially stirring up shit with?"

"The Dawn, or maybe the Alliance. Either of you got a problem with that?"

Mel shrugs and pulls out a couple of earpieces, handing one to Manu and one to Oriol. The snakes on her wrists say she doesn't have a problem stirring up shit with the Alliance.

"I hope it's the Dawn," Nacea says.

"Me, too," says Manu. "Let's move."

The smelter looks like it hasn't changed in decades. Graffiti on the walls, liquor bottles and drug paraphernalia mixed in with rubble at the base of the walls. Except for the freshly fixed perimeter fence and the trip field just inside, it still looks abandoned. The trip field itself is barely visible, only in the flash of insect wings that spark the tiniest hint of blue when they fly through or over the fence.

Nacea chooses a place on the far side of the smelter where the chain-link has been pulled back and crouches in the dust, staring at what looks like nothing. The lenses of her night-vision kit flicker the faintest green. She fiddles with her gauntlet, biosilk gloves drinking in the light.

She finally sits back on her heels and pushes her goggles up on her forehead. "Good news, they're cheap," she says, and pulls a long, thin rod with a pointed beak from her tool belt. She pounds it into the dirt in front of the chain-link fence, then slowly, carefully inserts the pointed tip into the trip field. And tilts her head to the night.

"Listening for alarm bells?" Manu asks.

She shakes her head. "These cheap ones, the frequency of the hum changes a bit when it's tripped, something about the extra energy heading to the alarm system. But we're good."

Nacea presses a button on her gauntlet and the beak slowly begins to open. A tiny shiver of gold spreads from prong to prong, widening until it's big enough to duck through. For Nacea, maybe. Oriol's bigger than her, and his prosthetic gives him more power than limberness. Manu is eying the opening dubiously himself.

"That get any wider?" Oriol asks.

Nacea rolls out her shoulders. "Haven't been keeping up on your yoga?"

"I've had a rough month," Manu says.

"C'mon, Nas," Mel says. "You can't expect me to get through that."

Nacea pushes a button and it gets a third again wider.

"That's as far as it goes," she says. And she shimmies through the gate and is standing on the other side before any of them can respond, smiling at them through a net of glowing gold sparks.

Oriol sends through Manu and Mel, then steps through himself, hairs rising on the back of his neck. They're inside the first round of security.

Nacea gathers up the contraption in a few heartbeats. "If we don't have time to set up the tripwire gate again, it won't matter if we trip the wire," she says reasonably. "And this thing costs an arm and a leg."

The second-story row of windows along the back of the smelter are all boarded up, and the row above is covered in yellowing stasis wrap.

"The teens I talked to said the plywood over the third window from the left is only attached in one corner," Manu says. Oriol eyes it dubiously. The rickety pile of junk below the windows could be a fairly solid ladder if you know what you're looking for. And if you're a teenager.

Nacea grins at them. "Thieves first," she says, then noiselessly scales the junk pile and drops through the window. Manu shrugs and follows her up, slightly less noiselessly. Manu's slower than he might have been, totally healthy, but Oriol doesn't see anything to give him pause. Doesn't mean he won't be keeping an extra close watch on Manu, though.

Mel's caught him looking. "He all good?" she asks.

Oriol shakes his head. "Help me keep an eye on him?"

"You got it."

Oriol takes up the rear once Mel is to the top. The rickety junk holds his weight at the last, but barely.

It doesn't take long for his eyes to adjust to the dark — there's enough ambient lighting coming through the high stasis-wrapped windows to make out the shapes of the ovens in the gloom. There are four rows of ovens, and Manu points them to the scaffolding on the north side. It seems stable enough, and the boards aren't creaking. Maybe this plan will work after all. When they make it to the last oven, Nacea crouches with one hand up, but Oriol doesn't need her warning. He can hear the voices, too. They fade as the guards walk past.

Oriol jerks his chin to Mel.

She has the first one on the ground as he hits the second with a slap of neutralizer against his neck. He catches the disposable cuffs Mel tosses his way, and in under a minute the two guards are out cold and locked in a closet.

"You two do that a lot?" Manu asks.

"Guardhouse," says Oriol. "Let's go."

The guard there isn't expecting them any more than the

two on patrol were, and Mel makes him comfy under the desk while Nacea gets acquainted with the security system.

Manu pulls the guard's gun from its holster and hands it to Nacea. "You do know how to shoot?" he asks.

"Not my thing." But she takes the gun, sets it beside her on the desk.

"Just don't shoot one of us," Manu says. "You good here?"

"I'm good." She pulls on the guard's headset, listens a moment. "Nothing interesting on the channel, but I'll keep you up on the gossip."

"Thank you," says Oriol. He jerks his chin at Mel. "I'll take point. Mel, bring up the rear."

"You saying I'm slow?" Manu jokes, and Mel laughs.

"I'm saying you're barely back from injury. Now let's go."

The glimmer of light coming from a stairwell in the far wall grows brighter as they descend. And with the light, voices, and the sickly vinegar scent of cleaning supplies and urine. Something snarls. Something else whines, high and scared.

Oriol shares a look with Manu. What the hell is going on in this place?

They creep to the bottom of the stairs and the basement room spreads out before them. One wall is lined with cages. Dogs, rabbits, mice. And with horror Oriol suddenly realizes the awful scent underlying the vinegar is from the furnace they've got running. He doesn't know whether the animals in the cages are successful experiments or simply haven't had their turn yet, but by the stench of charred flesh and hair, he knows where the unsuccessful experiments have gone.

The man from Manu's hologram, Moss, is strapped to a

table in the middle of the room. He's writhing, screaming against the rubber wedge in his mouth that seems to be more to keep him from biting off his tongue than to silence him.

He's got an audience. Two armed guards and a trio of people wearing lab coats.

"He's lasted longer than any of the others," says one of the guards. "That seems good."

"I'm not ready to call it a success yet," says one of the lab coats. She's dark-skinned, with a clipped accent that says she grew up off-planet somewhere in Durga's Belt.

"I thought you said you were certain about this version of the recipe."

"I said it was more certain," the woman snaps. "The animal tests have been promising, but we haven't done a human subject yet. Not that you lot seem to care about that. You can't just go dumping this in the water supply and see what happens. That's not the way you get results."

"I'd be careful what you're accusing us of," the guard says. "The Dawn doesn't take lightly to false accusations."

"I've read the prophecies the same as you," the woman says, but there's a hint of tremor in her voice. The man in the lab coat beside her shoots her a look: *Quiet.* She ignores him. "And it's right there in the name. The Gift of the Fallen is supposed to be a gift to humanity, not a plague. It's supposed to transform, not enable you to mass-murder entire communities in order to blackmail some corporation."

She doesn't say it with religious fervor, more annoyance. But as she turns back to Moss, the guard grabs her arm and spins her to face him, his pistol drawn and digging up under her chin. She cries out and drops the hand terminal she was holding as he tightens his grip. "Keep your conspiracy theories to yourself, Sister Zahra."

Oriol frowns. The last woman he met who called herself Sister died at the hands of Bennion Zacharia. She'd also been from an offshoot of the Dawn, fighting to get this Gift of the Fallen. Did everyone in the Dawn call each other brother and sister? Or is this woman part of the same group Sister Kalia had been from?

"Don't kill the lab coats," Manu signs to Oriol. He spells it out, "lab coats," obviously not trusting that Oriol will understand the USL sign. Which is fair. Oriol passes the order on to Mel in their own code, developed over years of working jobs together, and together they fan into the room.

They're going carefully, mindful of the animals, but one of them has caught their scent. The low growl is at first indistinguishable from the rest of the ruckus the animals are making, but the dog that spots them — a mongrel with uneven patches of silver and red that might mean one of its ancestors got romanced by a dziva hound — plants its paws and growls, hackles spiked tall, fangs bared and dripping bloody foam.

"Shhh, puppy," Oriol murmurs.

The dog begins to bark.

"Shut up!" one of the guards yells. "I have had it with these animals."

"A necessary part of the process," says Sister Zahra with disinterest. "Look!"

Oriol freezes, expecting their cover to be blown, but everyone is focused on whatever's happening to the man strapped to the table.

Oriol edges around a table, looking for a clean shot. The dog breaks out into a frenzy.

The big guard yells a string of obscenities at the dog, then pulls his pistol and pushes past the lab coats.

"Big one's coming your way," Mel murmurs in his ear. "I've got a shot."

"I've got him," Oriol says. "Take out the other one."

He waits for the sound of footsteps, listens to the litany of curse words the man hurls at the hound get closer. And when he hears the man almost directly behind his table, he shoves it up and back with all his might, sending it crashing into him. A shot rings out from the side of the basement Mel is on and someone screams — it's almost impossible to hear over the sudden crescendo of barking and shrieking from the animals.

The guard's back on his feet faster than Oriol thought possible, so he fires a round into the man's chest.

It doesn't slow him down one damned bit.

13

———

STARLA

They've been arching over the Jupari Desert for hours, the moon silvering an alien landscape of enormous, craggy mountain ranges and vast, smooth seas of rippling sand. Black chasms crack through ancient valleys carved by long-dry rivers.

The last time Starla flew over the desert she was fifteen and seriously injured, in no state to be admiring the scenery. Tonight she's trying to get the rest she knows she needs, but she's wired, and too transfixed by the landscape scrolling by below to do more than doze.

It's still dark when El taps her on the shoulder; if she's slept at all, she doesn't remember it. "Beto says we're just under thirty minutes to the drop point," he signs. After the initial bone-jarring liftoff, the Sikuda has been a relatively smooth ride. The parabolic trajectory they're flying is gentle, the moments of weightlessness near the top a reminder of home but not sparking the same waves of home-sickness she'd felt last time she was this close to breaking free of New Sarjun's gravity.

Starla sits up and rolls the stiffness out of her neck and

shoulders, rubs the sleep out of her eyes. The cargo ship wasn't designed with personnel transport in mind, even before it was stuffed full of supplies for the Alliance. Gia and Simca are strapped into the fold-down chairs opposite, eyes closed, if not sleeping. Beto and Arundhati probably have the most comfortable seats in the whole place, which is fine. They're the ones who're tasked to get them across the desert alive.

Kumail Anh is awake, sitting a few seats down from Starla on the same side. He digs his fingers into the back of his neck, stretches his jaw in a yawn. He sees her watching and says something with a rueful smile. Starla triple-blinks her lens on before she remembers the transcription isn't going to work without a network connection. She turns to El.

"To be young again and able to sleep anywhere," El interprets.

Starla laughs. "Barely," she signs to Kumail. "Not the most comfortable night."

"I've slept in worse conditions."

She supposes he has. Besides her cell in Redrock and a few rough nights trying to get some shut-eye on the road like this, she's had it pretty easy. Given the number of dangerous places he's covered as a reporter, he's probably got plenty of rough night stories. Maybe he'll tell her a few once they're on their way back home from this trip.

"Why choose the hard assignments?" she asks. "For the story?"

A faint line appears between his brows, like he's never considered the question. "Yes and no," he says. "I've never been north of New Sarjun's equator, have you?"

Starla isn't about to answer that. "I've been off-planet."

"Born there, right?" He doesn't wait for an answer, her

height makes it clear. "This is an important story, but the appeal to me is more than that. I want to see things nobody else probably ever will. To meet people other people can't."

"And tell the world about them."

"Sometimes." He frowns as though deliberating over his next words. "I've gotten to speak with hard-to-reach people because they understand I respect the privilege as much as the story. I lived with NMLF guerrillas in New Manila. I interviewed one of the most notorious Coruscan rebel leaders before he was captured." He smiles. "I've been curious to meet your godfather for a very long time."

"And why is that?"

"He has an interesting reputation. And the fact that Leti Diamante took him on speaks highly of him. I've known her for quite a few years, and I know how choosy she can be about her clients. Maybe after this we could have a casual chat."

That seems unlikely. She can't imagine Jaantzen having a casual chat with anyone, much less a reporter.

"We're getting close to our stop," she tells him. "I'm going to wake the others."

Kumail nods and yawns again, then begins absently massaging his knees.

Gia and Simca wake easily, if they were asleep at all, and begin to check their gear. They've already transferred everything they'll need with them to their packs and stowed the rest of the desert survival supplies in the *Coldfire*'s ingenious contraband compartments. No need to have the Alliance wonder why there are supplies for seven people on a ship carrying four when it lands at Redrock.

"Five minutes," El tells her, and she beckons him after her to the cockpit to check on the pilots.

"How are we doing?" she asks.

"Right on target," Benedicto Kulikutan says. Watching the screens with him gives her the stomach-churning feeling the ground is coming up too fast. "I restarted the turbines, and I'll hit the boosters to level us out right before you jump. We won't be low enough that anyone from Redrock should wonder, and you'll be tough to spot. But you'll still have plenty of margin for error on the parachutes."

They'll be nearly impossible to spot, rather — especially at night. The mimic silk parachutes she bought from Absolon Chevalier are the real deal.

"How much margin is plenty?"

"About five seconds."

Starla shares a skeptical look with El. "Plenty," she signs. "Thank you. You two play this by the book and you won't have anything to worry about except for boredom." Beto nods, still intent on flying. Arundhati glances back at her, a shadow on her eyes revealing worry. Starla smiles at her. "We'll be in touch for pickup in three days. I'll brief the others."

"Good luck," says Ari before turning back to her controls.

Simca and Gia are both suited up when Starla returns. Gia's calmly checking gear, Simca's all bouncy energy Starla knows better than to mistake for nerves. She punches her brother on the shoulder and starts up a stream of chatter at him as Gia helps Starla into her harness and checks her gear. Starla returns the favor, then looks over Simca's.

"Triple-checking never hurts," Starla signs. "Not when the margin of error is so small."

El catches her eye and gives her the thumbs-up, and the steady churn of butterflies Starla's been ignoring kick into high gear. She continues to ignore them, focusing on her breath, and the plan. El wrenches open the door and the wind rushes in, whipping against Starla's cheeks, sending Simca's braid dancing. El has secured the crate containing the trio of murdercopters and their own chute near the door; he rests a hand on the straps, ready to send it on its own journey as soon as Simca, Gia, and Starla are out of the way.

Simca high-fives her brother and tumbles out with a grin. Gia gives El a solemn nod before stepping out herself.

"Take care of them," Starla signs when it's her turn in the doorway. "And yourself. Toshiyo's expecting you home in one piece."

El's look of shocked horror is priceless — Simca's going to kill her for saying something when she wasn't around to watch her brother's face turn beet red — but in a flash of searing blue sparks, it shifts to actual fear.

He's flung away from the door, back into the belly of the *Coldfire*, and that mask of fear is seared on her retinas as Starla herself is thrown backwards, tumbling through the night above the waiting desert, almost too shocked to fumble for her parachute cord as another bolt of sizzling blue electricity hits the *Coldfire* from below and the ship begins to plummet.

14

———

MANU

Across the room, Oriol's firing into the chest of one of the guards, who isn't slowing. One of the supersoldiers, then — Manu sprints across the basement towards them. Oriol launches himself out of the way as the guard lunges, rolls with his karambit in his hand to slice across the inside of the guard's thigh. The man goes down howling — but it's in rage more than pain, and he swipes at Oriol, catching him around the neck in an unbreakable grip. The guard whirls with Oriol in front of him like a shield, bringing his own gun to bear on Manu.

Manu shoots before he can let himself think twice.

The guard — and Oriol — drop to the ground. Manu rushes to their side to find Oriol struggling free of the dead man's beefy arm. The guard is staring at the ceiling, a bullet buried in his skull.

He helps Oriol to his feet, then turns to see what Mel's up against. But the soldier she sniped must be the kind that can actually feel pain, because he's a crumpled heap on the ground. The lab coats have scattered, cowering.

"You attracted attention," Nacea says conversationally

through the comms. "Sounds like two guards on-site, back-up's on the way. Time to grab and go, folks."

"Cover me," Manu yells to Oriol, and he jogs to the table Moss is strapped to. The man is still screaming against the rubber mouth guard, flecks of froth dripping from his lips. When his eyes meet Manu's they're full of murder.

Someone grunts behind him, and Manu spins to find one of the lab coats, the blond, lunging at him with a scalpel in her hand. He sidesteps her easily and she crashes against Moss's table, then pivots and lunges again. She's untrained but scrappy, swinging at him wildly with her scalpel.

And drops, a spray of blood from her neck.

"I want them alive," he shouts.

"Wasn't me," Mel calls back, voice perfectly calm.

Manu ducks as a second bullet whistles by and shatters the distilling system behind him, sending shards of glass spraying across the floor. Manu leans out and wings one of the newly arrived guards; Mel decks the other in the jaw with a grin.

Between Oriol and Mel the guards are covered, but someone new is screaming. Manu whirls, trying to figure out where the sound is coming from. The male lab coat, who'd been hiding behind the distilling system during the fight, had caught the full brunt of the shattered glass and liquid when the bullet hit. At first Manu thinks his face has just been cut up by the glass, but it's actually sizzling, sloughing off down the front of his lab coat.

"Don't touch the liquid," someone says to Manu's left, and Manu spins in a crouch, gun in hand. The remaining lab coat, the one the guard called Sister Zahra, raises her hands. "Don't touch the liquid," she repeats.

"I see that." He looks at Moss, who's thrashing against his bonds. "I'm here for him. How do we sedate him?"

"I don't know," she says. "Every other time it seemed like an experiment was going wrong, one of the Dawn just shot him."

"That's not going to work for me."

"The experiment is working," Zahra says. "He's being transformed, but now's a dangerous time. Once he passes through to the other side, he'll be able to think again. But right now we can't let him loose — he'll react poorly."

"We don't have time." He lifts his chin to the gurney against the wall. "Help me move him."

"That's not wise," she says.

"It's not a request," he says. "You want out, you're coming with me — and we're taking this guy with us. You want to wait for the reinforcements, you can do it in cuffs."

Emotions war in Zahra's face: hope, fear, and something like opportunism. He can worry about that once they're out of all this. He wheels the gurney closer, then searches for a way to move Moss without breaking his bonds. The man thrashes at him, eyes wide and bloodshot, a guttural, animal noise in his throat. Zahra steps tentatively up to the other side of the hospital bed. She holds up a pair of restraints.

"We can secure his arms and legs before releasing him," she says. "But we need to be careful."

"Do it." Manu's not letting go of the gun around her, not yet. She reaches over Moss to put the restraints on his far arm, and Moss lets out a primal yell. Metal shrieks, and he tears free of the straps that are binding him to the bed. He grabs Zahra and flings her at the wall; she meets it with a sickening crunch and slumps to the ground.

Moss's movements are mercury quick as he turns from Zahra to leap at Manu. Manu fires twice, but the bullets go through him like water. Moss lands on his chest and sends his pistol flying, stabs at him with something that glances off his tactical vest.

He doesn't look like the sort of man who's used to being strong, and he definitely doesn't know how to handle himself in a brawl. Manu decks him in the jaw — it doesn't do anything but cut up his knuckles — then uses Moss's momentum to flip them. Too late, he realizes they're rolling towards the pool of shattered glass and liquid. They roll to a stop centimeters away, Manu's cheek pressed into the cold cement, the vinegar stench of the liquid searing his nostrils.

He coughs against the fumes. Moss is pushing him closer, grinding his cheek into the cement. Manu gets another lungful and his vision narrows, all the chaotic noise around him hushing until he can hear only his heartbeat. It's steady. Calm.

Moss shudders and howls as a bullet buries itself in his side, and Manu uses his surprise to push back with all his might. Moss goes fucking *flying*.

Manu palms his pistol once more and gets easily to his feet — he hasn't felt this good in years — to find Oriol and Moss circling each other, Moss with a wild flurry of punches, blood draining from the wound in his side, Oriol calm and precise, beating back every attack until he finally manages a pivot and roundhouse kick that sends Moss sprawling to the ground with his head at a sickening angle.

Oriol frowns down at Moss's body. The man they were here to save is sprawled in a heap, dead. Whatever he could have done to help them with Leone, whatever mysteries he could have cleared up for them, gone.

"The man's always got backup plans, right?" Oriol asks.

Manu bites out a curse. "At least we got some intel. Grab anything that looks useful." He sweeps a couple of data cubes into a bag, along with an unbroken syringe of whatever's still eating into the cement. Can't hurt to have a sample of whatever turned Moss into an almost-impervious homicidal maniac.

"Hope you guys are done down there," Nacea says. "Because we've got company."

"Where at?" Manu asks.

"Coming up the road."

Manu grins at Oriol. "Green ones," he says, and hits the switch for the green hornet tags — the ones the local teens planted for him. Seconds later, a faint rumble shivers through the ground beneath their feet.

"Slowed 'em down," Nacea says. "But they're still coming. We can't go out the front."

"Copy that," Manu says. "Meet us at the back door."

"This one's still alive," Mel says from over his shoulder. She's kneeling beside Sister Zahra. "We bringing her with or shutting her down?"

"Bring her," Manu says. So far she's the only one here who hasn't tried to kill them, and if she wakes up, could be she knows something useful.

Mel slings the smaller woman over her shoulder and stands with a grunt. "Let's get out of here."

Manu slaps a hornet tag on the seal of the fueling tank for the furnace, another one on the wall beside the door to make sure the short-wave relay makes it all the way down here, then sprints after Oriol and Mel two steps at a time. He's barely even breathing heavy.

They slip up to the level of the ovens as lights sweep the main floor, and Manu sends Oriol and Mel through the back window, hauling out Zahra's body. Before he follows, he hits the blue wave.

The room erupts in shouting as the blue hornet tags he left upstairs explode in scattershot fashion. It sounds like the place is under attack, even though this round wasn't positioned to do much damage.

But the red round?

Manu hits the switch and hauls himself out the window to the symphony of a series of increasingly quiet explosions as the relay of hornet tags explodes all the way down to the furnace fuel lines.

Manu feels that last explosion in his chest. The ground beneath his feet rumbles, and with a moment of silence for a venerable party spot probably lost forever, Manu jogs back to meet the others.

They end up back at Nacea's place, an unspoken agreement between the other three that Manu follows along with. Her flat is cluttered and cozy and she seems accustomed to it being a crash pad after jobs. She clears space on the couch for the injured woman, throwing down an old sheet to keep the blood off the upholstery.

"More getting shot at than I like," Mel says as she lays the unconscious woman on Nacea's couch. "But overall a pretty good time."

High praise coming from someone on your crew — it's what Manu wants to say, but he keeps his mouth shut. Probably the polite thing to do when hanging out with someone who used to run with Zmiya is to never mention that fact.

"Well, I was bored," says Nacea. "Lookout is a shit job."

"Learn to shoot and you can come on the fun bits," says Mel.

"I'm a thief, not a common mercenary," Nacea says, putting on a posh accent and fanning herself in faux outrage. Mel rolls her eyes as Nacea walks past her into the kitchen and begins rooting through the cupboards. "I'm starving," Nacea calls back. "Is everyone starving?"

"I could eat," says Oriol.

"You could always eat," says Manu. He frowns down at Zahra. Her dark skin is ashen, her lips bloodless. Black hair in tight ringlets that used to be slicked back into a bun. Her temple is sticky with oozing blood. Under all that, though, are signs she's had a rough few weeks. Her cheeks are sunken, a days-old scrape mars her jaw. The rope burns on her thin brown wrists are mostly healed.

Oriol disappears down the hallway without asking and reappears with a med kit. He pulls up a stool and starts to look the woman over.

"She Dawn or what?" Mel asks.

"I'm not sure." Oriol glances at Manu. "That job I did on the *Dorothy Queen*, right before I came home?" That one where he stole some data Aiax Demosga had planned on buying. "It was for a woman calling herself Sister Kalia. Seemed like she was some offshoot of the Dawn, but I didn't get much of a bead on her."

"Splinter group," says Nacea from the kitchen. Manu twists to look at her. "The hardcore members of the Dawn think they're heretics and have orders to kill or capture on sight."

"And how do you know that?" Manu asks.

Nacea's face clouds. "My daughter joined up. I didn't take it seriously until it was too late."

"Her intel is good," Oriol says.

"The enemy of our enemy isn't a friend just yet." Manu looks back at the unconscious woman in front of him. "The Dawn may be hunting down this splinter group, but Sister Zahra and her team are the ones that made the serum that turned Orris Moss into . . . whatever he was. She's a prisoner until I decide otherwise."

"No problems there," says Mel.

Manu rolls his shoulders, easing the tension of the night out of them. Ten minutes ago he felt like he could run a marathon. Now the aches and pains of a rough night are starting to show through. But some of the old wounds — his aching ribs, the lingering roughness in his lungs, the dull ache of the cut above his hip — aren't bothering him at all. He can't even remember which knuckle he split in the fight, since there's no sign of it.

Adrenaline? Or something in those fumes?

What he does know is he's starving. His stomach growls sharply as the scent of baking pastry and roasting garlic begin to waft from Nacea's kitchen. It's well after midnight, which means he'll be spending another night in the city, and Starla should be deep in the Alliance concession on northern New Sarjun by now. He wonders if she's jumped yet.

He opens up his comm and types a note to Toshiyo.

You got contact with S? I might have some info she needs.

The response comes almost immediately — Toshiyo is rarely asleep at this hour.

They're flying dark but I can send a message.

"Manu."

It takes him a moment to see why Oriol's calling him: Zahra's eyelids are fluttering, her lips moving faintly.

K one sec.

He slips his comm back in his pocket and rejoins Oriol at the couch. Zahra is blinking groggily, frowning at the faces above her until finally recognition comes. Her eyes widen.

"Where am I?" she asks.

"Safe," Manu answers. "For now. Are you part of the Dawn?"

She shakes her head, then winces at the movement. "I am something different."

"You seem awfully cozy with them," Manu says. "Nice monsters you're all making."

"We aren't making monsters." Zahra's indignant look fades to chagrin. "At least, that wasn't the end goal. The Dawn are the monsters, taking this world-transforming gift and using it as poison. The Gift of the Fallen can kill, of course. But it can also heal wounds, destroy infections, regenerate damaged tissue — even damaged brain tissue. Do you know what that could do? Give humans the ability to live longer. Indefinitely, maybe, with healthy minds and healthy bodies."

"That's what you gave Moss?"

"Who?"

"The man you were torturing."

The color drains from her face. "I didn't have a choice."

"Of course you didn't. Kill someone else or be killed yourself."

"It wasn't like that," she says; it's almost a whisper. "I knew it wouldn't kill him. I knew this time it would work."

"The Gift of the Fallen?"

"We've been attempting to replicate it. The true Gift is an incredible serum, but we hadn't gotten it right. Yet. Until now." She looks around, suddenly hopeful. "Is he here?"

"He's dead."

Zahra lies back against the couch, eyes closed in pain or regret. "All that work, lost. You didn't have to kill him. His mind would have been fine once he survived the transition."

"We weren't going to survive his transition," Manu says.

"This serum you've been replicating. Who else has the recipe?" Her gaze flickers to the side; she's thinking too carefully about what she's about to tell him, and Manu's suddenly tired of this woman who thinks it's no problem to play with the lives of people whose names she doesn't even know.

"No one," she lies.

He shares a look with Oriol, who raises a skeptical eyebrow. "Hey, Mel?" Oriol asks.

"Yeah?" Mel's been helping Nacea in the kitchen; she comes and leans a hip against the back of the couch, crossing her burly arms over her chest. The snake tattoos coiling around her wrists are black against her pale skin. Zahra's eyes go wide with fear.

"Sister Zahra's lying to us," Oriol says to Mel. "We need to know who she's been sharing her research with. Can you give us a hand?"

"Course," Mel says, and Oriol stands, elbowing Manu to follow.

Mel gives Zahra a friendly smile and takes Oriol's seat. She picks up the med kit, humming as she searches through it.

"Wait!" Zahra calls.

Mel cracks her neck.

"Wait." Zahra's voice is hoarse with adrenaline. "It doesn't matter if I tell you, you can't do anything about it." She boosts herself onto one elbow with a wince of pain, looking past Mel to make eye contact with Manu once more. "And you shouldn't. It's in the right hands."

Manu leans against the door frame, hands in pockets. "Tell me."

"All our work was shared with the prophet," she says, and Manu keeps his expression neutral, though that is absolutely not what he expected to hear from a woman whose splinter group is apparently being hunted by the prophet's organization. "He's the one that discovered the Gift, and he understands what it should be used for. The Dawn faction in Bulari is misguided, Bennion Zacharia was a disturbed man who never understood his brother's vision, and so sought to distort it. But the prophet's vision is pure."

Fuck these people and their twisted, secretive visions. Manu turns and walks out of the room, ignoring the frantic calls of Sister Zahra after him. Mel hasn't touched her, and he honestly wouldn't care if she did at this point. Whatever distorted version of the world this woman has, he's not going to listen to her justify it anymore.

Nacea offers him a garlic bun when he walks into the kitchen, but he ignores her and pulls out his comm.

TELL S THE DAWN HAS THE RIGHT FORMULA NOW SO WATCH OUT FOR SUPERSOLDIERS. AND TELL JZ I'LL CALL HIM IN A FEW WITH A REPORT.

This time full minutes pass before he gets a response from Toshiyo. He forces himself to stay calm, finally reaching for one of Nacea's garlic buns when he gets a connection request from Jaantzen.

"Hey, boss."

"What do you know?" Jaantzen's voice sounds strained, tinny through the poor connection.

Manu fills him in on the events of the evening, expecting frustration at Moss's death, but Jaantzen barely seems to hear him.

"We're trying to raise Starla," Jaantzen says when Manu finishes. "She's not responding."

A coil of fear unspools itself in Manu's gut. He ignores it. "You thought this would happen, right? The satellite connections?"

"She should be in the window right now." Jaantzen's voice is distant, precise. "We'll keep trying to contact her."

"She'll be all right," Manu tells him. "She's tough and she knows what she's doing. She's got Gia. They'll be fine."

Voices are rising in the other room, Oriol barking instructions to Nacea. Manu glances down the hall; Oriol is furiously searching through the med kit.

"I'll call you back in a few," Manu says, cutting the connection and jogging back down the hall.

Oriol is growling furious instructions at Sister Zahra to stay with him. She coughs weakly, takes a rattling breath, blood on her lips, and Oriol jams something into her neck that releases in a hiss.

Zahra convulses, then catches her breath in one last, awful rattle. Her eyelids flutter closed. Oriol sits back with a sigh, his fingertips brushing the woman's forehead, his lips moving in what Manu suspects is a prayer but knows Oriol will deny if he asks.

Oriol lets his hand drop and looks at Manu. "There's nothing I could have done for her. Maybe at a hospital, but."

Manu squeezes his shoulder. "Who knows how many people she hurt," he says. Hopefully whatever god she believed in will be kinder to her than Manu would be.

"Still." Oriol lifts his hands. "Did you talk to Starla?" he signs.

Manu's jaw clenches, he forces himself to relax. She's going to be fine. He shakes his head and Oriol gives him a concerned look. It has to be fine, he tells himself, just like he told Jaantzen. Starla can take care of herself, and she's got Gia at her back.

But fear is a cold drip down the curve of his spine.

15
———

STARLA

They crest the ridge at sunrise to find themselves dwarfed by a chain of massive stone spikes, crumbling and eroded by the winds of a hundred thousand years into an eerie backbone of spires. The one closest to Starla has an enormous crack about a third of the way up, and by the house-sized boulders littering the bases of the spires, when this one finally goes it won't be the first.

Starla gives it a long look, then settles at its base. That crack has probably been there for centuries.

The desert around Redrock is a different beast than the one Starla is used to, all channeled red-hued dunes held together by sparse tufts of grass and rocky outcroppings that glow spectacularly crimson and orange in the sunrise. The Maraka Valley seemed empty, but compared to here it's teeming with life. She's spotted no lizards or spiders or fire ants here — which hopefully also means no scorpion mites. The only trees they've seen are towering skeletons, bark sunbleached and limbs broken off short. Whatever water allowed them to grow hasn't been around in years.

Simca ditches her pack and scales the broken-off base of

one of the spires, shading her eyes against the morning sun to scan the valley below. Gia settles beside Starla, looking as tired by the hours-long trek as Starla feels. They're both covered in dust, Gia's dark skin ashy with it and Starla's pale skin smudged brown.

Starla often wonders how Simca has the energy for everything she does; today she knows exactly why. Her brother's out there somewhere in the smoldering wreckage of the *Coldfire*.

"Do you know this area?" Starla asks Gia.

Gia's brow furrows as she processes the USL, then she nods and waves an arm at the spires lining the ridge. "These, yes?" She's stumbling through the signs. "I was a few months working near here. Digging." She twists, then points at a jutting plateau across the valley. "There."

Before Starla can ask her anything else, Gia straightens and yells something at Simca, who's waving her arms at them.

"She sees it," Gia signs.

Starla leaves her pack where she dropped it and breaks into a jog, scaling the jagged tooth of stone to join Simca. There, in the middle of the valley, the *Coldfire* had skidded to a landing. Someone tried to cover up signs of its presence, using the desert camouflage kits — thermal shielding and optical cover — to break up the lines and obscure the shape. From the air it'll be difficult to spot. But at a low angle, in the rising sun, the hulking object is definitely the *Coldfire*.

They've also tried to obscure the tracks of the ship's crash landing. The tracks are long but not deep, a sign that makes Starla's heart leap with hope. If Beto and Arundhati managed to make a landing, even with the engines out . . .

"Let's keep going." Simca's expression is fierce.

"Ten minutes. We eat, we rest, then we go."

"We can eat as we go."

"We're in this for the long match," Starla signs sharply, and Simca's lips thin, but she nods. If they're going to make it through this, they need to conserve their energy — Simca of all people knows how hot she can burn. Her entire career has been built around managing her natural spike-and-crash energy cycles.

Simca sits, but doesn't relax, her toe tapping a frantic beat as they gnaw down protein bars. She's the first standing when Starla says it's time to go, and Starla's hard-pressed to keep up with her as they slide-trudge-hike down the dunes and into the valley to the site of the crash.

It's another two hours before they reach the *Coldfire*.

Starla pulls Simca back, and finally the other woman slows her pace, wary on the approach, cautious of a trap. The hull shows signs of fighting, scorch marks that could've come from a concussion grenade and a rainbow discoloration under peeling paint that probably came from a plasma carbine. Her crew weren't dead when they landed, they fought back.

But they're not fighting anymore.

Starla forces herself to move slowly, check for traps. She can't help anyone if she gets herself killed through impatience. Once Starla is assured it's safe, she opens the door.

On the far wall, a smear of blood. Bullet casings litter the floor. The air is stagnant and smells scorched, but there's no one inside. Someone went through the crates of supplies, sorting through the boxes and carting away what they could. Starla would bet anything that the neat piles they left behind are organized for a second trip. Her contraband stash of supplies wasn't touched — whoever ransacked the ship didn't find those panels. But they did take the murdercopters, Starla notes with disappointment. Wherever her crew has gone, they'll follow on foot.

Did her crew survive the fight? Were they marched off as captives? Or buried in the desert?

Simca taps her on the shoulder. "There's a trail of footsteps leading off to the east," she signs, her face pinched and streaked with sand.

"No other trails?"

Simca shakes her head. Which means that dead or alive, they'll find their crew along that path.

She turns to Gia and motions for Simca to interpret. "You know the area, right? That trail, where could it go?"

"Where we were digging you could see the beginnings of a cave system. A couple people got sent to explore it, not all of them came back. The Alliance must not have found anything worth going after, because after a few weeks we moved on to a new project. It would have made a hell of a hideout, though."

Starla cocks her head. "Hideout for who?"

"Escaped prisoners."

Starla and Simca both look at her in surprise. "I thought nobody escaped Redrock," Simca says and signs. She glances at Starla. "Present company excluded."

"No one crosses the Jupari Desert on foot," Starla signs. "And there's no settlements in the Alliance concession to run to."

Gia shrugs. "People try. Sometimes the guards would go after them and bring them back. Sometimes they'd just shoot them. One man, an Alliance guard just shot him in the back a hundred meters away and the rest of us had to keep working like nothing happened. I dug up bones twice while on a work crew."

"Then why run?"

"Why not? Maybe some people really did get away."

Starla hoists her pack once more. "Let's go find out."

"If they're watching, they'll be able to see us coming," Simca signs as they start to walk.

"They've already seen us."

There's nothing to hide them in the barren desert, and no way to approach the plateau without revealing themselves — yet. But to the south, a ridge of rock juts from the drifting sand, rising like a fin for a length of about two hundred meters before plunging back down into a washed-out riverbed that disappears behind the plateau.

"What do you think?" she asks Gia.

"That riverbed skirts along the far side of this plateau," she says. "It could get us close enough, while staying out of their view, that we could then find a less obvious way to make the rest of the distance."

"Let's go."

Starla's ankles are killing her from walking in the shifting sand, her back aches from the weight of the pack, and her eyes are dry and gritty from the heat and dust. The reclamation mask chafes against her cheeks, but she barely notices any of that over the throbbing determination in her heart. She needs to know what happened to El and the rest.

The fin of rock provides cover for nearly an hour, taking them to the base of the plateau and another stroke of luck: a field of broken boulders that will provide some cover. The sun is sinking low on the other side of the plateau — shorter days in this hemisphere — and the longer shadows will make it harder for them to be seen. Of course, as the light goes, so goes her ability to see well enough to communicate.

They knew that was a risk going in. And it's a bridge they'll cross when they come to it.

A worn-out sandal is the first human object Starla has

seen since they left the *Coldfire*. It's tossed carelessly up against a boulder, the tire-rubber sole worn thin and the leather thongs repaired and knotted so many times they couldn't have been comfortable. Whoever lives here doesn't have the luxury of buying a new pair of sandals when the old ones break.

A few steps later she stumbles across a wad of old rags black with grease and dust. To her left is some avian ribcage the size of her fist, picked clean and sunbleached. The sandal's mate is just beyond.

She looks back at the others. "Trash pile."

Behind her, Gia nods and points up. A cleft in the rock about fifteen meters above them. "It's whistling," Gia signs. "Cave entrance?"

"Check it out," Starla tells Simca. "If this is a trash heap, we can probably leave our packs here without worry that somebody will stumble on them."

Simca shucks off her pack and starts to climb, a coil of rope over her shoulder. Starla watches her a moment, looking for any sign of exhaustion, of the energy crash that's sure to come soon. But Simca is climbing as strong as ever, probably buoyed by the adrenaline buzz that they might be close to finding El. Starla and Gia obscure their packs and stow the water reclamation masks, then pull out as many weapons as they can. Starla straps on knives, a pistol, an electric barb, her whip belt. She checks the karambit Oriol gave her, it's snug in its sheath at the base of her spine.

Another bite of ration bar, another sip of reclaimed water, and a pebble lands at her foot. Simca tosses the rope out, it snakes down the cliff to fall into the boulders. Starla sends Gia up the cliff first, then follows herself once Gia's weight is off the rope. She uses it only when necessary, when she doesn't trust the fingerholds or the tiny cracks to give her good purchase with her combat boots. It's not the hardest climb she's ever done, but she can see why no one would bother to guard this entrance. Few can climb like Simca.

Inside, the light from the sunset only illuminates about five meters into the cave before fading into inky darkness. Starla squints at Simca's hands, attention so close that she doesn't notice if Simca is also speaking aloud for Gia.

"I heard voices while you were climbing," Simca is signing. "Two men."

"Alliance? Dawn?"

Simca shakes her head. "I couldn't tell."

A glimmer of light at the far end of the cave suddenly blooms, washes into the cave to illuminate a passage about as wide as Starla's elbows if she held them akimbo and about three meters tall. All three women melt back against the wall, but the light flashes over them and continues, as though somebody passed by holding a lantern.

Starla releases her breath. "Follow them."

Simca slips out first, trailing the light. Gia takes up the rear, fingertips brushing Starla's sleeve to keep up with her in the dark. Starla can see only the silhouette of Simca's cheek, inky black against the darker gray of the light ahead.

Until the light goes dark. Starla stops when Simca does, then slips her hand into the other woman's. "Wait," she fingerspells, then switches her lens to infrared and creeps ahead. She's been trying not to use her gauntlet because she doesn't know when she'll be able to recharge it out here, but if they don't get out of this now, it won't matter if it runs out of power.

At first the passageway looks empty, but as Starla inches forward, the faint glow of body heat appears on her lens. The person they've been following is pressed into a shallow depression in the wall, waiting, listening for them with his face turned their way. Starla carefully picks up a stone from the floor, then tosses it farther down the passageway.

The man's head whips around when the stone clatters to the ground and Starla leaps at him, coming up with her shoulder against his ribs, sending him crashing back into the wall. He grabs for her, but she has the element of surprise and the ability to see in the dark, and after a brief struggle she has him on the ground, her knee in his back, the point of her karambit's blade against his throat. His lantern was knocked over in the fight and is lying near his head; Starla switches it on and beckons Simca and Gia forward.

Probably not very subtle or quiet, but no one's running down the passageway to investigate. Yet.

She jerks her chin at Simca, who kneels beside the man, questioning him. He's clean-shaven and wiry, though not particularly big. Home-done tattoos wind down the backs of his hands and around his neck. There's real fear in his eyes as he talks with Simca.

Finally she sits back with a grim expression. "He says they're alive and he'll take us to them," she signs. "I don't trust him."

"Then cuff him. We'll leave him here."

The man protests as Simca slaps a pair of disposable cuffs around his wrists, but Gia stabs a needle in his neck and he goes limp.

"Thirty minutes," Gia signs. Starla gives her a thumbs-up, then rifles through the man's pockets to find a knife, but nothing more.

"Leave the lantern," Starla signs. "I'll lead." Stalactites and columns loom eerily in the glow of her infrared as she leads them through the dark. The passageway expands into a long, narrow room, with several other passageways leading away from the other end. It looks like this room is used as a sort of food storehouse. Braids of onions hang from racks, piles of squash, dried ears of corn. They're not close to the Alliance terraforming operation, but maybe whoever calls these caves their home has a small operation of their own? Or maybe they're stealing from the Alliance.

Simca's grip on her sleeve tightens. "Voices," she finger-spells in Starla's hand, then points towards the passageway on the right.

Starla leads them to the entrance, slipping up against the wall and motioning Simca to the far side as a light glows brighter. She pulls out her pistol, but Gia touches her arm. "Children," she signs.

Children? Here?

She keeps her gun ready, waiting as the bobbing light gets closer, pressing into her shadowy depression beside the entrance, her breathing shallow and smooth.

The lantern light is blinding when it comes. The man holding it doesn't look around as he enters the cave, the lantern in one hand and a child no more than five years old tugging against his free hand. Starla catches Simca's eye from the other side of the entrance and motions for her to continue on. She does, and Starla begins to creep out after her, stepping carefully to avoid kicking any loose stones.

She's barely taken her first step when the child turns, tugging on the man's hand with a big smile that turns to curiosity at seeing Starla there. Starla gives the child a smile, one finger pressed to her lips.

The child's mouth gapes open, eyes scrunched tight in a scream.

Starla bolts after Simca down the passageway, which is dimly illuminated from light at the far end, hoping it leads somewhere with a place to hide. Simca slows as they reach the next bend and presses herself into the wall, signs for the others to get back and prepare to fight.

Simca lets the first figure run past her, then tackles the next; Starla rams her shoulder into the first figure and he hits the wall, mouth gaping as the air is forced out of his lungs. Gia steps past her to help Simca, then her eyes widen with panic. She waves at Starla to get down just as Starla sees it: a grenade, spewing clouds of billowing gas.

Starla drops low and tries to hold her breath, but Simca's already hit her knees and Gia is stumbling. Beyond them a figure in a gas mask has joined the fight, and Starla launches herself. They've steeled themselves to meet her, so she switches at the last moment to a low sweeping kick that sends the figure to the ground. They roll back to their feet, and Starla stands — but her head is swimming, the edges of her vision going fuzzy. She lunges once more, clumsier this time, and the figure grabs her wrist and twists. Her head cracks against the wall. The world goes black.

16

PHAERA

Phaera flicks her thumbnail over the edges of the pair of mystix cards she's been carrying in the pocket of her jumpsuit. A fidgety gesture, she knows, but no one's watching her right now. Except maybe her security team, monitoring the Lorelei's feeds.

Or *her*.

As she'd expected, her apartment's security guard hadn't found a hint of the mystery woman with the heart-shaped face — or of anyone delivering the note with the Fallen Tower the night before last. His running theory is that Phaera had the note on her when she came home and it fell out of her coat pocket or purse in the shuffle of getting in the door. She just hadn't noticed it until later.

This may have satisfied Diego, but Phaera knows better. They can't see who delivered the note because Victoria Tierren doesn't want them to. Phaera has no doubts Tierren's the one who delivered the blood-stained mystix cards to the Devil's Table and the one who slipped the Fallen Tower under her apartment door.

Who had maybe already broken into Phaera's apartment?

Nice place. I love the couch.

Phaera barely slept that night, and she hasn't been home since. It isn't the first time she's stayed in her office at the Devil's Table, and it probably won't be the last.

Two out of the three fortune-killer cards: the Mask and the Fallen Tower. Betrayed trust and shattered stronghold. Phaera flicks her thumbnail over the edges of them both again, then forces herself to pull her hand out of her pocket. These cards may be meant to rattle her, but there's a warning worth heeding in them: The fortress and relationships you built to get you this far can't be trusted to take you where you want to go.

She trusts her people implicitly when it comes to running the Lorelei and the Devil's Table. But which of them will she be able to trust as she continues on her current path?

A sudden knock at the door sends her heart rate spiking; she knows she jumped, and she can't afford that. Anyone could be watching her for cracks.

Phaera takes the time to compose herself before she opens the door, even though she can see from the screen it's Jae Bakshi, her head of security at the Lorelei. The woman she trusts most — should trust most. Phaera catches herself. Jae will have her back, won't she? If Phaera can articulate what she needs from her.

Phaera opens the door. Jae's holding a covered plate. "I was bringing you dinner," she says, walking past Phaera to set the plate on her desk. Phaera's stomach clenches with nausea at the smell. "But you have a visitor."

"I ordered in from the 'Tercio."

"That was yesterday."

Was it? Phaera lifts the lid off the tray to find a mezze sampler from the Siren bar downstairs. Garlic, parsley, red onions, exactly the sort of thing one should eat before meeting a guest. "Who's the visitor?"

"A detective. Arman Falk? Sina's checking his credentials."

Phaera lets out a breath; everything's been too quiet these past few days. The few messages exchanged with Jaantzen yesterday were status reports more than anything: Aiax and Mizal are out, meeting's set with Teo Lordeur, any luck getting in touch with Leone's secretary in prison? She's heard nothing from him today, which doesn't surprise her. It's hard enough to get him to open up in person, he doesn't seem the type to get chatty in text.

She hasn't said a word to Jaantzen about the mystix card messages, and she doesn't know if Oriol mentioned the first one. Besides those, there's been no sign of Leone's next attack.

Even this visit from the police, she'd expected them to come asking her about Jaantzen days ago. She wonders what it means that it took them so long, and if it has anything to do with the fact that Leone has slowed her own rapid-fire pace. She's biding her time for something, because surely she didn't have a change of heart.

"Send him up."

"He'll be here in a few minutes. Oh." Jae's expression becomes uncomfortable. "Sina wanted you to know he's confirmed on the Chief Justice's payroll."

Phaera frowns, not quite understanding either the message or Jae's discomfort. "The detective?"

Jae clears her throat. "Apparently quite a few of the police are. Sina's been compiling a list for some time now."

"Oh." Of course. A chill slips down Phaera's spine. Who in this city does Leone *not* own? "Did you know that?"

"I haven't had to deal much with the police," she says, a hint of reproach in her tone so light Phaera's not sure she heard it. She files it away to probe later. Jae may not be one of the ones who will take this journey with her.

Jae crosses to the door. "I'll be outside. For the love of all that's holy, ma'am, eat something before you talk to him."

Phaera studies the selection on the tray, settles eventually on a handful of spicy harissa almonds that won't send the detective running from her breath — though maybe that's what she wants. With how little sleep she's gotten the last few nights, she's in no position to make rational conversation.

She knows, whispers a voice in her head. That's why he's here today.

If Leone's sending her goons to rattle Phaera with more head games, Phaera can play along. Leone needs to think the attack on her mother was her last straw, Jaantzen told her that night in the desert. Even so, Leone would have been suspicious if Phaera had come crawling back to her right away. The trick is letting Leone think she's winning without truly giving anything away. Let her think she's successfully planted doubts about Jaantzen in Phaera's mind.

The sharp edges of the mystix cards in her jumpsuit pocket are digging into her thigh: The place you thought you were safe is now a trap; you can no longer rely on those you trust. Maybe they were meant to unsettle her, but she'll take them as advice. She can't rely on what worked in the past to carry her into the future. She must build stronger and smarter, trust less easily.

Another knock on the door, and Phaera stands, smooths her palms down her thighs. Yet another showtime.

"Come in!"

Oriol opens the door, ushering in the detective. He's tall, with midnight-black skin and fine features, an impeccable suit, gleaming dress shoes. Perfect teeth when he flashes her a smile and holds out his hand. She steps forward warily to greet him.

Oriol shuts the door and leans against the wall beside it, a sharp eye on the detective. Out of habit? Or because he believes this man on Leone's payroll is here to hurt her?

The detective ignores him. "Ms. Harris, I'm Detective Arman Falk, with the Bulari Police." He gestures at her desk. "May I?"

"Of course," Phaera says, and he palms the signature pad on her desk. Phaera gives his ident card a glance before saving it for later study. It seems legitimate to her, and Jae said Oriol had already run his credentials. "Pleased to meet you, Detective."

"Likewise. If we could speak alone?" The false casual way he keeps his back to Oriol is excruciatingly deliberate.

"Of course. Thank you, Mr. Sina," she says, and Oriol frowns at her in surprise. "I'll call you if we need anything."

Oriol nods slowly, the slight hesitation in his movements a sign he's obeying her order under protest. She'd rather have him in the room, as much for security as to pick his brain afterward, but more than that she wants the detective's candor. And he won't hurt her; still, she twists the gold cuff on her wrist, reminding herself of the button that will trigger the self-defense mode.

Phaera waves Falk into the seat across from her desk. "How can I help you?"

Falk sits, one knee laid carefully over the other, tugging

at his suit so the crease of his slacks knifes towards his toe. "I have some questions about one of your associates."

Phaera waits, expression carefully neutral. She's been expecting this visit; he must know that, too. Now the game will be walking a thin line between giving away anything she knows about Jaantzen without appearing to protect him.

Falk glances meaningfully at her office door. "I'm here about Oriol Sina," he says, and she lets her surprise show. The corner of Falk's mouth twitches.

"What about him?"

"You're aware of Mr. Sina's relationship with a man named Manu Juric?"

"I am."

"Then can I assume you're comfortable with Mr. Juric's criminal record?"

"I run background checks on my employees, not their spouses. Is Sina in trouble?"

"It depends, ma'am," Falk says, hand up as though to calm her, though she hasn't raised her voice, has she? "Can you vouch for his whereabouts five nights ago?"

"Things have been hectic since the Lorelei was attacked," she says, pulling up her calendar. "Forgive me if all the days are blurring together. Five nights? He was with me. My mother took ill. We took her to a clinic, then home, where he stayed with us through the night until we were sure she was all right."

"Does he often stay with you through the night?"

Nothing in his tone adds to the impropriety of the question, but it's in the gleam of his eyes nonetheless. His tone and expression is perfectly skirting the line between inquisitive and patronizing, so much so, she can't tell if he's trying to get a rise out of her on purpose or if she's simply on edge and overreacting.

"Odd hours are a job requirement for a personal body-guard," she says crisply. Let him think she's offended at the innuendo; she is.

"You don't remember anything strange about his behavior that night? Maybe he received a call? A message?"

"I'm not sure I would know if he did. He's very private and my attention was on my mother. What's this about?"

"Your Mr. Sina's partner is wanted in connection to the murder of BPD Detective Timo Cho that same night."

Phaera blinks at him, honestly shocked.

"May I?" Falk leans forward, sliding his comm across her desk to show a picture of an older man in a police uniform. Salt-and-pepper hair, light skin, somber lines carved around his eyes and mouth. Phaera leans in to study the photo, but she's watched enough of the street magicians on the drag to notice Falk's other hand disappear beneath her desk.

"My old partner from a few years back, in fact," Falk says, and his patter is a little too fast, a little too rehearsed. "A good detective and a good man, slain in his home in what looks to be a professional hit." He leans back in his chair, slipping his comm back into his pocket. "Can I assume you're comfortable with that, Ms. Harris?"

"Of course not! But I don't know anything about that. And I doubt Mr. Sina does, either."

"You say Mr. Sina is private. He might not say anything about his partner's professional work." He pauses delicately, a predatory gleam in his eye, giving her a moment to pretend to ask what he means by "professional work." She's not playing the clueless damsel, though. She waits for him to ask the inevitable next question.

"Do you know anything of Willem Jaantzen's where-abouts that same night?"

Phaera takes a slow breath. "He was also with me at the clinic."

"And when you and Mr. Sina went home with your mother?"

"Jaantzen left."

"Did he say where he was going?"

"No."

"Is he often so secretive with you?"

"He's also very private."

Falk holds up his hands again as though to calm her, as though her last comment was the fiery outburst of an emotional diva rather than the simple statement it was. Her blood boils at that, but she keeps her game face on. She's sat across the table from a hundred men just like him and walked home with their cash.

"You don't seem to have a problem with hiring someone with ties to a murderer, but I wonder if you're comfortable being linked yourself to a man who orders the assassinations of police officers."

"I don't have any comment." Now the room does seem like it's crushing in; Phaera straightens her shoulders to keep it all back. "I'm sorry, I can't help you, Detective Falk. If you have any other questions, please get in touch with my lawyer."

Some triumph flashes across his face — he should be upset at getting shut down here, but he thinks he has her trapped. This air is suddenly hard to breathe.

"It might make more sense to speak down at the station," Falk says.

Phaera gives him a tight smile. "Please let me know how I can help, and I'm sorry for your loss." A blink of confusion on Falk's face before he catches himself. "For your partner."

"Thank you. We'll talk again soon."

He shuts the door behind him, and on the security screen she watches the brief, cordial exchange he has with Oriol before heading out across the casino floor. Oriol settles back into an impossibly relaxed posture beside her door, no sign whatsoever if he's ruffled.

Phaera watches him on the feed a moment, gathering herself. Gods, he's so fucking calm — and calming. He's gone from a suffocating reminder that she needs protection to a reassuring presence and sounding board in a matter of weeks. The coming road is treacherous, and she doesn't know whom she can trust of the people who got her this far. Jae Bakshi has her back, but she's obviously not comfortable in Jaantzen's world. Hiro Matapang is, but he's not going to be her confidante. Vanessa Dosantos may be one of her best friends, but Phaera can't drag her into this morass. She needs Oriol, now more than ever.

But that doesn't matter.

Especially if Falk's patter about his old partner was distracting her from what she suspects it was.

She crosses to the other side of her desk and sits in the chair he vacated, peering under her desk until she finds it: a barely noticeable surveillance tab adhered to the bottom of her desk. Falk didn't think he'd get anything out of her by asking directly; this visit was a way to get into her office and bug it. That's why he didn't press much.

Phaera sits back in the chair, trying to think. Leone wants her paranoid and alone, wants her to sell Jaantzen out and come crawling back. Phaera will, but she needs to time it exactly right. Leone knows Phaera has too much pride to make that decision lightly, she has to believe Phaera is at her breaking point.

She leaves the surveillance tab where it is and returns to

her chair, straightening her shoulders to steel herself for what comes next.

Oriol's been waiting patiently, but he palms open the door immediately when she pages him. "Is Bakshi out there?" she asks.

"No, ma'am."

"Have a seat." She opens up a channel to Jae. "Jae, I need you in my office, now."

Oriol's studying her with wary curiosity, and whatever he sees keeps him from taking the chair Falk left. Phaera could sit here forever trying to find the best words, but it's best to rip the bandage off. She takes a deep breath.

"You're fired."

She didn't think anything could surprise Oriol Sina, but she's managed to do it. His lips quirk to the side, like he's not sure if she's serious. "Ma'am?"

"You're fired." Phaera swipes open her desk and pulls up his file. "I'm revoking your security clearance. You'll get a full month's severance immediately, and if you need a recommendation I'll be happy to make one."

Now he's frowning. "Phaera. What is this?"

"Did Manu kill that police detective?"

That doesn't get a reaction. "What police detective?"

"I know none of us are saints, Sina, but I've managed to pretend it's all for some greater good. But that's not true, is it? And no matter what you tell me, I know where your loyalties really lie. I've been an idiot not to see it before now."

Oriol rests his fingertips on her desk, voice quiet. "Phaera, I don't know what he told you, but don't do this. You need me."

"I need someone I can trust," she snaps. "The night my mother had her heart attack." She gives Oriol a beat; his lips part but he doesn't say anything. They both know that's not what happened, but her office isn't safe anymore and he needs to understand that.

She lifts her chin. "That night. Did Manu kill a police detective?"

Oriol's jaw tightens. "Of course not."

"You were with me. You can't know for sure."

"It wouldn't make sense."

"It wouldn't make sense, or it wouldn't be right?" He's silent, and something shifts at her core, a deep fracture that has nothing to do with this charade and everything to do with the truth of the world as she knows it. "Tell me, Sina," she murmurs. "Tell me Jaantzen's not the kind of man who'd order Manu to kill a police officer."

Oriol takes a deep breath, but he can't tell her no — Phaera knows that, with the sickening dizziness of realization that she may be putting on a show, but every word she's said here is true. She's long been wondering what skeletons Jaantzen might have in his closet. But maybe the better question is, how long will she keep fooling herself he doesn't?

"Phaera," Oriol says quietly. "Protect yourself."

"From what? From him?" She forces herself to breathe. "From you?" He's searching her gaze, and a part of her is watching his gun hand, knowing there's nothing she could do if she actually had overplayed this game, if he really thought she needed silenced. If he really was Jaantzen's man.

Jae Bakshi's knock on the door breaks the moment. "Come in," Phaera calls. Oriol steps into parade rest, untroubled as granite.

"Please escort Mr. Sina out," Phaera tells Jae; her chief of security's eyes go wide. "I've revoked his clearance. If he's checked out any equipment please see it's returned."

Jae glances at Oriol, about to argue, but he gives her a faint shake of the head. "Of course, ma'am." The reluctance in her voice is clear.

"Thank you."

Phaera forces her attention back to her desk as Jae holds the door open for Oriol, keeps her expression smooth as he looks over his shoulder.

As her heart breaks.

She's truly alone, now. But if that's what Leone wanted, she'll soon find out that Phaera on her own has more to fight for. And less to hold her back.

17
____

JAANTZEN

It's been more than a full day since Starla left, and she hasn't checked in. Every ninety minutes an alarm has gone off as the satellite crosses over the Alliance dead zone, sending him into a cycle of anticipation, disappointment, and increasing worry. Jaantzen is pacing the small space of his bunker office, continuously checking his desk to make sure she hasn't pinged him and it failed to notify him.

Nothing.

The satellite is less than a minute from leaving the communications window when the desk finally chimes with an incoming message, and he slumps into his chair, pulse pounding.

But it's Oriol, not Starla.

BE ADVISED I'M OFF PHAERA'S DETAIL PER HER REQUEST. I STILL HAVE EYES ON HER.

Jaantzen's been wondering how long she'd be able to keep Oriol at her side, given her plans to make a break with Jaantzen look realistic, but he had hoped it would be longer. He doesn't like her unprotected like this. He forces himself to wait until the satellite's out of the communications window, then another ten breaths in case. He knows if Starla's message does come through, he'll see it even if he's on a voice call. But he doesn't want to take any chances.

Oriol answers immediately when he opens up the connection. "Yes, sir?"

"What happened?"

Oriol clears his throat. In the distance, a siren wails. "A detective came to see her, asking about the murder of a Detective Timo Cho? I believe he implicated Manu, and she thought it best to let me go."

"Manu wasn't involved."

"I know."

Good. Then Jaantzen doesn't need to worry about Oriol being upset, only Phaera.

"Do you think she believed the detective?"

"Hard to tell. But she called her mom's poisoning a heart attack. She thinks someone has her office bugged, is my guess."

"What was the detective's name?"

"Falk," says Oriol. "Arman Falk. He's on Leone's payroll."

"And he was . . ." Jaantzen's trying to dislodge the man's name from his memory.

"Cho's old partner. Back when."

"Right." Oriol might not be angry with him now, but *back when*, Oriol had been furious that Jaantzen sent Manu to dampen Cho's curiosity. At Leone's request. "Who's with her now?"

"I am." On the other end of the line Jaantzen can make out rustling fabric, distant traffic. "I've been working shifts with people I trust. Just now it's all remote."

"Thank you."

"Course. Is Manu with you?"

"He is."

"Okay. I'll let you know if anything changes."

That Leone is using Cho's death to make trouble for Phaera and Oriol isn't a surprise. After the PR backlash of publicly announcing Jaantzen as a suspect in the Alliance Embassy bombing only to have the Alliance itself deny it, the BPD has moved more cautiously in naming a suspect in Cho's death. Though internal sources have told Jaantzen that Manu's the popular candidate.

One more loose end. But unlike resurrecting Orris Moss, bringing Starla home, or protecting Phaera himself, this is something he may actually be able to do something about.

Manu's door is shut and his light is out, but Toshiyo's door is open at the end of the hall. Light and the sound of humming spill out. He pauses in the doorway, mentally routing a path to her desk. They've been here less than a week and she's apparently already dragged half the rubble from the bunker complex back to her room to poke at; his skin crawls at the clutter. A monitor at his elbow shows a diagnostics scan running on an autodefense bot, one of the kind that bury themselves like sand vipers and release a volley of neurotoxin darts when triggered.

He tells himself Toshiyo probably removed the darts.

Every surface is piled high, except for a low shelf at her left elbow which holds only a ragged blanket. Maybe she gets cold down here — with all the whirring electronics, Toshiyo's lairs have always been uncomfortably warm to Jaantzen, but she's wrapped in an oversized sweater.

He knocks and gets no response; she's still humming, head bobbing faintly to whatever's playing in her ear. Jaantzen picks his way through the maze to get in her peripheral vision and she blinks at him and drops her headset to her shoulders. Blaring static and frenzied drum riffs flare until she turns it down. "Yeah, boss?"

"You know you can use the hangar if you want to dismantle things," he says drily. "Especially dangerous things that might get us all killed." He nods towards the door. "Please tell me you disarmed the autodefense bot."

"It's perfectly safe," Toshiyo says. "I found a whole stash of them in one of the sealed bunkers I opened yesterday. This guy was prepared to fight off an army. Land mines, assault rifles, and two whole cases of wasp drones. You know, the ones that swarm out at proximity? I've always wanted to see what I could do with those."

Jaantzen glances over his shoulder, but if there are any dormant wasp drones nearby he doesn't see them. "Please play with those outside."

"Sure thing." She cracks her neck. "What's going on?"

"Do you have a minute? I need you to help me put some pieces together."

"Of course."

She swipes a few keystrokes, and whatever she was working on disappears. But before Jaantzen can say anything more, he's cut off by a rattling click and a leathery flap of wings from the other side of Toshiyo. With a hoarse cry, the creature lands on the ratty blanket at her elbow. Jaantzen's hand is halfway to where his pistol would be if he carried it at home; he reaches for a hefty spanner instead, grip tightening around the handle.

"Hey, Lucky," Toshiyo says warmly to the creature. "You can put that down, boss, it's okay. Sign hello. Look friendly."

The alien creature had slowed its initial rapid growth at about Toshiyo's waist height, though if it stretches its wings and gets onto its hind legs it can now reach her shoulders.

And it's starting to put on muscle. It watches him with an expression of protective wariness and distrust. Jaantzen lowers the spanner, but doesn't set it down.

"I thought we had a home for our friend," he says carefully, keeping his gaze locked on the creature's. It's watching him like a predator. "Somewhere a bit safer."

"It's fine, he's not going to hurt any of us."

"Tell that to Manu."

"He was just protecting me."

"Toshiyo. This thing should be — "

In a cage, is what he's about to say, when the creature nudges Toshiyo's shoulder. It extends three claws and taps them against its lips. Toshiyo obligingly pours water from a bottle into a dish and it settles into the blanket to lap daintily, cooing a deep, guttural purr.

Jaantzen stares at her. "It can sign?"

"Basic words. If these guys are smart enough to get to a whole new star system, they have to be able to communicate. It doesn't seem like little buddy's going to be able to speak our language, and I haven't figured out if the sounds it makes are supposed to be speech. But we both kind of have hands, so Starla and I figured, why not?"

The creature is watching her with an expression that could be called concentration.

Toshiyo points to Jaantzen. "He's a friend," Toshiyo signs to Lucky.

"A friend who's uncomfortable with the idea that this creature is roaming free."

"Lucky."

"That Lucky is roaming free."

The creature's curious expression is slowly shifting to mistrust.

"He's not roaming, he's with me."

"He?"

Toshiyo nods. Jaantzen's not about to ask how she knows.

"Put the spanner down. Lucky needs to get used to you. And know that you're not a threat." She turns back to it and makes his namesign. "That's Jaantzen, he's a friend," she signs again. She points to herself. "I'm Toshiyo. I'm a friend. You're Lucky. You're a friend. We're all friends."

It settles back on its haunches and mimics her sign for friend.

It occurs to Jaantzen he's been thinking this whole time of the creature as a pet, a feral thing with no training that Toshiyo has taken a fondness to. Like one of Starla's cats — underfoot yet far more dangerous. But Toshiyo is right. Lucky may be a juvenile of his species, but others like him managed to build starships that can span galaxies. This whole thing began beyond his scope of knowledge, and it's rapidly spinning past what his team is capable of dealing with.

This isn't developing a new technology or expanding into a new territory. Lucky and his rapidly growing little sibling need to get into the hands of experts.

But first, they need to survive.

Jaantzen gives Lucky a solemn nod, and then puts the idea of him back into the compartment in his mind labeled Deal With This If We Live Through Leone.

"I need to find out who killed Detective Timo Cho." He finds himself signing as he speaks out of an uneasy sense of politeness.

"It was Tierren," says Toshiyo. With a few keystrokes she calls up video footage. "After I first saw her with him, I cloned the security feed of his building. And a good thing, too — she erased the original after her visit."

Lucky is watching the footage with interest, he growls when Tierren walks through the frame.

"Not a friend," Toshiyo signs to him. He raises his bony claws and copies her.

"You have evidence?" Jaantzen asks.

"That she actually killed him? No. But we do have vids that link them together multiple times, and she's the only one who entered the building during that time."

"And we can link her to Leone, correct?"

"Yeah." She frowns. "But why would she kill him, then? It seemed like she had a nice tame lapdog."

"Because he met with Manu. She went to see if her lapdog was still taking orders, and he must not have been any longer." Jaantzen breathes out a curse. "Which means Manu was probably right that he was more interested in finding the truth than carrying out his vendetta."

"But asked questions to the wrong person."

"Apparently. Can you get into his network logs and see if he communicated with anyone after he talked to Manu? Maybe he had someone else he trusted."

"Sure." Toshiyo's black-lacquered fingernails click on the desk as she types. Jaantzen watches her until he becomes aware of the creature's shiny black eyes studying him.

What does one talk with an alien about? "I'm Jaantzen," he signs, using his namesign and tapping his chest. He does it again, and finally the creature lifts a clawed, webbed hand and copies him. Then it coos gutturally and gestures at Toshiyo, makes her namesign.

A shiver runs down Jaantzen's spine.

"Here we go," Toshiyo says, ignoring the exchange. "He sent a series of messages to this comm. It belongs to some-body named Hector Ngara."

The name rings a bell, but the alien in the corner is a distraction. "Major Hector Ngara," he says after a moment. "Of the BPD. Did he respond?"

"It doesn't look like it. Is he one of Leone's?"

"I'm not sure." He thinks back through her dinner parties, through every comment she's made about the Bulari Police Department. The chief of police is definitely on her payroll, and Jaantzen knows he's built a close cohort of loyal stooges around him. But is Ngara in that cohort? Did Cho's messages back to him trigger a visit from Tierren, or was she already planning on shutting him down?

"Can you find me files related to the investigation of Cho's murder?"

More clicking, and Jaantzen leans over Toshiyo's shoulder to read. "I've seen plenty of shoddy cover-up paperwork," he says. "They were investigating Cho's murder for real."

"For a day or two, at least," Toshiyo says. And she's right, the log entries are detailed and frequent for the first day and a half, then they take on the lackluster performance of someone doing a job for show. External notes show why. The first entries were from Cho's partner, Officer Ossandre Samson. Then the case was given to a more senior detective, Cho's old partner Arman Falk. The change of personnel should have gone through Major Ngara, but it went above his head — the approving signature is from the police chief himself.

"Falk is definitely on Leone's payroll," says Jaantzen. "Even when he was Cho's partner a decade ago. What was Cho working on last week?"

Click, click. "Interviewing victims of the Alliance Embassy bombing."

"Nothing about investigating the murders of Naali Hinoja and Chase Ratham?"

Toshiyo shakes her head. "By the time that case shows up in the system the files are already complete and there's a warrant out for Manu's arrest. Signed by Ngara. Cho is listed as lead detective, even though he didn't work murder."

Which means Cho was investigating the case outside the BPD system, and Ngara knew about it.

Jaantzen frowns at the files on Toshiyo's desk, trying to put together the pieces. Cho obviously didn't trust many people in his department, and for good reason. But at least one person was honestly trying to solve his murder — his partner, Samson. And if Major Ngara had wanted to cover up Cho's murder, he wouldn't have let her investigate it in the first place. Or at least his name would have been the one giving the case to Falk instead. But that order came from over Ngara's head.

"I want your gut feeling," he says to Toshiyo, and she winces. "Did Cho trust Ngara?"

"I don't know," she says. She cups her chin in her hands, staring at the open files on her desk, pale fingers digging in behind her ears. "How would I know?"

"There are patterns in people like there are in data," Jaantzen says. "What's your instinct?"

Toshiyo sighs. "Yes?"

"I think so, too. And he may have been right to." Jaantzen is done sitting around; it's time for action. "Open a secure connection to him, please."

Toshiyo shoots him side-eye, but does as he asks. It's late; in the underground bunker his schedule has shifted, his already night owl tendencies becoming exacerbated, especially with Toshiyo for company. But not everyone is still awake. After a long round of connection requests, the line finally opens up. The voice that answers is gruff and sleep-dulled.

"Major Ngara? This is Willem Jaantzen. I'm sorry for waking you."

A beat, and now Ngara sounds more alert. "What do you want?"

"You lost a good man last week," Jaantzen says. "I don't think everyone at the BPD appreciated what Detective Cho was trying to do, but I think you did." He can hear Ngara's breath on the other end of the line. "Prevailing opinion seems to be I was behind his murder. Is that what you believe?"

"No. It's not."

"Would you like to know who was? Or are you content to let Falk sweep Cho's death under the rug?"

A deep breath. Jaantzen's pulse beats slow and steady, measuring the time. Dozens of alternate plans spool out from this moment while he waits for Ngara to make a decision.

"Tell me," Ngara finally says.

"I'll send you a location." Somewhere on the road to the valley, far enough out in the desert that they'll be able to see if Ngara brought backup, but close enough to Bulari he won't be able to guess which direction Jaantzen came from. "Meet me there in one hour, and I'll give you what you need to bring down the person behind Cho's murder. And give yourself some breathing room again."

"In an hour? But — "

"Come alone."

Jaantzen cuts the connection, and Toshiyo gives him a resigned look.

"I want you to come with me and monitor the conversation. Keep an eye out and make sure everything is safe."

"Of course. If Manu or Starla were here, it would be their job to talk you out of this, right?" She sighs. "I'm terrible at talking you out of doing things."

"You are. But we should wake up Manu and tell him the bad news."

"Not it." Toshiyo swipes the files they've been looking at into a nearby data cube. "Anything else you want on this?"

"Our file on the police chief and Leone."

"The whole thing? Or the 'for public consumption' version." More than a few of the things that implicate the police chief and Leone involve Jaantzen, too — at least back in the days of the civil war. It's not a time that needs to be dredged back up today.

"The latter."

"Course." Another few keystrokes and she copies that file, too. She waves the desk to standby and gets to her feet. "Give me a few minutes to get Lucky comfortable and grab my gear and I'll be ready to go."

The meeting spot is an intersection with good sight lines; Jaantzen doesn't want Ngara to feel he's walking into an ambush, and Jaantzen needs to know the same. They've gotten here a little ahead of schedule, giving Manu time to slip into the night and cover the meeting spot from another direction.

Jaantzen parks the Dulciana in a clear spot, then Toshiyo rolls down the window and releases a handful of beetle drones. They're dealing with the tail end of a dust storm and the winds are still high, though visibility has improved. The drones' batteries won't last long with so much energy devoted to mitigating the effects of the wind. But this meeting shouldn't last long, either.

Jaantzen shifts against the tightness of the tactical vest he's wearing under his shirt and jacket. His stats are part of the stream of data flowing across Toshiyo's tablet, along with reports from the drones.

"We've got a vehicle incoming from the road to Bulari," Toshiyo says after a moment. She maneuvers the drone closer, and in the grainy footage Jaantzen can make out a tall, dark-skinned man driving alone. "No other life signs in the spinner with him," says Toshiyo.

Ngara slows as he approaches and Jaantzen gets out of the driver's seat so Ngara can see him. Wind whips at his suit, grit scours his eyes, and that poetry shrapnel in his mind twinges once more. *Death on the desert wind,* was that it? Headlights sweep over him and away, and Ngara finally pulls off the road a dozen paces from Jaantzen.

"I've got a clear shot," Manu says in Jaantzen's ear.

Ngara leans over to shove open the door to the passenger seat as Jaantzen approaches, and Jaantzen settles into the seat and shuts the door behind him. The howling wind is replaced by the hum of the engine, the quiet strains of an Alusinian ballad, until Ngara switches off the music.

"I've spent my whole life in the city," Jaantzen says. "It's easy to forget how fierce the wind can be out here. There's a poem about it, something about death on the desert wind."

Wariness sharpens the lines around Ngara's eyes and creases his lips, but it's tinged with curiosity. He's wearing a holster under his jacket.

"I haven't heard it," Ngara finally says.

Jaantzen extends a hand. After a moment's hesitation, Ngara takes it.

"Thank you for coming out," Jaantzen says.

"Don't make me regret it."

"You won't." Jaantzen slips a hand into his jacket pocket — Ngara tenses — and retrieves the data cube. He sets it on the console between them. "Detective Cho was murdered by a mercenary who is currently in the employ of Chief Justice Geum-ja Leone." There's no hint of disbelief or shock in Ngara's expression; he must suspect who's behind the bribes his fellow officers are taking. "The mercenary is a woman currently going by the name of Victoria Tierren, real identity as yet unknown. This cube contains evidence she and Leone are working together, as well as that she knew Cho. She was also the only person to enter and leave Cho's apartment building during the timeframe in which he was murdered. The evidence is circumstantial, but I believe you can fill in the links."

Jaantzen glances at him. "Incidentally, Tierren was also the reason your star witness pinning the murders of Hinoja and Ratham on Manu Juric changed his testimony. She had his daughters held as collateral for him to testify against Juric. After we secured their safety, Ajesh Paiman felt able to tell the truth."

"Acheta killed Hinoja," Ngara says. "Apparently everyone in the underground knew it was Acheta."

"He liked to brag."

"And who killed Acheta?"

"I believe that's out of the scope of our conversation tonight."

"It was you?"

"No."

Ngara frowns at him, then at the data cube. "And what do you want in exchange?"

"The same thing you do. To get Leone's influence out of the police department."

"That influence has protected you," Ngara points out.

"And you," Jaantzen says, and a muscle in Ngara's jaw jumps, but he doesn't deny it. "But that arrangement is no longer working for either of us, is it?"

"So you want a new arrangement."

Jaantzen shakes his head. "This isn't a bribe. I'm not asking you to exchange one master for another. I have information you need, and if you use it, we both benefit. You get justice for your detective, I get Leone to stop using the BPD as her personal attack hounds in our private dispute. I don't expect anything from it but your trust."

Ngara scowls. "Cho was a pain in the ass," he says finally. "But he was a good detective."

Jaantzen nods; the silence that follows feels almost ritualistic, a moment for a dead man who'd been a thorn in Leone's side, in Jaantzen's side, in Manu's side. And, apparently, in Ngara's side, too.

Jaantzen clears his throat when the moment seems to have concluded. "What did Cho tell you the night he died? He called you four times."

Ngara looks away. "I don't know. I didn't answer."

"Ah." Jaantzen takes that tinge of guilt in Ngara's voice as a good sign. "Incidentally, the data cube also contains evidence the police chief is close to Leone and has been taking her bribes."

"How did you get that?"

"I've known them both for over a decade. It seemed like something worth keeping a file on. You'll probably recognize some of the other names in that file." He pauses, letting that sink in. "In case you're in the mood to clean house. Find yourself a promotion."

Ngara gives him a sharp look, tempered by a gleam of intrigue. He rests his fingertips on the data cube. "I recorded this conversation."

"I assumed as much." Though Ngara will have to be in a tight spot to admit who he got this information from. Jaantzen holds out a hand. "It was an honor to meet you."

"How will I get in touch with you?"

Jaantzen shrugs. "If you need to, I'm sure you'll figure out how. Good night, Major."

Outside, back into the night, where the desert wind howls once more.

TIERREN

"What a lovely scarf!"

"Oh my god, thank you!" Tierren smiles at the young woman waiting at the streetcar stop with her. She leans in, conspiratorial, voice hushed. "I stole it."

The girl giggles. "You did not."

Tierren waves a hand. "It was a gift." She readjusts it around her neck and the black and white floral silk wafts a tantalizing hint of Phaera: warm skin and citrus and cardamom and a touch of cigarette smoke.

She knows why the woman is talking to her. She doesn't care about the scarf, she cares that Tierren is the sole other woman at a sketchy streetcar stop and she's seeking backup against the vicious things that lurk in the dark beyond the streetlights.

Tierren smiles at her, reassuring.

It *was* a gift, this leisurely night she had wandering Phaera's apartment, knowing the other woman wasn't coming home. Exploring what Phaera surrounds herself with, what makes her feel safe. She's awfully sentimental. A collector of knickknacks, some so odd and ugly they must have stories attached. Her furniture, her decor, everything has the feeling of accumulating over the years, as opposed to being deliberately curated. The result is comfortable and unassuming, with a combination of tidy yet disorganized that says whoever lives here is too busy to be home much.

Tierren had had the luxury of time on her side tonight, to browse Phaera's closet, page through Phaera's recipe collection to see what she saved aspirationally versus what she actually cooked. And she does cook for herself when she's home, mostly survival rations for one like beans and rice or stir-fries without protein, but also the occasional extravagant meal made even without a guest to partake in it. A recipe labeled *Grandma R's Korris* gets called out of the archives for date nights. Grandma R uses cardamom, which seems unorthodox.

The couch — Tierren had admired it through the window the first night she stopped by — is incredibly comfortable. Tierren had stretched out for a while, thinking through the patterns of the apartment, trying to understand two things: what Phaera Dalvinia Harris fears the most, and where Willem Jaantzen has been hiding himself. Because Phaera's putting on one hell of a show, and Tierren herself can't quite decide if it's for real.

Which makes this gig even more fun.

Tierren would have been a hell of a catch for the Alliance special ops, she's thought it before. If they'd've just worked with her instead of always enforcing such inflexible rules. Unfortunately, when you come from an occupied country like Corusca, flunking out of an Alliance training program means getting put on a watch list.

Tierren's watchers had become her first game. Her first

game with real stakes, at least. How many times could she slip past them? How many different ways could she unnerve them? And in the end, she hadn't even had to touch them. Her head game had been good enough, she'd not only gotten them to secure her false paperwork to leave Corusca, but one of her watchers was dead and the other was standing trial for the murder.

That experience had taught her everything the Alliance had refused to.

"You're heading downtown?"

Tierren had hoped the girl was happy with proximity, but seems she wants to make conversation. Ah. That's why. Two drunk men have joined them at the streetcar stop. They're not talking to the girl, they're harmless if you know their soft spots, but their boisterous, obscene laughter washes across the sidewalk.

"Yeah," Tierren lies. "You?"

"I live there." The girl gives her a bright smile. "I was meeting a friend for dinner."

"It got late."

The girl laughs and blushes. "It did."

"You had a good night, then," Tierren says, because it doesn't seem like the girl is going away. "A new fling?"

The girl giggles in surprise. "Is it obvious?"

"You look happy." Tierren gives her a wink. With a soft hum and a flash of lights, the streetcar finally floats around the corner. Tierren debates waiting for the next one — she's done with this conversation — but it's been a long night, and with what Leone's got planned tomorrow it'll be a long day. She lets the girl get on first, sits a reasonable distance away, and ignores the drunks. Before the bus even pulls away, though, the girl has slipped into the seat beside her.

"Do you mind? It's nice to chat."

"Of course not," Tierren says, though all she wants to do is stay lost in her memories of Phaera's apartment, mulling over the details, playing back the vids she recorded on her lens and trying to spot the key. Phaera's apartment is intimate, but it's not her life. No, her life is at the Lorelei and — even more so — at the Devil's Table. If you really want to make her scream, that's where you cut.

The girl is chattering, not paying much attention to the fact that Tierren is barely nodding along. Alcohol on her breath, a hint of it ghosting over the perfume she's doused herself with for this date tonight. Maybe that's what's made her chatty. Or maybe it's her nature.

"I'm never out this late," the girl says. "I couldn't when I was working full time. But that's a whole scandal in itself." She throws it out like a particularly uninteresting lure — oh, goody, let's talk about your past work drama. But this streetcar won't go any faster if Tierren ignores the girl, so she might as well bite.

"Oh?" she says.

The girl ducks her head, ready to dish out the dirt. "Have you been following the news?" She doesn't pause for Tierren's indifferent shrug. "About the Alliance Embassy bombing?"

"Right, some local NMLF affiliate finally claimed credit for it?"

Confusion crosses the girl's face. "Did they?"

"Yeah," says Tierren. She waves a hand. "Trying to disrupt the trade agreement, something like that." She doesn't actually care. The NMLF hadn't stopped the Alliance from acquiring New Manila, the rebels hadn't stopped them on Corusca, and when the Alliance finally decides they're ready for New Sarjun, they'll get what they want without a fight.

"Well." The girl's determination to tell her story musters itself once more. "My *boss* was originally accused of it."

Tierren blinks at her, suddenly not too tired to be the gossip queen tonight. "You're not serious," she says breathlessly, and the girl's wide-eyed smile says, *I know, right?* "You work for Willem Jaantzen?"

"Worked," the girl says smugly. "For RKE. I quit as soon as I found out he actually owned it."

"Did you work in the warehouse?" With that manicure the girl obviously didn't, but Tierren aims low to get a rise out of her pride. She's rewarded.

The girl lifts her chin. "I *managed* the place."

"So you reported to Jaantzen himself?" Tierren leans in to whisper the name, and to get a glance at the girl's young, unmarked palm. Have the girl's credentials been revoked? Or could the biosign of her palm still unlock some interesting secrets if Tierren decides to take her identity for a spin?

"No, some guy named Manu Juric."

"Oh." Tierren feigns disappointment; the healing bullet wound in her left arm twinges.

"But get this." The girl's trying to reel her back in with more gossip. "Manu was definitely in on it. I've thought about going to the police. Oh, the things I could tell them." She sits back, arms crossed, waiting for Tierren to ask. God, she loves a scandal, doesn't she?

"Like what?"

"Shady paperwork. I think they might have been smuggling, like drugs or something. I mean, RKE was obviously a front, right?"

Tierren's stop is next, but she's not getting off this streetcar until the girl does. A plan is starting to form in her mind. "This is incredible," she says. "What's your name?"

"Cedra," the girl says.

"Victoria," Tierren says. "It's nice to meet you."

19

STARLA

Starla wakes from a dream of her cats burrowed under the blankets with her, the gentle rise and fall of Pepper's body curled in the small of her back, the radiating warmth of Mango behind her knees. But she's not lying on her bed back in Bulari, or even her serviceable cot at the deathtrap in the Maraka Valley. Hard edges dig into her shoulder blades and hips, a wad of cloth cushions her head. Someone's arm is over her ribcage, suffocating, and Starla forces her eyes open, her mouth tasting of ash and bile. Her stomach churns and she rolls onto her side, heaving, but nothing comes. Hunger is a dull, nauseating ache. Her right temple throbs.

Someone gently squeezes her shoulder. Gia's beside her; they've been sharing the same emergency blanket, and as it slips off Starla's shoulders she understands why. Wherever they are, it's freezing.

"Drink," Gia signs, handing her a cup. The water tastes fresh and slightly of minerals, without the over-purified tang of reclamation.

"Simca?" she asks, and Gia nods and points. Her eyes

are starting to adjust, and now she can see they're in a cave — or, more of a tunnel that collapsed on one end and is barred on the other with a simple but effective iron grate. Ten steps and she'd walk end to end, five steps and she'd span the width. If she jumped she could probably touch the ceiling. Figures are huddled in lumpy piles for warmth under emergency blankets. Beto and Arundhati are dozing side by side. A few feet from them, Simca, El, and Kumail share another pair of emergency blankets.

Starla sits up, her joints painfully stiff and aching.

"How is everyone?"

Gia makes a gesture Starla takes to mean mostly fine. "You I worry best about," Gia signs clumsily, then her lips thin. "And El."

"I'm fine." Nothing seems to be worse than bruises, though that splitting headache could be a bad sign. She'll pay attention to it. She pushes off the emergency blanket. "Are those from our supply?" Gia looks confused. Starla points to the blanket in her hand, at the others around the room. "Ours?"

Gia shakes her head. "Here before," she signs.

So whoever's keeping them prisoner cares enough to keep them from dying of exposure. The blankets, the water . . .

"Food?" Starla asks. She mimes eating. Gia shakes her head, so Starla ignores the empty pit in her gut and crosses the narrow room to check on El.

He's lying between Simca and Kumail, who are both pressed against him for warmth. Even in the dim light his brown skin has an ashen cast, his lips are nearly blue as his hair.

"Has he woken up?" she asks Simca, who shifts up to a

seated position to use her hands, thigh still pressed to her brother's shoulder.

"A few times before we got here, Kumail said. And Gia talked with him for a few minutes when we first got here."

"How long ago?"

"A few hours. We were all gassed, but you hit your head."

She turns to Kumail, who's watching her wearily, lips pinched in pain.

"What happened?" Starla asks, sitting back so she can see Simca's hands.

"Right after you jumped, we got hit by some sort of disruptor charge," Kumail tells her. "That's what Ari thinks, at least. It disabled us but didn't destroy the ship."

He glances down at El's prone form. "Everyone was strapped in but him, and he hit his head when we were shot. I was afraid he might fall out the open door, so I managed to get us both mostly strapped in before we crashed."

"Mostly?" Starla asks.

He smiles wryly and extricates his left arm from under the emergency blanket. His forearm and hand are encased in a splint. "Believe it or not, this is the first bone I've broken on assignment," he says. "We were down about an hour before they came for us. El had woken up by then, and he and the pilots fought back, but there were too many of them. They sorted through our supplies, then forced us to help carry things back. I figured we were temporary labor until they threw us in here."

"Any idea who they are?"

Kumail shakes his head. "They wouldn't tell us, and hadn't been back until they dragged you three in."

"Thank you." She unfolds from her crouch and turns to take in the space. The lens in her left eye is gritty and dry —

partly because she slept in it, partly due to dehydration. The thing's useless without her gauntlet, which is missing, but she doesn't have anywhere to put it where it won't get destroyed.

Kumail and Simca both look past her. Light glimmers at the doorway, a pair of torches held by shadowed figures approaching the barred gate, casting the cave in a flat and flickering yellow light. The unmistakable silhouette of rifles points their way and Starla gets slowly to her feet, lifts her hands. Finally a woman steps into the light. She has a thick mane of blond hair tied back in a series of braids, weather-browned skin lined from sun and wind, tattoos feathering down her muscular forearms and up her neck to coil over her cheeks. She says something, her lips obscured by the light.

Starla feels Gia stepping up beside her, and turns on her with a glare. "I'll handle this," she signs, but Gia's staring at the tattooed woman like she's a ghost.

A faint, mocking smile pulls at the tattooed woman's lips. "Hello, Giaconda," she says. "Nice of you to come back."

Starla takes a step forward before Gia can respond, and both of the guards' rifles track her. She holds her hands out in an *I'm harmless* gesture, then points over her shoulder to Simca without breaking eye contact with the tattooed woman.

"My name is Starla Deyva," she signs; the woman's attention flickers over her right shoulder to Simca. "These are my people. I'm deaf, and Simca will be interpreting." Simca takes careful steps into Starla's line of sight as she speaks.

"You're with Giaconda," the tattooed woman says to

Starla; it's not a question. "What the hell are you doing up here?"

Before she can answer, Gia's fingers brush her arm. *May I?* her expression asks, and Starla nods for her to go ahead. She moves with deliberate slowness to get herself in a good position to watch Gia and also see Simca as she's interpreting. Rifles track her every move.

"Matí?" Gia asks. The tattooed woman lifts her chin. "It's good to see you."

"Jury's still out," Matí says. "Looks like life's been good to you on the other side."

"It has. I thought you were dead."

"That was the plan." Matí sweeps her gaze around the cell before turning back to Gia. "What kind of trouble are you getting into up here? Having a walk down memory lane?"

"Doing a job," Gia says. "And we could use your help."

Matí snorts. "You're in no position to be asking for favors."

"How about offering them? I'm a doctor, remember? A surgeon. Any of your people need medical attention?" When Matí doesn't answer, Starla lifts her hands.

"If you were going to kill us, you would've done it before this," she signs. "So cut the posturing and let's talk."

The tattooed woman exchanges a long, inscrutable look with the guard beside her. Something silent passes between them, and he lowers his rifle and lifts the heavy iron bar holding the grate shut. Matí jerks her chin at Gia, then Starla. "You two."

"And my interpreter," Starla signs. "Unless you have someone fluent in USL." Suspicion narrows Matí's hard eyes, but after a moment she nods and steps out of the way of the grate. The barrels of two rifles motion for them to step out of the cell. Simca says something to Kumail before she follows Gia and Starla.

They're led single file through a cool, dark passageway, the jagged lines of the stone illuminated by flickering torches. The passageway is obviously natural, though enlarged by human tools. Matí walks ahead, her easy swagger saying she isn't worried about being attacked by her prisoners. Either she trusts Gia or she thinks the armed guards walking behind them will hold them in line.

Maybe she's right not to be worried. It would be so easy to signal Simca and Gia, to take advantage of one of the passageway's many bends to grab Matí from behind and take the knife from her belt, to drop one of the rifle-holding guards with a razored kick — they took all of Starla's weapons but didn't find the blade in the sole of her boot. But even if they won that fight, they don't know the cave system. They don't know how many other people are here, or how to get out. Or how to get back to Bulari.

Eventually the passageway starts to show more signs of use and is lit by some sort of bioluminescent pack that casts a soft greenish light over the stones. After a few minutes it opens out onto a scaffolding near the ceiling of a cavern twice the size of the hangar at the deathtrap, lit by the bright sun at its mouth. It's much warmer than the passageway they just left; Starla lets a shiver run through her at the heat on the breeze.

There's freedom, Starla thinks — but in between them and the cavern's mouth are dozens of people. A handful in one corner are sorting through the supplies scavenged from the *Coldfire*. Another pair are working on a rusted hopper, its engine torn apart in a mess of wires and belts. Someone's cooking — Starla can't see them, but the aroma of roasting meat rises above the earthy scent of the cave and the unwashed humanity calling it home.

And a knot of children are playing a ballgame, whipping through the rest of the room with wild grins and wilder hair. Starla stares at them. Were they born here, living their entire lives in hiding? Do they care what they're missing? Or are they like Starla had been, blissfully unaware of a world larger than Silk Station, where her parents kept her — all of them — hidden from the Alliance?

A rifle prods at her kidney, the guard behind her nudging her out of her reverie to follow the others across the scaffolding and around to the right. There, Matí pulls aside a curtain and motions them through.

The room beyond is a bit larger than the cell, but not by much. Instead of bare stone and darkness, though, it's layered in fabrics and lit by the same bioluminescence as in the passageway. As she follows them in, Matí runs a hand over the wall and the light brightens into a pleasant glow. The room appears to be a bedroom: a mattress piled with blankets in the corner, clothes hung on pegs in the wall, and a circle of cushions in the middle. One of the two men with rifles takes up a position by the door. The other sits on a cushion beside Matí, his knee brushing hers companionably, rifle laid across his lap, cloak pooled on the floor around him.

Starla can't hide her surprise at the cushions. They're made of hide; Starla sits and sinks her fingers into the thick fur. It's coarse and dark, not from any animal she can identify. The cushions seem handmade, with primitive tools, but the materials — the leather, the furs — they would fetch a fortune on livestock-poor New Sarjun.

"Several of my people are injured," Starla signs; Matí's

attention flickers to Simca, then back to Starla. "We need access to our medical supplies, and food."

"We'll get there," Matí says. "But let's start with what you're doing here. And don't tell me a fucking supply run for the Alliance — the three of you jumped before we shot down your ship, and there's nothing out here for hours." She leans in, teeth bared. "How did you know we were here? And who else is coming after us?"

"We had no idea you were here," Starla signs. "Your secret is still safe."

Matí's scowl remains fierce as she searches Starla's face for the lie. This is the most important question on the woman's mind, she thinks. This is Matí's fear: that her secret haven is about to be discovered, her people endangered. Those children playing ball in the cavern, is one of them hers?

"My parents were wanted by the Alliance," Starla says. "I grew up in hiding, in a secret station with my family in Durga's Belt. When I was fifteen, the Alliance found us and destroyed our station. Killed my parents. Believe me, I would never bring that on you."

The man beside Matí brushes his fingers over her knee; she relaxes, a fraction. "We'll see," she says shortly. "If you're not here for us, why are you here?"

Starla's been considering her answer to this since she first woke up in the cell. No lie is plausible, and if they're going to get to the Alliance research facility now, they need help.

Time for the truth. "We're here to learn about the Alliance terraforming operation," she signs.

Matí glances at the man beside her.

"Because of the terraforming?" he asks. "Or the aliens." He grins when his reveal doesn't have the intended effect on the three women, revealing a chipped front tooth. "So you've heard about the aliens."

"Jude was there when they found the crash," Matí says.

Starla leans forward in excitement. "Then you can help us. Any information —"

"And call attention to ourselves?"

"Your secret is safe with us."

"Of course it is. Because you're not going anywhere." Matí's smile is hard.

"Our ship isn't damaged beyond repair," Starla signs. "It can still take us home. And you."

The man at Matí's side — Jude, she called him — straightens. Matí shoots him a glare Starla can't decipher. Surely she'd want to go home? They took the supplies, but more food and fuel pellets only prolongs the inevitable. The *Coldfire* can actually help Matí and her people get to freedom from the Alliance, and back to civilization.

"We don't need you to repair your ship," Matí says.

"You're right," Starla signs. "But what will you do once you're south of the Jupari? The Alliance may think you're dead, but the instant you try to buy food, you palm into a hotel room, your face gets picked up on a security feed? Someone's going to get an alert. You'll be hunted by the Alliance." And by her godfather, Starla thinks, but if she's resorting to threats they've already lost.

"If you help us, we can help you," she signs. "Get you new identities. Jobs if you want them, safe passage off New Sarjun if you don't. A new life where you won't be constantly on the run. It's been, what? Twenty, thirty years since you were sent to prison? Whatever network you had is gone. But my godfather is a very connected man."

Matí's chin lifts slightly. "And who is your godfather?"

"Willem Jaantzen."

She blinks in surprise. Jude leans forward. "You work for that guy?" he asks Gia. His expression holds distrust, but also intrigue. Starla wonders what version of Jaantzen's reputation has filtered up to Redrock; probably depends on how many of the convicts used to work for his rivals.

"For the first decade after I got released," Gia says. "Off and on since then. He's good for his word, and Starla's word is his."

Starla's gauging Matí's body language — she's still uncertain, though Jude has lit up at the idea of returning home and doesn't seem to be too bothered by the fact that it's Willem Jaantzen offering him the opportunity. Starla channels Oriol's effortless zen, Manu's relaxed readiness, Jaantzen's stone-faced calm.

"We need each other," she signs. "You're our key into the Alliance research facility, and we're your ticket home. My godfather will send you supplies. Transport."

"If we help you, we call attention to ourselves."

"Which is a problem if you want to stay up here the rest of your lives. But if you want to be free?"

"I am free," snaps Matí. "I've been free for twenty years. About a third of us were born here — they don't know any other life. What does Bulari have for us?"

"Running water?" Starla asks, incredulous. "Real beds? Food you don't have to shoot down supply ships to get?"

"I've lived in the city," Matí says. "Civilization isn't always too civilized. None of us have anything to run back to."

Jude lays a hand on her thigh. "Some of us do," he says gently.

It's five long breaths before Matí finally nods. "Call an assembly," she says to Jude. A muscle jumps in his jaw.

"The sooner you make your decision, the better," Starla

signs. "We want to leave tonight for the Alliance research center."

"You're not going anywhere until we have a consensus from the group, and half of us are away until evening. We'll have an assembly tonight."

"My people need medical attention," Starla signs. "Food."

Matí lifts her chin to the guard at the door. "Move the prisoners to the spare room in the south tunnel and get them some food," she says, and he salutes and leaves. "What else do you need?" she asks Starla.

Starla motions for Gia to answer. "I have a duffel with all my medical supplies in it. One of our crew has lost a lot of blood and possibly has an infection. And at this point he's possibly hypothermic. Matí, he could have died being left there all night. Why didn't you come to us earlier?"

"My apologies," Matí says. "But we were occupied all night on a hunt."

"Hunting?" Gia asks.

Matí breaks into a slow smile and reaches into her pocket. She pulls out a fang, it's nearly the length of her palm. "This bastard," she says. "They taste like shit, but they're meat. Plus this one's been picking off our people for the last few months. We finally tracked it to its lair."

"What the hell is that?" Starla asks.

"Wolf." Matí shrugs. "Or, used to be. Not sure what you'd call it these days. All sorts of strange creatures have been showing up in the past few years."

"Since the Alliance started terraforming?"

"Since the Alliance and the Dawn started playing God with biology," Jude says. "You've heard of the Dawn? Good. Because if you're breaking into the alien crash site, you're dealing with the Dawn. They're hand-in-hand out there since the prophet started converting the guards."

Starla straightens. "Felipe Zacharia? He's there?"

"He was part of the team that discovered the alien wreckage," Matí says. "With Jude."

"Felipe was digging right beside me," says Jude. "And the instant we uncovered enough of the thing to see what it was, he dropped to his knees and started — I don't know. Worshipping it. At night he'd talk nonstop, about how these aliens had fallen from the stars for us. How they were a gift, and he'd seen something like it once before, out in Durga's Belt."

A shiver traces Starla's spine.

"The Alliance quarantined us out there so we wouldn't spread rumors, but that backfired. Because we had time to talk in isolation, and Felipe's good at talking. Pretty soon even some of the guards started to believe it. When new blood got sent out, they'd catch Felipe's fever just as fast. Started calling him the prophet, passing around copies of his journals."

"How did it spread outside the prison?" Starla asks. "Through his brother?"

"Bennion?"

"Did you know him?"

"I've heard stories," Matí says. "Fucked-up stories."

Starla suppresses a shudder. She still can't think of the man without a corresponding image of being bound and helpless on the floor of Julieta Yang's greenhouse, staring into his ice-blue eyes while his finger slowly squeezes the trigger of the pistol aimed at her head. She pushes the image away.

"He's dead," she says.

"Good riddance," says Jude. "Yeah, at first he sent journals to his brother, but eventually the guards helped him, too. He has half of them wrapped around his finger with his promises of living forever with his magic serum."

When Starla doesn't ask, Mati raises a tattooed eyebrow. "So you've heard of that, too."

"We've ended some of his experiments," Starla signs. "Almost impossible to kill."

Mati holds up the enormous wolf fang once more. "Almost," she says with a faint smile.

Jude's face is serious. "Felipe Zacharia is vicious, and so are his followers. I played along to keep them off my back, but Felipe could tell I was faking it and he — " Jude shakes his head; his expression is haunted. "The world would be better off without him. And you're better off leaving this alone."

"I'm not leaving it," Starla says. "Felipe Zacharia is the one who told the Alliance how to kill my parents' station."

Simca blinks at her in barely concealed surprise, but Starla ignores her, because Mati is finally starting to look interested. The tattooed woman breaks into a grin, then rolls her neck. "A vendetta against that asshole, I like it," she says. "We'll get you fed and cleaned up, then we'll figure out a plan."

"I'd like a chance to present our case at your assembly."

"No," Mati says, and even Jude's shaking his head. "No outsiders attend assembly, and you're an outsider until we all decide you're not. Get some rest, get some food, and we'll talk in the morning."

20

———

PHAERA

For the first time in more than two weeks, business at the Devil's Table feels normal. The tables are filled, the kitchen is hopping, and the wealthy elite of New Sarjun and beyond are perched on her couches and armchairs to make small talk and business deals.

There's an electric hum in the air; the sense of unease she's sensed from her staff finally has lifted.

Phaera's own sense of unease is still coiled in the pit of her stomach. She's slept better the past few nights on a cot in her office at the Devil's Table than she could have in her compromised apartment, and she swung home this afternoon for a shower and another change of clothes.

Whatever gets her through this week.

She's wrapped in black silk tonight, an off-the-shoulder style that bares one arm while the other is encased in sheer black mesh to the wrist. A Meherzad, one of his new collection, and it's been attracting compliments all night. One of the earliest things Cavy had taught her about the high-end casino business was to set aside a wardrobe budget. "Everything is going swimmingly at the Devil's Table" is what the new dress says as Phaera mingles with politicians and heirs and magnates.

Phaera may still be on edge, but at least her patrons look relaxed. And they should be. The liquor's been flowing tonight, her policy for the last few weeks being that giving away a case or two of the nicest bottles every night as a compliment of the house is worth it if it reminds regulars why they love coming here.

And the regulars have been returning. There are her two favorite aging matrons — both retired from the pharmaceutical industry and spending their golden years people-watching and dining at the finest spots throughout Bulari. They're set up at the usual table, trading gossip with their waiter like nothing has changed. A few cabinet ministers are in one of the private dining rooms, showing a good time to the CEO of an Alliance edtech corporation. And Teo Lordeur is wheeling himself towards her with a smile.

The Lordeur siblings are among Bulari's most respected financiers, both for legitimate businesses and for less scrupulous ventures. Teo's older sister has been housebound since before Phaera met Teo through Leone, so she's never met her. But Teo is pleasant company even though she's never needed his funds. Jaantzen, on the other hand, has worked with the man for decades.

Which is what brings Teo here tonight.

Phaera bends to greet Teo with a kiss on the cheek, then settles into a chair beside his wheelchair. "You're looking wonderful," she tells him.

He laughs, hollow, wrinkled cheeks transformed by mirth. His eyes are bright and clear as water. "Less so sitting next to you, my dear."

"You're too kind." She squeezes his hand, then flags

down a passing server. "And thank you for coming. Another limoncello?"

"If you insist." But Teo's smile dims a touch. "Now, what's our boy gotten himself into?"

"Leone hasn't warned you away from him?"

Another laugh, this one mirthless. "Her head's gotten too big for her own good, but even she knows better than to issue ultimatums to Tara and I. He's going to try to supplant her, is he?"

"Do you think it's possible?"

Teo frowns, accepts the new glass of limoncello, sips it in silence while he thinks. "How many rebels does he have in his little guerrilla band?"

It's a good question, one Phaera isn't sure how to answer. She hides her rush of frustration. "No one will commit until there's a critical mass."

"But it's hard to create a critical mass if no one will commit." Teo purses his lips. "Well, if the Lordeur name is good for anything, it's good for rallying skittish investors around a shaky new venture."

"That's why he would be so grateful for your support, Teo. With your and Tara's expertise and influence, this little coalition could be quite influential."

Teo takes another sip of the liquor; light catches like molten gold in the tiny glass. Phaera's stomach clenches, waiting for the answer.

"We'll back that boy," Teo says finally. "And you can tell anyone you need to if it gets them on board."

After a week of bad news, Phaera wants to jump up and hug Teo; she reins herself in for a dignified yet grateful smile. "Thank you," she says. "May I ask why?"

"The boy's always a sure bet, and he's homegrown to

boot — I'm sick of that woman's fake Indiran airs. And her Indiran friends."

Phaera tilts her head, attention piqued. "Her friends?"

"She's been lining her pockets with Alliance gold." Teo pitches his voice low. "That trade agreement is going to be bad for all of our businesses, and you wouldn't believe what Tara and I have spent to scuttle it, but she and her Alliance buddies can spend more. You tell your boy if he does something about *that*, I'll move the stars for him."

"I'll let him know," Phaera says, something like hope kindling in her belly. If the Lordeurs are on board, everything is a bit simpler. "I'd be delighted if you would join us here at the Table two days from now for a conversation among like-minded businesspeople."

"Absolutely, my dear."

"Thank you, Teo."

A voice in her earpiece catches her attention, and she turns from Teo with a smiled apology. "V? What is it?"

"Government inspectors to see you, ma'am," Vanessa says. Phaera's front-of-house manager sounds pissed off. "I'm making them wait down here, but they're not happy about it."

A cold flush washes away any sense of relief Phaera may have had at winning Teo Lordeur's support. "I'll be right down."

Teo's watching her with concern. "What is it?"

"Leone's next move," Phaera says as calmly as she can. She pats his hand. "Whatever happens, I'm her target. You stay out of her crosshairs and I'll see you in two days."

She keeps her smile light as she crosses the floor of the Devil's Table, tossing out waves and compliments with a levity she doesn't feel. She has nothing to hide, and she's been meticulous about her record-keeping since far before this business with Leone started. But none of that will mean anything if Leone has chosen tonight to teach her a lesson.

"It's so easy to let little things slip," Leone had told her. "Permits, licenses — it's easy to miss a payment. Especially when you're distracted with someone like *him*."

Leone had tacitly threatened Phaera's mother, and then she'd had her poisoned. She'd threatened Phaera's business, and here are the inspectors. Phaera beckons over the bartender and leans into the young woman's ear.

"We've got a potential problem with inspectors," she murmurs. "I'm going down to meet them."

The bartender frowns at her. "Everything's up-to-date," she says.

"I know. Just be warned things could be ugly, and be prepared to help me and V out if we need it."

Vanessa's voice chimes in her ear. "Fay, they're getting restless."

"I'm on my way." Phaera shoots a friendly smile at a New Manilan businesswoman who glances her way, and makes her way down the black-lacquered stairs to where Vanessa is arguing with a pair of men in jackets emblazoned with the Gaming Commission logo.

As she expected.

White-hot fury rises in her gut and she fights it back with an iron will. The same will she fought to build this business with in the first place. To rebuild after Acheta tried to tear her down. All these people who rely on her for their income, all of these people she promised steady jobs to, all of those times she threw her success back in the faces of those who had doubted her. Every single sleepless night spent solving problems, every skipped meal — all of it spent building a glass house Leone is about to throw a boulder through.

"What is this?" Phaera asks, and for all she meant it to come out politely to soothe the situation, her voice is acid sharp.

The more senior inspector is a jackass in a suit crumpled from days' worth of sitting at his desk — this is probably the first time he's been out of the office all week. He's got a hundred pounds on Phaera, but it's all belly paunch and extra height. Even so, he tilts back his head, looks down at her past the end of his nose.

"Are you Phaera Harris?"

"I am," she snaps, then forces herself to sound like a hostess. "How can I help you gentlemen? If you like, we can head to my office and have a talk."

"No need to talk, ma'am," says the tall man with the paunch. He takes a holoprojector from his jacket pocket and slaps on the outside of the door. It adheres to the door with a sharp fizzle, then begins to project: Business Closed for Violation.

All her patrons will walk through that door on their way back to their rides tonight. She can feel the heat rising in her cheeks; no matter how much she expected this, nothing could have prepared her for the humiliation she's about to experience.

"What violation?" asks Phaera. "All of my paperwork is in order."

"Take it up with the city," the inspector says with a shrug. "You don't have all your paperwork on file."

"Yes, I do. Every single license is on file with the city. Every single one of my dealers' licenses is on file."

The inspector shares a glance with his friend. "Not according to our system."

"We *just* renewed our licenses," Vanessa says. Light plays on her red-smoked lenses as she searches files. "I can show you the receipts." The last word comes out slowly as Vanessa's dark-red lips purse quizzically. Phaera can guess what she's about to say. "I need a minute."

If she didn't see them in the right spot, she's not going to find those files.

"It's fine," Phaera tells her.

Because of course the permits are gone. Of course the receipts are deleted. Because just as she knows without a doubt her permits are up-to-date, she knows Leone could have them deleted from the system with the snap of her fingers. Which leaves Phaera's word against cold hard fact.

The inspector gives them both a put-upon look. "Take it up with the city if you think there's been a mistake."

He starts to walk past her to the stairs, but startles back as he sees the massive shape of Hiro Matapang looming there.

"Who the hell are you?"

"My chief of security," Phaera answers.

"And what are you hiding with all this security?"

"I don't know if you've ever been in a casino before," Phaera snaps. "But they tend to have a lot of assets around. And my clientele are very high-net-worth individuals. They appreciate feeling safe — which is something you're not helping with."

"Not my problem," the inspector says. "Excuse me." He edges past Hiro, heels clicking on the stairs.

Vanessa's blinking at her in horror. "It's okay," Phaera says again, as much to herself as to Vanessa.

"Fay. I know we — "

Phaera grabs her tightly in a hug. "I know. It's fine. But it's happening, and right now I need you to help me make this go as smoothly as possible."

Phaera turns on her heel and rushes up the stairs after

the men. If she's going to be humiliated she'd rather it be to her face. The two inspectors in the Gaming Commission jackets are at the top of the stairs when she catches up to them, and she calls for them to wait. It doesn't matter, they're already turning heads.

She steps in front of them and cuts the music with a touch of a button on her cuff, then raises her chin, shame burning in her cheeks. She desperately hopes her voice won't shake. "I've been notified we'll have to cut our evening short," she says to the room. "I apologize for the inconvenience, and appreciate your patronage. I'm sure we'll have this cleared up in no time."

"What's going on?" someone calls from near the bar.

"Wrong permits," the lead inspector says loudly. He turns to Phaera with an apologetic shrug. "It's an easy mistake to make if you're new to business."

If you don't come from the right background, he means. If you're not the right sort of person. If you're just trash wrapped in fancy dress and jewels.

Phaera notices the whispers start, but she doesn't spare their audience a glance. "There's been a misunderstanding," Phaera says, jaw clenched. "And I'm sure the Gaming Commission will have a good excuse for why they're inconveniencing some of the most powerful people in this city tonight."

Across the room, Teo Lordeur is rolling his wheelchair forward. She shakes her head — *Please, please stay out of this* — and he stills.

Phaera keeps her chin high as the next excruciatingly long moments play out. Some of her patrons are watching her in pity. Those she marks — she hates their pity, but she needs allies, and if she's going to recover from this she can't be too proud to ask for help.

But plenty aren't looking at her at all. It's an embarrassing end to their night, as Leone intended when she chose a busy night where important people would be affected. This message is as much for them as it is for Phaera: Don't come to the Devil's Table, Phaera D is marked.

And they're getting the message. One of her two favorite retired society matrons squeezes her arm as she walks past. "You poor dear, I'm sorry."

"We'll get it sorted out," Phaera says, and the two women walk past.

"And to think I almost hired him to do my security," one murmurs, and Phaera's fury kindles anew. Is it only their guess, that whatever is happening tonight has to do with Phaera's relationship with Willem Jaantzen? Or does that rumor have its origins with Leone, too.

In less than half an hour the Devil's Table is empty of all but essential staff. Hiro, Vanessa, the kitchen and bar managers. "I need to make some calls," Phaera tells them. "Get things shut down and head home. I'll talk to the city tomorrow and be in touch."

"I'll give you a ride home, Fay," Vanessa says.

"I'll be here late."

"One of us can be here as late as you need," Hiro tells her. "It's fine."

"It's not fine." She didn't mean for her voice to break. She grinds her jaw until she knows she can speak evenly, measured. "You all go home, I'll call you in the morning."

She shuts down the Table, then locks her office door behind her and sets the security overrides that mean even Hiro can't come in. She pours herself a mezcal, sipping it while she watches the security AI feeds to make sure the

Table's gone dark. A pleasant green circle symbol pulses to let her know the building is secure.

She downs the rest of the drink and lets herself feel the night until the backs of her eyes are burning and her throat is raw with the tears she's not going to let herself cry. Because crying right now won't do her any good. But being on the edge of tears is the look she wants for this next call. She swipes fingers over her eyes, smudging mascara in the few fiery tears that have seeped through like traitors.

Her hand is shaking as she calls up the connection; she's not sure it's an act.

Leone answers in seconds, hologram flickering onto Phaera's desk. Leone is still dressed, apparently working late. Or waiting for this call.

"Phaera?"

Phaera lets her voice break. "I'm sorry to call you so late, but I don't know who else to go to."

"Honey, is everything all right?"

"I swear I filed my permits, but something went wrong. The Table got shut down tonight, and I know it was a mistake. I didn't know who else to call."

"Oh! How horrible!" Leone's expression is kind. "I can talk to some people tomorrow and make things right."

"I *know* everything is in order, I don't know what happened."

"Mistakes happen. But on a weekend evening? What terrible timing."

Phaera bites back a curse, coaxes her voice to contrite. "I've made a horrible mistake," she says. "I wish — "

"Shhh, shhh. Honey, let's have lunch tomorrow and talk this all over."

Phaera sniffs. "I can't go out in public. Not after this."

"You can with me," Leone says, her voice syrup, and

nausea roils in Phaera's gut. She chases it with mezcal. "We can make this all better."

"Thank you," Phaera forces herself to say.

"Of course. I'm glad you called." The smugness in Leone's voice is a knife in Phaera's eardrums. "I'll see you tomorrow."

Phaera cuts the connection and squeezes her fists until her nails leave sharp brands on her palms. Deep breaths, she thinks to herself. Deep breaths.

When she thinks she can do so without tearing it to furious shreds, she shucks off the Meherzad dress and changes into the sleeping clothes she brought: drawstring pants and a slouchy sweatshirt. But when she hangs up the dress in the closet something about the silhouette strikes her. A hard edge in the pocket. Even before she draws it out she knows the embossing by touch.

A mystix card, slipped into her pocket some time during the chaos of the evening.

It's the third of the fortune-killer cards, the Mirage: What you thought to be true is actually false; you've built your hope of salvation upon a lie.

Maybe she has. But if he is lying to her, does she have time to change her path?

She flicks the card face-down onto the coffee table, then pours herself another drink and calls Jaantzen.

21

STARLA

The room Jude takes them to is a larger version of the bedroom, but a rocky protrusion and curtain makes it feel like two rooms. It's the cave dweller version of furnished, with fur cushions scattered over stiff woven mats, the walls lit by bioluminescence. It's warmer than the cell, heated by a cobbled-together solar-charged slow-release unit like the kind you see charging up on front porches throughout the Fingers during the day. There's no door to lock. It's not like there's anywhere to run here in the desert.

Their packs are already there — someone must have figured out how they got in and gone searching for any gear they left outside. Starla's itching to search through them and find out what's missing, but Jude is leaning in the doorway, watching them.

"We used to have a few more souls around here," he says, in explanation of the room. He waves down the passage to the main cavern. "Reclamation units are down there to the right."

"Where are the rest of my crew?" Starla asks.

"On their way." Jude answers Simca; maybe he didn't

see Starla speaking. Starla tries not to let her anger spark —
it's been a long few days and her temper is too close to the
surface. "We're sending up some food, too. Ah. Here
we go."

He steps out of the doorway and smiles warmly at Benedicto Kulikutan; Beto doesn't return the smile. Ari's right
behind him, followed by El and Kumail. Her crew is ragged
and wary, but El has a bit more color in his cheeks and lips,
his eyes are focused and clear as he leans in to say something to Kumail.

Two unfamiliar guards are behind them. They're
armed, though their weapons are holstered — apparently
they've gotten the memo Starla's crew are on their side. For
now. The last guard is carrying a canvas bag and a jug,
which she sets inside the door with a general announcement
to the room.

"Food and water," Simca tells Starla. "And apparently
there's a well to refill the jug down the passageway to the
left."

A well? That explains the refreshing, nonreclaimed
taste of the water Starla had tasted earlier. And the fact that
these people have managed to live here this long. Decades,
at least, if Gia knew Matí in Redrock.

Jude dismisses the guards before Starla can thank them,
then lounges back in the door. "Need anything else?" he
asks her.

"My gauntlet."

"It won't work up here."

"It helps me communicate." Let Jude think she needs it
because she's deaf — it will help her type messages when
Simca or El aren't around. But she's not ready to let Jude
and Matí know she has a link to the outside world.

Jude shrugs and pulls Starla's gauntlet from the pocket

of his cloak and tosses it to her, then his attention shifts over her shoulder. "You're at the Cavern," he says. "You're our guests."

Kumail is the one who asked the question that must be on everyone's minds.

"We are guests of a group of convicts who escaped from Redrock," Starla signs. She's expecting more surprise around the circle, but they've probably already speculated as much. "They shot down our ship for the supplies, but they don't intend us harm." Any more harm. El is on his feet, but barely. And probably only because Jude is still in the room.

Kumail raises a hand. "Are we free to explore?"

Starla cuts in before Jude can answer. "This is Kumail Anh," she tells him. "He's a reporter, working on a story about Redrock Prison. We were giving him a ride."

Jude's face closes down. "There's no story here."

"He's here for a specific reason," Starla signs. "Not to expose your people to danger. He's chasing a story about New Sarjunian prisoners whose sentences were changed to send them to Redrock instead of the local penitentiary. Certain officials in Bulari are getting kickbacks for this, and the prisoners then disappear off the register."

Jude's frown deepens as Simca interprets.

"We think they're being sent to work at the crash site," Starla signs, and a muscle jumps in his jaw. "If he uncovers this story, he can keep it from happening to anyone else." When Jude doesn't answer, Starla leans forward. "The story of what the Alliance is doing up here is getting out, whether or not you help us. Kumail isn't the only one searching for missing New Sarjunian citizens. People back home are putting the pieces together, and when they do, they'll be going over the Alliance concession with a fine-toothed comb. You can't stop it, but you can control your part in it."

Resignation and relief war behind Jude's eyes. "Then you'll want to talk to Jae-jin," he says finally.

"Armed robbery, right?" Kumail asks. "About five years ago?"

"I believe so," Jude says warily.

Kumail smiles. "I would love to talk with Jae-jin."

"You had to know this couldn't last forever," Starla signs gently.

Jude gives her a firm nod, then straightens out of the doorway. "I'll send Jae-jin back to talk with you," Jude says. "Stay close to here for now and let us tell people our way. You don't want an angry mob."

"Thank you," Starla signs.

"Don't thank me yet."

Starla peeks out the door after he leaves, catches a glimpse of his back turning the corner. No one's guarding them. She buckles on her gauntlet and checks the charge — low, but it should last another day if she's sparing with it. She blinks on her lens to see the familiar stats and time-stamp. No signal. She'll have to go exploring if she's going to get a message out.

El has slid down the wall and onto a cushion, sitting with his head tilted back and wrists propped on his knees. Ari and Kumail are talking at her, but Starla ignores them both to crouch beside El.

"How are you doing?"

"I'm going to be fine," he signs back, speaking aloud as well. He runs a hand through his shoulder-length blue hair, making a face at the grease. "You trust these assholes?"

Starla glances over her shoulder to find that Beto, Ari, and Kumail are all watching for her answer. She motions for

Simca to interpret — she doesn't need to have this conversation multiple times. "We're among allies," she signs. "And you're right to all be skeptical. They're going to work with us. I'll explain, but first, food."

Gia kneels on the other side of El with her med kit and gives Starla a faint smile; Starla goes to find him something to eat. Simca has spread out the contents of the bag the guard left on a canvas blanket and the others are picking through the options. It's a strange feast made up of rations from their own kits, the Alliance supplies, and, presumably, whatever was already on hand in the Cavern.

Like the grayish strips of dried, salted meat. Ari tears off a piece of jerky in her teeth and chews curiously. She says something to Beto, her lips distorted with chewing, and he takes a piece himself. His face says it wasn't as bad as he expected it to be.

Starla picks one up tentatively and sniffs. "Enormous wolf?" she signs to Simca, who grimaces. Kumail looks curiously between them, but neither woman explains. The civilians have enough to worry them without stories of enormous wolves.

She gathers a few ration bars and a tube of energy paste and turns to take them to El, but he and Gia are joining them in the circle. He sits between Starla and Simca and accepts the ration bars with a smile of thanks, then pops the cap off the energy paste tube. Simca says something to him that makes him laugh and cough on the paste; he wipes his lips on the back of his hand and throws a piece of jerky at her.

Starla relaxes. A fraction.

The water is cold, the ration bars bland and dry, and the meat not too bad if you don't imagine it coming from a wolf with teeth the length of a person's hand. Starla eats slowly, letting the others get their fill, and when she notices them starting to slow down she makes eye contact with Simca. Simca crumples a wrapper and tosses it onto the blanket in front of her. "Ready."

"Our plans haven't changed," Starla begins. "We've offered the convicts supplies and transport back home in exchange for helping us complete our mission. They're meeting tonight as a group to discuss it. Kumail, we didn't get you to Redrock, but this could be the next best thing. Beto and Ari, what's your estimation on the *Coldfire*?"

Beto gestures for Ari to go ahead. "The pulse they hit us with shut down our electrical systems," she says. "But the *Coldfire* wasn't damaged much in the crash. We always run with extra repair parts, and we have everything we need in our inventory."

"Good. We'll spend tomorrow getting it working again.

Ari's mouth opens, then closes again without a word. It's Beto who says what she probably was thinking. "We're supposed to trust the people who shot us down?" He looks around the circle. "You really trust a bunch of convicts to keep their word?"

"I can count the people I trust in this world on two hands," Starla signs. "And half of them are in this room. We'll get out of this, I promise you." She turns to Gia. "Matí: Do you trust her?"

Gia wobbles her head, noncommittal. "I knew her," she says. "Matí was in for life, a freedom fighter with the Fist, in for blowing up Alliance outposts in Durga's Belt."

Starla nods for her to go on. But she remembers even her anti-Alliance parents called the Fist terrorists rather than freedom fighters.

"She slipped the guards during a work crew we were both on, hit a dry creek bed with a little bit of cover — they fired off a few shots but didn't hit her, but they didn't chase her, either. Didn't want to waste the resources, I guess." Gia shrugs. "Suicide by desert, we always called it. Sometimes lifers wanted to die and Redrock Prison wasn't killing them fast enough."

Gia's staring past Starla, past the wall, caught in some memory. "The night before, she tried to talk me into running with her, but I told her no way. Even if there was some mythical colony of escaped prisoners, I only had a couple of years left. I wasn't going to spend the rest of my life in a cave living off snake meat and drinking my own piss when I could make it back to Bulari if I waited it out."

"Do you think she'll help us?"

"She'll have to," Gia says. "She may want to get old and die out here, but you saw how Jude lit up at the idea of seeing civilization again. I'd bet more people feel like him than her."

Starla hopes she's right. "Get some sleep tonight," she says. "Tomorrow, Kumail goes after his story, Beto and Ari fix up the *Coldfire*, and at night Gia, Simca, and I will complete our mission." Whether the convicts help them or not.

Kumail gives her a small smile. "Your mission is . . ."

He'll probably find out tomorrow if he can get anyone to talk to him. She flexes her fingers — here's the dry run for a conversation she'll be having over and over in the next few months.

"Our mission is this: The Alliance has discovered wreckage we believe to be an alien ship. The technology contained on that ship has allowed them to begin terraforming part of the desert. That technology? For obvious reasons, they're attempting to keep it secret." She turns to Kumail. "But they need extra bodies to work it. Ones no one will come looking for later."

He nods slowly. "That's where you suspect the missing prisoners ended up."

"Yes. We didn't want to influence you in case you found out something different, but that's our theory."

"Alien?" Beto asks.

"Yes."

"How can you — how do you . . ."

"We know."

He's frowning at her and shaking his head. It's an unconscious gesture, not of disbelief, but more like he's trying to shake this newfound knowledge out of his head and go back to the universe as it was seconds ago. Beside him, Arundhati is staring at Starla in awed horror.

Kumail wears an expression of mild surprise. "Just the wreckage?"

It's not Lucky and his brethren's time in the spotlight yet, so she skirts the question. "A wreck which contained technology that allowed the Alliance to begin terraforming the desert. We're going on a research trip."

"When your godfather said my name would be on the biggest story of our lives, I admit I wasn't expecting aliens."

"There's more than one career-making story here," Starla signs. "And we'll share details with you when the time is right for the story to break. But for now, stay focused on the story you came here to find."

"Are we allowed to leave this room?" Beto asks.

"We're not being guarded, but best to stay close for now. Reclamation units are back towards the main cavern. We'll be meeting with the leaders again tomorrow morning, so for now, everyone get some sleep. Any questions?" When she doesn't get any, she stands. "I'm going to find a signal," she tells Simca, keeping her back to the others. The fewer people who know Willem Jaantzen has a spy satellite in the skies above Redrock, the better.

She heads the direction of the reclamation units, then blinks her lens on and keeps an eye on the signal bar. Nothing yet, but according to the timestamp, the satellite should be sweeping overhead any minute now. She reaches the main cavern to find the sun has set since they've been talking and the cavern's mouth has been sealed shut with a vast metal door that looks welded out of scrap. The area near the reclamation units is lit by a few blinking lights and smears of bioluminescence, but the rest of the cavern is blazing with torches and filled with people.

Starla melts against the wall, watching.

There's maybe fifty people of all ages, and no hierarchy in the way they're gathered. Matí is talking, but when she finishes an old man with a scar-slashed face starts, the crowd paying as much respect to him as to her. A young woman with a shaved head speaks next; maybe she's one of those who were born here?

With that crowd, it will be hard to cross to the cavern's mouth unseen. She thinks back through the maze of passageways they've already been through, trying to guess which would lead outside.

A hand falls on her shoulder.

Starla whirls and has the man who touched her on his knees with a wristlock in a breath, the razor in the sole of her boot clicked out, foot poised to strike.

The man holds up his free hand in surrender. His face is a mask of pain, but she recognizes him instantly.

Jude.

She releases his wrist and he rubs at it gingerly, giving her a rueful look. It's too dark to see what he says, but she does have her comm back. She hands it to him and mimes typing.

Sorry for sneaking up on you, I called your name.

Sorry for overreacting, Starla types on her gauntlet, though she's not. She still has no idea if she can trust Jude, or if he really did call her name.

What are you doing? Reclamation units are back that way.

Starla has auditioned a dozen excuses, but so far, Jude has played level with her. She studies the crowd once more, trying to figure out which way the winds are shifting. Whether her having a way to communicate will be seen as a blessing or a curse.

Have they made a decision? she types.

Jude spreads his hands in an exaggerated shrug, then begins to type.

This is home for most of us, but you're right. Word is going to get out eventually. This is our chance to choose before someone else makes the choice for us.

Starla nods, and decides to take the risk.

I need to send a message, she types.

Jude's lips part in surprise, and he points at the ceiling, one eyebrow raised in a question. Starla nods. He stares out over the assembly, emotion warring in his face: wistfulness, hope. Finally his smile quirks to the side and he thumbs over his shoulder for her to follow him.

Starla at first isn't certain if he's going to take her back to the room where she and the others are still ostensibly being held prisoner, but after a few twists and turns she realizes they're going a new way. The breeze freshens, and soon they're standing on a ledge overlooking the desert. It's not big. If Jude wanted to silence her, he could push her off now and no one would be the wiser.

But the signal bar on her lens is suddenly strong, and Jude hasn't moved. This is her chance. Starla takes a seat with her back against the cliff. It's not the most secure place she has ever sat — and she's trying not to look down — but at least she'll be a lot harder to push off-balance here. After a long moment, Jude sits, too.

WE'RE SAFE, she begins. MISSION IS STILL ON.

She describes their situation as briefly as she can, letting Jaantzen know about the revised timeline for raiding the Alliance research facility and asking him to prepare potential transport and supplies for the convicts, if that's what they decide.

When she presses Send, she breathes a sigh of relief.

Jude is still sitting beside her, staring out over the desert.

No, not at the desert. At the *stars*.

The night is dazzling, more stars than she's ever seen on New Sarjun — if she thought the Maraka Valley was dark, this desert valley is the perfect pitch-black showcase for the heavens above. It takes her a moment to realize she's smiling.

She turns to find Jude watching her.

WHAT'S THAT CONSTELLATION? she types, then points to a U-shaped grouping of stars a few degrees above the north horizon.

THE WINTER QUEEN. YOU CAN ONLY SEE HER THIS TIME OF YEAR.

Starla gives him a genuine smile. Of the very few people on New Sarjun who have seen the stars of the northern hemisphere, even fewer have seen this particular set because of its rarity.

"Thank you," she signs.

Did you get your message sent?

She nods.

His brow is furrowed as he types something new, but he stares at the screen a long time before erasing it and starting over. Not before Starla catches a glimpse. Can you send a message to a woman named Bea

Her lens tells her the connection has failed again, right on schedule as the satellite completes its pass. Once again her family is out of reach. Starla blinks off her lens and lets the sea of diamonds above her fill her vision.

Jude shows her the comm.

Will you really help us get home?

If you want to go.

She can't tell by looking at him if he does. He hands her comm back and stands. "Let's get sleep," he says, or she thinks he says. In the dark it's nearly impossible to read his lips. But when he turns his back and begins walking, she takes one last, long look at the stars and follows.

22

JAANTZEN

We're safe.

Jaantzen stares at the message on his desk in relief — Starla is alive. Gia's alive. And apparently they've found more than they bargained for in the desert.

A colony of escaped convicts, potentially willing to help in exchange for transport home. Not the first time Jaantzen has harbored refugees from Redrock Prison, but she's promised his help to several dozen. Should be interesting.

Toshiyo's countdown clock has already reset, and his fingers flex over his desk.

I'll prepare transport and supplies. Say the word and we will send them. Be advised the Dawn has managed to replicate the serum and watch out for their soldiers. Let me know what else you need.

He hits Send and the message heads into the queue for her to download when she can log back on. Right now, Starla's sleeping in a cave peopled by others who ran from the Alliance and shouldn't have lived to tell the tale. If he hadn't been there the night she tried to run, would she have found them fifteen years ago?

The shrapnel fragment of a poem digs at his mind once more: *The desert wind brings me the voice of my lover* — but he still doesn't quite have it right.

After a few moments of staring at his dark desk he realizes he's waiting for a response that won't come, and he plants his hands, ready to force his stiff right knee into action.

His desk chimes softly with an incoming call.

He lets himself sink back into his chair.

Phaera.

There's already more than a touch of blurriness to the edge of Phaera's words when she greets him. Her video is off, he hears the clink of ice cubes. He frowns at the clock, it's still early in Phaera's world. "Are you at home?"

"The Table. My night was cut short and I'm having a sleepover at the office — I think Tierren broke into my apartment."

Jaantzen opens up a new message pane. "Is she there now?" Oriol needs to know, if so.

"Who knows? I'm not. It's a feeling. Someone slipped a note under my door saying they liked my couch."

He can make out his own reflection in the glossy black surface; he wishes he could see Phaera's face instead. "You're sure it was her?" he asks.

Silence, then, "No. You think I'm being paranoid?"

"Not if you think the Table is safer." He certainly feels it's safer. The security system Starla and her team installed there is the best on the market. "What do you mean your night was cut short?"

A harsh laugh. "Closed down by the feds," she says. Ice clinks again. "Apparently all my permits have disappeared, so they needed to come in and bust the place up during the dinner rush. A lot of very influential people got to watch me take a public beating tonight."

"I'm sorry."

"It's not your fault."

But it is. The clipped, matter-of-fact tone, the strain in her voice when she laughs again — it's all a knife to his heart. He wishes he could hold her, if she'd let him. Or at least be there to pour her into bed; he hears the liquid glug of another shot hitting her tumbler.

"But we've got the Lordeurs," she says suddenly. "I told Teo two nights from now, and Teo said, 'That boy's always a solid bet,' and that he doesn't like Leone's Indiran friends. And he'd love for you to find a way to scuttle the Alliance trade agreement."

Now that's interesting. "He did?"

"Yeah. And Jaantzen, if you've got that card up your sleeve, it might be the thing to bring over the Demosgas and Seti, too. They're all too fucking scared to throw their weight behind you still."

"I'll see what I can do."

"Oh, and Cavy thinks you're poison."

"He's right."

"We need some heavier hitters." She sighs. "And everyone I was going to approach tonight will probably never speak to me again."

"Or they'll understand exactly what it means to cross Leone and be willing to help."

The sound she makes behind the clinking ice could be a laugh.

"I'm having lunch with her tomorrow. I think I've hit rock bottom convincingly enough for her."

Jaantzen parses this, trying to decide how to ask. "And

have you?" he says finally.

"I'm not at rock bottom until Leone's there dying alongside me."

"Be careful." Another laugh, but she doesn't answer. "You're not going to hit the bottom. Get some rest."

"I'm drinking it right now," she says brightly, then takes a sharp breath. "Oh, I almost forgot. A detective came by yesterday afternoon and said they're looking into Manu for the murder of another detective, and how did I feel about my bodyguard being married to a murderer? Or about my own connections ordering such murders?"

Jaantzen goes cold; he knows what she's about to ask, and he desperately wishes he could see her face when she asks it.

"Yes?"

"Tell me you didn't order Manu to kill that detective, Jaantzen." Her voice is suddenly crystal clear.

"Of course not."

"Why not? Because it wouldn't be smart?"

"No, Phaera." Though she's exactly right, and there was a time he wouldn't have thought twice about it. But business works differently these days. And that's not the answer she wants to hear. "Oriol told me you fired him," he says instead. "He thought it was a ruse and he's been keeping an eye on you from a distance."

"Bastard bugged my office." The slurring speech is back.

"Oriol?"

"Falk."

"Ah." That explains why she had been so convincing about firing Oriol, rather than letting him in on her plan. "Is that all right? About Oriol?"

"Firing him?"

"No, that he's keeping an eye on you."

"Yes." Her laugh now is tinged with something he doesn't recognize. Something wild and exhausted and so, so far away. "Tell him thank you."

"I will. Good night, Phaera." The words seem inadequate, and listening to her quiet breath on the other side of the line, he wonders if she feels the same.

Ice clinks. Liquor pours. "Good night," she finally says, and cuts the connection.

The message pane Jaantzen opened to Oriol is still blinking on his desk.

She's having lunch with L tomorrow. Thinks T broke into her apartment, she's sleeping at the Table now.

Oriol's response is immediate.

I've got her. Will send someone by the apartment.

Thank you.

Jaantzen folds his hands over his mouth, thinking. She's set the meeting for two nights from now, and they're both burning vastly different lengths of fuse. Starla should be on her way home by then, if everything goes well tomorrow night, which means he'll have some good news to share with the Demosgas about their terraforming business, and some powerful ammunition to throw at the trade agreement. He could use a few more days to solidify that attack, but Phaera . . . doesn't seem like she has long left to wait.

The Lordeurs are on board, which might influence others his way. Lhasa Demosga will happily go against Leone, but not without her brother, Aiax. And Aiax and Mizal Seti are both more afraid of Leone's wrath than they are of a lifetime stuck under her thumb.

He hadn't honestly held out hope for Phaera's connections, at least not while Leone is still a threat. Wiljo Cavenaugh and Ayisha Amadule are both far too on the straight and narrow to get involved in an underworld brawl. But if he can bring on the Demosgas and Seti, add to that Julieta Yang's family . . .

It still won't be enough.

But his biggest advantage may be the Alliance agent and her bid for amnesty. If that destroys the trade agreement, he'll not only be able to count on bringing Seti and the Demosgas on board, he'll also pull Leone off-balance. And reopen himself to attack from the Alliance — but this truce with Deputy Chief of Mission ó Lauris was always only a temporary shield.

It's a nuclear option. But it might just work.

Manu's light is off but the door's open, and after standing until his eyes adjust to the darkness, Jaantzen can see his lieutenant's bed is empty. Voices are coming muffled from farther down the hall. Toshiyo and Manu must both be up, in Toshiyo's makeshift conference room across the hall from her office.

Jaantzen gives a slight tap on the door before he turns the handle, but the voices don't pause. Water rushes in the distance, ominous music flares — he's not hearing a conversation, then, but a vid. Jaantzen cracks the door to find Manu and Toshiyo on the couch, a horror vid projecting in front of them a pair of misshapen black beasts stalking scientists through an Indiran jungle.

Manu's watching it with his feet kicked out on the coffee table next to the holoprojector, one arm draped over the back of the couch. Toshiyo appears to be fast asleep, tucked under Manu's arm with her head on his chest and a curtain of black hair falling over her eyes. Pepper is curled in Manu's lap; Mango is tucked in the crook behind Toshiyo's knees.

Manu looks over and raises an inquisitive eyebrow when Jaantzen opens the door. Toshiyo snores softly.

"Do you have a minute?" Jaantzen signs.

Manu nods, then gestures a finger at the top of Toshiyo's head. "Do you want her, too?" he signs with his free hand. Jaantzen shakes his head and Manu carefully extricates himself without waking Toshiyo, settling her onto a pillow and tugging the blanket off the back of the couch to cover her. Pepper gives him a reproachful yowl and pads through the door, disappearing down the long, black hall and into Jaantzen's office. Presumably to make trouble.

On the holoprojector, the black beasts pounce on a young woman in a scientist costume, snarling as she screams. Gouts of hologram blood spray out. Manu glances back at it with a wince and lowers the volume, but leaves it playing.

Out in the hall, Manu leans his shoulder blades against the wall beside the open door. "I don't know how she can sleep through that," he says. "But she normally watches shit that's way worse — she and El have some sort of contest going as to who can find the most disturbing horror vid. She picks the tame ones when I'm going to watch with her."

"That was one of the tame ones?"

"Man, you have no idea." Manu rolls his neck. "What's going on, boss? Any word?"

"Yes. They're alive."

Manu's chin jerks up. "Just now?"

"Apparently the *Coldfire* was shot down by a colony of escaped convicts who have been living in the desert for decades. She's offered them supplies or transport home if they help, and they're making that decision tonight. Can you arrange that?"

"Transport for how many?"

"Around fifty."

"Fifty? Shit. Yeah, that's fine." Manu scrubs his hand over his jaw. "Is that all we know?"

"They'll attempt to break into the Alliance facility tomorrow night, if the convicts decide to help."

"If."

"She seems confident they will."

"Well, at least we know where she is so we can come in guns blazing." Manu's eyes must have adjusted to the dark, because he tilts his head, studying Jaantzen. "What is it?"

"The Devil's Table got shut down tonight," Jaantzen says. "I just spoke to Phaera. I don't think she's all right."

Manu winces. "No shit."

"She also thinks Tierren broke into her apartment, so she's been sleeping at the Table. I told Oriol."

"How much longer do you think she can hold out?"

"I'm not sure. She set the meeting for two days from now. So far it'll just be Teo, us, and the Yangs."

"Unless?"

"How much backlash do you think we'll get from ó Lauris if Calanthe files the Alliance agent's amnesty plea?"

"And start fanning flames to derail the trade agreement talks, you mean? Even though he asked us nicely not to?" Manu shoves his hands in his pockets and rocks back against the wall, gauging ó Lauris's reaction. "He's gonna be pissed. But are we looking for allies in the Alliance? Or on New Sarjun."

"Exactly."

"Let me know when you're gonna pull the trigger. Maybe I can soften the blow." Manu shrugs. "Of course, if he'd figured out a way to off us without it blowing up in his face, he would've done it. His loyalty is to keeping the Alliance's diplomatic mission running smoothly. We're a wrinkle in that plan, so we just need to keep reminding him that *his* people are the bigger wrinkle."

"Keep him focused on cleaning house?"

"Exactly."

There's a bloodcurdling shriek from the other room and Jaantzen glances in; Toshiyo is still dozing on the couch, while the vid pans out to hurricane-force winds shredding the tents of the jungle scientists. And all of a sudden, the fractured line of poetry resolves itself: *When death comes in on desert wind it brings me the voice of my lover.* He knows now where he heard it before.

Jaantzen clears his throat. "Tae had some books." He says her name carefully. "She kept them beside the bed, back at the house on Seventeenth Street."

If the poetry shrapnel in his mind has been dangerous, bringing up Tae's books places hairline cracks in carefully constructed walls. Memories jostle behind, pushing at the cracks: the exquisite shiver of bare toes brushing his calf, irritation at her reading light late at night, contentment at rolling over when she rose for morning prayer onto a pillow still warm and scented by her hair.

He shuts the memories down. Manu is still watching him.

"A handful of religious texts and a book of poetry." Jaantzen anchors himself in fact, in describing dusty tomes. "Do you know what happened to them?"

Manu hesitates, and Jaantzen is annoyed to find that he's steeling himself to hear they were given away, too. Wasn't that what he wanted? For every trace of his family to vanish without a trace, just like Tae and the children had?

"Oriol has them," Manu says finally. Jaantzen blinks at him. "Do you want them back?"

"No," Jaantzen says quickly. "She would've wanted him

to have them. The religious texts especially."

Manu laughs. "She would've wanted you to have those, and to read them. She always hoped she and Oriol could convert us both."

When Jaantzen had first met Tae, he'd kept her separate from his business. But her presence in his life had changed the makeup of his crew. He slowly severed ties with people he would be uncomfortable inviting over for dinner. He hired Gia and Toshiyo, then Manu, whom he's trusted to vet every employee or mercenary he's worked with since.

Like Oriol, whom Jaantzen would have kept firmly at arm's length, until Manu made him part of the team by default. He'd been surprised, the first time he introduced the reticent ex-soldier to Tae, to learn that they shared a faith; he hadn't expected the man to follow any credo but money and freedom. He'd been even more surprised to watch Oriol bloom as she coaxed stories of the ocean out of him.

She'd always wanted to see the ocean.

Jaantzen clamps down on that line of thinking. He can't continue this conversation with how many emotional land-mines are here, but he's not sure how to gracefully exit. "Does Oriol still practice?" he finds himself asking.

Manu shrugs. "He doesn't talk about it, but I'm pretty sure he does."

"Then I'm glad he kept the books. I'm going to bed."

He expects Manu to dig, but his lieutenant just rolls his neck and glances back through the doorway, where the music has gone shrill along a pouncing sound effect and the sound of crunching, wet bones. Manu makes a face. "Me, too. I'm tapping out of this one."

Jaantzen follows his gaze. Toshiyo is snoring where Manu left her. "Should we turn it off?"

Manu shrugs. "She'll just put another one on if she wakes up." He yawns, then claps Jaantzen's arm as he walks past him down the hall to his room. "Night, boss."

Bed isn't where Jaantzen's feet take him, but back to his office, where he finds himself staring at the box on the corner of his desk.

He doesn't keep much around for sentimental value. Leaving the penthouse suite at Cobalt Tower meant packing a suitcase and erasing his files — he couldn't care less now, thinking of the police pawing through his things. What will they find in a set of dishes? A collection of shoes and ties? Toiletries?

The only sentimental items he has are in this box: a pair of children's handprints cast in glass, never to get any larger. There's a pocketknife his childhood friend Paz had been carrying the night Jaantzen got him killed by convincing him to join him in breaking out of the orphanage. The titanium goddess Coeur left in the explosion that killed his family but was meant to have killed him. A wire-wrapped stone Tae had always worn around her neck but had somehow left home that day.

At the penthouse, he'd stored the box deep in a closet, out of sight. Maybe that had been a mistake, not to have the constant reminder. Because by all rights it should have a few new items. The vial of antidote he'd nearly been too slow to administer to Manu. An earpiece, empty of Toshiyo's voice, from when he'd left Cobalt Tower undefended and allowed her to be attacked. The cheap Maribi Station trinket Starla brought him when she traveled there, years ago. And Phaera —

He can't think about that.

It's late. He should sleep, but Jaantzen sits down at his desk to work once more.

23

STARLA

Breakfast is a savory gruel with a rich, gamey flavor Starla can't place. Probably giant wolf fat; she pushes the thought out of her mind and focuses instead on Jude and Matí.

They arrived this morning to invite Starla and her crew out into the main cavern for breakfast. The main doors have been thrown open, and now morning light is flooding in to bathe the scene in a soft yellow glow. Starla hadn't taken the time to appreciate it yesterday in the harsh light of the afternoon, or been able to properly see much last night. Now the Cavern's residents are slowly beginning their routines and the place could almost be Nidaly Square in the mornings when Starla looks out at it from her apartment window. People waving greetings to each other, kids running after a ball, workers breaking open crates that are definitely stolen from the *Coldfire*.

There's even a food truck with a solar-powered cooking stove, the type mining co-ops use in their early days before they can afford to have regular supplies shipped out to their claims. The old man there is dishing gruel to anyone who brings him a bowl.

Her crew has occupied a pair of low stone tables against a far wall, and although people are curious, no one has come to speak with them. Warned off by Matí's glare, maybe. The vote last night obviously didn't go her way.

"We'll take you up on your offer to help," she's saying. "Some of us want to go home, but the rest of us aren't quite ready." She shoots a sharp look at Jude. "We know we'll be discovered soon enough, but we want to make the decision to leave on our own time."

"How many want to go?"

"Eighteen."

It's fewer than Starla would have expected, barely a third of the entire population. She glances at Beto. "Can the *Coldfire* hold that many?"

"Now that it doesn't have cargo," he says wryly.

"We'll leave all the supplies we brought for the Alliance at the Cavern," Starla signs. "Give me a list of what else you need and I'll have it sent to you today."

"And another ship," says Matí.

"Another ship?"

"For us to keep until the rest of us are ready to leave."

Manu's going to love that request. "Done." She looks back at Beto and Ari. "Do you two need any help repairing the *Coldfire*?"

Ari shakes her head. "So long as nothing we need got removed from the ship." The words are innocuous enough, but there must've been something in her tone to earn side-eye from Jude, a warning nudge from Beto.

"El, do you feel well enough to go with them?"

"Of course."

"Thank you." She turns back to Matí. "Kumail would like permission to talk with people here."

"I understand how delicate your situation is," Kumail says. He's polished off his gruel, probably accustomed to eating much stranger things on the road. "My intention is to help you tell your own story, not expose you. And, of course, to continue researching the story I came up here to find."

Matí's nostrils flare, but she turns to Jude. "Make sure someone's with him at all times. What else?" she asks Starla.

"We'll leave tonight to find the Alliance research facility. Any information you can give us will help."

"I'll go with you," Jude says. "Some of us raid the gardens there on occasion, we know how to get in and out without being seen."

Of course, that's where the produce they'd seen when they were sneaking in had come from. All those onions and squash, stolen from the Alliance.

"Thank you. One last thing. We brought personal transport to get to the facility. We need those."

"You mean your . . ." Jude frowns, apparently at a loss for words. "Your flying machines? They're right over there."

It takes less than half an hour to get the first murdercopter operational, and by then they've attracted quite the crowd.

"You and the pilots can take these out to the *Coldfire*," she tells El. "Hopefully it's enough time for repairs and to get back so we can head out to the facility at sunset." El regards the machine skeptically. "It'll be fine," Starla signs with a grin. "Come on, help me put the next one together."

The murdercopters are relatively easy to assemble: fold out the blades and lock each section into place, then telescope up the harness and controls. The standing platform spirals outward above the blades — it seems flimsy but it's stable. Finally, a set of self-inflating runners elevate the blades and make it easy to land on multiple different rough surfaces. Potentially even water — Starla would love to try that someday, should they come across a body of water large enough to attempt it.

"You've actually ridden this thing?" Beto asks.

"We all have." She gestures to Gia, Simca, and El. "They're perfectly safe if you keep them flying even. It's all in your legs and balance. Here."

She mounts the platform and motions for everyone to get back, though not many people were standing too close to begin with. She checks to make sure it's in neutral, then hits the starter switch until she feels the hum of the engine below her feet, feels the shudder of gears grinding to life through the controls. She carefully eases it into gear and the blades begin to spin below her, blowing her short, choppy hair into her eyes. So far, everything seems to work as it did back at the deathtrap. A twist of the throttle and the rhythm of the blades becomes a smooth purr.

She rises.

Lean forward to go forward, back to slow down — it's all in the hips and legs in order to steer the thing. It feels intuitive, almost like the microadjustments she grew up learning to make to maneuver in zero G. She soars out of the mouth of the cave, stirring up sand below her, executing a wide turn, and then settling easily back in front of the crowd. She grins and cuts the engine.

"Want to try?"

Beto's eyes are wide with delight. Beside him, Ari sports an expression of begrudging interest. "Absolutely," she says.

El already has practiced, and it doesn't take long for the

two pilots to get up to speed on the murdercopters. Soon they're specks in the desert heading out towards the *Coldfire*.

Starla watches them go with a smile, then turns to find Kumail standing behind her, a young man who must be his escort lounging back against a boulder with a bored expression. Starla waves Simca over.

"Did you find the man you wanted to talk to?" she asks the reporter.

"Yes. I actually spoke with one of his cousins in Bulari before we left; his family is going to be happy to find out what happened to him." He turns, taking in the rest of the Cavern. "All these people's families will be. It's an incredible story. The oldest person who was born here is twenty-three. She's never lived anywhere else, she doesn't know anything other than this life being on the run from the Alliance. And no one back home has any idea this is going on up here."

"It makes you wonder what else the Alliance is hiding," Starla signs. An alien crash site, terraforming the desert, disappearing New Sarjunian citizens?

"The concession is up for renewal as part of the trade agreement," Kumail says.

Starla doesn't pay much attention to politics, but that tidbit had caught her attention when the NMLF splinter group who claimed to be behind the Alliance Embassy bombing gave refusing the concession renewal as part of the reason behind the attack. No one had taken them seriously — the Alliance concession on New Sarjun has been a fact of life for nearly a century, since before Arquelle had started pushing the idea of an Alliance even to other countries on Indira. The concession would be renewed without argument, everyone thought.

Unless there's suddenly a compelling reason to revoke the Alliance's access to New Sarjun.

Realization is flickering across Gia and Simca's faces, too. "Do you think our government knows what's going on up here?" Gia asks Kumail.

"I wouldn't be surprised if certain people do. This is a lot for the Alliance to hide from the public of New Sarjun without help."

"And we already know people are getting kickbacks from the Alliance to move prisoners from Bulari up to Redrock Prison. Like Chief Justice Leone."

Kumail gives her a lopsided shrug, his broken arm immobilized against his chest. "We'll see if the facts play out. One of my colleagues is digging into the account information you gave me, and if there's anything there, they will find it. Meanwhile, I'm getting more here than I could have ever anticipated. I might've gotten somebody to talk to me at Redrock, and I might have been able to piece together some of the puzzle from observation. But here?" Kumail waves his good hand around the Cavern. "Almost everybody here knows somebody who was sold to the Alliance. And besides his own story, Jae-jin was able to confirm what happened to other prisoners on my list — and introduce me to a woman who was sold to Redrock for running out on an indenture with an Alliance corporation."

"That's incredible."

"And you were right. Everyone I've confirmed so far was brought here to work at the Alliance terraforming facility." Kumail leans forward. "I'd like to see it."

Starla shakes her head. "Absolutely not. You have a broken arm, and this will be dangerous enough without someone babysitting you. Stay here, collect more stories, and we'll share information with you when we get back."

Gia cuts in before he can argue. "I promised Matí I'd do screenings on some of the kids. You've been building up a rapport with people, come help me wrangle them up."

Kumail looks like he has more to say, but he inclines his head to Starla and follows Gia back towards a knot of kids. Kumail's escort pushes off the boulder with a yawn and pads after them.

Feeding information to the reporter without tipping their hand is going to be a challenge. The whole story will come out eventually, but it will need to be carefully controlled. He seems to understand that, though, and Leti wouldn't have passed the story off to him unless she trusted him to do the job the way Jaantzen needed it done.

Her gauntlet buzzes with a notice: the satellite is back overhead. Time to share the good news with the folks back home. She's just finished composing an update to Jaantzen with Matí's supply list and demand for a ship when Simca puts a hand on her arm. The older man who was serving up the gruel earlier this morning is approaching. His face is lined and deeply tanned from the desert sun, brown eyes and gray hair shorn to stubble. A scar bisects his lips, pulling one side up into a permanent sneer. His broad shoulders and arms are roped with muscle and spattered with burn scars.

"He's been watching you all morning," Simca signs. Starla knows. It's been hard not to notice that constant sneer.

She presses Send, then stands and lifts her chin to him, inviting him to speak his piece but ready for whatever he might try. This is the most exposed she's been all morning, alone but for Simca. He's been waiting for this opening.

"Can I help you?" she asks.

The man glances at Simca as she interprets. "Tell her — "

Simca cuts him off. "Tell her yourself." She shifts subtly. She's been acting as interpreter all morning, neutral, but she can switch into fighting mode on a dime and there's no one Starla would rather have at her back except for Oriol.

The man's lips twist, but he turns to Starla. "Where are you from?"

"Bulari," she signs warily.

"No, originally."

"Durga's Belt." If he's just here to chat up a stranger, he can stop being so awkward about it. "You?"

"Corusca," he says, and with the way he's studying her face, with his age, she has the sudden, vertiginous feeling she knows what he's here to say to her.

"You look exactly like Lasadi Cazinho." When she doesn't answer, he drops his gaze and taps his fist over his heart, a strange gesture Starla remembers her mother making in those rare cases when she ran into people from back home. "We fought together, during the independence wars. She made it out right before it all went to shit, I ended up in Redrock. You were that girl I kept hearing rumors about, right? Raj and Lasadi's daughter who ran? We all figured you were dead, but I knew Lasadi. No kid of hers was going out that easy."

His certainty is faltering as Starla still doesn't answer. She's not sure what to say. *I never knew the woman you remember? Tell me what she was like, back in those days? Am I anything like her?*

"It *is* you, isn't it?" the man finally asks.

Starla nods, and he breaks into a grin and holds out his

hand. The smile distorts the sneer even more. "Henri," he says. "It's a pleasure to meet you."

"It's nice to meet you, too."

"Your mother saved my life once. She was a good woman to have on your side."

Simca and Henri are both watching her, but she's still not sure how to answer. A strange jealousy kindles in her chest, jealousy of this man's memories, that he knew her mother in a way Starla never will. Jealousy, and resentment. The rare times someone recognizes her as the daughter of the infamous Dusais, she ceases to be herself and instead becomes a vehicle for them to reminisce about some daring adventure they went on with her parents, or how Raj made them laugh, or what an amazing pilot Lasadi was. When they tell her, they always seem lighter, as though telling the story is a relief after all these years. For Starla, though, each person's story adds weight to her parents' legend, making it that much heavier for her to carry.

She's saved from having to answer when Jude approaches.

"Good, you've met Henri," he says. "He'll be coming with us tonight. We go on raids together all the time, he knows the place like the back of his hand."

"Thank you," Starla signs. "I'd be grateful, but you don't both need to go. I can't ask you to put yourself in danger."

Henri grins. "And miss a chance to fight alongside the daughter of Lasadi Cazinho? Not a chance."

Starla forces a smile, then turns to Jude. "I sent the supply list to Jaantzen," she signs. "The ship may take a little longer, but he'll get it to you as soon as he can."

"Thank you." He glances over his shoulder; Matí is laughing with Gia. "I don't like the idea of them staying up here with everything that's about to happen, but at least they'll have a way out when they need it."

"And you have our way in? To the research facility?"

Jude nods and spreads a roll of paper out over a crate, anchoring the corners with rocks. "I drew this map based on memory. Henri?"

The scarred man bends over it, considering. While he does, Starla brings up the satellite images of the facility Toshiyo had taken. Jude's hand-drawn map is startlingly accurate: rows of rectangles on the north side of the complex, a smaller V-shaped building with a circular addition at the base of the V to the south. A short runway leads out of a building that must be the transport bay.

"Looks right to me," says Henri.

"It fits with the satellite images we have," signs Starla. She snaps a still of it with her lens.

"These are the barracks for prisoners and guards." Jude stabs a finger at the northern buildings, then points to the V-shaped building. "This is the research facility. It's built around the crash site — that's this big circular room. Everything you want to know will be in there. Security is all focused on keeping prisoners from getting out, since the only people who come here are vetted by the Alliance before they get on a transport at Redrock. Security at the research facility is just a deterrent."

Henri takes the pencil from Jude and draws a square near the barracks. "This is the power distributor. The research facility has a backup generator, but it's to keep the experiments alive. The external security is all run through this."

"How do we shut it down?"

"Leave it to me," says Henri with a smile.

"The researchers all stay in this wing," Jude says,

pointing to the left leg of the V. "I helped build this facili-ty — the residential wing is designed to be automatically cut off from the rest of the building in case of emergency."

"What kind of emergency were they expecting?"

Jude shakes his head. "With what they were experi-menting on in there? Who knows. But they won't get in our way once the power's out."

"Guards?"

"They'll be at the barracks, making sure nobody escapes during the outage."

"And if anyone comes to check on the research facility, we'll be ready for them," Simca signs and says aloud.

Starla takes a deep breath, then checks the time. They still have most of the day left to prepare. "All right," she signs. "I like this 'sneak in and out without a trace' plan. But tell me what you've got in the way of weapons."

24

PHAERA

"Eat something, sweetheart, you've barely picked at your food."

Chief Justice Geum-ja Leone gives Phaera a motherly smile brimming with saccharine concern that turns Phaera's already sour stomach.

But she returns the smile and stabs at the rich pasta with her fork, forces herself to take a bite.

The last time Leone invited Phaera to meet, it had been in the formal setting of her office. Today they're at the nicest cafe in the courthouse complex, which serves Arquellian favorites to tourists and expats looking for a bland bite of home. Is the location out of convenience? Or is Leone afraid of exposing herself outside these walls? Maybe she worries Phaera is bait to get her into the open, maybe she just likes pretending she's on Arquelle. Surrounded by tourists, Leone's own accent has caught a hint of an Arquellian drawl.

Phaera has ordered one of the few dishes on the menu with actual heat, and the waiter brings her one of the chile grinders they keep around for locals who get stuck taking unadventurous Arquellian clientele out for lunch. She'd hoped something rich would kindle her appetite but instead the smell is turning her stomach.

"I'm so sorry about what happened last night," Leone says. "I looked into it this morning, and you're right. It was all a clerical error. Believe me, I'm furious at whoever allowed this to happen."

Leone's lips purse in manufactured anger; Phaera wonders what poor soul Leone picked to sacrifice as scapegoat for her little game.

"I knew it had to be a mistake. But everything lately has just been . . ." Phaera shakes her head and forces down another bite.

"I know you've had a hard week." Leone gives her a pitying look. Phaera is letting her exhaustion show — it's not far from the surface — and Leone has been barely able to hide how much she's reveling in Phaera's weakness. Or resist prodding her wounds in the guise of concern. "With your mother. I was so sorry to hear what happened."

Phaera's spent all night rehearsing reactions to Leone's inevitable mention of her mother. Can't throw her glass of wine, can't slap the traitorous bitch across the face, can't curse her out. Fortunately, she's so tired this morning all her emotions are smothered in a damp, lifeless blanket.

"I took her to another specialist to get a second opinion," Phaera says. "But she simply had a shock. At least it finally helped me convince her she and Dad needed to go on a vacation."

"Oh?" Leone smiles kindly. "Where did they go?"

"To visit family," Phaera says. She's not going to say south to Alusina, though Leone could find out easily if she wanted to.

"Well, I wish her the best." Leone cuts another tiny bite

of her paprika chicken and chews it delicately. She leans in as though about to impart a scandal. "Darling, I couldn't believe it when I heard. But Willem had the gall to visit your mother at the hospital? After the shock she'd already been through?"

Phaera can't come up with an answer that doesn't get her kicked out of this restaurant, so she shakes her head at her plate and finds the most palatable bite of her pasta, filing away that Leone knew Jaantzen was at the clinic. Those doctors were definitely working for Leone.

But is Leone letting her know how much of Bulari she owns? Or is it a simple snipe, insinuating that Jaantzen was the reason for Phaera's mother's shock? Phaera can't tell. She can't do this, she's too tired for these games. Or she's not wily enough today. Maybe she never was.

Phaera digs a thumbnail into the pale underside of her wrist. The pain spikes and fades, leaving another half-moon mark alongside the growing collection she's made this lunch already. Stop worrying about Leone's head games, she tells herself. Worry about planting the bait with your own.

"Have you heard from him since?" Leone asks. "No? After everything he put you through, I'm not surprised. He had to know you couldn't forgive him for what happened to your mother. She could have died."

At the comment, Phaera nearly loses her fragile control. But maybe losing it is exactly what she needs to do. Phaera lets the tears well up, then wipes them away impatiently. Leone drinks in the sight, the faint spark of delight in her eyes belying her expression of concern. Phaera pretends not to notice.

"Do you know he was having me watched?" she asks bitterly. She clenches her jaw against more tears, and Leone pats the back of her hand. Her skin crawls.

"That bodyguard he made you hire?"

"Sina told me he wasn't reporting to Jaantzen, and I believed him." She tries to laugh, fails. "Gods, how many times have I sat with a friend in some shitty dive bar, listening to her talk about her ex and secretly rolling my eyes because her story is all one red flag after another. You must think I'm an idiot."

"I tried to tell you," Leone says, tone soothing, papery thumb gently caressing the back of Phaera's hand. Phaera forces herself not to pull away. "But love can cloud judgement. You haven't lived until you've let someone make a fool of you for love."

"Still."

"It hurts every time." Leone pats her hand once more, then mercifully releases it and goes back to eating her salad. "But he hasn't tried to get in touch? That's a surprise. Controlling men don't normally give up their targets so easily."

"He left town," Phaera says. She takes a sharp, angry breath. "And now he's not taking my calls."

Leone gives her a disapproving look. "Ah, there it is. If you'd ignored him, he would be after you. But while you keep crawling after him — I'm sorry sweetheart, but it's the truth — he knows he holds all the cards. Stop calling and he'll try to reel you back in. And when he does, let me know."

What kind of terrible advice is that?

Phaera picks up her fork, sets it back down. Pushes back her plate. "I will."

"I'm worried about what he might do, Phaera. Not just to you, but to me. To everyone in our little circle. You know how men like him can get. Think back to your conversations. Did he tell you any of his plans?"

"No, he was always so secretive. Like when — " She shakes her head. "This is so stupid."

Intrigue blooms in Leone's eyes. "What is it, dear?"

"After Acheta attacked the Lorelei, Jaantzen told me Acheta had it out for me. But later I learned it was because Acheta knew Juric was visiting the Lorelei right then. Jaantzen made me believe it was my fault when it was actually his."

Leone drinks up the lie with gusto. "Of course it wasn't your fault."

"And then he used me as bait to get Acheta away so Blackheart — Blackheart! — could take over the territory." She lets real frustration color her tone, because that part is true. She'd been furious at the time. And, if she's honest with herself, she's not quite over it.

"Oh, honey," Leone says soothingly. She waves the waiter over for another glass of wine for Phaera — Phaera hadn't quite meant to drink hers so fast, but the glass is empty and the heat in her blood isn't only her anger at Leone or her frustration with Jaantzen. The wine arrives and Phaera immediately takes a sip, then leans back in her chair with the glass in her hand. When Leone's not looking, Phaera tips some of her wine into the plant beside them. If Leone's trying to get her sloshed, she can put on a good show. But she can't afford to actually lose her head. Especially since she's barely managed a few bites of lunch.

"I don't know how they got so cozy, though," she says, shaking her head.

Leone frowns. "Who?"

"Jaantzen and Coeur. I suppose that should have been my first red flag." She laughs bitterly and pretends to drink. "Or one in a long chain of many, I suppose."

"What do you mean?"

"I don't think I'm supposed to know." Oh, gods, Leone's dying of curiosity, isn't she? Phaera takes a steadying breath and sets her glass back on the table. "I think that's where he is. In her part of the Fingers? Because, the police won't set foot in there, it's supposed to be a hellscape."

"It's a leap," Leone says doubtfully.

"I overheard his man Juric talking about meeting in Altamira with Sina. That's Coeur's territory. It got me thinking."

And hopefully it'll get Leone thinking, too.

"I trusted him about so many things because he told me to," Phaera says, steamrolling past her last comment like it wasn't important. "And then? Radio silence. I was useful, and then I wasn't. And now he's sitting back while everything I've built its torn apart. You tried to warn me he was using me, and he was — to get to you." Any good bluff needs enough of a kernel of truth in the lie. "Because of the trade agreement."

Leone's gaze narrows. "What about it?"

"He's *obsessed* with it. He says it's about his import business, but I think he just hates the Alliance. He told me once Coeur was his ticket to tanking the whole agreement, and he was happy it would make you angry. Why, because you have Arquellian friends? Of course you want to work nicely with the Alliance."

Leone is still. "Think, honey. What does Coeur know?"

"I don't know the specifics. She has a lot of dirt on Alliance diplomats, and he's trying to blackmail people on the New Sarjun side to get them to vote against the agreement." She lets a shiver run through her — it's not hard; it's freezing in here to cater to the Arquellian tourists. "Some of it is horrible. Threatening their kids? I couldn't be a part of it."

She takes another gulp of her wine — a real one, this time, Leone is watching — then decides it's time for Distraught Phaera to pull herself together.

She set the glass down with too much careful deliberation, then straightens her shoulders and lays her hands on the table. She catches Leone's glance at her fingers. She's due for a manicure anyway, but even that won't fix the raw, torn red of her cuticles. A habit she has got to ditch.

"I apologize," Phaera says primly. "I've been out of line. I don't know what to do and I feel like an idiot." She gestures to the waiter, then swipes marks to cover the bill. "My treat, with my thanks."

"It's all right, we've all made bad decisions." Leone pulls her into a strong hug when they rise, engulfing her in a cloud of perfume, her voice a poison hum in Phaera's ear. "Don't forget again who your real friends are." The steel behind those words makes Leone's subtext clear: Phaera had better not screw up a second time.

Leone's grip on her arm is going to leave bruises, but when she releases Phaera from the embrace she's smiling like they're old friends. Phaera's not entirely certain Leone bought the act of contrition, but she's willing to play along. At least for now. And she definitely took the bait about Jaantzen's plans.

Phaera steps out of the air-conditioned courthouse into the brilliant sunshine, drinking in the heat after the chilliness of the cafe. She still has goosebumps down her bare arms, from the cold, or from the mental image of Leone watching her from one of the building's many windows. She starts walking in no particular direction, trying to put distance between herself and the courthouse, ignoring the whistling of passing pirate cabs who've marked her as a fare.

A few blocks later she's calmed down enough to notice

the green-and-white union cab slow to pass her, hot-pink runners indicating that it's free. She holds out a hand and it stops; she's halfway in the door before she realizes someone else is already sitting in the back.

"Oh, I'm sorry," she says, but the older man makes no attempt to get out.

"Hey, Fay," says a familiar voice from the front. Dal Jaxon, the lanky head of the cab drivers union, is folded behind the driver's seat of the cab. "Get in, I've got a friend I want you to meet."

Phaera doesn't move. The older man is wearing a suit he's not comfortable in — he looks like he'd much rather be pulling a gun on you in a dark alley. But there's no arrogance or threat in the way he's sitting: a polite smile, hands carefully visible on knees. He's not trying to intimidate her.

And she's known Jaxon over a decade, since her days volunteering with the service industry workers' union. His friendship has helped keep her honest since she transitioned from service worker to one of the bosses, and he wouldn't put her in danger.

"Come on," Jaxon says. "They're watching."

Phaera slips in and shuts the door, heart racing. "I didn't know you were pulling shifts anymore, Jaxon," she says.

"Special request. Phaera D, meet Aden Damyati. Blackheart's lieutenant. She wants to meet with you."

The goosebumps rise on her arms once more. "About?"

"Your common interests in the prosperity of North Bulari neighborhoods," says Damyati. "You'll be perfectly safe, ma'am. Though, for obvious reasons, she can't leave the Fingers."

Jaxon's watching her in his security mirror with his usual friendly ease.

"And if I don't want to go?"

"Then I drop you wherever you want," Jaxon says. "No hard feelings."

"From you, maybe. What about Blackheart?"

"I'm your collateral," Jaxon says. "Word'll get back to the man who took you to see her. And believe me, I know what he'll do to me if anything happens to you."

"You're under Blackheart's protection," Damyati says solemnly. "Nothing will happen to you."

Nothing, except for Blackheart.

Phaera takes a deep breath that does nothing to loosen the tightness of her chest.

"Fine," she says. "Let's go."

25

MANU

"I'm flattered she thinks I can just find a ship for a bunch of escaped convicts," says Manu. "I really am."

He's kicked back in a chair in Toshiyo's office, feet up on the corner of her desk, Pepper a warm, purring blanket in his lap as he scrolls through Starla's list of demands on his comm.

"You can though, right?" Toshiyo asks.

"I'll figure it out."

The rest of the list is straightforward: food, weapons, medical supplies. Antiaircraft missiles? He might forget to include that last one.

His fingers dig in behind the cat's ear and the purring dials up another notch. Pepper's always liked him, while Starla's other cat, Mango, tends to give him the cold shoulder. Currently she's curled up on the table beside Toshiyo's desk, tucked happily under Lucky's wing. Both creatures appear to be asleep.

"That cat's got wires crossed," Manu says.

"I think we all do." Toshiyo's brow furrows as she says it — something's bothering her beyond tracking down a dozen solar cells and two spools of industrial electrical wiring. Manu thumbs off his comm and raises an eyebrow at her. "Do you think the boss is doing all right? He's been bringing up stuff," she says in explanation. "Like the house on Seventeenth. And poetry."

"We're all getting too much time to think out here." And new relationships tend to stir up ghosts of the old. Manu would've tried to dig deeper last night when Jaantzen asked about Tae's old books if he thought the man would actually talk to him about it.

Manu skritches Pepper's head and in gratitude the cat flexes needle-sharp claws into Manu's abdomen. He winces and extracts clawed paws carefully from his shirt. "You're probably the only one who actually likes being out here," he says to the cat.

"I like it," Toshiyo says. "The network sucks, but otherwise, I guess it's not much different than home."

"Some of us have lives, Tosh."

"Hey, I went out with Starla last week."

"I'll believe it when I see it." He winks at her and she rolls her eyes, turning back to her desk.

"Wait, why do they need so much ammonium nitrate?" she asks, making a face at Starla's list. "We're not really going to send them that, are we?"

"Definitely not."

His comm buzzes with an incoming message from Cedra Ardz, RKE's office manager. It's marked Urgent as always, and he almost ignores it before he remembers she doesn't work for him anymore. Remembers that moment of joy he felt upon finding out she'd quit and he'd never have to deal with her blatant disregard for the Urgent tag again.

The subject line is *A Proposal*.

He scans through the message with a growing sense of

disbelief; she's got to be kidding. Manu pours Pepper back onto the ground and drops his feet off Toshiyo's desk. "Hey, Tosh, do you mind if I make a call?"

He dials up a connection request on speaker and props one elbow on Toshiyo's desk, drumming his fingertips against his temple. Maybe Cedra won't pick up. Maybe she was brave enough to type the message out, but not to talk with Manu in person.

Finally there's a tentative breath on the other end of the line. "Hello?"

"Hey, Cedra, it's Manu. How're you doing? You doing good?" He catches Toshiyo's eye. "Record this?" he signs, and she starts tapping at her desk.

Cedra clears her throat. "Hi, Manu."

"I got your message." He scans back through it. "Blackmail, huh?"

"No!" He's trying to listen past her to the background noise, but he can't place where she is. "Of course not."

"What are we calling it, then?"

"It's only fair." Her voice gets stronger, more confident. "I was working for you under false pretenses, and my reputation has been damaged. I can't get another job with RKE on my résumé, no one will hire me after I worked for . . . him."

"I wouldn't worry, Cedra," he says. "I'll write you a — scratch that. I'll have Lo write you a recommendation. You'll get a job in no time." And Manu'll send a bottle of whiskey to whatever poor sap hires her, they'll need it.

She's out in public, he can make out the sound of traffic behind her, voices and footsteps rising and falling away. She says something he can't hear and another voice answers her. A waiter at a cafe? Or a conspirator? He's having trouble believing Cedra came up with this brilliant idea on her own.

"What do you think you have on us?" Manu asks.

"Years of shady paperwork," she says. Sure she does. Jaantzen's accountants and lawyers have been all over RKE from the beginning, knowing any business Jaantzen launched would get more scrutiny than most. There's not a single cent placed in the wrong column. "There's some very suspicious stuff here — honestly, I've been worried about it for years."

Right. Manu sighs; he doesn't have time for this. "Cedra. Drop it, okay? If you're worried about a job, I'll help you out. But this is a dangerous game."

There's that voice again, muffled and low. Toshiyo frowns at her desk and cocks her head, listening. At her elbow, Lucky rustles his wings and bares his fangs, sending Mango running.

"I'm serious, Manu," Cedra says firmly. "I like you, but you lied to me for years. I have to think about myself and the damage you caused my reputation. Meet me tomorrow after dinner at Diva's in the Tamarind. Bring five hundred thousand marks on an unlinked chit, and I'll bring all the evidence I have." She's practiced saying that line, he can tell.

"Course," he says. "I'll see you then."

He cuts the connection and stares down at the desk. It's a familiar feeling: pieces are falling into place in his subconscious, and if he relaxes and lets them, in a minute or two he'll finally see the pattern.

"You really think she has anything damaging on Jaantzen?" Toshiyo asks.

Manu shakes his head. "I can't imagine what."

"But she thinks you'll pay for whatever she has?"

"She does." And this is the missing piece. He leans back in his chair, staring up at the mottled ceiling once more. "She does, but this wasn't her idea. Cedra wouldn't come up with this on her own."

"A friend? A partner?" Toshiyo asks. "Who would talk her into trying to get you to pay her off?"

Does Cedra have a boyfriend? Girlfriend? Manu can't remember. But that doesn't quite ring right. "Anyone who'd try to talk her into this would have to be more clueless than she is. *Or?*" This is it, he can feel it in his bones. "Or someone's trying to set her up. Someone knows she doesn't have a case, but *does* think I'll show up tomorrow and try to shut Cedra down."

"She's bait."

"Yeah." He calls up Cedra's file on his comm and flicks it onto Toshiyo's desk. "Here's her home address so you can get a bead on her. I want to know who she's been meeting. Who talked her into this? Start by figuring out where she is right now, and who's with her."

Toshiyo's already called up Cedra's address by the time he's finished talking, and he watches in silence as Toshiyo traces the other woman's path. She finds a nearby camera, then scans back through the footage until the moment Cedra emerges from her apartment, about an hour ago. She gets on a streetcar and Toshiyo follows it from stop to stop until her scan spots Cedra getting off in the parks blocks of the Tamarind District. The cafe she steps inside doesn't have a camera on the grid, but the parks blocks are smothered with them to help keep the tourists safe.

"She must have made the call from here," Toshiyo says. She pulls up three different angles on the cafe, studying the screens. "You think we're looking for Tierren?"

"Could be. Can you get me a catalogue of every face

that walks in there from thirty minutes before Cedra until the call was made?"

"Sure thing." Toshiyo's black-lacquered nails click against her desk as she types in the sequence and then plays back the footage, a flickering row of still shots stacking themselves on the corner of her desk as her scan runs. Manu flips through them as they pile up. An old man in a turban, his arm around his grandson. A waitress in and out for a smoke. A pair of young men in Arquellian fashion, shopping bags slung over their elbows. A trio of businesswomen on their lunch break.

Manu's felt like someone's watching him for weeks, and he can feel eyes on him again. When he glances up, Lucky has fixed him with his strange reptilian stare. "You want to help?" Manu signs and says aloud. He mimes looking at the snapshots. "Help look?"

He can't quite shake the feeling of ridiculousness when it comes to talking with the creature, but he seems to understand more and more each day. So long as Manu doesn't actually think of Lucky as an alien, he doesn't run the risk of his mind imploding.

"Help look," Lucky signs. Manu files that in the mental compartment labeled This Is All Totally Normal, and starts flicking stills down to the other end of the desk when he's done with them.

There's a middle-aged woman in a shabby suit — Manu zooms in on her face, but it's not Tierren, not anyone he recognizes. A gray-haired man and a woman young enough to be his daughter, though the way his hands are roving Manu hopes she's not.

And he jumps, his heart racing, as Lucky's piercing screech splits the room.

"What the fuck, buddy?" he signs and says when his

adrenaline spike levels off. Toshiyo has a hand pressed over the ear closest to the alien. The cats are both long gone.

Lucky taps a claw on the still of the three business-women Manu passed over earlier. Toshiyo tosses it up above the desk, blowing it up so they can all see it clearly.

"It's her," Toshiyo says.

It is. The women are all chatting as they walk in, and because they seem like they're together Manu hadn't looked as closely as he should have. But the one on the right, loose dark curls and a smart suit? That's Victoria Tierren in one of her many disguises. Forty minutes before Cedra made the call.

Manu's pulse picks up. "Is she still there?"

Toshiyo dials in the scan and fast-forwards — the other two women leave the cafe about an hour after they entered, and Tierren and Cedra both leave separately a few minutes afterwards. Toshiyo tries to follow Tierren, but loses her. She sinks back in her chair. "I'll see if the AI can pick her up in another neighborhood."

"At least that confirms Cedra didn't make this up on her own."

"Then you're not going to go meet her?" Toshiyo asks.

Manu winks. "Of course I am. If Tierren thinks she can trap me twice, she's fucking wrong."

26

PHAERA

Phaera had used the word *hellscape* to describe Coeur's territory in the Fingers; she'd been funneling general middle-class paranoia when she said it, but in reality she has no idea what to expect. Some of her employees — like Hiro Matapang — have told her things are actually nicer since Coeur came back to power. But in her mind she's still expecting . . . anything from abandoned buildings and tent encampments to an all-out war zone with teenage paramilitary soldiers carrying assault rifles.

It's simply a neighborhood. A bit shabbier than her own, a bit more crowded. Two-story townhouses packed shoulder to shoulder, their front doors opening into gated yards that are mostly bare dirt, though there are children playing on the stoops. Laundry strung over the street, political graffiti from last year's mayor's race peeling off the walls or covered over in posters for concerts and fights. The streets are potholed and sidewalks crumbling. Jaxon is driving slowly to keep the jostling down; he gives a wide berth to a woman carrying an ungainly bundle and shepherding a pair of toddlers a few feet away from the busy road. She waves.

"Have you ever been out to the Fingers, ma'am?" Damyati asks.

"I've been to Carama Town."

"Barely counts," says Jaxon from the front. He edges his way through oncoming traffic to turn left off the main boulevard onto a market street.

"I never had occasion to visit," Phaera says. She can't see any signs of the fighting that was said to have torn this neighborhood apart — the news vids have all been showing smoking rubble and bodies. "It seems pleasant."

"Dry Creek ravine's in way worse shape," says Damyati, "but the crew that ran it before us left it in bad shape. We've got work crews out fixing up the damage — the pay's good, and for some Dry Creek residents it's the first real job they've been able to get in years."

"We're in Altamira ravine?" Phaera guesses. Phaera's seen maps of Altamira, streets all cut at odd angles to accommodate the terrain. She's grateful she doesn't have to navigate — and hopes she doesn't have to find her way back out of this maze alone. They're on a market street now, stalls lining one side of the road, the other made up of storefronts advertising barbers, set-menu restaurants, shoe repair, used electronics. Not dissimilar to the neighborhood Phaera grew up in, though hers had had middle-class money to put a polish on the signage. Jaxon eases the cab through a sea of bicycle carts and moto taxis before ending up on another residential street, this one a bit wider.

A few minutes later they arrive at a plaza surrounded by old-fashioned facades. A church made of broad steel plates and rivets presides over the eastern edge. In another neighborhood this church would have been restored to its colonial splendor as a tourist destination; here it's streaked with rust.

"There aren't many of those older buildings around," Phaera says.

"It'd be on a historic register, for sure," says Damyati. "If the people who make those sorts of things weren't too afraid to come out here."

"What type of church is it?"

Damyati and Jaxon both laugh. "You'll see," Damyati says.

The plaza is filled with people and tables piled with goods, blankets stretched overhead for shade from the afternoon sun. Jaxon steers carefully around kids playing ball in the street, then pulls up in front of the church. Here are the armed guards Phaera's been expecting: a half-dozen of them with rifles slung over their shoulders, dressed in paramilitary fatigues and combat boots. Phaera makes no move to open the door.

"They're here for your safety," says Damyati. "No one's going to hurt you."

Phaera knows Coeur and Jaantzen have some sort of agreement, but she has no idea what it is. Does Coeur just want to talk? Or has she been brought here as part of some grudge? The one thing she does know is that with all those guards, she's not walking back out of here unless Coeur decides to let her go.

She steels herself as one of the guards approaches the spinner and opens her door. "Right this way, ma'am." The guard has a pleasant smile despite the vicious weaponry she's wearing. Jaxon gives her a thumbs-up from the front seat. Damyati is waiting for her at the door to the church.

Phaera squares her shoulders and follows Damyati inside.

After the brightness of the sun, the interior of the church is dark and cool; her eyes take a moment to adjust.

Inside, any trace of the church's original religion or denomination has been erased. The frescoes on the walls have long been painted over, the altar taken down, the sanctuary turned into a training gym full of equipment and mats, heavy bags and weights, a row of weapons lockers. A boxing ring at the far end has room for plenty of spectators, though at the moment only a few people are shouting encouragement as a pair spar.

Damyati leads her past the gym to a set of stairs. They've been repainted recently over layers of paint that had already peeled, creating a pitted topography. The hollow click of Phaera's heels on the metal stairs echoes up and down the stairwell.

She's made a hobby of imagining a person's natural habitat before she actually arrives, and she enjoys getting it right as much as being surprised. Walking into Jaantzen's penthouse suite for the first time, for example, had been completely unexpected. His home was surprisingly stylish, but it was almost sterile, nothing out of place. An environment as tightly controlled as his emotional life. On the other hand, Geum-ja Leone's home had been exactly what Phaera had imagined, down to the Arquellian antiques and stylistic flourishes that mimicked the elite from back on Indira.

Phaera has been imagining a cartoony underworld throne room for Blackheart, especially once she saw the church. She'd half expected Coeur to be doing business from a gold throne where the altar should be.

She's not expecting the simple, cluttered office overlooking the plaza. It looks more like it belongs to an overworked grassroots politician, the large desk piled with paperwork and layered in open files, stacks of books, overflowing crates in haphazard piles. The desk is a newer model, but the rest of the furniture is shabby and functional. Phaera guesses Thala Coeur doesn't spend much time entertaining.

Blackheart herself looks up from her desk when they enter, spares Phaera a glance before she turns to Damyati. "All good?" she asks her lieutenant.

"Yes, ma'am."

"Give us a sec, then."

Damyati smiles encouragingly at Phaera, then shuts the door behind him. Leaving her alone with Bulari's most vicious crime lord.

Coeur stands and tilts her head like a predator, studying Phaera with glittering eyes.

Phaera has seen vids of the woman. She remembers being charmed by a younger Thala Coeur on the campaign trail, at least until stories about her criminal past started surfacing. In the end, Phaera had voted for the incumbent, as had everyone she knew, so when Coeur won it was easy to believe she'd stolen the election. Phaera hadn't hated everything about Blackheart's time as mayor though. She'd fought the federal government to keep the Alliance out of New Sarjun, after all. But government corruption had gotten worse, violence in the city had spiked, and then everything had dissolved in a fiery mess of scandals. Coeur had run to the Alliance for amnesty — after railing against them for so many years — and then vanished from the news cycles.

Though her influence hadn't vanished from the city.

Phaera had been shocked when she first began attending Leone's dinner parties and met Coeur's former lieutenant, Naali Hinoja. And realized Blackheart was still running her business quietly from exile.

She remembers Blackheart as a woman who lit up the

news feeds with her fiery rhetoric about how the city should serve all its citizens, no matter the neighborhood they lived in. Back in those days she'd had an athlete's body and a head of black braids, each tipped with gold. Now her shorn scalp is hidden under a knit cap, the edges of burn scars dapple her red-brown cheeks. She's stick thin and rangy, all angles under the maroon silk blouse and black trousers, boxer's hands encased in therapeutic gloves.

But then she grins, and there's the woman Phaera remembers. Bright white teeth flash in a trickster's smile. A jaguar's smile. One of her eyeteeth has been replaced, it's blood red and extra sharp.

"Thanks for coming in." Coeur holds out a hand and Phaera shakes it gingerly. She's heard the rumors: the Dry Creek crew broke every bone in Blackheart's hands before Jaantzen rescued her.

"I didn't have much choice."

"Bullshit." Coeur sits back down behind her desk, gloved fingers playing over the silver head of the black-lacquered cane beside her. "You always have a choice."

Phaera sits as well, though she wasn't invited. The rickety wooden chair wobbles under her and she tries to force her body language to be calm though her heart is beating in her throat. "The choice was to say yes, or say no and your lieutenant would drag me here against my will."

"There, you see?" Coeur gives her a feral smile. "You always have a choice, even if the alternatives aren't pleasant. Have you been to Altamira before?"

"I've never been to the Fingers."

"Too scared? You don't look like you get scared."

"I'm not."

Coeur narrows her gaze. A chill touches Phaera's bare

arms, despite the heat of the day, despite the shouts of children playing drifting through the open window.

"It's healthy to be scared, it's what keeps the species
alive," Coeur says finally. She swipes off her desk and leans
her elbows on it. A vicious handgun sits like a paperweight
at her right elbow. "I've been hearing about your idea to
form the North Bulari Business Alliance. I want in."

Phaera blinks at her in surprise. "As a business owner?"
she asks delicately.

"My crew is the biggest business in the north end of the
city. I employ half of two neighborhoods."

"I'm not sure if — "

Coeur begins ticking items off on her fingers. "The
delivery business. The work crews rebuilding Dry Creek.
The gaming hustle. The bus lines — the city won't run
transport out here, so who do you think organized that?
The, ah, let's call it the import business."

Phaera's intrigued despite herself. "You run everything
personally?"

Coeur shrugs one bony shoulder. "I delegate. Sometimes it needs done so I find the people to do it. Sometimes
someone comes to me with an idea, I give them the
resources they need, they give me a cut."

"Resources?"

"Startup money. Connections to buy what they need.
Help with, well, let's call it a secured share of the market."

"Reduced competition?" Phaera offers. She can guess
where this is going.

"Competition reduction services." Coeur laughs. "I like
that. You want to do something for real in Bulari, I'm part of
your ecosystem."

"I understand that," Phaera says. "But I don't think
other people will. Like Mizal Seti?"

"I don't have a problem with Mizal. I had a problem with his dad." A sly grin flashes her red eyetooth. "And I took care of that problem."

"That's exactly what I mean. How can anyone trust you?"

Coeur's fading smile says Phaera's skirting awfully close to the line. Phaera's gaze flickers to the gun sitting inches from Coeur's hand, heat warming her cheeks.

"Fair," Coeur finally says. She stands, then grabs the gun off the desk. Phaera stiffens, but Coeur holsters it in the small of her back and grabs her cane. "Let's go for a walk."

"Is this another one of those false choices I get to make?"

"It's a free city." Coeur knocks her cane against the door and Damyati opens it for them. Locked from the outside? Or simply too painful for her to grip the handle. Phaera wonders if she can actually shoot that gun she's carrying. "Try it and see. There's something I want to show you."

Phaera follows Coeur to the lift at the end of the hallway. A pair of the guards at the entrance to the church break off to trail them with rifles in hand as Coeur strolls out into the plaza. Damyati walks a few paces ahead, a pistol at his hip. The show of force doesn't seem to worry people in the plaza — Coeur returns a steady stream of waves and smiles as they walk. A ball comes rolling towards Damyati and he blocks it with a well-placed foot, then kicks it back to the kids playing soccer at the edge of the plaza.

Jaxon's nowhere to be seen. Phaera tries not to think about what that means.

The street directly behind the church leads up a steep residential road. Coeur leans heavily on her cane, walking slowly but casually, as though she's merely enjoying the stroll. Phaera matches her pace.

"Altamira wasn't originally part of the Bulari settlement," Coeur says as they walk. They've reached a set of stairs carved directly into the ravine wall, and she gestures with her cane for Phaera to go first. She's hiding how out of breath she is, and Phaera's surprised she risked this walk at all. She was under the impression Coeur ruled by strength of might; wouldn't showing this weakness to her people plant the seeds for revolt? But if anything, the guards around them seem proudly protective of their broken queen. Phaera begins to climb, slowly. Behind her, Coeur keeps talking.

"Altamira was relatively wealthy back when it was first settled, and they resisted being annexed by Bulari for a long time. But eventually Bulari took Altamira over. And as the poor got pushed out of the city proper and started building their own communities in the rest of the Fingers, it meant being from the Fingers was a bad thing. Even if that Finger was rich little Altamira."

The staircase leads to a small park built into the side of the ravine, a promenade about a city block long. It's high enough they can see all the way down Altamira ravine as it spreads open into the city, embraced by craggy cliffs.

"The elite wanted to live closer to the center of power, and as they moved out of Altamira, they took their money with them. Now? Bulari may have wanted Altamira when it was rich, but it sure as shit doesn't want anything to do with us now."

"I didn't know that," Phaera says.

Coeur settles on a concrete bench. "Where'd you grow up?"

"Near the university."

She expects Coeur will give her shit for that, but she nods. "Nice area."

"You didn't bring me here to talk about history or joining a business association," Phaera says. "So why am I here?"

"I have one question." Nothing in Coeur's body language shifts, but that of her soldiers does. Phaera's acutely aware she's standing above a three-story drop, with a pair of Blackheart's soldiers, Blackheart's lieutenant, and Blackheart herself as the sole witnesses if something were to happen to her. "Is he playing me?"

"Of course not."

Coeur leans forward, hands draped over the head of her cane. "Are *you* playing me? You're getting together a nice collection of upright citizens, and there's no room for someone like Blackheart. But you'll need a bargaining chip, and I make a nice one. Sell me out to Leone, to the Alliance, and Jaantzen can have a sweet deal."

"That's not his plan."

"Ah." Coeur smiles without humor. The look in her eye is calculating, cold. "I'm starting to think I need some insurance."

"I'm not a bargaining chip to get to him," Phaera snaps.

"You're not Tae, you mean," Coeur says. Phaera can feel her cheeks flushing. "I thought this was just a business deal between the two of you."

"Whether it is or isn't is none of your business." Coeur's words shouldn't wound her so much, though it's true. This thing with Jaantzen was a business relationship gotten out of hand, and it may need to be reined back in. "But I'm still not a bargaining chip."

"No. I'm not an idiot. You're the one to be bargained with."

Coeur pushes herself to her feet and closes the distance between them. Phaera's pulse pounds in her throat, she waits for Coeur to reach for her gun. But Coeur steps past her to lean against the railing. Either she doesn't think Phaera would try to hurt her, or she's sure Phaera wouldn't succeed.

"You know," Coeur says after a moment. "You're going about this the hard way. You want to get yourself power in this city, getting in Leone's good graces is the way to go."

"There's no fixing the rift between her and Jaantzen."

"So fuck him. Why tie your star to his, anyway?"

"It's good for business."

"The best thing for your business would be to let Leone hold your leash."

"I'd rather go back to waiting tables," Phaera snaps.

Coeur's cheek twitches in a smile.

"I'm doing this because I want my independence," Phaera says.

"Bullshit. I can recognize an ambitious bitch when I see one. What do you actually want?"

Phaera stares out over the ravine, sifting through possible responses. She wants to be successful in her business, of course. She wants to make a positive difference in her community. She wants to be remembered. And she wants to stop having to fight so fucking hard to get any of those things done.

"I want people to believe what I'm capable of when I tell them the first time," Phaera says. "I want my name to mean something."

Coeur's smile grows slow, then flashes her blood-red eyetooth. "My kinda woman," she says. "You know, it only takes killing a couple people before the rest start to take you seriously. Like three, tops."

Phaera can't tell if she's serious. "I'll stick to the hard road."

Coeur laughs and turns back to the view. Outside of the city proper the breeze is warm, but not stifling, and they're out of the direct sunlight. It must make for a gorgeous place to watch the sun set over the city, Phaera can imagine the ravine walls lighting up with the colors of the sunset. And then you're stuck in Altamira at nighttime. She may have revised her opinion of the slum since coming out here, but she's not going to be caught here after dark anytime soon. Even as a guest of Thala Coeur.

"You know I rigged the election to win, right?" Coeur says suddenly.

Phaera turns back to face Blackheart, leans a hip against the low railing. "I've heard that."

"Wanna know how? Vote collector AIs."

"You hacked the vote collector AIs."

"Not the AIs. I hacked the *system*." Coeur straightens from the railing, pain ghosting across her face. "Here's the trick. I found all the dirt I could on every one of those fuckers on the city council, then squeezed as hard as I could until they gave me what I wanted: the same ratio of vote collector AIs per capita in the Fingers as in the rest of the city."

Phaera blinks at her.

"Hasn't happened before or since. They gave the Fingers a vote and they got me. They're too afraid of what folks might say next."

"You're saying you won the majority of the vote fair and square."

"Not according to the people at the top of this shitpile."

"Why are you telling me this?"

"Because this is the kind of fight we're in. Leone couldn't touch me last time without bringing in Jaantzen, but now she's stronger, and she knows his weaknesses. And

I don't have a tenth of the power I had when we last fought." She smiles. "But Leone has weaknesses, too."

"Teo Lordeur told me she's lining her pockets with Alliance gold."

"Selling my people to Alliance work camps," Coeur says. "And getting kickbacks from Alliance corporations for helping them pass this trade agreement."

"Do you have proof?"

"Yep." Coeur lifts her chin to Damyati, who pulls a data cube out of his pocket and hands it to Phaera. "Jaantzen asked me to look into her relationship with Redrock Prison last time I saw him. I still have some friends in high places — and on Indira. So here's a little gift. You two just let me know when you need the streets filled with angry protesters."

"You'd manufacture a riot?"

"I don't need to manufacture shit," Coeur says. "I got a lot of close and personal relationships with people who are missing sons, daughters, and job prospects because of Leone. I'll just give them a place to put their anger." She shrugs. "And it's not like people need my help to be pissed at the Alliance trade agreement. They already bombed the embassy over it."

Phaera slips the data cube into the pocket of her dress. "Why are you helping him? I thought you two hated each other."

"I've seen plenty of people try to put Jaantzen in the corner over the years and end up dead for it," Coeur says. She smiles, slow. "I might be the one exception to the rule."

"If there's one exception there can be others."

Coeur just laughs. "Leone's tough, but she's not half the vicious bitch I am." She turns to Damyati. "Get Jaxon to take her home. I'm going to stay here a minute more and admire the view."

Maybe climbing is easier than descending and she doesn't want Phaera to see even more of her weakness. Whatever it is, Phaera holds out her hand. "It was a pleasure to meet you." And somehow it's true; for the first time in a week Phaera feels like she can breathe.

Jaxon's waiting for her at the foot of the stairs, and Phaera slips into the front passenger seat of the spinner and presses herself back against it, takes a shaky breath. He looks her over. "You all good?" Phaera nods. "Good. Means I am, too."

"Do you trust her?"

Jaxon shrugs. "She's been good to me and mine. You heading back home?"

Phaera thinks it over briefly. She still has a change of clothes at the Devil's Table. "Take me to the Lorelei," she says. She pulls the data cube out and scans it with her phone as he drives. It seems to contain what Coeur said it did, so she sends the files on to Jaantzen, praying something good can come of it.

Her phone chimes almost immediately, but it's not him. It's Wiljo Cavenaugh.

I heard what happened at the Table last night. I'm so sorry. Is there anything I can do?

Phaera stares at the message, considering.

Come to the Table tomorrow evening. She hesitates before she presses Send; her stomach churns as she waits for a response.

I will be there.

Phaera lets out a deep sigh, almost ready to laugh hysterically. Thank you, she writes. And she leans her head back against the headrest of the spinner.

"Everything all right?" Jaxon asks.

"Maybe. Hey, Jaxon. Do you own a suit?"

He looks at her sidelong. "Depends on why you're asking."

"Dig it out of storage. Things are changing around here, and I need everyone I can trust. I want you to meet us tomorrow night at the Table."

"Sure thing," Jaxon says. "Just tell me when, and I'll be there for you."

27

STARLA

The sun is setting over the desert as they fly, long shadows streaking rust red over the sand and soil and rock. Taking the murdercopter for a spin around the death-trap property was fun — but for the nearly ninety minutes it takes for them to cross the distance to the Alliance facility, it's exhausting. Starla sets hers down gratefully and flexes her wrists, rolls her shoulders, stretches her calves. Nearby, Simca and Gia are doing the same.

"Glad I've been doing core work," Simca signs, gestures exaggerated in the dark so Starla can see.

A minute later, the rust-bucket skiff Jude is flying lands nearby, roiling up a cloud of fine red dust that obscures him and Henri.

They've landed in an abandoned quarry; in the dark, with only the rapidly fading glow on the horizon to guide them, everything is featureless and flat. Starla follows Jude's silhouette along a well-worn dirt road he's told them leads back to the facility, which must be the faint ambient light over the hill ahead. After nearly half an hour, the road curves out of sight. Jude slows, then motions the rest forward.

The small valley below is washed with light from the compound.

Starla calls up the map on her lens, orienting herself to the place. Those are the barracks on the northern side, an ugly and utilitarian design built around a central courtyard. To the south is the research facility: two wings jutting off a vast, domed building made of opaque panels that radiate a soft yellow in the black night.

At the far side of the valley, the airstrip stretches out into the black. A pair of transport hoppers with Alliance markings squat near the hangar. Starla catches Simca's eye. "There's the ship they need to get home," she signs.

"Oh, yeah, let's just steal an Alliance ship," Simca jokes back.

The others are watching them, so Simca explains.

"Can't tell you how many times we talked about that," says Henri. "No way to do it without making life hell for those of us who didn't want to go home, though."

In the central part of the small valley, light hits something with a very different texture than the rock they've been walking through. A breeze touches Starla's cheek as a wind picks up, and the crops in the valley ripple. Crops. In the desert valley. Starla's accustomed to Julieta's greenhouse, to the lush indoor gardens at the Jungle and in Jaantzen's penthouse. But she's never seen anything like this.

Starla's brought a pair of Toshiyo's beetle drones, with a short-range connection strong enough to stream video to her lens. They're also programmed to sync with the satellite whenever it's in range, so they should get a good bit of intel even if everything else goes wrong. Starla checks the time on her lens. The satellite should be passing overhead in twenty minutes, which will hopefully be perfect. They'll be inside, ready to transmit the instant the satellite comes online.

She slaves the beetle drones to her gauntlet and sends them on a perimeter sweep pattern, then turns to Simca. "You and Jude go first. Gia and I will follow. And Henri?"

The man's scarred lips twist into what she's learned to recognize is his grin. "I'll go hit the light switch."

While Henri heads north along the ridge, Starla and the others follow Jude down as he picks his way through boulders and slickrock rather than taking a more direct route through the loose sand and soil. Whatever happens, it won't do to leave tracks and tip the Alliance off that they should be looking for raiders from someplace like the Cavern. If everything goes according to plan, Henri's power disruption will appear to be a glitch, rather than drawing attention to the possibility of an outside attack.

Something about the air changes as they reach the floor of the valley, the residual heat of the stones around them replaced by a fragrant, cool breeze. Starla breathes deep: rich soil, the sharp bite of vegetation undercut by a touch of sweetness. The spear-leafed plant growing in rows in front of them is nearly as tall as she is. She traces her fingers over one big leaf, tentatively touches the tightly wrapped fruit; the leaf's rough as a cat's tongue, the tassels silken and still warm from the sun.

"Corn?" she signs to Jude. He's grinning at her.

"If we could've grown food like this, my parents' commune would still be going," says Gia. "This is amazing."

It is. And it belongs to everyone, not the Alliance.

"Let's go," signs Starla.

They slip into the rows of corn, crouching to stay out of

sight, walking carefully to avoid rustling the crops. They can sneak within twenty yards of the research facility this way, then hunker down and wait for Henri.

Starla sends one of the beetle drones to circle the building while they wait, the other one to examine the biosign keypad beside the door to the laboratory. When she still had access to Ximena Nayar's files, she saw orders from a company called MSK, the military-grade subsidiary of a popular home security brand Admant no longer carries due to its irritating tendency to reset all the security override codes to default whenever there's a power outage. A little digging on security forums told her the flaw extends to the MSK product line, too.

And this biosign keypad?

Gotcha. There's that proud MSK logo.

She waits, trying to focus on her breathing and not on the fact that Henri should have gotten to the barracks by now and what is taking him so long? She shares a look with Simca — relying on an outsider for this part of the plan isn't ideal, but she does trust Jude won't do anything to endanger his people. Which means he wouldn't have brought Henri along if he thought he couldn't be trusted to pull this off.

Suddenly the others flinch at something Starla can't hear. She can't read Jude's lips, but his expression says he's cursing up a storm. "A siren," Simca signs to her. "I think it's coming from the barracks."

Starla may not hear the siren, but she feels the explosion rumbling through the ground. "What the fuck was that?" she asks Jude, but his eyes are wide. That wasn't part of the plan.

The lights go out in the research facility; emergency bulbs at each corner flicker on as the generator boots up.

Whatever's going on at the barracks, no one has come to investigate here. Yet.

It's now or never.

Starla sprints across the open field to the door and punches in the twelve-digit factory override code from memory. The biosign pad glows green and she shoves the door open, swinging in rifle first to check the hall. Empty. She motions the others inside.

The lights are dim, and the faintly flashing strobe doesn't feel fast or bright enough to be an alarm, more like the gentle pulse of a heartbeat. Blinking panels remind her the building is under an automatic shutdown procedure, and residential access has been cut off. So far that's exactly what they were hoping would happen when Henri set off the alarm — it should keep any scientists confined to their quarters and out of Starla's hair.

"Stay here and watch for Henri," she signs to Jude. He nods, and she posts up one of the beetle drones to hover in the doorway.

Ahead of her, Simca swings with her plasma carbine pointed into an open doorway; she motions Starla past her to take the next one. They make their way down the hall, finding supply closets, a kitchen, the generator room — the countdown timer in Starla's vision lets her know Toshiyo's satellite should be overhead in less than five minutes.

So where the hell is a computer access terminal she can try to find her way into?

They're getting closer to the domed part of the facility; the lights are dim through the frosted double doors, calling to her like a beacon.

The next room in the hallway is some sort of conference room with an unconnected table, beyond that is a closet. Starla's chance to connect will be under the dome.

She kicks open the double doors. And stops, stunned.

There's the alien spaceship, sure. She's seen the shape of it in a few stills Ximena Nayar managed to sneak out with her when she left Redrock. Even broken as it is — cracked in half, fins sheared off, dissected and dismantled by researchers — it's an impressive craft.

But the showstopper is the alien on the other side of the room.

It's dead, or sleeping, or drugged, but even laid out on a table it's terrifying. It's a more mature-looking version of their Lucky, and larger — maybe ten times larger, Starla thinks, with a horror that fades to pity. Its nearly translucent skin has a gray cast, and it appears to be malnourished, with ribs jutting sharply from its sides and skin hanging from atrophied muscles. One impressive wing has been torn, the membrane badly healed. Tight leather straps cut into its fragile skin, holding it down to the oversized operating table. And all over its body are a mess of surgery scars healed over. What did they get out of cutting the poor thing apart over and over again?

An operational desk is blinking beyond the alien.

She snaps to get Simca and Gia's attention — they've been as transfixed as she was by the alien. "I'll send the data. You two, we need the terraforming sample. Spread out."

Starla skirts the alien, wondering if it's still alive, then sits behind the desk. She uses the fake credentials Mona sent her to log in, accesses Toshiyo's data stick, and runs the code.

She's counting down the seconds until the connection goes through once more, hoping against hope the satellite will actually be here for another pass. It's been a miracle so far the Alliance hasn't yet noticed and stopped their fun.

She takes a deep breath. Another.

And the connection blinks green.

Initiate upload Y/N.

Starla stabs at Y, tentative relief flooding through her. Even if this doesn't work, Toshiyo's mistletoe program will thread its way through the file system and copy the files back onto the data stick, so Starla can at least have a physical copy to take home. She composes a message to Toshiyo on her gauntlet.

At the facility, sending data, she types. Her fingers flex over her gauntlet, waiting.

An incoming message blinks on her lens. I've got you.

Toshiyo. Starla breathes with relief. Do you see the files?

Coming through. And a second later: Hold on. Getting some interference.

And the connection blinks twice and goes dark.

No. Nonono. Starla types in the connection code again. And again — but the satellite isn't there anymore. How much of the data went through?

This is why they have backup plans, she tells herself, checking the mistletoe's progress on copying the files. Twenty percent. Once it's done, she'll clone it to her gauntlet and give the stick to Simca. One way or another, Toshiyo is going to get her hands on the data the Alliance has collected about the alien and the terraforming.

Simca's waving at her across the room, and Starla leaves the data stick to do its thing, catches Gia's attention, and sends her to secure the far door.

On the far side of the wrecked ship, Simca has found a sealed vat filled with a roiling substance an unearthly shade of neon green, its depths glimmering like emerald. One vat is labeled Original Algae Sample, and another is labeled with a version and batch number. The refrigerator behind the vats contains smaller vials labeled with previous version numbers. Failed attempts? This last version seems to be the successful one, since there are multiple vials labeled as batches of the same version number.

Whatever this is, it's the key to making the terraforming plans Toshiyo has been studying work.

Starla grabs two vials each of the Original Algae Sample and the most recent batch number, puts them into a safe carrier, and hands it to Simca. She makes up another set and shoves the second carrier deep in her bag. Time to get out of here.

She jogs back to the desk, where the data stick is blinking to let Starla knows it's finished.

Gia's movement at the doorway catches her attention. "Bullets," Gia signs, pointing back to the door they came from. Starla switches to the feed of the beetle drone she left with Jude; her eyes go wide. A lone man has emerged sprinting from the cover of the corn, a wide, ferocious grin on his scarred lips. Bullets chew up the crops at his feet as he runs, firing wildly over his shoulder, Jude covering him from the doorway. Henri dives through the door as a half-dozen Alliance guards — no, marines? — come tearing through the corn. Two fall to Jude's and Henry's bullets before the closest ones reach the door and Jude slams it shut, blasting the lock sealed.

Jude helps Henri to his feet and they both jog towards the domed laboratory. Starla meets them at the frosted double doors.

"Can't go out that way," Henri says with a grin that gapes open as he sees the creature over her shoulder. "Is that . . ."

Starla waves a hand in his face. "No time. What happened?"

Henri shakes his head like it'll clear the vision of the alien strapped to the table. "The Dawn," he says. "I hit the barracks power first to keep the guards busy, but as soon as the power went out, the Dawn started rioting. Half the guards here are sympathetic, but apparently they've got some marines here tonight, too."

"There's another exit this way," says Jude, leading the way to where Gia has secured the door. But Gia yells something at them, motioning for them to get back.

"The Dawn," Simca tells Starla. "Prisoners, and they're armed."

Starla readies her weapon as Gia hits the ground.

The panes in the door above her explode in a hail of glass and bullets.

28

STARLA

Starla scrambles forward over the broken glass to grab Gia's arm and help her to her feet, and together they run to get cover from the door. By the amount of firepower currently battering it, the Dawn prisoners are heavily armed. That flimsy piece of metal won't keep them out for long.

And the Alliance marines? A flash through the frosted double doors says the marines have forced their way in, too.

"Get in the ship," Starla commands — with both exits blocked by hostile enemies, it's the only place they can escape to. She hopes the Alliance marines aren't as sympathetic to the Dawn as the normal prison guards are.

Henri is the last of her crew inside the alien ship, and Starla ducks in after him just as the Dawn break through the door. She plasters herself against the far wall, rifle trained on the ship's entrance.

She can feel the staccato of bullets against the hull of the ship, taste sharp ozone as plasma charges sour the air. A shower of sparks fills the ship's entrance as a stray bullet shreds metal above. The marines and the Dawn obviously have no love lost between them — and maybe, if they're lucky, the two groups will wipe each other out without realizing there's a third band of intruders hiding out in the ship.

She presses her back against the wall, thinking. Simca's across from her, gaze raised to the ceiling like hearing people sometimes do when they're listening to something they can't see. Jude is checking his weapon; Henri is panting, teeth gritted. Something's wrong with him besides the cut on his temple that's pouring so much blood down the side of his face. Starla catches Gia's eye and motions to the older man, and she scoots over to him, slipping her med kit out of her bag.

They're inside an alien spaceship.

Inside. An alien spaceship.

And every one of their little group is so focused on surviving that no one is bothering to gape at their surroundings. Starla's lost one of Toshiyo's beetle drones — not a problem, she has records of the video — but the other one's hovering at her shoulder. She sets it on a 360-degree survey inside the ship. She has to believe she'll get through this, that she'll get a chance to see Toshiyo's delight, Jaantzen's disbelief, when they go through this footage together. That Manu will crack jokes about the decor — "You think they're colorblind? Or did the contractor have a deal on purple and yellow paint?"

Right now, she has to focus.

"Sounds like things are calming down," Simca signs. She flinches. "They're finishing off the wounded."

"Who are?" Starla's not sure if she'd prefer to end up facing the Dawn or the Alliance.

Simca listens a moment longer. "The Dawn," she signs. "The Dawn won. But I don't think they're looking for us. They're talking about moving the alien."

"To where?" She's been assuming that if the Dawn escaped, it would be to take control of the facility, not to head out into the desert. Maybe there are more places like the Cavern around, and they plan to find refuge. After all, the Alliance isn't likely to ignore what happened tonight.

Simca's eyes go wide as she listens. "Transport. They're stealing the Alliance transports and flying back to Bulari."

With the alien, whose venom is the serum they've been trying to replicate. They've already been dumping the replicated serum in water supplies in rural areas of New Sarjun — what will they do if they have a supply of the real thing? In New Sarjun's capital city?

"We have to stop them," she signs. She risks the beetle drone through the doorway. Five men in a combination of prison and guard uniforms are standing around the alien, undoing the leather straps and replacing them with ropes; the friction tears into its already fragile skin. A dozen bodies in Alliance marine armor and prison uniforms are slumped around the facility.

"Five of the Dawn, all around the alien," she tells the others. "They don't know we're here." She runs down their strengths, coming up with a plan on the fly. She saw the way Jude took out the Alliance marines who were chasing Henri earlier, and Gia's the best shot of their little group. And Henri? He's obviously not afraid of a fight even if he's now sporting a bandage Gia secured around his left shoulder. He gives her a thumbs-up.

Starla points to Gia and Jude. "You two cover us. Henri, take right, get behind that desk. Simca and I will go left to that stack of crates. Try not to hit the alien. Objective is to clear out the Dawn and get out of here as clean as possible. Ready?"

And she's out the door and firing. The two Dawn

members on this side of the alien's table drop almost immediately, but the remaining Dawn return fire as Starla dives behind the pile of crates, Simca on her heels. But not all of the return fire is coming from the direction of the alien. Bullets chew along the corner of the crate pile from the door the Alliance marines came through originally; this time it's more people in prison uniforms.

Starla waits for a lull, then leans out and takes a shot, using the beetle drone above to guide her. The Dawn member she was aiming at — the one with the nastiest rifle — hits the floor. The man behind him fires back, and as she ducks the hail of splinters she realizes in shock she knows him.

She knows those eyes.

She sends the drone in closer to confirm: it's Felipe Zacharia. That ice-blue gaze pierces hers through the beetle drone and he raises his pistol. Before she can swerve, the vid feed in her lens disintegrates in a blinding flash of sparks. Simca pulls her back as Starla blinks her lens off, stunned by the light.

Simca's screaming a name.

Starla risks a peek out to find Henri charging the half-dozen Dawn members at the door with his rifle held like a club, a wild grin plastered on his face. Starla shoots past him and one of the men drops, clutching his thigh, a shot from Gia catches another man in the chest. But Henri's still outnumbered.

"Let's go," Starla signs.

She sprints towards the door, knowing Simca is at her back. She can't get another good shot with Henri in the midst of the melee, so she drops her rifle and pulls the karambit Oriol gave her from its sheath in the small of her back. Slashes it down the back of the man who's about to drive his own blade into Henri's back, then kicks the man in the jaw when he falls. He's out.

She whirls to the left, the curved blade in her fist biting deep into another man's bicep and slicing away as easily; his shot goes wide and his pistol hits the ground. Henri breaks the man's neck.

Simca's a few feet away, crouched over another fallen Dawn member, and the battle's been won. But Felipe Zacharia?

There.

She spots him running for the frosted double doors they both came in, a few of his men at his back. Starla sprints after him, but as he pushes through the doors, he hits a panel beside them and then turns with a grim smile. Her skin prickles with electricity, and she stops just short of running headlong into the forcefield that sizzles into place over the doorway. Zacharia tilts his head, studying her quizzically. She can't be sure what he says to her, but puzzle pieces are snapping into place behind his eyes. *I know who you are.*

Zacharia slams his fist on another button beside the door.

The breath disappears from Starla's lungs; the ground disappears from under her feet. The world flashes white.

The concussion of the blast throws her halfway across the room, but Starla lands on something soft, and her gear absorbs the worst of the impact. She pushes herself back up, choking on the smoke pouring out of the ruined doorway, head throbbing.

Whatever she landed against moves beneath her.

Starla rolls over and finds herself staring into a single yellow eye.

Lucky's big sibling is awake.

She scrambles back from the creature as it throws back its head, jaw wide and screaming — she can feel the sound vibrating through her chest, and all around her weapons drop as everyone else slams their hands over their ears.

Starla takes advantage of the confusion to scramble beneath the table. A few Dawn members, both prisoners and guards, are still fighting with her crew. Gia and Henri are posted up at the second door, and Jude and Simca are pinned down behind a desk nearby.

Above her, the table shifts. At first a fraction, then in great lurches as the creature thrashes against the ropes the Dawn had tied around its wrists and legs. Then it buckles, ropes snapping like thread, wind rushing around Starla as wings pound at the air. The table crashes to one side in a rumble of tearing, twisting metal.

The alien is free.

It fans its wings, one clawed tip lashing a stinging line along her cheek. She scrambles back on all fours, glad for her gloves as glass crunches under her hands, and the creature turns on her, hissing, fangs bared.

Starla rolls as it strikes, rolls again as its tail whips towards her and knocks a table over on her. It rears to strike again, and then stops short, blood blooming from its shoulder.

Gia. She's standing over Starla, rifle in hand, and the creature whirls on her as she shoots again, jaws wide and gnashing, those triple rows of teeth tearing into her forearm as she raises it to protect her face. Gia falls to her knees, screaming, and Starla lunges towards the creature, slashes at the tendons in one clawed ankle. It drops Gia and Starla ducks and rolls under it, out of view of those gleaming, raging eyes. It whirls, searching her out.

And shudders as something hits it from behind.

It rounds on the newest threat — a handful of Alliance guards who've just arrived though the other door. Its tail sends one flying, and the angle of the guard's neck after they hit the wall turns Starla's stomach. She doesn't stay to watch the rest of the fight. She grabs Gia, hauling her up by her good arm. They run.

It's dark on the far side of the building, and most of the Alliance guards are either fighting the alien creature or tracking the running Dawn members, so they sneak out the way they came with no one following them. Henri helps her and Gia climb, and they all settle behind a rock once they're over the ridge.

For a long while, no one speaks. Then, "I think we tipped the Alliance off," Simca says and signs.

Laughing hurts, but Starla can't help it. "That wasn't very subtle," she signs. "I blame Henri."

"Hey, you did a great job of bashing the place up yourself," he says. "Glad I was on your side."

He looks like he's about to say something more — something about her mother, probably — but Jude has gone serious. He points solemnly behind them and Starla cranes to see around the shelter of the boulder. Both of the Alliance troop transports are lit up; one after another they rise into the air and soar away.

"The Dawn finally escaped," he says grimly. He looks to Starla. "Zacharia must be with them, he got away, right?"

She nods. "Did they manage to take the alien with them?"

"I couldn't tell," says Jude.

The prophet has escaped and is on his way to Bulari with what remains of his followers here, and possibly with their own living source of alien venom. But there's nothing she can do about it now — their murdercopters and rust-bucket skiff are no match for state-of-the-art Alliance transports.

A problem for tomorrow. Tonight she got what she came for, and her little crew is out safe. Almost.

Gia's eyes are glassy, her dark face gleaming with sweat. "Can you walk?" she asks, and Gia nods wordlessly.

They make it nearly to the quarry where their vehicles are hidden when Gia suddenly pushes herself away from Starla and falls to her knees, vomiting until she's dry-heaving. When Starla smooths a hand down her back, the other woman is shivering.

It's shock from the lacerations on her arm. Her sleeve is ragged and shredded where the alien tore into her, the fabric slick and black with blood. Maybe she's lost more blood than Starla thought — they should have taken the time to bandage it back on the ridge. Starla pulls Gia's pack off and pulls out her med kit. She scans it along the arm, but the bone doesn't seem to be broken, so she wraps it in a quick bandage. Gia could just be in pain. Or it could be something worse.

The serum, the alien's venom.

The Gift of the Fallen.

Starla pulls Gia's good arm carefully over her shoulder once more, then makes her way towards the quarry. They have to get Gia home.

Gia's shaking so badly by the time they reach the quarry she can barely stand. Starla's about to suggest Jude take her back in the skiff when Gia begins thrashing uncontrollably, lashing out like caged animal. Her fist catches Starla in the temple and she sees stars, then barely ducks the next wild punch. Henri grabs her wrists, twisting her arms behind her and wrestling her to the ground, where she bucks against him, furious.

"We have to sedate her," Simca says.

Starla shakes her head; Gia bares her teeth and lunges against Henri. "What if it makes things worse?" Starla signs. "She got bit. We don't know what's in the venom. What if the sedative keeps her from surviving whatever's happening to her?"

"Or it lets her go to a peaceful end," Simca signs.

"She's not dead yet."

"You saw what happened to that shard pusher at the Brujería," Simca signs. "If a sedative helps her sleep through that — "

Starla shakes her head. "The shard pusher, he started blistering almost immediately. Gia is . . ." Not fine, but she's not covered in awful black blisters. She turns to Jude. "We put her in the skiff."

"Not if she's thrashing," Jude says. "It doesn't have the stability. If we sedate her, sure."

Starla huffs out a breath of frustration. "Then you three go back for help. I'll stay here with her. You come for us in the *Coldfire*."

"I'm not leaving you," signs Simca.

"You are, because you're the only one here I trust with my life," Starla signs back. She's nearly certain Jude and Henri would come back for her, but she's not staking any of their lives on it. "She's either surviving this and coming home with us, or she's not. And either way I'm not leaving her body here, so we need the *Coldfire*. Simca. Go."

Henri helps her secure Gia with a pair of restraints, then settles on the sand beside her. "I'll stay with you," he says. Jude pulls emergency rations and a blanket from his pack, hands her his rifle and an extra magazine, his canteen. Simca wraps Starla in a bear hug.

"We'll be back at sunrise," she signs.

"We won't go anywhere."

———

Starla doesn't remember falling asleep, but she wakes with the first rays of the sun peeking over the horizon. Gia is still beside her, her hand cold as ice. Henri isn't here; tracks lead around an outcropping.

Starla pushes herself to one elbow, palm on Gia's cool cheek. Her eyes are closed, but she's not moving, she doesn't seem to be breathing.

No. No, she can't be dead.

Starla pulls off her glove and searches Gia's neck for a pulse and — there, faintly behind everything, her heart is still beating steady. Starla lets out a breath, then pats Gia's cheek. Has the venom worn off, or is this another stage of the poisoning?

Gia's eyelids flutter open. Her eyes are bloodshot, a starburst of red in her right sclera, her lips cracked and dull with dehydration and sand. Her lips move but Starla can't tell what she's saying. When she raises a canteen to Gia's lips the other woman drinks thirstily, then lays her head back against the pack.

Starla touches her cheek again and Gia opens her eyes, forces them to focus on Starla. "How are you feeling?" Starla asks.

Gia blinks at her through eyelashes dusted with sand.

"Rest," Starla signs. She mimes sleeping. "Help is coming."

Gia shakes her head and struggles to sit, so Starla helps her. Gia stares at the blood-soaked bandage on her arm. "What happened?" But before Starla can answer, Gia digs through her med kit and pulls out a pair of scissors, slicing through the gauze. It falls away to reveal unmarked skin. Gia shivers, then straightens, her gaze refocusing over Starla's shoulder.

Starla turns and sees Henri returning from around the outcropping, the unmistakable silhouette of a Sikuda slingshot beyond.

The *Coldfire*.

They're going home to Bulari — and so is Felipe Zacharia.

And her crew may have made it through alive, but they're not unscathed. Beside her, Gia cracks her neck and smiles.

29

JAANTZEN

Jaantzen's been lying awake most of the night, well before the early footsteps in the hall, the murmured argument, the scrape of chairs being pushed back. The smell of coffee lures him to the kitchen and he finds Manu and Toshiyo sitting around the table, having a heated conversation in low tones.

Manu glances up at him, then heads to the coffee maker to pour Jaantzen a cup. "Morning, boss."

"Good morning." Jaantzen settles gingerly at the table, hiding his wince at the pain in his bad knee. Toshiyo notices and gives him a pointed look, which he ignores. "Do you have news?"

"Amazing news," Toshiyo says, tucking a stray lock of hair behind her ear. She doesn't look like she even went to bed. "They broke into the facility and started to upload their files, but we finally ran out of luck with the satellite. It was disabled just after it started crossing the Alliance concession. I was up all night trying to reestablish contact. But we heard from the *Coldfire* about twenty minutes ago." She smiles tiredly. "They'll be here tonight."

"Casualties?"

"She said they're all safe." Toshiyo cracks her ring fingers in unison; *safe* and *healthy* are two different things.

Jaantzen takes a long sip of coffee, feeling one of the last knots of worry smooth out of his gut. There's nothing more he can do to influence what happens tonight until the meeting, and his goddaughter is on her way back home. For the first time in days, he feels eerily calm.

"Does she have the sample?"

"Yes. And the complete set of files. She'll transmit when they're in better range. I went through the files that did make it through — it's going to be a goldmine of information on the terraforming operation. With that sample and these files, we're going to save a ton of trial and error." Toshiyo stares into her coffee mug, then blinks as though remembering. "Oh, and we might have a problem with Lucky."

"Which is?"

"He'll get pretty big."

Jaantzen glances at Manu, who's got one hip propped against the counter by the coffee maker. Manu gives him a *What are you gonna do?* shrug over the rim of his coffee mug.

Toshiyo clears her throat. "Like, maybe the size of the Dulciana. Or bigger. I guess they have one of their own they've been experimenting on. There was a lot of good biological data on the aliens that I haven't gotten into yet."

"Oh." Jaantzen realizes that he's smiling when he notices Toshiyo's quizzical look. "If only figuring out what to do with an alien the size of the Dulciana was our most pressing problem," he says. "Wouldn't that be a wonderful life."

Toshiyo laughs ruefully, but her hands are cupped around her mug, shoulders hunched protectively.

"Let me know what you find," he says to Toshiyo. "But I doubt you two were arguing about Lucky when I walked in."

"The meeting with Cedra," Manu says. "It's just before the meeting at the Devil's Table, which means I can go and still meet you at the Table."

Ah, yes. "Is the timing a coincidence? Or a trap."

"Trap," Toshiyo says to her coffee mug.

"Hard to tell," says Manu at the same time. "Cedra obviously wouldn't know anything about the Devil's Table, but Leone could have found out and be trying to lure us somewhere for Tierren to attack."

"Then we treat it as a trap," Jaantzen says. "You aren't going."

Beside him, Toshiyo relaxes a fraction. Manu tilts his head in surprise.

"If Tierren is planning on being there, this is our opportunity," Manu says. "You're willing to risk that?"

"I'm not willing to risk any more of my people," Jaantzen says. "Or myself. Maybe Leone did find out about the meeting at the Devil's Table. And maybe she had Cedra plan the timing to draw my right-hand man away from me and leave me exposed." A muscle twitches in Manu's cheek. "I need you at my side, but that doesn't mean we miss this opportunity."

Manu arcs an eyebrow.

"Major Ngara," Jaantzen says. "If he's taken a real look at the evidence, he'll also come to the conclusion that Tierren killed Detective Cho. He'll probably appreciate the tip-off as to where his suspect might be tonight."

For a moment it seems as though Manu will argue. But he just refills his coffee and brings the pot over to top off Toshiyo's and Jaantzen's cups. "You got it, boss."

"Thank you. I'll make the call. Do you have someone who can shadow Cedra? Not Oriol, I need him with Phaera."

"He and one of his merc buddies are watching the Table today. I'll find someone."

Jaantzen turns to Toshiyo. "Are you coming into town with us, or staying here?"

"Somebody should be here when they get back," Toshiyo says. Manu's lips twist in secret amusement, and when she catches his eye, her cheeks redden. She turns her attention back to her coffee. Jaantzen glances back and forth between them, but before he can decide if he wants to ask, his comm chimes with an incoming call: Calanthe.

Jaantzen excuses himself and heads back into his office with coffee mug in hand, the sound of Manu's teasing and Toshiyo's protestations following him down the hall.

He takes the call at his desk; Calanthe's image flickers on the wall screen, and even in the grainy resolution she looks terrible: bags under her bloodshot eyes, the healthy glow of pregnancy washed out of her skin. When she greets him her voice is hoarse and low.

"What's wrong?" Jaantzen steels himself for what she's about to tell him, fear tightening his chest. A wisp of steam rises between them from his mug; in the kitchen, Toshiyo is laughing at something Manu said.

"The doctors have been here all night," Calanthe says finally. "With Mom." She swallows and lifts her chin, light catching in her wet eyes. "They don't think she's going to make it."

Something's ringing, loud enough to drown out almost everything but Calanthe's voice. He almost turns to find the source when he realizes it's in his ears. His pulse is suddenly sharp and strong in his temple.

"She took a bad turn last night. Her fever's back, and the doctors think her lungs are failing. Half the time she's sleeping, and the other half she doesn't seem to know where she is, like she's not really in the room anymore. I wanted you to know." Calanthe impatiently scrapes a tear from her lashes with one elegant fingernail. "She was asking for you."

"Give her my love."

"Tell her yourself, Willem. You need to come see her."

Julieta's turn for the worse could be just as much a trap engineered by Leone as the meeting with Cedra, an attempt to draw him into the open before he has a chance to meet with Phaera and the others at the Devil's Table.

Or it could be a natural progression of the pneumonia that has racked her body since Leone had her arrested.

"Will you come?" Calanthe says. "Today, Willem."

In the end, it hardly matters if it's a trap. Jaantzen isn't going to let fear of Leone keep him from paying his respects to the woman who helped him become the man he is today. "You said people have been coming by all week. Are they still?"

Calanthe barks out an exhausted laugh. "It's worse, it's a constant stream. But if you're worried one of my mother's society friends will be scandalized, you know what she'd say. Fuck them if they get the vapors. You're as much her son as Liatris is, you know that. Willem, she's asking for you."

"I'll be there as soon as I can."

She closes her eyes, her shoulders dropping. "Thank you."

She cuts the connection and Jaantzen means to stand, to move into action, but he finds himself staring past the blank wall screen where Calanthe's face just was, a slow numbness seeping through his chest.

It had been hotter than usual the spring day his life had irrevocably changed, nearly forty years ago. He'd been hung out to dry one too many times by his old crew, and had turned to freelancing. A series of muscle jobs for a Bulari-based smuggler who'd hired him on the recommendation of Raj and Lasadi Dusai. "She won't meet you," Raj had told him, "but Yang pays well and she does solid business." And so long as the unlinked chits had the agreed-upon amount of marks at the end of every job, Jaantzen hadn't cared much what the work was or if he ever got to meet his reclusive boss. And then one day, when he was drenched in sweat and helping unload the cargo at the end of another successful run, a strange hush went through the warehouse.

He'd never even seen a picture of his new employer, but the guard-flanked woman walking towards him was unmistakably Julieta Yang.

Calanthe shares her mother's strikingly handsome features and impeccably styled glossy black hair, but where she tends towards subtle feminine colors that give people the wrong first impression of her in the courtroom, Julieta always preferred her colors bold. That day she'd been wearing a pantsuit in emerald green, with ivory heels and an embroidered silk scarf that probably cost more than Jaantzen would make all year.

She'd stopped in front of him, not a drop of sweat on her brow; his shirt was completely soaked through. If she noticed how very far below her she was, though, it didn't register on her face.

"You're Willem Jaantzen," she said; he nodded. "Would you join me for tea when you're done?"

He'd joined her for tea after nearly every job from then on, fueling rumors that Julieta Yang had a taste for men half her age, though their relationship had never strayed beyond that of mentor and mentee. When he'd gotten the nerve to ask why, years later, she only said she'd thought he was interesting. At the time her children had been young and not particularly interested in the family business, and he suspected she was considering successors or partners and had heard positive things about him from the Dusais. But Liatris and Aster eventually came around, and Calanthe became a skilled advisor despite keeping a careful distance for professional reasons.

And so Julieta taught him how to build his own empire, using every hard-earned trick in her book and introducing him to her own connections, like her old, dear friend Geum-ja Leone.

Grief is sudden and strong as a storm, the first unexpected raindrops becoming a torrent in the blink of an eye, washing through his body like flash floods through the street; and when it fades it leaves a strange hollowness. And rage.

Julieta had introduced him to Leone. Leone, who'd pushed her *dear* friend's already failing health past the breaking point out of spiteful retaliation for siding with Jaantzen rather than her. Was the pneumonia Julieta caught during her night in jail another coincidence? Or part of Leone's revenge?

He pushes himself up from his desk. This cold, furious thirst for revenge is preferable to grief — it sharpens his thinking and helps him home in on the essentials, so he lets it bloom, lets it fill him to the brim.

Footsteps approach his door just before he opens it, Manu's easy saunter. Manu lifts his chin in greeting. "Heard from Oriol, he's watching the Table now, and we've got someone on Cedra. We're all set." His face falls as he studies Jaantzen's. "What's going on, boss?"

"Julieta," Jaantzen says, holding fury bright as a torch. "We need to leave now."

30

PHAERA

From inside the windowless Devil's Table, it could be midday or midnight; staying here has twisted Phaera's sense of time. Or maybe it's the sleepless nights, lying awake for hours and falling asleep to stress dreams. Vanessa's smile sporting a blood-red eyetooth, watching Jae fall from the roof of the Lorelei, following a siren song that's always out of reach until she realizes she's waded into a river, the banks unreachable, the water closing over her head — her hands claw at the water and something catches around her ankle to pull her down to the bottom of the river, where she finally realizes she can indeed breathe if she allows herself to, if she opens her lungs up to the water and lets herself relax. And at the bottom of the river, a dinner party, the guests arriving and nothing's been done. Phaera wakes in a cold sweat from this dream over and over until she finally gets up and lets the scalding shower ease the stiffness out of her muscles.

The Table will stay closed through tomorrow. Leone kept her promise to make Phaera's paperwork troubles go away, but even she can't make the Gaming Commission's bureaucracy move at more than a snail's pace. Which means the only people at the Table tonight will be those who are coming to meet Jaantzen and the staff she trusts the most.

Hiro Matapang is providing security, a team picked from people he trusts and people Jaantzen recommended. She didn't need to worry if Hiro would be up for the task, not like Jae or Vanessa. Hiro's from this world; Phaera knows only a fraction of his résumé is legitimate work. He understands the unspoken rules Phaera is barely beginning to grasp, and he's comfortable there.

She's scrounged breakfast from the Table's kitchen when her comm chimes with an incoming call. It's been a long time since her heart has done that particular little flip of excitement at seeing a man's name appear next to a string of text, and the events of the last few days apparently haven't diminished it. Real excitement to see him tonight? Or simply relief that this exhausting week is about to be over?

"Good morning, Jaantzen."

"Good morning." She closes her eyes, letting his rich voice roll through her. "I wanted to let you know Manu and I are heading into town early, to see Julieta. We're driving now."

Her eyelids snap back open. She's known Julieta was doing poorly, but for Jaantzen to deviate from the plan, to risk visiting her rather than coming straight to the Table — it can only mean he thinks he won't get a chance to see her again if he waits.

"What happened?"

"Calanthe says she took a bad turn last night. She thought I should come before." Whether before the meeting or before he misses her for good, he doesn't clarify.

"I'm so sorry, Jaantzen."

"I'm not certain if Calanthe or Liatris will make it tonight."

"That's fine. That leaves us . . ." She pushes her half-eaten plate of scavenged leftovers aside and digs fingers into her temples, willing her exhausted brain to think. "Teo Lordeur. Cavy's coming, and Dal Jaxon. From the cab drivers union?"

"I know him. Cavy's coming?"

She'd wondered how Jaantzen would react to the cab union leader's inclusion; she can't tell if his unfazed reaction is positive or negative.

"Cavy called after he heard Leone shut down the Table. One silver lining, I guess."

"Those three?"

"Aden Damyati." Is the silence disapproval? Or does he not know the name? "He works for — "

"I know. How did you get in touch with her?"

"Damyati took me to her yesterday. It was a bit of a surprise." At the coolness in his voice she decides to leave Jaxon out of the picture. "It was fine. She was . . ." Not pleasant, exactly. "Helpful. We came to an understanding."

He takes a deep breath on the other end of the line. Gods, she wishes they were having this conversation in person, it's driving her mad that she can't see his face to get some insight into what he's thinking.

"Damyati," Jaantzen says finally. "Anyone else?"

"You, me, Calanthe and Liatris if they can come."

"Thank you," he says. "This is a good start. I know this has been a struggle." It's not enough, is what he means. They need more people who are willing to oppose Leone if they're going to make this work, more people from Leone's immediate circle. She should have fought harder, dug deeper.

"I'm looking forward to seeing you," Jaantzen says, his tone oddly formal, and she closes her eyes once more, leaning back in her desk chair and willing her mind to stop playing guessing games.

"Likewise," she answers. She'd say something more, but he's with Manu and the other man's probably listening in. "Give my love to Julieta."

"I will."

He cuts the connection.

Jaantzen is right — it *is* a good start. But it's not enough.

Phaera heads to the little bathroom attached to her office and checks her face in the mirror, adds the right touches of makeup to falsify a few extra hours of sleep, then puts through the call she swore she wasn't going to make.

Aiax Demosga looks surprised to see her hologram on his desk. "Phaera, nice to hear from you."

"I'm calling to tell you to make a choice," she says; she doesn't want to be talking with him already, and she's not going to waste precious time on small talk. "You can't bet on both of them in this race."

Aiax's laugh rumbles from her desk. "You're feeling pretty good about your man, aren't you?"

"Given what I've seen, I'm feeling pretty poorly about Leone," she says. "And about the success of that trade agreement she's been talking up behind the scenes."

Now she has his attention. "Is that right?"

"That's right. In fact, I'd say supporting her right now isn't just going against your own business interests, it's going against your own country."

His eyes narrow. "Is that a threat, Phaera?"

"Aiax. If I thought the only way to get you in the room with him was to threaten you, I wouldn't want you here at all. It's a statement. Your agricultural businesses are under pressure from this trade agreement, and I've sat through enough of your blowhard speeches about supporting New Sarjunian industry to know you actually do believe them."

"My blowhard — "

Phaera cuts him off. "You may be insufferable and you may have a skewed, out-of-touch view of what actually will help the common person, but I think somewhere in your narcissistic heart you actually do care more than the other rich assholes I know." She straightens her shoulders. "So are you going to do something useful for a change or not?"

For a moment she thinks he's going to cut the connection. Until the disbelief clouding his face fades and Aiax Demosga begins to laugh so hard he can barely speak.

"Sure, fuck it," he says when he can breathe again. "Let me know when."

"Tonight." Relief is a wild thing winging through her chest. "At the Devil's Table."

He frowns at her. "I'm in orbit."

"If you'd listened to me two days ago you'd already be here," Phaera says impatiently. "Get your ass down here or don't."

Aiax waves a hand. "Fine, fine. You want my sister, too?"

Phaera doesn't want either of the Demosgas there, but she's making this particular call for Jaantzen. "Please."

"I'll let her know."

"And bring Seti, if he's in your pocket. He'll listen to you."

Aiax winces. "The Coeur thing, though."

And Aden Damyati will be at the meeting. A shitty thing to surprise the man with, but Phaera's too exhausted to care who's mad at who.

"She's back in power, and he's going to have to get over

it sooner or later. Or have her killed, and at this point I don't care which so long as he's at the Table tonight."

Aiax nods. "I'll see what I can do. Thanks for calling, Phaera. And I do look forward to seeing your Devil's Table. I hear it's quite the place."

She can't quite tell if he's trying to compliment her or insult her. Knowing Aiax it's probably a bit of both, so she ignores him. "I'll see you tonight." She cuts the connection and sits back, palms damp, blouse clinging to her clammy skin.

Phaera of five years ago — of five months ago — would be staring at her in shock at how she'd spoken to one of the richest men in New Sarjun. She's still not sure what gave her the nerve, or why he listened to her. The weight of Jaantzen's name? Or is it something else.

And who knew all it would take to convince Aiax Demosga to get on board would be to finally give him a piece of her mind?

While they were talking, a message has come in from the head chef at the Lorelei's Siren bar, clarifying her appetizers order for this evening. She's ordered from Siren before when hosting a gathering at her home, so it won't raise suspicion the way bringing in some of the Devil's Table kitchen staff would. And of course there's plenty to drink on hand, though Phaera's wary of taking on the role of bartender. It's one she enjoys when hosting parties, but she's spent too much time and energy convincing this crowd that she belongs among them to let them get back in the habit of giving her orders. She needs staff beyond Hiro's security, and she isn't sure anyone she knows will be willing to cross this line.

She pings Hiro: Do you have someone who might be willing to help me with hosting tonight?

He doesn't answer, but a few minutes later her desk chimes with an incoming call. Vanessa.

"Hiro said you might need me tonight?" Vanessa says when Phaera answers. "He didn't say why."

Dammit, Hiro. The point was to leave V out of this, not suck her under, too. Though maybe he knows Vanessa better than she does when it comes to this. And maybe Phaera needs to learn to trust help when it's offered.

"I'm having some people at the Table tonight," she finally says. "Some important people, and I need to be discreet. I didn't want to assume you'd be comfortable."

"With being discreet?" Phaera can hear the sharp intake of breath. "He'll be there?"

"Yes."

Yes, Willem Jaantzen, the man who's been accused of everything from murdering a police detective to planting a bomb in the Alliance Embassy, will be there. "You need to decide whether or not you want to take this bullet for Jaantzen," Vanessa had said. "Whether or not you want one of us to take it."

"You know I'm always there for you, Fay. So be honest with me. Is this for you? Or for him."

"You know me, V. You really think I'd risk everything because a man asked me to?"

Vanessa laughs. "I thought I was going to have to talk some sense into you."

Phaera lets her smile fade. "I want this. And I need help."

"Then I'm fucking there. What time?"

31

JAANTZEN

Outwardly, everything at Julieta Yang's estate seems normal. The damage to her greenhouse has been repaired, the sole sign of violence the patches of new glass among the old. Manu parks the Dulciana among the other vehicles in the driveway with a clear run at the exit in case things go sour. Jaantzen doesn't recognize any of the other spinners, he wonders if he'll recognize the people who arrived in them.

It would be too much to hope they won't recognize him. After the way Leone has been smearing his face and name around the news feeds, there can't be many people in Bulari who don't know who he is now.

Jaantzen checks the pistol holstered under his jacket, not caring that Julieta would be upset if she knew he was armed in her home. The last time he was here ended badly, and Leone may be expecting him to make this visit. He's not going anywhere without a gun.

Or without his lieutenant.

Jaantzen knocks, Manu a few steps behind him, and Alex Yang opens the front door. Calanthe's husband is haggard, a dusting of black stubble on his square jaw, gray eyes crinkled with worry. He greets Jaantzen with a warm handshake and Manu with a one-armed hug, then beckons them in. Jaantzen slips his shoes off into the neat row with at least a dozen other pairs. Julieta's house is filled with the scent of baking treats, coffee, with the faint cloying overtone of bouquets and clashing perfumes. A quiet murmur of voices comes from the sitting room, but Alex leads them past it to the kitchen where Calanthe is sitting at the kitchen table with her feet up.

"Oh, thank the gods," she says when she sees Jaantzen. "If you were another one of her horticultural society friends I was going to lose my mind."

"Don't get up." He bends to kiss her cheek, then settles in the chair beside her. He can't remember when she's due, but it has to be soon. If she gets any bigger she'll snap her small frame.

"Coffee?" Alex asks. "Tea? Something stronger?"

"Tea, thank you." He accepts the delicate cup Alex hands him; Manu settles in the doorway with a mug of coffee and the sort of vaguely unsettling yet polite smile meant to keep the curious from wandering in.

"I hate this," Calanthe says. "All these vultures here, swooping in to watch the great Julieta Yang die."

"They're friends, Cal, they're grieving, too." Alex's tired tone says they've had this conversation before. He finishes arranging pastries on a tray, kisses his wife on the forehead, then maneuvers past Manu to deliver another round of finger foods to the guests.

"How is she?" Jaantzen asks.

"The same." Calanthe pinches the bridge of her nose so hard her fingernails leave tiny half-moon dents in her pale skin. "Or worse. She was sleeping when I left her a few minutes ago. Liatris is in with her now." She sighs and sets her swollen feet on the floor with a wince. "Shall we?"

"If she's resting . . ."

"She's been sleeping most of the morning, Willem. And when she's not, she keeps asking if you're here. Let's not keep her waiting."

Julieta's home is one level and sprawling, the walls are decorated with artwork and carvings. The triptych of stylized dancers in the hallway is a set he bought her on a trip to Alusina. The furniture is mostly New Manilan antiques that have been in the family since Julieta's great-grandmother moved her family here over a century ago. And of course there are plants, an ever-changing entourage of plump succulents and flowering orchids brought in from the greenhouse. The pile of cut flower bouquets overflowing the sideboard is no match for them.

He remembers suddenly the jadau cutting she gave him the day she told him Coeur was dead. He'd finally remembered to plant it, but it should be watered. He should have brought it with him to the Maraka Valley, not left it to presumably wither and die, but back then it had been yet another in a long line of cuttings Julieta Yang would continue sending him home with. He hadn't known it would be the last.

A touch at his elbow. Manu, urging him after Calanthe. Jaantzen realizes with a start that he's been staring at the pile of bouquets, lost in thought about the jadau cutting, while a half-dozen well-wishers he doesn't recognize stare at him in a mixture of shock, suspicion, and wariness.

He nods solemnly to the room and follows Calanthe down the hallway to where the faint beep of a scanner and the breathy whir of autodoc bots gets stronger.

Julieta is in her own bed, leaning back against pillows

with eyes closed. She strikes him as insubstantial, barely making a mound in the blankets, her limp gray hair braided simply, the skin of her hands nearly translucent.

Liatris is sitting at the foot of his mother's bed, talking with a nurse. He stands when he sees Jaantzen. "Thank you for coming, Willem," he says with a handshake — the nurse does a double take. "Though it might not be . . ." He trails off, fixing his sister with a grieving look. "We tried to wake her for her medication a few minutes ago, and, nothing."

Calanthe nods fiercely, jaw set and eyes glistening. "Well, we wait," she declares. "And she'll — she'll make her way. One way or another."

Jaantzen squeezes Calanthe's shoulder, she's rigid as a board. "Can I sit with her a while? We have nowhere to be until tonight." Until the meeting Julieta should be at, that Calanthe and Liatris had been planning on attending in her stead.

It's a good start, he'd told Phaera, and he believes it. He's not surprised it's been this hard to get support. Leone's grip is too tight, her punishments too severe for people to take the risk. Especially when all any of them have seen is how badly she's beaten him and the people who dared stand by his side. All that's about to change, though, and the tide will change with it. Those who trust him now — the Yangs, the Lordeurs, inexplicably Coeur — are just the beginning.

Julieta's hand feels lost in his, papery, her pale skin mottled more purple and red with bruising than not.

Calanthe sinks into an armchair on the other side of the bed with a small groan, Liatris settles on the window seat. Manu sets his shoulder blades against the doorframe with a view down the hallway and gives the nurse a polite smile as the man excuses himself and edges past.

"Where are the boys?" Jaantzen asks.

"With my cousin," says Calanthe. "Safe. They'll stay there overnight so we can . . ." She trails off with a sigh. "Willem. I can't leave her."

"I know." He glances at Liatris. "I understand. Starla's on her way home with Ms. Diamante's reporter." He assumes Calanthe has kept her brother up to speed. He's been ignoring the buzz of Toshiyo's incoming status updates for the last few minutes, but now he pulls his comm out with his free hand and lays it on the bed beside Julieta and begins to scroll through them. "I haven't had a chance to talk with Starla yet, but it sounds like the reporter was able to piece together an incredible story."

There's a draft of it in the messages Toshiyo's sent him; he skims it, then forwards it to Calanthe and hands his comm to Liatris.

As the Yang siblings read in silence, punctuated by Liatris's surprised whistles, Jaantzen studies Julieta's face. He's not much of an escapist, but he's watched a few fiction vids in his lifetime, enough to have experienced a range of mother characters from aloof to smothering to supportive to restricting. He's never thought of Julieta that way. A cherished friend. A respected mentor. A trusted guide. But, "You're as much her son as Liatris," Calanthe had said. How had Julieta thought of him?

When Calanthe looks up, her eyes are wide with shock. "How much of this did you already know, Willem?"

"Some." He takes his comm back from Liatris and scrolls back through the draft. "I knew the Alliance had been successfully terraforming the desert around Redrock, and we suspected they had been conscripting prisoners from New Sarjun to do it. And that they have been giving some considerable kickbacks to high-ranking politicians on

New Sarjun in order to cover their tracks and get the trade agreement passed."

Calanthe leans forward. "Are you fucking serious?" she whispers, then shoots a chagrined look at her mother's sleeping form, smooths a hand down her arm. "How long have you known about the terraforming?"

"The shipment your mother did for Coeur? That case Bennion Zacharia wanted?" The Yangs both nod uncertainly. "It contained some of that technology." It's technically true; it had contained Lucky, at least.

"The same case the Alliance agent broke into Cobalt Tower to steal," says Calanthe, understanding dawning on her face. "Does Leone want it, too?"

"I don't believe so, but she is working with the Alliance to cover up their operations at Redrock. So it's possible."

"Possible. But her vendetta with you isn't about some terraforming technology," Calanthe says. "It's personal."

"I'm so sorry," Jaantzen says.

Calanthe laughs; a tear spills over her lashes and she ignores it.

Liatris clears his throat. "You have nothing to be sorry for, Willem. Mom always said if she died unexpectedly, Leone had probably done it. We thought it was an old lady joking about her friend, but I think Mom knew her the best of any of us."

"She warned me," Jaantzen says. "She told me how dangerous Leone was."

"It was probably already too late," Calanthe says. "Leone could have been holding a grudge against you for years."

Jaantzen looks down at Julieta's pale hand. "Did you check for poison?"

"There were sedatives in her blood when she came

home from the police," Liatris says. "They claim she asked for a sedative to help her sleep, but she doesn't remember. And Leone might have slipped her something, before."

They may never know exactly what happened to Julieta, but there's no mystery as to who's at fault.

His comm buzzes again, this time with a message from Letizia Diamante. Just saw the draft. Kumail will file final this evening. We're cutting together the footage Starla sent — say the word and the whole world knows.

"It's time to act," Jaantzen says. "Calanthe, I'm sorry. But the amnesty plea for the Alliance agent?"

"It's ready to go whenever you are. I saw her two days ago, and she's ready to testify."

"File it first thing tomorrow." She nods. "The story will break then, too." He glances down at Julieta. "I'm sorry. We shouldn't be talking about this here."

"And let Mom miss out on all the gossip?" says Liatris.

Calanthe sighs deeply. "I need to go lie down for a bit," she says. "Willem, will you stay for lunch?"

"I'll stay as long as I can."

"Thank you." She bends awkwardly to kiss her mother's forehead, then leaves.

He stays through lunch, through nervous visits from the nurse, through multiple attempts to wake Julieta to give her medication. Some of the time he spends in quiet conversation with one of the Yangs, some in awkward small talk with Julieta's friends when they come back to see her — he's not leaving her alone with someone he doesn't trust. And in the midst of it all, fielding a flurry of messages.

Aiax and Lhasa will be here, Phaera writes. He is going to work on Seti.

Aiax finally grew a spine? "She convinced the Demosgas," he tells Julieta. He's taken to narrating his activities whenever he's alone with her. He carefully extricates his hand from her still one to type out a response.

Thank you. Still uncertain if the Yangs will come. Possibly Liatris. I'll be leaving soon.

Jaantzen checks the time. He can't bear the thought of leaving Julieta like this, but he has no choice.

"Phaera sends her love," he says to Julieta. "I've never thanked you for that. I might never have entertained the idea if you hadn't put the thought in my head. I wish you — "

An emotion purely crystalline and extremely breakable waits at the end of that sentence, and he lets it drift away, unsaid. "She is very good for me," he says instead. "I intend to keep her in my life as long as she'll let me."

This week has been one of the longest of his life, and only part of it has to do with the desert exile and his goddaughter's dangerous adventure. He'd had one night with Phaera D before the world crumbled around them, and the taste of that pure, stunning peace he felt having her in his arms had left him hungrier than he thought possible. After tonight, he's never letting her out of his sight again.

If, after this week, she still wants him.

He's so lost in thought it takes him a moment to realize the rhythm of Julieta's raspy breathing has become more irregular.

"Julieta," he murmurs. The autodoc bots whine into motion.

32

TIERREN

Major Ngara has been sitting outside Diva's for the past hour, which is truly fascinating. Tierren had looked into Ngara when she was picking apart the puzzle that was Timo Cho, and she'd dismissed him as the type of man who liked to play it safe, who knew about the corruption running rampant all around him — who'd profited from it, of course — but who tried to stay neutral. He hadn't gone after bribes like some of the others at the BPD. Hadn't found himself a patron. Hadn't *really* let himself get caught in someone's pocket.

And yet? Here he is, staking out the cafe where Cedra Ardz is supposed to meet Manu Juric.

Which means he's finally found a bribe he's willing to take.

Willem Jaantzen's? Seriously?

Of all the crooked people in this city, he finally bends for Jaantzen. Either he's finally snapped, or Jaantzen found some exceptional dirt. She should have dug into Ngara more.

Tierren's found herself a perch in an apartment across

the street where a sweet, trusting old man made the mistake of letting her in. She left the news playing at high volume, since the neighbors are probably used to it and will come investigating if she shuts it off, and now she's perched at the kitchen table overlooking the old man's little balcony. He has quite the collection of hardy succulents and kitchen herbs in pots along the railing, making a perfect screen behind which to watch the scene below.

She's been watching Ngara for the past hour. He's been watching Diva's.

There are two ways this plays out, Tierren decides.

First, Jaantzen has decided that getting rid of Cedra the old-fashioned way is too risky and he's going to try to have her arrested, instead. In that case, Juric may or may not still be planning on showing up.

Second, she's been made, and Jaantzen suspects that Cedra's just bait. And Manu agreed to the meeting in order to draw Tierren out of hiding.

Either way the question remains: Will he be showing up?

She drums her fingernails on the sniper rifle in her lap, antsy with waiting in a way she hasn't been in years.

Her arm still aches from the bullet wound Juric gifted to her, and although this isn't what she prefers, she's not an idiot to make the same mistake twice. She'd been reckless last time — it had been too long since she'd had a good hunt. If Juric shows this time, though, she doesn't need to get close to finish him off.

Now that Leone's finally agreed sometimes you need to spill a little blood if you really want to get a point across.

From the other room, the newscaster is droning to his captive audience about the Alliance trade agreement talks, which have been an interminable hum in the background of her trip to Bulari and must be coming to an end soon. She'd been a kid when Corusca was pressed into the Alliance but she remembers the same thing — politicians and talking heads explaining and explaining why it was such a good deal, playing the game of public opinion. Like anyone on this rock will get a choice when the Alliance finally decides it's done playing coy and is ready to take New Sarjun once and for all. New Sarjun has already given up so much — the concession, the corporate tax breaks, the policies favoring Alliance territories over independent ones. All it will take is a few more tripping steps and they'll fall.

Not that Tierren cares. At this rate, most of the places she goes are Alliance territories. That's never gotten in the way of doing a job.

Ah, there.

Cedra is right on schedule, and dressed like she's the femme fatale in a thriller vid. Like if she shows a flash of cleavage in a tight dress her old boss will be too confused to properly negotiate.

In his spinner down the block, Ngara notices her and sits straighter.

Tierren smiles and lifts the sniper rifle.

She'll give Juric fifteen minutes before she moves on to check her next trap.

After all, a smart hunter always sets more than one.

33

―――――

PHAERA

There are three private dining rooms at the Devil's Table. This one, the largest, is decorated in warm red velvet and lit by a pair of onyx-and-brass chandeliers salvaged from one of the first casinos to be built in this neighborhood more than a century ago. The sideboard and mirrors are from the same salvage, stately pieces designed to impress, and Phaera commissioned the long dining table to match.

It's subtly ostentatious; by contrast, Phaera's dressed in a simple, classic gray linen dress that flares over her hips and falls to her knees. It's a warm summer's night, so she's left off the matching jacket. Her earrings are single sapphire drops, and she's finally gotten that manicure she's been desperately needing, a holographic magenta that matches her hair and almost hides her ragged, picked-apart cuticles.

"Everything looks perfect," Vanessa says from behind her.

"We should set water glasses and pitchers out on the table," Phaera answers. She calls up the time on her cuff — her guests will be arriving any moment.

"On it, Fay. You ready for showtime?"

Phaera nods. She expected butterflies, but her nerves are oddly calm going into this meeting. The hard work of convincing all these people to be in the same room with Jaantzen has been done, and although she assumes there will be surprises — there are always surprises — she can handle whatever comes next.

And tonight she won't be going it alone.

Right now the building is empty but for Vanessa Dosantos, Hiro Matapang, and the dozen security guards he hand-picked to be here. They still have a few more minutes to make sure everything is perfect.

Vanessa taps a finger to her red-smoked lenses. "I have a whole checklist here. Including water glasses and pitchers. You asked me here tonight, Fay, so you go get your game face on. I'll call you when people start showing up."

Phaera sweeps her gaze over the room one last time and Vanessa gently takes her by the elbow and leads her to the door. Phaera squeezes her into a brief hug.

"Thank you."

Vanessa winks. "Get outta here."

She's spent all day trapped in her office, so she heads to the roof. The night is clear, stars faint overhead in the ambient light and atmospheric dust, but the real show-stopper is the city of Bulari itself. She's always admired this view of the drag, but she doesn't always take the time to lift her gaze to the skyline beyond. The skyscrapers of down-town Bulari are brilliant in all their creative glory: this one a spiraling light show, that one a piercing spire, this other dripping with gold lights. It's a beautiful city at night, painted in light and color against the blackness of the surrounding desert. Vibrant and strong-willed and flashy and fierce, just like its people.

No one but her has been up here since the Table was shut down two nights ago, and her staff left it a mess due to the way the night was cut short. Cigarette butts in overflowing trays, half-empty shift beers, an ice tub that someone hauled up here for Lord knows why now melted and brimming with water.

She's never going to turn this into a bar, she decides. This is her people's place, and that's how it will stay.

Phaera keeps back from the edge out of habit, leaning against the makeshift bar, filling her lungs with the cooling air. She flicks her thumbnail over the three fortune-killer mystix cards in her pocket.

One night, years ago, she'd almost gotten fired from Orveto's Thousands because of a fortune killer. The Fallen Tower, the worst one.

Working the mystix tables at Orveto's had been her first job as a dealer. That night, a player on a winning streak was completely cleaning her out. The floor AI alerted her manager, who started buzzing in her earpiece and coaching her on every hand. She finally turned her earpiece off so she wouldn't have to hear him — she was a better player and he was getting in the way of her instincts.

She was sure the player was counting cards, but so was she. And she was positive he had the Fallen Tower in his hand, so she bet large. But when he lay down his cards he had a double marriage: Loup-garou with Moon, Lorelei with River. The only two marriages that aren't broken by the Fallen Tower, and he had them both.

It had been an incredible game, and even if it'd lost her her job it would've been worth it to play and shake that man's hand.

Whatever reason Victoria Tierren had for leaving her fortune-killer cards, Phaera has taken them to heart. She's shored up her stronghold, she's made certain of her people, and any doubts she still has about whether or not to trust Jaantzen no longer matter. She trusts herself.

It's showtime.

She straightens to go back inside; as she turns a glimmer of gold on the wall overlooking the drag catches her eye.

Yet another piece of debris her employees left behind? If Oriol were here he'd tell her to stay back, but curiosity gets the better of her. She takes a step, aware of the distant sound of traffic, the clicking of her heels, the faint pulsing of music from Ayisha's Palace.

She recognizes the cards before she reaches the wall, her heart beating faster and faster.

A pair of mystix cards, light glinting off the embossed gold river on the cards' backs.

Phaera turns the cards over with a shaking hand.

The Loup-garou and the Lorelei. Just like the first set Tierren sent her days ago.

This time both are smeared with blood.

JAANTZEN

Julieta's hand twitches, clutching at the blankets, and Jaantzen slips his hand back into hers. "Julieta?" he murmurs.

Footsteps in the hall, and Manu appears in the doorway. "Get the others," Jaantzen says, and he disappears once more.

Julieta's fingers tighten around his, her eyelids slowly flutter open. She focuses on his face, then smiles. "I thought I heard your voice," she says, so quietly he can barely hear the words.

He bends closer. "I'm here."

"Good." Her eyes close. Her breathing is a shaky rasp. She may be awake, but she's far from all right.

"Julieta? Stay with me, your family wants to talk to you."

Her eyelids flicker back open and she gives him a ghost of her old mischievous smile. "I don't know why it took you so long to listen to me about Phaera," she whispers. "I'm always right."

A smile tugs at his lips. "Have you just been pretending to be asleep this whole time?"

Her laugh turns into a cough so feeble it breaks him.

"You have a good heart, Willem," she says when she can speak again. Her eyes are still closed, her lips barely moving. "Don't be afraid of it."

He squeezes her hand gently, there's no answer to that. "Thank you for everything."

And the quiet is over. Calanthe and Alex are at the door, Liatris and the nurse following. "I'll let you see your family now," Jaantzen says, but Julieta's hand tightens around his.

"Mom?" Calanthe slips into the chair on the other side of her mother's bed. "Mom, stay with us." The room has become crowded with the Yang siblings and Alex, the nurse, Manu standing at Jaantzen's side.

"I need some room," the nurse says.

The Yang siblings aren't leaving, and Julieta's grip on his hand is firm. Manu pauses beside Calanthe. "It was good to see you, Julieta," he says.

Her head rolls on the pillow, and when she sees him, she smiles.

"In such a state," she murmurs.

"You're stunning as always, my queen." A single tear traces the curve of Manu's smile as he bends to brush a kiss over her gnarled knuckles. He slips back out into the hallway.

Calanthe takes her hand. "Mom, the nurse is here. He's going to — "

Julieta shakes her head, but at the motion she begins coughing, horrible, weak sounds that rack her whole body. Her grip loosens, and Jaantzen steps back to let Liatris in.

One of the autodoc bots keeps trying to land on her arm;

she waves it away again until, "Shut those goddamned things off," Calanthe snaps at the nurse, who obeys then steps back, hands raised in surrender.

Liatris is sitting in the seat Jaantzen vacated, holding his mother's hand; Calanthe is doing the same on the other side, Alex standing behind her and rubbing his wife's shoulders in a way that seems unconscious. Jaantzen stands at the foot of the bed, studying the woman in the bed. Through the frail arms, the bruising, the dullness in her hair and skin, the wet shine of her yellowed eyes, he can clearly see the woman who hired him, who taught him, who welcomed him. Her face may be lined, but the spirit behind it is as strong and fiery as ever.

Nothing will ever diminish Julieta Yang.

She blurs, and he blinks to clear his vision, ignoring the streak of hot salt down his cheek.

She's whispering something to Calanthe when her spirit decides it's time, and her head settles gently back against the pillow, her purpled eyelids flutter closed, her chapped lips part.

And the room is silent but for Calanthe's weeping, Alex's gentle murmur as he holds her, Liatris's whispered prayer.

Jaantzen sits heavily on the window seat, watching her face. Time passes — he's not sure how long — and a motion in the doorway catches his eye. Manu.

"It's time," Manu signs. It's beyond time; he'd hoped to be there before everyone else, to have a moment to talk with Phaera alone, but that won't happen now.

He takes a deep breath and stands. "I'm sorry," he says.

Calanthe sniffs loudly and lets out a curse. "I'll go."

"Calanthe," Jaantzen says, at the same time Alex says, "Come on, Callie."

But she shakes her head, dashing a hand over her eyes. "You're still trying to convince people to help, aren't you? Let them try — let them *fucking* try to tell me to my face tonight that Geum-ja Leone isn't a threat to us all." She looks at her brother. "You'll stay with Mom? Good." She straightens. "Give me a second to put my face on and I'll be ready."

Moments later, they're in the Dulciana, Jaantzen and Calanthe in the back seat while Manu drives. They're not speaking — there's nothing left to say — and when a chime cuts through the silence, Calanthe flinches.

Jaantzen reaches for his comm, expecting Phaera. It's Oriol.

Security breach at the Table. Do not approach until advised.

35

PHAERA

"It's a gorgeous view, isn't it?"

Phaera spins; the mystix cards fall from her fingertips, fluttering down to the street below.

The woman beside the door tower is slim and athletic, dressed in black, and even though she's still half in the shadows, Phaera recognizes that pointed chin and faint smile. She's spent the last week studying it, having nightmares about it, waiting for Victoria Tierren to appear.

She can't remember how to breathe.

"A beautiful view for a beautiful night," Tierren says, taking a step towards Phaera. "A momentous night, I suppose you might say."

She's casual, hands in her pockets like she's no threat, but Phaera knows exactly how dangerous this woman can be. She's calculating the distance between herself and the door. Tierren is in the way, but if Phaera can keep her talking long enough, Hiro will be here. He's watching the security feeds. He'll notice what's happening. Phaera pretends to adjust her gold cuff, pressing the panic button that will alert him. Tierren's gaze flickers to the cuff, but if she realizes what Phaera's doing, she doesn't seem bothered.

"I've been getting your messages," Phaera says.

Tierren lifts a narrow shoulder in a shrug. "It passed the time." She moves closer; Phaera steps back reflexively and hits the wall around the rooftop. The sharp edge digs against her lower back. She plants her hands on either side to steady herself.

"Do you know Leone actually thought she'd broken you?" Tierren says. "That little show you gave her at lunch? But you're far more interesting than she gave you credit for."

"That's nice. What do you want?"

Tierren's close enough Phaera could reach out and touch her. She braces herself, willing Tierren to take another step.

"I'm just here for my payday," Tierren says. "No offense, but this was never about you."

Phaera's heart skips a beat. "Your payday is Jaantzen."

"The one and only." Tierren smiles. Phaera can feel her warmth. "Sorry, kid. It's been fun."

With a shout, Phaera shoves against Tierren, grabbing the other woman's bare wrist and gripping with all her might. The tiny electric barb in her cuff is insulated against Phaera's hand, but it sears into the other woman's flesh; Tierren cries out and tries to wrench away, but Phaera holds on as tightly as she can, the stench of burnt flesh filling her nostrils. It seems like eternity until the charge runs out, but it can't even have been a second. Phaera shoves Tierren away and runs for the door on shoes not meant for sprinting, her mind racing. Even if her panic button malfunctioned, the electric barb discharge will automatically call for help.

So where the hell is Hiro?

And what's wrong with the door? The edge of the metal door where it sits into the frame is lumpy and warped, glowing with heat that's slowly fading.

A blow from behind when she's steps from the door and Phaera stumbles on her impractical heels, hits the ground on one knee, then scrambles to her feet again and lunges for the door handle. Hands seize the back of her dress and yank, send her crashing back into one of the tables that's bolted to the rooftop, and Tierren is on top of her.

Phaera lashes out, her fingers clawed, as much in fury against this woman who tried to murder her mother as in fear for her own life. She drives one sharp heel into the other woman's instep, hands scrabbling for anything and closing around an empty pint glass turned ashtray. She smashes it against the side of Tierren's head and is vaguely aware of the hail of cigarette butts and glass shards that explodes between them.

Tierren growls and backhands her — stars burst behind Phaera's eyes — then shoves her backwards over the table. Phaera lands badly against the wooden tub of melted ice. Before Phaera can move, Tierren grabs the back of her neck and shoves her face-first into the water.

She's too strong.

Phaera's hands claw the edge of the tub. She tries flailing one arm behind her, it only loses her the small amount of purchase she'd managed to gain and drives her need to breathe to bursting. Her diaphragm spasms with the urge to expand.

She's vaguely aware of the hand tangled in her hair, the elbow digging into her back, of Tierren's voice — it's a low, mocking drone and Phaera can't make out a single word with her heart thrashing in her ears and her own strangled, watery screams. She chokes down water now, pain searing through her chest, and the roaring in her ears sharpens, elevates, until the entire world is focused to a single, high-pitched whine in the black.

Her hand slips; she collapses.

The grip on her neck releases.

Hands pull Phaera from the water with as much violence as they held her under, slamming her against the wall beside the door. She barely notices the pain as she retches up water, forces air screaming into her lungs. When she finally catches her breath, Tierren is crouched back on her heels with hands dangling over her knees, watching her curiously. The back of her left wrist is blistered raw and oozing.

"Didn't expect you to fight quite so much," Tierren says, and Phaera can't think of a comeback. She's not sure she could speak even if she had one. But speaking is the one weapon she has left. Hiro isn't coming or he would be here already. Her cuff doesn't have enough charge for a second attack, and even if she'd carried a knife or a gun, Tierren would have disarmed her immediately.

She lets her head roll like she's dazed — she is — and spots a fork lying a few feet away. She's never been so grateful her staff don't pick up after themselves on the rooftop.

Her fingers inch towards the fork.

"Do you think your security team is watching this on the feeds and laughing?" Tierren asks. She tilts her head, studying Phaera. "Maybe they're taking bets."

"Fuck you," Phaera manages to choke out.

"You must be wondering how I got up here. Which one

of your team gave me the access code? Jae? Hiro? I bet he's downstairs in your office, breaking into the special liquor stash you've been keeping from him, enjoying this little show. He's been patient for so many years."

"Not Hiro." She locks her gaze on Tierren's. The woman doesn't seem to notice what Phaera's reaching for.

"No? Or maybe you're too full of yourself to see? Fancy new clothes, fancy new friends, treating your old ones like servants. Like Vanessa."

"Not Vanessa."

Tierren smiles, slow and lazy. "She told me some things, girlfriend. Who the fuck do you think you are that Vanessa should take a bullet for you and appreciate the opportunity?" She shakes her head. "I admire ambition, but I've got no respect for those who leave their friends behind for it."

Phaera's been listening to this too long.

Her fingers close around the fork and she drives it tine-first with all her might at Tierren's head. Tierren's arm whips up to block the blow, though her gaze never wavers from Phaera's. She catches Phaera's hand in hers and twists. A sickening crunch. Searing pain shoots up her arm.

Tierren shakes her head in disappointment and lets go. Phaera falls back against the wall, cradling her injured hand.

"Nobody's coming for you," says Tierren. "And nobody's going to miss you."

"Jaantzen — "

"Ah, well of course. He needed you, and he's got enough of a conscience he'll feel guilty. But you already know he's the same as you. He planned to drop you as soon as he got to the next level."

"He's not — "

"He is. In the end the only thing that will bother him about your death is that he was downstairs drinking wine and schmoozing while it was happening. But don't pretend either of you want anything more from the other than power."

Tierren shifts as though to stand, and Phaera readies herself to strike — to do anything.

She doesn't see the rope in Tierren's hand until it's too late.

She tries to get up a hand, but Tierren throws the loop of rope over her head before she can block it. She claws at the coil, choking, as Tierren hauls her to her feet and hooks the end of the rope over a light fixture. Tierren yanks, pulling Phaera onto her toes.

Phaera stretches for height, gasps for air, fingernails digging into her own throat as she tries to loosen the rope; it's slick with water and blood.

"Don't worry, no one will think this was suicide," Tierren murmurs in Phaera's ear; her breath is hot on her cheek. "They'll all pretend it's a shame, but every one of them will think you deserved it." She ties off the end of the rope, then stands back to watch Phaera struggle. Her eyes are bright with curiosity.

A shot rings out, cracking like a whip through the blood rushing in Phaera's ears.

In the fuzzy black edges of the world she sees the other woman fall. Something explodes, a crushing noise that rocks her forward and cinches the rope even tighter around her throat. The entire world is smoke and shouting and rumbling and she can't tell if it lasts a second or an hour.

She's still fighting, but she can't feel the noose against her raw fingertips anymore. And in the shrinking dark she can't tell who is walking towards her. They're moving so, so slowly. Not to help her, then. Maybe everything Tierren has been saying is true.

Whoever killed Tierren isn't here to save her. They're here to watch her die.

36

PHAERA

An arm tightens around Phaera's bruised ribs, and she tries to push it away, but whoever has her is too strong. It takes her a moment to realize the person isn't pulling her down — they're lifting her up with one arm, other hand at the back of her neck to loosen the noose. The rope around her neck comes free all at once and air rushes back in like fire. When the grip around her releases, Phaera falls to her hands and knees, sobbing for air, ignoring the shattering pain in her right hand for the glorious, desperate agony searing her throat and lungs with every blessed breath.

Someone's talking to her. Has been for a while. She tries to calm the rasp of her own ragged breathing to hear Hiro. He's got his hands on her shoulders, steadying her.

Another voice says her name, and Phaera blinks away water and tears to see Vanessa crouched in front of her. Oriol is beyond Vanessa, bending over Tierren's prone form. Vanessa says her name again, and Phaera doesn't trust herself to speak so she nods in response. She pushes herself back. Lets Hiro steady her until the wall's against her back.

She tries to ask what happened, but when she takes a breath to speak she doubles over again, coughing.

Hands gently help her sit back.

When she opens her eyes again, Oriol is kneeling at her other side. He smooths back the dripping hair plastered against her cheeks and cups his hands around her face. "She's dead, Phaera, and I need you to breathe," he says. "Deep breaths, all right? With me. In, out. In, out."

She focuses on his rhythm as his fingers spread her eyelids, turn her chin to examine her temple — his fingers come away bloody — and tilt her head to see her neck.

At the movement she realizes the rope is still coiled there, a snake draped around her shoulders. Her calmed breath spikes rapid once more, she claws at the rope to get it *gone*.

Hiro catches her wrists. "It's okay, ma'am, we've got you." The coiled weight disappears as Oriol untangles her, and Phaera forces her breathing to smooth out again. Hiro swears quietly. "Her hand," he murmurs to Oriol.

Her hand. Phaera holds it up, seeing it for the first time. The pinkie on her right hand is bent at an angle that sends a wave of nausea through her. She leans her head against the wall once more. "No wonder it hurts," she whispers. "So damn much." She bites back a curse as Hiro prods. She managed to say that much, so she takes a shallow breath and tries again. "What happened?"

"I was keeping an eye on the feeds when you came up here, and I saw her. I tried to raise you but couldn't get through, and when we came up after you the door was sealed shut." The strange melting she'd noticed around the door — even if she'd gotten away from Tierren for a second there'd been no place to go but over the side of the building.

"Tierren blocked communication with you," says Oriol.

He's examining her temple again; belatedly, she realizes he's holding a compress there. She raises her uninjured hand to her face, stares at the blood on her fingers.

"Oriol climbed the building," says Vanessa. She's still crouching in front of Phaera, past her bare feet. Phaera blinks at that — when did she lose her shoes? — then forces her attention up to V's face. "He shot her and Hiro blew a hole beside the door."

So that had been the explosion. She can breathe now without concentrating, though her lungs are still on fire. She coughs, and everything from the lump on her temple to her dislocated finger lights up like a bonfire. All she wants to do is curl up against the wall until this stops.

Something settles over her shoulders. Hiro's jacket. She hadn't realized she was shivering until she felt the silk lining vibrating against her bare arms. Her dress is soaked through. Her hair is drenched. She reeks of adrenaline and blood.

And the Devil's Table's dining room is filling with guests.

"Is everyone here?" she asks Vanessa.

"Fay, it's all right. You don't need to — " She cuts off at the look Oriol shoots her way. "She's a wreck, cowboy. We're not sending her in there."

Phaera forces herself to focus. "Is everyone here?"

"Almost," Vanessa says with a glare at Oriol.

"What do you want to do, ma'am?" Oriol asks her.

Phaera takes a deep breath — too deep, she doubles over until the coughing fit subsides. "I need thirty minutes," she says when she can talk again.

"Ma'am, your hand," Hiro says.

"How bad is it?" she asks, and because he's the only one who truly seems to understand the show must go on, she rolls her head back to Oriol. "Sina?"

Oriol takes her hand gingerly, examining the damage. "Dislocated," he says, handing it back to Hiro with a lifted eyebrow. Hiro nods. "Tell us what you need," Oriol says to Phaera. "Focus on me, ignore Hiro, he's just going to take a look at it."

"Liar." Phaera hisses through her teeth at the pain of Hiro's touch, but she stays focused on Oriol, trying to relax. To run through logistics and keep her mind from anticipating whatever Hiro's about to do. "V, tell Cavy what happened in private, he can keep the others in line while I get cleaned up. I have a change of clothes in my office. I need to dry my hair."

"I'll find you a hair dryer, and some ice," says Vanessa as she stands.

"And some meds," Oriol says. "Are there any painkillers in the building?"

"Yeah." A shadow crosses Vanessa's face. "And you left a scarf in the valet stand, I'll grab it."

A scarf? Gods, she hadn't thought — she reaches to touch her neck with her good hand, suddenly realizing how bad the damage must be.

Oriol catches her hand. "We'll get you cleaned up, it's fine," he says; that's not what Vanessa's face says. "What else do you need us to do?"

She's thinking so hard about the question she's almost managed to completely forget Hiro. Until he grunts and her hand erupts. She gives an animal howl and doubles over, cradling her wounded hand.

The pain ebbs, and when she finally opens her eyes, her finger is in the right place again.

"Thank you," she whispers.

"We'll get you to a doctor," says Oriol. "After."

"Okay." She tests how deeply she can breathe without

triggering another coughing attack and finds improvement. She coughs once and slumps back against the wall. "I look like hell, don't I? What am I going to tell them?"

"The truth, ma'am. That Leone sent her woman to assassinate you because you tried to get out from under her thumb."

"I look like a victim."

"You were the victor." Oriol's voice is low but fierce. "You have Leone terrified. Go down there and show everyone what you're made of."

"It takes more than an assassination attempt to intimidate Phaera D," says Hiro. His faint smile fades. "I'm so sorry, ma'am."

"Your job is to protect our guests," she tells him. "You acted fast when you found out something was wrong. You can't blame yourself."

"It's almost like you should have a personal bodyguard," Oriol says.

"It might not hurt," Phaera says. She manages a smile. "I don't suppose you're still in the business."

"I never left it."

"Thank you." She takes another deep breath and finally doesn't cough. She's not ready to move, but thirty minutes will go fast enough as it is. She doesn't have time to let herself break down. And speaking of which? "Is Jaantzen here yet?"

"No, ma'am," Oriol says.

"Good." She's one stray thought from completely losing it and she's not going to be able to compose herself in time if she has to explain what happened to Jaantzen before heading into that dining room.

"Shall we?" Phaera holds out her uninjured hand to Oriol and Hiro takes her elbow.

It's time to end this.

Her legs are unsteady at first, but it's only nerves, and she shakes off Hiro's arm as he tries to shepherd her down the stairs. Oriol says something to him when they reach her office, and he disappears. Phaera heads to the attached bathroom, Oriol following behind.

"Let me take care of your hand and this cut on your temple," he says. "Is there anything else that can't wait until after?"

"I don't think so."

She sits on the toilet lid and lets him wash blood off her face — she's not ready to face the mirror yet. A surprisingly small plaster closes the cut on her temple, and a larger one covers the oozing scrape on her knee she doesn't remember acquiring. With a few strips of tape he secures her little finger to the one beside it.

"That'll keep it from moving until you can see a doctor," he says, stepping back. "How else can I help, ma'am?"

"I have another outfit in the closet," she says. "White pants, blue blouse." She closes the door behind him and reaches for the zipper at the base of her neck with her uninjured left hand, then swears and opens the door again. "Wait, Sina? Zipper?"

When he's gone, she wets a towel and scrubs at herself with her left hand, trying not to catch a glimpse in the mirror until she absolutely has to. She's freezing cold. Her lungs still burn and she's aware of how her voice sounds, like an old man's, well seasoned with whiskey and smoke. She doesn't let herself think about it.

A moment later she hears Vanessa's voice, a knock on the door. V has the clothes Oriol had been searching for draped over one arm, a tumbler with a healthy pour of mezcal in her hand. "Tia keeps a hair dryer in her locker," she says, laying the slim device beside the sink and handing Phaera the glass. The liquor burns. Phaera shudders at the sudden heat. "You need help?"

"Please."

Dressed again, Phaera finally turns to face the mirror. Her makeup is smudged into bruised circles around her eyes, one cheek is blaze red where Tierren hit her. And her neck: the raw red band around her pale throat is punctuated by long bloody scratches she left herself.

Phaera's hands grip the edges of the sink, her stomach churning.

Vanessa appears in the mirror over her shoulder. "Sit down, Fay. We'll get you fixed up. Cowboy, can you grab that gray jacket in the closet?" She hands Phaera an ice pack for her hand, then palms the hair dryer and smooths it gently through the tangled, damp strands of Phaera's magenta hair. Phaera closes her eyes while Vanessa expertly retouches her makeup — she's caught in a flashback, the two of them in the break room at the Aterciopelado, rooting through each other's makeup bags for fun, to experiment, because one or the other had a date.

What dreams they'd had in those days.

What a nightmare this night has been.

"You're gorgeous," Vanessa says after a moment, snapping the cap back on a lip pencil. She pulls out the black and white floral scarf that Phaera must have left at the valet stand and wraps it carefully around Phaera's neck. Phaera catches a hint of citrus and cardamom, and something bitter beneath. It's familiar but she can't place it, maybe a touch of the perfume V is wearing herself, or the adrenaline of the night. "That all right? Good." Vanessa slips an arm around Phaera's waist and meets her gaze in the mirror. "I'm proud of you, Fay."

Phaera's eyes are bloodshot and the bruise on her cheek still shows through Vanessa's magic, but otherwise she could pass for fine. She smiles back at Vanessa. "Thank you for everything."

Oriol clears his throat in the doorway, and Vanessa gently squeezes her waist and lets go.

"He's here," Oriol says. "Should I have him come back?"

"No." Phaera shakes her head. She can melt down later, after this is all over. "Let's end this."

Toshiyo Ravi is used to solitude. Before the onslaught of the last few weeks, she'd spend full days alone in her office, daydreaming and dabbling on her own work, tinkering on a project for the boss or for Admant, communicating with other humans entirely through text. Nobody tried to include Toshiyo in their hologram conferences, not anymore.

Her brain feels muddled from so many days in a row of being *on* around other people, the constant whiplash of conversations and pressure for results.

And so she'd expected to breathe a sigh of relief when Jaantzen and Manu left this morning, to luxuriate in these hours she has before the *Coldfire* returns with its cargo of chatty crew. She was supposed to love this blessed, blissful solitude, without the chance of tripping over Jaantzen brooding in the kitchen or Manu and his constant banter or Starla with her steady supply of new projects and theories to run by Toshiyo.

But the deathtrap feels empty in a way the fourth floor at Cobalt Tower never did. Somehow knowing that the closest people to her are strangers — and well out of earshot — has her counting down the minutes until the *Coldfire* arrives with company.

She's been chasing the sensation away with headphones and music, familiar and loud and thrashing, that drowns out the constant whine of her electronics and soothes the chatter in her mind. Classic, well-worn tracks deliver a frenzied, pulsing beat she feels in her throat and between her shoulder blades, and within a few minutes she's humming along with the chorus and bobbing her head in time with the screaming staccato strings.

Starla sent ahead the rest of the files and the footage from the beetle drones as soon as the *Coldfire* hit a reliable signal, and Toshiyo is in awe of the goldmine of answers that has landed in her lap.

Like proper nutrition recommendations for Lucky, which she's delighted to realize they've already more or less discovered through trial and error. Good thing the little buddy kept picking the foods his body needed rather than junk that tasted good. If Toshiyo had been given a wide range of random foods by an alien in order to figure out what she ate, she'd have ended up on a steady diet of berries. Which probably wouldn't keep her alive.

The files also contain the missing pieces of the terraforming puzzle she's been trying to figure out. Starla has confirmed she's got several samples of the mysterious substance, which means Toshiyo can stop losing sleep about the Demosgas. Jaantzen's been making unwise promises to them in the belief she has the ability to figure literally anything out. Flattering, sure. And stressful. So incredibly stressful.

Also among the files are records and observations about Felipe Zacharia and the Dawn, which Toshiyo has already started paging through. It's unsettling, the amount of control he got over his followers in such a short amount of time. And morbidly fascinating to piece together his rise to power as seen through notes from his captors.

She's never been one to hold grudges — holding grudges requires giving space in your mind to the memories you're supposed to hold grudges about, and Toshiyo would rather shut those deep away. But the Dawn tried to kill Manu, and the boss, and Starla. They killed Ximena, who she'd started liking. And they'd slaughtered the entire population of Blacklode mine.

Maybe she doesn't spend time thinking about Black-lode. Maybe there are a few people she's glad to know writhed in painful death after drinking the tainted water. But most of the people there were indentured workers, like she'd been. Scared and exhausted and lonely and just trying to make it through their years until they could find life on the other side. They didn't deserve to die like that.

And so Toshiyo Ravi is going to see what it's like to hold a grudge.

It's all this reading about the Dawn that has her para-noid, she thinks. That's what's giving her the image of someone standing behind her, watching. She checks the feed running in the corner of her desk to make sure she's still alone in her office.

No one else can get into the compound. The gate to the hangar and the front door are both keyed only to her people's vehicle signatures and biosigns, and she's restored most of the old owner's ingenious perimeter defenses in case a stranger starts poking around. She built the same redundancies into the security feeds that she'd had at Cobalt Tower, along with a fresh new snippet of parasite code that will automatically follow the stream back when tripped and give her access to their systems.

She's also restored the several kill chutes the old owner built in the maze-like corridors of the deathtrap. Of course, she modified them from the original plan of "bullets everywhere" to a much less bloodthirsty tranq dart option, and set them to manual rather than the hair trigger he'd had them on. All together, the deathtrap's defenses would slow down all but the most determined army of attackers.

Toshiyo pushes aside the paranoia and turns back to the files.

Something shifts on the feed above her desk.

It's too fast for her to see what it is, and she whirls and drops her headphones, studying the room. Nothing. No one. A trick of the light, maybe. Her imagination running away from her.

Chill, Tosh.

She's setting headphones back on her ears when sharp claws clutch her shoulders, pulling her from her chair. She lands in a tangle of chair legs and cables, striking her elbow and head on the hard floor. Her headphones fall away. A horrible shriek splits her ears.

Something lands on her chest in a flurry of wings and fish-reeking breath, and when the stars clear from her eyes she's staring into Lucky's bared triple row of razor-sharp teeth.

He crouches, the duller claws of his feet bruising her stomach and digging into her sternum, one set of needle-sharp finger claws poised over her neck. He hisses, but it's not at her. He snaps his teeth together like a spring trap, then bares them menacingly at her headphones.

Toshiyo moves slowly, heart beating like a jackhammer in her throat. She stretches an arm for the headphones, but

Lucky snaps at her. "It's okay, buddy," she signs and says aloud. "That won't hurt me. It's safe." She gives him her most encouraging smile, though her animal instincts are screaming at her to fling him off, find cover, run for her life.

Lucky narrows his gaze at her, then watches her hand like a hawk as she carefully, slowly reaches for the headphones. She smooths a finger down the volume control and the music disappears.

Lucky hisses at the headphones again — this time with smug triumph — and hops off of Toshiyo's chest. His claws click against the floor as he stalks towards the headphones; Toshiyo swoops them up before he can get any ideas about destroying them, then sits back at her desk. She calls up one of Starla's playlists, trying to ignore how badly her hands are shaking, and hits Play on a random song. Something syrupy sweet and bass-heavy starts pumping out of the desk's speakers. Lucky hops happily.

"You're too big to go pouncing on people," Toshiyo signs and says to him. She points to her elbow and makes a grimace of pain. "Ouch."

Lucky's face falls.

Toshiyo sighs. "It's okay. Just . . ."

Just what? Don't be an unknowable, terrifying alien? She saw the stats in the Alliance files about the fully grown alien they'd been studying. Lucky may be able to pull her off a chair now, but his older cousin could throw her across the room with the flick of a wing. At least Lucky seems to feel bad about hurting her — but how will that change as he matures?

What the hell are they going to do with this little guy?

And — she realizes with a chill — didn't she lock him in his room after Manu and the boss left? She totally did. How did he get out?

An alert bleeps through the cheesy anthem chorus and Toshiyo turns back to her desk, trying warily to keep an eye on Lucky at the same time.

It's the *Coldfire*, getting ready for approach. Thank the stars.

"C'mon, buddy," she signs and says to Lucky. "Let's get you back in your room. We have friends coming." She makes the sign for *friends* again with a bright smile, hoping he gets it. He signs it back and points at her. This morning it would have made her heart melt. Tonight, though?

She pastes on a bright smile, hoping he can't sense her fear.

"Right, friends. C'mon, little guy."

ABOUT JESSIE KWAK

Jessie Kwak has always lived in imaginary lands, from Arrakis and Ankh-Morpork to Earthsea, Tatooine, and now Portland, Oregon. As a writer, she sends readers on their own journeys to immersive worlds filled with fascinating characters, gunfights, explosions, and dinner parties.

When she's not raving about her latest favorite sci-fi series to her friends, she can be found sewing, mountain biking, or exploring new worlds both at home and abroad.

Author photo by Robert Kittilson.

Connect with me:
www.jessiekwak.com
jessie@jessiekwak.com

DID YOU LIKE THE BOOK?

As a reader, I rely on book recommendations to help me pick what to read next.

As a writer, book recommendations are the most powerful way for me to get the word out to new readers.

If you liked this book, please leave a review on the platform of your choice — or tell a friend! It's the easiest way to help authors you enjoy keep producing great work.

Cheers!

Jessie

The Bulari Saga

Double Edged

Crossfire

Pressure Point

Heat Death

Kill Shot

Bulari Saga Prequel Novellas

Starfall

Negative Return

Deviant Flux

Standalone Novels

From Earth and Bone: A Ramos Sisters Thriller

Nonfiction

From Chaos to Creativity: Building a Productivity System for Artists and Writers